NO MAN WANTS A TEMPEST FOR A MISTRESS ... OR DOES HE?

"You say you never mix business with pleasure. What then of mixing pleasure with pleasure? I have a pair of dice. Throw for me, your Lordship. If you win ... you win. Will you cast?" Rue tilted her head back to regard him, her fine blue eyes shining, her mouth slightly parted with an emotion the earl knew well—gambler's fever.

"Of course," he said casually, and picked up the small velvet box in his right hand. His other hand went behind her back and he swept her to him, kissing her deep and hard on her startled mouth. Rue heard the dice chatter as if chuckling at her and then roll sharply across the wood.

"You didn't even wait for the cast," she gasped.

"See for yourself," he said softly.

"Six ..." said Rue through stiff lips. "The highest winning number ... and you knew! You *are* luck incarnate, you *are* the devil!"

He laughed, his eyes moving intently over her features as though they were both about to be plunged into darkness and he must memorize them first.

"I am your lover now, Rue Morgan, and that is all about me you need to be concerned with."

Carole Nelson Douglas delectably mingles
the mystery of romance
with the romance of mystery ... and more

GOOD NIGHT, MR. HOLMES,

A NY Times Notable Book
American Mystery Award: Best Romantic Suspense Novel
Romantic Times Award: Best Historical Romantic Mystery

"Introducing Irene Adler—the only woman to dupe Sherlock Holmes—as a detective in her own right ... truly original ... readers will doff their deerstalkers."
—Publishers Weekly

GOOD MORNING, IRENE

"This vibrant creature is back ... a carefree, romantic romp."
—The New York Times

IRENE AT LARGE

"A perfect Chinese puzzle of a book, with layers of mystery, history, romance, and intrigue. An irresistible read."
—Mary Jo Putney,
author of *SILK AND SECRETS*

CATNAP and PUSSYFOOT:
Midnight Louie Mysteries

The tomcat detective introduced in the Las Vegas romances,
CRYSTAL DAYS AND CRYSTAL NIGHTS, returns!

All now available from Tor Books

And look for
FAIR WIND, FIERY STAR

A lady swashbuckler and a Cavalier sea captain
fence with hearts and swords from London ballrooms
to tropical Barbados during the English Civil War
On sale in October '93

Tor books by Carole Nelson Douglas

MYSTERY

Irene Adler Adventures:
Good Night, Mr. Holmes
Good Morning, Irene
Irene At Large

A Midnight Louie Mystery:
Catnap
Pussyfoot

HISTORICAL

*Amberleigh**
*Lady Rogue**

FANTASY

Sword and Circlet:
Keepers of Edanvant
Heir of Rengarth
Seven of Swords

Taliswoman:
Cup of Clay
Seed Upon the Wind

SCIENCE FICTION

*Probe**
*Counterprobe**

*also mystery

LADY ROGUE

CAROLE NELSON DOUGLAS

A TOM DOHERTY ASSOCIATES BOOK
NEW YORK

LADY ROGUE

Copyright © 1983 by Carole Nelson Douglas

Cover art by Deborah Chabrian

A Tor Book
Published by Tom Doherty Associates, Inc.
175 Fifth Avenue
New York, N.Y. 10010

Tor® is a registered trademark of Tom Doherty Associates, Inc.

ISBN: 0-812-52265-6
Library of Congress Catalog Card Number: 82-91198

First edition: August 1983
First mass market printing: September 1993

Printed in the United States of America

0 9 8 7 6 5 4 3 2 1

For Sam,
typist then and true believer,
then and now

Chapter One

The wind came off the open sea and hurtled inland with a demon's speed. It wrenched the cloak from the night watchman as he made his grumbling rounds through Fetter Lane. He chased it, cursing, tripping over the feet lolling into the street; like the dead, they slept, when the gin mills closed.

He caught his sturdy worsted at the corner where the streetlamp glowed dimly through the fog of London's pre-dawn limbo. He cursed again and wrapped it well around himself, but the gust had howled away down broader streets, seeking grander prey. It wafted against second-story windows and rattled the panes, occasionally bringing mob-capped matrons bobbing out of their linens with a start.

It turned sharp corners, trailing disembodied fingers through the grooves in the cut-stone quoining on great houses and weaving up among the rooftops to play tag among a forest of chimneys.

It came finally to the sprawling London residence of Black Harry Morgan, and there it tiptoed past, as if even the November wind knew better than to rattle Morgan's doors in the night. The wind contented itself with breaching a half-ajar rear casement in the mansion's service area, blowing cheekily at the maids' candles.

"Now that's done it! Left the window wide, didn't you just?" The late-working kitchen maid rushed to secure the casement. "That's all we'd need, burnin' the master's candles unasked and then a fire to send us to hell beforetimes."

"Not 'im. No fire'd send 'im to 'ell aforetime."

"Rebecky Bartle, you've served in this house more years than I've been livin', but you've learned no wisdom of it. If anyone hear you take to the master thataway—it's more than the wind gives me a chill to think it. He's blacker than the darky Heliotrope, now there's a truth. But it's one thing to know and another to say."

The young maid shivered again, for effect, and caught her coarse red hands tight around her arms. Her mobcap nodded once for emphasis at the older woman bent over a piece of lace she was pressing by the candle flicker.

"Oh, pooh, girl! I've been in this 'ouse long enough to fear neither wind nor Black 'arry's 'earing. Thank the Lord 'e's got ears that are only mortal, if 'is temper be devilish vile. But, look, will she like it, you think?"

The older woman, whose aproned garb revealed her to be an upstairs maid, lifted the delicate web of lace. Perhaps a bit of the wind remained, for the fragile stuff trembled in her hands.

" 'Tis lovely." The kitchen maid advanced, her roughened hands reaching longingly for the lace as pale and intricately veined as a moth's wing. "Beau-ti-fulll. But Rebecky, why do ye work yer eyes raw on such a thing only to give it to *her?* Mistress Rue is a high-handed piece that'd as soon see us kicked down the stairs as curtsy to her when she passes."

" 'As she ever kicked you, girl?"

"Noooo. But I see it in the way she tosses that coal-black hair of hers and looks past with her ice-blue eyes. Ay, that one, she's got her father's temper for sure."

" 'As she, then?" The old woman let the lace drift to the

tabletop and caught her veined hands to her sides. " 'As she got her father's temper?"

"Oh, here now, Rebecky. I didn't mean to give you a turn, and you workin' half the night. You been here longer'n me. I've no right to tell you the lay of the land."

"Aye, no right, but you young'uns will." The woman straightened, whatever had pinched her features passing. She looked around the dimly lit pantry with its single, now shuttered window to the outside world.

"Eighteen years, it'll be tomorrow, Eliza. Eighteen years I thought meself a girl like you then, though likely I was foolin' meself. *She* was just a girl, though, upstairs in 'er fine, grand, wide bed. 'Owling like one o' Paddy the Coachman's banshees. Or 'owling like the wind. A November wind it was. Cheeky. Like her. Like the little Rue. I never come to a November without rememberin' that one."

Rebecca Bartle folded the lace into a triangle and draped it across one wrinkled palm. " 'Tis fine, isn't it, Eliza? Fine enough for 'er to wear. It's one thing I can do. Looky, even folded I can read my lifeline through it. Or that mad gypsy Fenelia could."

"Don't be talkin' o' lifelines! Lord help us, 'tis glad I am I'm no Papist like Paddy and would be believin' in All Souls' Night. For they'd be walking now, 'tis certain."

"I wonder if *she* walks?" The old woman's eyes were cast up, a gesture that carved wrinkles of mock worry into her brow.

"Mistress Rue? Go on, Rebecky, even she keeps to her bed at night. She's only eighteen."

"I don't mean Mistress Rue," said Rebecca firmly, setting the iron on its triangular rest and moving to the candle. The older woman looked around the plain room. "It's always windy on Mistress Rue's birthday. Sometimes I think it's 'er cries I 'ear and not only a bit o' breeze from the channel. She cried enough to wake the dead that night, the old mistress. The night Mistress Rue was born. Mayhap this lace will settle round Mistress Rue's shoulders and keep the cries from 'er. I mean 'er no ill, Eliza, which is more'n you can say for 'im."

"Him? Oh, Rebecky Bartle, you don't mean the master?"

"I mean what I mean, an' it's for you to find out. Blow out the candle when you leave. Wouldn't do to have the master know we'd been up, and up to something."

The old woman sailed out, the lace across her palms like a ceremonial cushion.

Eliza shivered again and watched the single candle throw her shadow on the wall. She spit upon her thumb and forefinger and pinched out the light.

In the instant dark, her light footsteps sounded out the door and down the passage, tapping with the stuttering chatter of a blind beggar's cane.

Eliza's guttering candle winked once through a chink in the ground-level shutter before going out.

Something black and huddled, scurrying by, paused as if caught in the light of a thousand suns. What was left of the coastal wind rippled through its cloak-swathed shape, painting it into a monster amid a courtyard full of shadow-engendered monstrosities.

The figure hissed forward again, shuffling stealthily past the house's wing to the stables beyond.

It was black, black night. And chill. Even the horses slept on their night-locked legs. The figure cracked open the tack room door, edged through, and waited.

"Rue? Here, over here. Close the door, and I'll fetch the lantern."

Flint struck steel and a yawning mouth of pale glow enveloped first the man that held it, then the glittering metal of bit and spur on the walls around them, even the glimmer of kitten eyes slitting open in a furry mass on a pile of straw.

One of the last things the light revealed was the cloaked figure. The black enshrouding fabric seemed to draw all light to itself and swallow it. But the lantern did outline a sickle moon of silk lining the dark hood. Flame-colored silk.

"Rue!" The man hung the lantern on a hook and drew her into the candlelight, catching her hands so she couldn't stop the hood from sliding off the back of her sable hair.

She was a remarkable young woman, no wonder he almost trod on a kitten while leading her to the lantern. Her dark glossy hair was piled into a concoction of sausage curls and tendrils, its blackness painting her pale skin paler. Her face was piquant, each feature strong but abbreviated. This feral sharpness trembled on the brink of the unattractive, which only made her more intriguing. Her eyes were blue, a particularly vibrant shade that made all who encountered them rack their brains for mental comparisons.

The young man enfolding her hands now had settled on April ponds reflecting a clear spring sky. It was not the most original attempt among her admirers, but he was dear to her for many reasons and intellectual invention was not foremost among them.

"Graham, I've missed you so this past week."

He took her confession for permission to draw her closer, his red-uniformed arms encircling the black of her cloak as if he were afraid to close them and find only limp fabric within.

"I had to go, Rue, though I loathed it. My uncle would tolerate no absence from the ranks, not even that of his favorite nephew."

"Well, you are not *my* favorite nephew, Captain Graham Winthrop of His Majesty's Seventeenth Lancers," she teased.

"Thank God for that, dear aunt-never-to-be, or we could hardly announce our betrothal at your birthday festivities tomorrow."

Graham tilted his powdered head to her face when she didn't reply. "Not worried, sweet, are you? 'Twill be a grand affair, with witnesses by the score to our troth—"

"One witness too many, I fear." She pulled her hands free

and walked away, a frown between the dark brows that slashed across an otherwise lineless forehead like wounds.

"Your father . . ."

"Yes?" She turned, the black cloak front splitting to reveal a billow of white nightshift cascading frothy lace, which made the young man's expression turn suddenly tender.

Captain Winthrop straightened to his nigh six feet, one leg still bent in its glossy black knee-high boot, his left hand resting by habit on the shining sword pommel at his side.

"Your father cannot deny so public a declaration. I've a fine commission, a noble family behind me! And if I'm older—then it's only given me the time to discover that there is no other woman I want more than you." He strode over to her, the lantern light winking from all the military brass that marched in rows down his buttoned-back coat flaps.

"I won't say I adore you, Rue, or that you're the moon of my existence or any of that goose-quill nonsense the fops go around dispensing like snuff. But I do love you and will be true. And if your father steps forward from the crowd tomorrow night and forswears us, I'll take you away with me then and there!"

He caught her close again, as if to make good his promise, and she curled her arms around his stiffly uniformed shoulders and let the warmth of his kisses wash over her in reassuring wave after wave.

He was one-and-thirty, 'twas true. And he'd had mistresses and doxies aplenty, as soldiers will. But he was a good man—she sensed it with her still half-formed emotions. She would have him and no other, forever. She would be true until death. She would be true even if it meant facing the wrath of Black Harry Morgan, which stronger souls than hers had quailed at before.

Her forefinger found the familiar cleft in his chin, which it had discovered on other occasions when their position had been more supine than upright. Tracing his features was a fond occupation that could easily be indulged. London was not so great a city even in this year of 1795 that a man and a woman could not outride it, could not find a country hedgerow for a bridal bed.

For Rue Morgan was not one to bridle her feelings. And what she felt for Graham Winthrop was an alliance with another human being that she had only known before, in a vastly different manner, in her relationship with her dusky Caribbean maid, Heliotrope, who had been reared in Blackstone House with her almost from birth.

There was a third in her field of affections, and the lowest. Her favorite Pekinese, Piquant, who of all the yapping, tongue-lolling flock had an intelligence that matched his beauty. Rue Morgan was careful not to let her father see that she had a preference; the last time she had done that, her lemon canary from Great Aunt Ninevah was sent winging off into the rooftops of a London winter, one dimming flash against a leaden sky.

"Graham," she said suddenly, her wax-white hands curving into the wool of his lapels. "I know you love me and you . . ." Her fingers dropped to the watch-chain at his side and dredged up the golden sun of his timepiece. From its top ring dangled a teardrop of bezeled sapphire.

"True blue," she said, letting the pendant sway in the lantern light. "I have given you this as a token, Graham, the centerstone from my mother's sapphire necklace, which father doles out to me stone by stone on each birthday. He made the mistake of working round from one end to the other, and thus gave me the center-cut prize when I was ten. I have given you this, and my heart, and something more—"

"Rue, hush. We'll wed soon, and then it won't matter. But would you wish back the days we had together?"

"No." She welded herself into his arms, made her mouth molten, and let the precious metal of her love run liquid through all her veins. His lips were warm and infinitely fascinating, as were his hands, somehow now within the cloak, tracing a tantalizing pattern across her back.

"Hush. Graham, you heard—?"

"Nothing, my admirable Rue, but your heart. You see, you've made a poet of me!" He laughed, not releasing her. It seemed for a moment that the spurs and bits around them rang with the echo of his laugh, though it was a low one.

"Graham." Her fingers fanned across his mouth. "My late mother named me Rue for a reason. I must go back. Soon none of it will matter. Tomorrow. I live for it. Don't make me worry."

"I swear, I swear I'll be so prompt the butler will have me polishing silver with the footmen."

She smiled and opened her left palm, in which his watch was still pressed. "Time flies. I'll leave your time with you so you will have something to remember me by. Until tomorrow."

She slipped the flat engraved circle, still warm from her hand, into his waistcoat pocket, stepped back from him as a soldier in a firing squad might retreat from a victim, took a deep breath, turned, and melted into the night outside the door.

Graham watched her, withdrawing his watch again only after she had gone. With his thumb he flipped back the lid. Past midnight, almost morning. Slipping back into the barracks would require bribing McMasters again. Fortunately his uncle kept him on a long leash, well weighted with pounds.

What was worse, there'd be the infernal baiting of his fellow officers, certain that doughty Captain Winthrop had been for another ramble along Stew Lane. These several months they'd been making free with his evident tastes in entertainment, ever since Black Harry's immediate realization of Graham's attachment to his daughter had made the old tyrant declare that she was not to see Graham for two years to "test" their love.

The lantern light flickered. He'd left the wings half-shut

so no betraying glimmer should alert the house and Black Harry. Graham clicked the watch lid shut and thought he heard—no. He turned to collect the lantern from its hook. It hung yet, swaying. No wonder he had noticed the wink of its light. It hung now from the curled fingers of Black Harry Morgan.

"B'Gad, sir, you've a nerve," said Morgan, almost admiringly.

"I beg your pardon, sir," Graham replied stiffly, blood rushing to pound his ears with the thunder of regimental drums.

"I forbid you to see my daughter and you take it manfully, then sneak into my stables of a night for a rendezvous with a maidservant. A versatile lad, I call you, captain. Which hussy was it, now? I'll know where to look for my own entertainment then."

"Sir, I feel the identity of the young woman . . . That is, I'm honor bound—"

"Honor! Honor's a word for priests and geldings. And you're a right manly fellow, isn't it so? Which was it, young sir? Or not so young, I recall that was a problem. Was it that darky shadow of my daughter's, that high-talking black beauty Heliotrope? You surprise me, captain. I'd no notion you hankered for the garden's more burnished berries. I thought it was medicinal herbs you were after—camomile, bittersweet, rue . . ."

Black Harry Morgan paused and regarded his frozen victim. Captain Winthrop was a fine figure of a fellow, no doubt about it. A solid, steady man who'd make any father a good son-in-law. But Black Harry Morgan was not any father. He'd spent eighteen years proving just that, and he wasn't about to stop now.

His powdered hair was caught at the nape of his neck by a simple black ribbon. But that was not why they called him Black Harry. His strong, square face was ruddy and drooped with the exhaustion of fifty hard-lived years. Its most remarkable feature, other than the hard hazel eyes and aquiline nose, were a pair of thick, bristling, black brows. And they were not why he was called Black Harry.

That reason was written in thirty-five years of his personal history, and Captain Graham Winthrop was about to receive a history lesson.

"Which gel, lad, tell me now, which backstairs slut o' mine have you been delvin' in?"

Captain Winthrop flinched. "It—it was just a common girl from the kitchen, sir. I don't know her name, I—"

Black Harry's brocade sleeve swung out in a powerful arc, and with the back of his hand he knocked Captain Winthrop to the matted hay on which they stood. The lantern never even wavered in his other hand.

Graham sucked the hot salty sea welling around his tongue and brought a hand to the burning slash that was his mouth.

"S—sir," he began thickly.

"That, puppy, is what you get for lyin' to Black Harry Morgan. Something you'll avoid in future even if I make it simple for you. If you believe I'd swallow the idea that it was only a servant of the house you were takin' for a roll in the hay, you'd think I'd swallow a fistful of snuff as readily."

"You know, then, sir," began Graham, struggling to his feet. "But I'm not ashamed of loving Rue."

"Aren't you now? Brave lad. Spirited, you know." Black Harry rocked back and forth on his high-tongued shoes. Captain Winthrop stared down at cut-steel buckles incongruously gleaming from the dusty straw. "Tell me about it, lad," said Black Harry through his teeth softly, his hands clasped behind his back as he still rocked on his heels.

"T—tell you, sir? About what's between Rue and me—?"

Only silence answered him, and the brush of Black Harry's clothing against itself.

"There's naught to tell you, sir, and a Christian gentleman would not so inquire, not even a father."

Black Harry arched one thick eyebrow at that. Captain

Winthrop took it for skepticism until he heard shuffles behind him and felt his arms pinioned by someone who knew what he was doing. Two someones, the reek of gin still heavy on them, their roughly clothed arms twining around his smart red sleeves.

" 'Tis not good to lie to a father, Captain Winthrop," said Black Harry, baring a sliver of white teeth. "Been seein' her, haven't you, lad?"

"No, no, I swear—"

The man at his left spun Graham to face him, his right fist driving into his captive's stomach. Graham doubled over the stunning blow, half-hanging over his attacker's stinking shoulder. That, more than anything, brought his head up, his light eyes gone even lighter with unfocused pain.

"No, captain? Still no?"

Graham's head sagged forward as his stomach regurgitated wave after wave of fire. His lips slacked, and the blood behind them trickled warmly down his chin and moistened his fresh white cravat.

"Now, think first, captain. Is not this most sensitive father correct in assuming that you have not only made a calf of yourself in this affair, but a woman of her?"

His quarry gasped—whether from residual pain or the sharpness of the accusation—even Black Harry couldn't tell.

Graham straightened again in his warders' grasp.

"No. You impugn your daughter, sir, and that I will not tolerate."

A moment's silence greeted this assertion. Black Harry raised a black brow, the other, in fact, though Graham did not notice Morgan's facial ambidexterity. The second ruffian stepped round to confront the officer, then struck him full in the face with a beefy fist.

Graham's body lurched with the blow, his involuntary grunt of pain trailing away to a moan. His attacker stepped back quickly to support him before he fell to the floor.

Now, his head lolling on the blood-brocaded cloth at his neck, his knees bent almost to the straw, and his shining black boots dusty, filmed from heel to knee-guard, Graham was beyond defiant gestures.

"Well?"

"You want—what do you want?"

Black Harry had to lean down a bit to hear the question bubbling out between the bloody lips.

"Less lyin', lad. And you seem to have been doin' enough of it with my daughter."

"Not . . . . not what you think," Graham began groggily.

The answer was not what Black Harry thought acceptable. He nodded slightly to his lackeys. They heaved the almost unconscious man up only to pummel him with crashing blows to the ribs. This time when Graham sagged they let him crumple to the straw.

"Well?" Black Harry's hands spread on his bent knees as he leaned down to continue his verbal prodding. "My daughter's no virgin now, thanks to you and half your regiment, for all I know. That's true, isn't it?"

Graham was not unconscious. "Yes," he hissed finally.

Black Harry straightened. "Excellent."

Graham's eyes rolled up in confusion despite the effort. Surely he had not heard right with the drumming of his own pain in his ears, surely the man was not pleased to learn of his daughter's ruin? Though God knows, they would marry and then—

"It's as I thought," said Black Harry softly. He glowered at the waiting ruffians. "Well, assist the lad up, you pair of mutton-headed oxen. And dust off his pretty bright coat."

They hauled Graham up again, their clumsy brushes at his sides buffeting his damaged ribs. His groan of protest was faint.

"So." Morgan moved around his quarry, pausing finally between him and the lantern so all Graham saw was his devil-dark outline and a halo of bright, pulsing, painful light.

Morgan reached out for Graham's coat and dusted a brass

button between his thumb and forefinger. It was an avaricious gesture.

"You'll clear out then, young sir. Nothing to loiter for, my dear captain. Your piece of petticoat is snug in her deceitful little bed. And you'll not see her again."

"T-tomorrow," Graham mumbled. But the word was an incantation, a faint memory throbbing through his pain, not a promise.

"Not tomorrow. Not any day. You'll never see her again."

Graham shifted drunkenly on shaky legs, groping toward protest.

Morgan's eyebrow saluted the thug on Graham's left, who suddenly dropped the grip on his arm, waited for Graham's infinitely slow sag to the floor, and administered a savage kick to his midsection.

Graham groaned and rolled into a passive ball. The other man half-lifted him up by the uniform reveres, then struck him powerfully across the cheek. This time Graham crumpled without the accompaniment of a groan, and Black Harry sighed.

"I'd not done with him, Wilkes. This is not one of your crimping house johnnies with twenty-four hours to sleep off in the bowels of a ship before he's needed again."

Graham's head rolled back on the straw, perhaps instinctively in search of a pillow. It found the rough boot of his tormentor. But that boot-toe was still, for Black Harry's brows remained level.

The lantern light was not kind to any of the faces in that ill-lit room. Black Harry's was shadowed and deeply lined; the two men's beard stubble painted them heavy-faced and brutal. But Graham Winthrop's face was as red as his coat, his features swelling unrecognizably. The cleft in his chin filled with a rivulet of blood trickling from his mouth.

"Now listen well, captain. You've violated my house. I could have you horsewhipped, transported, sent to a crimping house and on the next ship to the slave markets of Constantinople. I could cut off your ear or your hands or your privy part, and none would stand forth to accuse me of it."

Graham gagged on his own blood and pulled himself up on an elbow to vomit into the blood-slick straw around him.

"But," continued Black Harry, rocking steadily on his heels as Graham's retching subsided from sheer weakness. "But I'll let you go now, lad, and say no more into the bargain, if you'll give me your word as an officer and a gentleman to see my daughter no more. Some may be harsh and deny you your rank as a gentleman after your behavior with my Rue. But bygones be bygones, I hold no grudge, if you will see her no more."

Graham said nothing.

"Never again!" Morgan leaned down. Graham's eyes lifted only enough to focus on the backs of his hair-tufted hands.

"Yes," said Graham.

"What, lad?" Black Harry cupped his hand over his ear and cocked his head on his bullish neck.

"Yes," said Graham tonelessly.

Morgan nodded, and the crimping house men pulled Graham upright, though he sagged between them almost to his knees.

"Ah, a pity," noted Morgan. "Look, lads, you've taken a bit of a crimp out of our captain's finery. A shame, for his watch is more dimpled than a country wench's bum."

Morgan pulled the crushed chain from Graham's waistcoat and held up the broken watch like a trophy. His dark eyes narrowed and fastened on the single blue stone swinging from the bent ring of metal atop it.

"Aahhhhh. Sweet, ain't it, lads, what tokens love will buy? Or give away." He wrenched the stone from its anchorage, bending the watch ring more, and thrust it into his own dark waistcoat pocket. The timepiece he spit upon, polished on the flap of Graham's jacket, and thrust back into its customary pocket. A nod, and Graham was dropped again to the floor, a blow he seemed beyond feeling.

"If he doesn't drag himself out by dawn, you two linger a bit and deposit him back on his barrack stoop. They'll think a cutpurse had at him."

The men nodded and followed Black Harry out into the crisp night air, leaving the lantern flickering softly over the crumpled scarlet form in the straw.

Later, much later, one of the sleeping kittens untwined itself from its fellows and tottered over on dainty feet. It brought an inquisitive gray-striped face down to Graham's, tiny whiskers brushing the unresponsive flesh. It extended a narrow, pink tongue and experimentally licked. Warm and liquid, but not milk. Something other, something that hummed through its predatory nature like wine. But not milk.

The kitten turned and made its way back to its littermates.

By morning Graham Winthrop was gone, and the bloody hay had been turned to leave no trace of his ordeal. But whether he'd walked away or been carried, none but the kitten could say. And it only dreamt of mice.

Chapter Two

Deep blue the gemstones twinkled, like reverse stars against a background of soft white silk.

"Thirteen," said Rue Morgan, counting the members of the constellation sparkling from the oblong jewelry case. She shut the moiré lid. "An unlucky number, Heliotrope."

"Luck is not in numbers," replied the maid bent intently to the shining black edifice that was Rue's festive hairdress.

Barbados-born and maid she was, but Heliotrope had been reared with her mistress in benign neglect. They were more friends than mistress and servant, and Heliotrope irritated all who encountered her by speaking with the clarity of one of the King's English born.

Now her able dark hands arranged the final tendrils of the hair that massed at Rue's temples and cascaded down her back in the latest fashion of loose curls.

"Thirteen. Three more to be pried out of Father, and then, of course, Graham's. I wish I had this whole, Heliotrope. I'd wear it tonight, and every night thereafter, I promise you. Don't grin, you vixen. Haven't I seen you fluttering demurely past Sir George Lancaster's footman, Cyrus?"

"Stay still," retorted Heliotrope, thrusting a flowered frill into Rue's hair and holding her stationary on the brocaded dressing table stool.

Rue frowned at herself in the tabletop looking glass. At her tender years, she merely produced dark down-slanted brows that made her look elvish. She rose despite her attendant's protesting flutter of fingers.

"Enough. Father will thunder if I'm not there to receive my guests. But what for the neck? If not sapphires, what?"

She confronted herself in the long glass near the bedchamber door, a gilt curlicue-framed affair with wavy glass. It seemed Rue Morgan found other flaws in it. She studied the full, flowing skirt of figured yellow taffeta that just brushed the toes of lemon velvet slippers. She sighed.

When she had been born, women of fashion wore elaborately curled and piled white-powdered wigs and full, hooped skirts thrusting out from tiny waists. Their bared bosoms had thrust out as imposingly from wide, angled necklines edged in lace. The French had refined the décolleté and underlined it, so to speak, by edging necklines with transparent frills they called *"tatez-y,"* touch here. Even within Rue's memory, when the daring had first cast off hoops, women had still contrived a fullness at their skirt rears balanced by a forward inflation of bosoms through the fountaining projections of snowy shoulder handkerchiefs. Such women resembled pigeons both coming and going.

Now, fichus had expanded to cover the once swelling bodice, and while soft wide sashes around uncorseted waists were girlishly attractive, Rue feared that her vivid looks were somehow dampened by the stylistic changes wrought by the French's current fever of antiaristocratic republicanism. The guillotine toppled not only heads, but hairdresses and fashion.

"Be damned to the French!" she fussed, jabbing feathers and pearls by the string into her midnight hair.

At least the tax on wig powder favored her. Now only the stodgiest went about whitened from temple to pigtail and ringlet. Of course, military men like Graham and judges and such still kept to their floured whiteness. Rue envied them their drama, even though she knew her own black locks were the opening curtain to her beauty.

Her fingers pulled the fichu that ruffled below her collar bone lower and fixed it there with a pearl brooch. Heliotrope watched this haphazard rearrangement of her fastidious dressing with hands on hips.

"And you're to announce your betrothal tonight? What would your late mother say?"

"Nothing," retorted Rue. "Her life was short enough and sad enough for her to name me 'rue' in token of her own regret, and then take swift leave of life and me. I am called after a bitter herb whose very name means repentance, and I warrant my mother repented mightily of the marriage that bred me. If she were here, she would begrudge me nothing." Rue gave the fichu another downward tug.

"Young Captain Graham will learn to keep half an eye on you if he's wise," said Heliotrope, appealing to the living if the dead would not second her.

"Heliotrope!" Rue laughed and squeezed the woman's green and white-striped waist, half-shaking her, until the full, violet lips widened in a smile. "You've no experience of men, silly goose," she chided. "I know what they like."

"Ay, and should not," said Heliotrope, shaking her trimly sheared black head. She herself was not yet twenty, but despite sharing so much with her mistress, she had been a servant all her life and therefore grew older earlier.

"Duenna," accused Rue lightly, pulling downward on the offensive alençon lace once more before collecting a bespangled ivory parchment fan. She dangled it from her wrist while tying a scarlet ribbon around her throat and teasing its ends into a full rosette.

"Your gown and sash are yellow—red will never do unless you wish to play sunset," said Heliotrope tartly.

"It will for me. I'll match my captain. He's so splendid in full dress, isn't he, Helia? Well?"

Heliotrope acceded to the sparkling sapphire eyes. Captain Winthrop was, she granted, a festive and breast-stirring sight, perhaps even one deserving of a plunging fichu.

"Now then," said Rue, who would tolerate only agreement on this most splendid night of her young life, "where's my Piquant? I must kiss him for luck."

"Where do all lazy beasts go besides hell? Your fine brocade coverlet, where he no doubt drools on the linens."

Rue flounced to the bed's foot, kneeling under the towering, carved wooden tester like a subject to a king. The jonquil skirt foamed up around her narrow sashed waist.

Heliotrope felt a momentary friendly envy for her mistress's shatteringly lovely looks, fevered vitality, and ability to wear stunning yellow gowns that would look equally as well on velvet coffee-colored skin. Then Heliotrope recollected Black Harry's moods and petty houndings of his daughter's every little happiness, and she was glad she wore white cap and apron and faded into the servant-sentried background of the Morgan household.

"You pet! You king of canines," cooed Rue to the complacent accumulation of strawberry blond hair curled into her coverlet. A jaded face of pushed-in black muzzle and wide olive-dark eyes lifted reluctantly from dainty paws.

"Piquant! Give me a kiss for luck," Rue demanded, presenting a smooth and naturally flushed cheek to the oddly sour little face. The Pekinese complied, tongue lolling out lazily, face returning to his pillowing legs almost instantly.

"Monster of indifference! It's why I love you, I think. You are uncommon haughty for a dog." Rue ruffled the long silky ears fountaining from black velvet ribbons.

She stood, jerked again at the fichu that had ridden up, and met Heliotrope's reproving liquid brown eyes.

"And you are marv'lous haughty for a maid, my jewel," Rue said, "and, blame me, but I must love you for it." She fluffed the fichu upwards a conciliatory quarter of an inch. "There. When next you see me, Heliotrope, Piquant, I shall be the happiest woman in the world!"

A circle of gay saffron skirts, black curls bouncing down her back to joust mockingly with the great sash bow at her waist, fan folded and ready for a flirtatious unfolding, and Rue had danced out of her ornate bedchamber and downstairs where awaited servants, syllabubs, punches, towering delicacies, guests, Graham Winthrop, and her father, Black Harry Morgan.

Rue's birthday galas were always splendid occasions; no one could fault her father there. True, the guests were predominantly his friends and associates, but they were a respectable lot and Rue had learned early to revel in being the youngest, gayest and brightest at an otherwise exclusively adult affair. They were kind to her on their annual visit. She relished their undemanding amusement and affection. It was almost as if Black Harry could only muster fatherly feelings through his kind-hearted dependents.

Tonight, as each year, Morgan himself was resplendent in claret brocade coat with full pocketed skirt over a jade-green embroidered waistcoat. It was also true that younger men wore double-breasted frockcoats to formal occasions now, instead of such elaborate old-fashioned apparel. But Morgan had not changed his fashion in twenty years and still wore a tightly rolled wig in the wings-of-pigeons style.

His ship captains would be there, also bewigged or powdered, men of authority being the last to relinquish dignified symbols, however ludicrous. And their wives, who would often slip Rue some birthday token from the rare and distant Orient—her favorite was a strangely speckled egg painted with odd designs. And Morgan's fellow investors from the City, where his mercantile holdings were managed, though they were flung as wide as the East and West Indies. His great wealth flowed most sweetly, however, from the Barbados sugar plantation where hundreds of enslaved black backs promised that Morgan should never have to flex a muscle for himself if he so wished.

But Black Harry Morgan did not choose to absent himself

from the coarser duties that attended his wealth. In fact, he seemed to relish them. He was intimate at the crimping houses that lured unwary Londoners into the hands of crimping men who would drug them, beat them, and convey them to out-going ships where they would wake to begin arduous, and often fatal, unwilling apprenticeships in the Indies trade.

If Black Harry's antecedent had been the redoubtable Sir Henry Morgan himself, the West Indies' first respectable pirate, the hundred years since Sir Henry's heyday had not watered down the Morgan stock of rapacity at all. When or why people had come to call him Black Harry was not clear; it was before Rue was born. Certainly Morgan's treatment of the young and delicate second wife who bore Rue had done nothing to earn him a nickname of brighter hue.

Black Harry Morgan, in the second half-century of his life, feared neither man, woman, child, God, nor Devil. It made him many enemies and more friends. But that was the way of London in the year of Our Lord Arrogance 1795; people starved for want of bread while the army and navy powdered fine wheat flour on thousands of military heads spread across the British empire. Black Harry Morgan made fortunes that could have brought humane conditions to the hard-driven sailors on every ship of his line. Instead he supported crimping houses to drag unlucky men from their families and country. He had fathered a daughter who could have been the keystone of his mature years and instead. . . .

Rue sometimes watched her father's powerful face, hoping to catch those hard features relaxed. He did not even fancy women, as far as she knew. Or if he did indulge in such pleasures, it was with the painted, vulgar whores, far from the elegant streets of Marylebone and Paddington.

She watched him, this night of her eighteenth birthday. As great a pleasure as this annual affair gave her, the occasion was deeply underlaid with primitive fear. It was unnatural for Black Harry Morgan to lavish anything on his daughter.

And now, in defiance of this man who had seemed to demand defiance from birth, Rue would watch and wait for her red-coated captain to come blazing into the candle-lit atmosphere. She would listen for the hard sound of his gleaming black boots among the soft-slippered steps of lavishly attired civilians.

This was her father's one vulnerable point, the night when he presented a false picture to the world. If she and Graham could paint him into his own composition, could join hands under the dripping crystal chandeliers and declare what her father had denied them, even Black Harry Morgan would have difficulty preventing her dearest hopes from being achieved.

So Rue smiled and inclined her much decorated head to the familiar faces sweeping past, each announced by the footman who stood at the double doors leading into a long drawing room with arched plaster-decorated ceiling. So many powdered wigs and heads were abroad tonight; her father's set grew stodgier each year.

She stood beside him, aware of his own white-wigged head nodding on a muscular neck hardly softened by the flowing ghostly folds of his stock, aware of each rustle of brocaded coat sleeve against brocaded body. She was intensely wary of him, as one is of a snake whose attention one desperately hopes to escape.

"That's the lot, then," said Black Harry abruptly, turning to her with eyes narrowed. "You're looking cunningly lovely tonight, my dear."

She looked quickly to see for whose hearing the remark might have been really intended. No one was near them now; she must have been dreaming.

"Oughtn't we to wait here, Father, for the last guests?"

She glanced imploringly to the footman. Would that his tall cane were a wand to produce the desired person at will. Graham—where was he on so important a night?

Black Harry commandeered her elbow. "They're all here, my dear. Don't you remember greeting every man jack and lady jill on the guest list? Tsk, so sad to grow forgetful at your age. No doubt your mind is on other matters."

He led her briskly to the tall, Italian marble fireplace under whose looming mantel he had niggardly presented her with each sapphire in the necklace rightfully hers since she was old enough to remember to whom she owed such largesse. Rue had received her first sapphire at three. The guests gathered round for the ritual they regarded as charming proof of Black Harry's otherwise insignificant humanity. He did dote on the girl, at bottom. Of course, despite the disturbing tales.

Rue stood beside her father, facing the open semicircle the crowd automatically gave them. They made a gaudy pair—he in his fusty claret and green, and she cheerful as a tulip with a slash of carmine through its yellow petals. The red rosette around her neck trembled slightly, as did the frilled edges of her fichu.

"Since it is my eighteenth birthday, Father, perhaps I should save your gift for opening later—"

"Nonsense. No daughter of Black Harry Morgan puts off her pleasures. Is that not right, my friends?" he retorted with a rough laugh. A few in the semicircle laughed with him. Rue skimmed them for an answering flash of red and found none. The scarlet ribbon around her throat tightened with each moment's passing, like a gory noose.

She picked up the small, square jewelry case, the same shape and color every year, always containing the same perfectly cut sapphire each November—save for her tenth birthday, when a great watery teardrop had lain tremulously on the pale silk interior, the centerpiece of her mother's fabled necklace. Only three sapphires were left. Only this and two more years. And if her marriage to Graham justified her father in keeping the last two stones, well, then she should wear her necklace askew and regret nothing.

Rue opened the hinged lid, her fingers pressing into the box's padded ivory moiré.

Her mouth dropped, and some in the crowd giggled nervously. How touching to see a young woman surprised by her father on her birthday. Give Black Harry credit—the fellow was original.

Not one stone, but more, more round sapphires. Three at one blow. No more birthday rituals, no more empty smiles, no more torture standing next to the brocaded adder who had fathered her and—

And a fourth. A fourth stone so large and so unmistakable she had literally looked around it rather than at it, and even now its glittering facets wavered in her sight, for her eyes were abruptly adrown in some stinging clear liquid. Graham!

She stared at it, speechless, while the crowd murmured and asked to be shown the prize. She stared until the water in her eyes gathered into pendants like the sapphire and dropped beside it on the light blue silk, soaking through the fabric instantly, blotting and swelling and darkening.

"Now your set is complete, daughter," said a harsh voice from someplace so remote she looked up to the overbearing mantel and found only the laughing frozen faces of the cherubs carved there. Or were they Cupids?

"Let us see, let us see," came a soft chorus of female voices, giddy, uncaring voices.

Rue snapped the case shut and bolted from the room, light soles tapping through the astonished silence in her wake, the footmen's staffs bowing away from her abrupt exit, the footmen themselves resembling startled fairy godfathers found wanting.

When she reached the central hall, she heard the hissing waves of comment rising behind her and clattered quickly up the long curving staircase. The ivory moiré box was folded against her artfully arranged neckline, now forgotten, and her hand skimming the mahogany balustrade felt it slide over splinters rather than polished wood. Near the top, one of the flimsy slippers swiveled off her foot and tumbled halfway down the steps.

Rue stopped, turned, froze, watched her footwear bobble

away like a severed head into a basket. She whirled and mounted the last three steps, then savagely kicked the other slipper down the long carpeted passage, running along again on silent, white-stockinged feet so rapidly that she nearly passed her discarded shoe before it had stopped tumbling.

"Mistress Rue!"

Heliotrope had been dutifully sorting the furbelows in an ornament box. She stood, her dark face graying as if her blood had remained seated, and the trinkets floated to the floor in a gaudy pile.

Rue paused, her back to her white-painted bedroom door, the jewel box still folded to her breast, and that breast heaving for air as if something had caught in her throat, choking her.

"For pity's sake," began Heliotrope, rustling forward.

Sensing the uproar, the dozing Pekinese started up from the coverlet, barking raggedly, and then bounced to the floor to yap sharply at the general air of tragedy.

"Hush, you fat, blue-blooded nuisance," chided Heliotrope.

Rue stared unseeingly at her favorite's raised little muzzle. Her pale complexion, of which she was so vain, was now too white to be attractive. It was as if all the color in her body had drained into the scarlet band around her neck, and even the yellow of the gown looked jaundiced.

"Ah, *ma pauvre petite*," began Heliotrope, falling into the fashionable French phrases she had learned from Rue's gay chatter.

Rue moved from the door, her posture curved around the box she carried as if eggs rolled inside it instead of precious stones. She advanced to the room's center and watched Piquant recognize her and break into a series of circular turns, his plumed tail waving excitedly.

She stared down at the dog uncomprehendingly.

"Mistress Rue, what is it? Can anything be so awful—?"

"Only Father, Heliotrope. And sometimes God. But only Father can be so consistently awful." Her voice sounded strangled, but a little color leaked into her cheeks. Rue spun fiercely to a spindly legged table and deposited her burden upon it, opening the lid so wide the hinge-pin snapped and rolled to the floor. Piquant waddled over and sniffed at it.

"Four?" Helia said. "And what is so awful in his anticipating a few years' gifts? He gave you four."

Rue elevated the large, tear-shaped sapphire.

"And this, don't you know it?" she asked tonelessly.

"Know it? It is from the set—oh, it is the center stone. You had it earlier—another, he has given you a matching stone, a mate?"

"No, the keystone. I received it when I was ten, tucked it away, and only looked at it on rainy days for years . . . Until this year. Then I got it out and gave it to Captain Graham Winthrop of His Majesty's Seventeenth Lancers to wear on his watchfob. I never told you, Heliotrope, that I had done so. I never told Piquant. I most certainly never told Father. Yet here it is."

Rue wandered to the candelabrum still blazing on her dressing table and held the stone before one leaping flame, looking through it as through a quizzing glass with her dark head thrown back and her eyes narrowed speculatively.

"And it came into your father's possession because—"

"Because he knew I was meeting Graham despite his forbidding it, because he knew we planned to defy him and marry, because he has taken it from Graham and Graham from me. And now it doesn't matter if I have the stone because it is a very bitter thing to me, which must be a great satisfaction to Father."

"Even he is not such a devil!"

"What do you know of devils, Heliotrope? You are not even Christian."

Rue tilted her head, the candlelight painting sapphire highlights in her gleaming black hair. She had spoken, since returning to her bedchamber, in a light, remote singsong that stirred some faint memory in Heliotrope's non-Christian blood. Perhaps she remembered the lilting, repetitive slave songs from the cane fields. The mechanical, singsong refrains of those who have no hope.

"Your father has thwarted you 'ere this," the maid said briskly, extending her palm for the sapphire as if it were only one more trinket in need of efficient putting away.

Rue examined Heliotrope's waiting hand through the gemstone.

"They have such clarity, sapphires, yet are so dark. You can't quite see through them." Rue dropped the jewel into the maid's cupped palm, then examined her own fingertips, indented from the hard-cut edges. "I shall have it mounted and wear it on a ribband. You will find me one."

She knelt to stroke Piquant's head, drawing away the hinge-pin upon which he sucked noisily.

"If your father had the stone, but Captain Winthrop had it before—where is Captain Winthrop? And how—?"

"It does not matter, Helia," said Rue gently.

"Not matter? But it is all the matter."

"No. What matters is that my father had the stone, that he knew and was able to prevent Graham from coming to me. That is all that matters, all that ever mattered. He always knows. I thought I had learned when he sent Aunt Ninevah's canary winging into icy skies. It was only that I waited a while before risking again, and then risked all. And Father knows it. Perhaps he even forbid me to see Graham because he knew that would make my captain but more precious to me." She knelt again to the Pekinese on the floor lying with legs splayed to the world's four corners.

"But you, my jewel, he did not guess. Perhaps because you are so lazy and monstrous vain he deemed you beneath my affections . . . And you, Helia, he has let me keep you."

The black woman cast her eyes down to the dismembered jewel box, then dropped the great sapphire in it.

"I? I am as good as a slave, though your Parliament says such things no longer exist. I was bought on Barbados and freed here only when law made it necessary. Your father has surveyed those island slave fields, so perhaps he thinks such as I have little to offer."

Rue rose and shook out her crumpled taffeta skirt.

"Where are the rest of the stones? Fetch them and put them all together. And fetch more candles. I will need much light to pack by."

"Pack?"

"Yes. The footmen must remove the trunks from this house early, before my father's party sleep wears off. He will drink heavily of canary this night. We must be gone before he wakes."

"We?"

"I know you are loyal, Heliotrope; I do not know if you wish to trust yourself to a homeless orphan. And Piquant, of course, must come. It will so annoy Father to have overlooked him so long. I will take all of my things and, thanks to Father's generosity, the complete set of sapphires."

"But where, where do we go? And the young captain, can we find him—?"

Rue looked down at the open jewelry box. "No, he is lost, Heliotrope."

"Lost? He may be . . . delayed, drawn away, wounded . . . Dead."

"He is lost to me. I never wish to hear his name again. Father has proved quite satisfactorily that he can take anything I love. Very well," said Rue Morgan, untying the wide sash at her waist. "I will never love again.

"But I will hate. Oh, yes, Heliotrope, I will hate quite professionally. And when I am done, Black Harry Morgan will know this day was blacker than any he ever dreamed of. Well, don't stare. Will you help me remove this, this . . . dreary gown? I tire of it. It's yours, an' you'll not wear it when I may see. Then fetch my wrapper. We will pack all night and in the morning leave."

Rue paused by an alien piece of lace folded triangularly on the table. "What's this?"

Heliotrope returned to examine it with a troubled frown.

"Ay, a frippery that queer maid Rebecca tatted for your birthday. She left it with some raving that it bear you company in a troubled world."

Rue fingered the fancywork, then shrugged and moved on. She and Heliotrope emptied every wardrobe and chest and filled every trunk and bandbox the footmen Rue bribed brought them when the house had settled to sleep. They packed every last sash and shoe and white kid glove. The sapphires in their oblong box were stowed away in the reticule that accompanied Rue's best morning gown, which she instructed Heliotrope to leave hanging alone in the empty wardrobe.

When the room's contents had been siphoned into the pile of baggage at its center, she called the footmen to take it to the stable and prepare a coach for departure at five. She dimmed most of the candles and sent Heliotrope to bed.

Then she went to the windowseat in her last unpacked nightshift and stared at the distant trees set dark against the horizon in a predawn glow. A bit of wind rattled the panes in their mullions. The candle she had brought with her flickered reflectively in the window glass, a moth of dancing light.

She thought she saw a tiny red figure walking across the landscaped parterres surrounding Blackstone House. A small red figure in the dawn, Graham Winthrop passing through the copper beeches . . .

But then she studied the scene more closely and discovered that the dark dawn and the candle had conspired to paint a faint ghost of herself in the glass and that she had forgotten to remove the broad red ribbon from her throat.

Rue began sobbing then, setting her broken heart afloat on an endless salt sea within her. Somewhere in that tide Graham Winthrop died and Rue Morgan drowned. Deep she went, spiraling to unsounded depths of forgotten rage that had plunged like an anchor to the bottom of her consciousness. Treasured hopes as fragile as seaweed drifted through all her memories. She felt herself netted, flapping fishlike for air. And Black Harry Morgan sailed those internal oceans of hers, as he had for as long as she could remember, as piratical as his forebear.

She battled to the surface, breasting the tears and the despair, breaking to the surface, seaweed twining her as hopes never would. No hopes, she felt them slither away and drift deep to the bottom again. On the horizon of this empty world in which she bobbed she saw a carmine sun and a ship full-sailed against the glare. It carried a Jolly Roger grinning eternally.

Was there any weakness there, any unarmored part into which the rapier of her revenge could plunge to the hilt?

Yes. Appearances, always appearances. It was why she had never lacked for gowns, although birds and boys in pretty red coats went winging into exile; why the sapphires returned to her each year, bestowed in contemptuous reminder of power; why he gave the annual celebration that even now saw the house below her empty but used, wine-stained glasses waiting for the morning wash-up, flowers wilting in tall classical urns, long tables still bearing emptied platters.

Then appearance should be her weapon. She would take the Rue Morgan her father had made and make her the most outrageous blot on the Morgan name yet. She would take the only thing her father could not wrest away from her—his name—and forge it into a blade to rip his reputation, even the disreputable part he so prided himself upon, to shreds.

Rue got up from the windowseat and went to find a handkerchief to wipe her eyes. The only unpacked cloth she discovered was Rebecca Bartle's lace. She brought it back to the window and let it absorb the last silent tears that would still come and watched the dawn turn the sky rosy-yellow.

It could have been a sunset, Rue Morgan realized. A sunrise and a sunset were the same, according to one's point of view. Her sun, she resolved, should rise until it dried up all of that vacant, mindlessly undulating salt sea within her and left the dark pirate ship stranded on a Sahara-sandy bottom, dried weeds around its anchor, rusted red upon its chains, and its crew bleached bone white.

Rue's white teeth flashed in a Jolly Roger grin at the dawn, but the sun was already too high and there was no reflection in the glass to smile back at her.

Chapter Three

"No, I'll give you your revenge another time, when you are not so indifferent. You are thinking of something else now and play too negligently."

The speaker, an elegantly attired man in a frockcoat of most fashionable cut, collapsed a hand of cards into a single stack on the table, then fanned them carelessly in a semicircle. The slightest hint of a sneer curled his lips as he continued analyzing his opponent's indifference.

"The coldness of a losing gamester lessens the pleasure of a winner." He nodded with lowered lids to the one he addressed. "I'd no more play with a man that slighted his ill fortune than I'd make love to a woman who undervalued the loss of her reputation."

The flat of his palm slapped the table, and he stared steely eyed at the face opposite him. "No damme, it won't play!"

The face confronting the gamester was as grim as his own, and why not? It was his. He faced a mirror.

The man who had spent the last two minutes addressing himself lifted a lace-edged handkerchief to his cheek and dabbed at a bit of light powder clotted there.

The woman who had spent the last minute standing in the nearby doorway listening to him, crossed the threshold.

"And why, sir, won't it play?"

The man glanced idly over his mauve broadclothed shoulder. " 'Tis Congreve, and he is all wit and no warmth. I am a fool to fiddle with him." The handkerchief returned to dab fastidiously at his cheek. But his mirrored eyes focused on the figure behind him.

And little wonder. She wore a deep rose-colored spencer jacket, its cuffs and caped shoulder reveres edged in black velvet. The unhooped skirt fell gracefully to the floor. A snowy stock cascaded from her chin to where the Spencer's deep vee met the top of her narrow waist. Somehow this modesty but veiled an implied wickedness. Her white hat was high-crowned and wide-brimmed, caught up at one side with a diamond buckle, its brim lined with pink silk and latticed with black velvet appliqué. In one black kid-gloved hand she carried a slim walking stick bowed with rose velvet.

The man, who by profession took a deep interest in attire, had summed up his visitor's ensemble in a flick of his lashes over piercing blue eyes. It was her face his thoughts dwelled on, and not unremarkably, for Quentin Rossford had been partial to pretty faces since he'd glimpsed one more attractive than the midwife's who'd birthed him. And that would have been when his unfocused infant eyes had first chanced upon a pretty country housemaid.

He had made a study of faces, and the one that confronted him now wore all the surface beauty and inner contradictions that stirred his actor's soul to its wellsprings.

"Like Venus, you have pried open the clam shell of my frightful curiosity. Are you only a passing vision, or may you light for a moment in my humble dressing room?" he invited in the modulated baritone that had tingled in the eager ears of London's loveliest ladies for years.

She inclined her hatted head and stepped to the rather tumble-down chair he indicated. He anticipated her with perfect grace and flicked it first with his handkerchief before the rose folds could arrange themselves on it.

"I thank you, Mr. Rossford." She nodded to the door. "You may wait in the foyer."

Rossford realized that a dusky hatted shadow bearing a blond muff—nay, a canine with rose velvet bows at its ears—had loomed behind his visitor all the while. He chided his aging eyesight—or perhaps it was simply his aging vulnerability to a fair face—and leaned back against the dressing table, for he sat only upon a stool.

"I must tell you that I have thought you quite marvelous since I was first allowed to attend Drury Lane," she told him. "Such occasions have not been often, but you have always risen to them, in my humble opinion. Your Sir Teazle was brilliant."

"You honor me, and concur with our esteemed manager and author, Mr. Sheridan," he said with a smile. "But I would comfort myself more if I could be assured you had seen me in more dashing circumstances than playing the diddled husband. It is a role which on the stage, as in life, takes great greedy bites out of one's dignity."

"Ah, but it was your dignity that so impressed me, sir. I hazard that you are well thought of in the company?"

He inclined his head again, still powdered from his previous night's role, though his true iron-gray color showed through the waning flour.

Quentin Rossford had been blessed in many ways during his fifty-some years of life. Chief among his blessings was the good fortune of keeping his hair. It had allowed him to essay romantic roles well past the normal lifespan of such careers. It had endeared him to London matrons as well as the new generation of daughters they brought to see their favorite. He assumed he was being honored by just such an offspring now.

"So ardent an admirer deserves a name. Have you any besides Diana?"

She smiled, and he was startled to see an admirably

straight row of white teeth, pearls beyond price in this age of early poxed complexions and blackened teeth. She was almost impossibly lovely—skin of snow, raven hair tumbling loosely to elegantly collared shoulders, and eyes of blue satin starred by dark lashes. And yet behind them lay some cold calm ocean that screamed warning at his Lotharian instincts.

"Rue Morgan. Do you think it will serve?"

Quentin Rossford's long, handsome face had frozen. It gave Rue an opportunity to survey him. A pity, he was much older than he appeared from a seat in the Drury Lane's cavernous auditorium. Not unhandsome, of course, simply all the well-modeled flesh drooped sadly at his fine eyes and sensuous mouth. But he was handsome enough; he would serve.

"Serve for what, Miss Morgan?"

She started, her drifting eyes anchoring again on his face. Was he so intuitive that he had read her thoughts? Ah, no, it was about her name he queried her.

"For a theatrical undertaking."

Rossford stirred uncomfortably on his stool. His cheeks, still painted slightly from his role, seemed more rouged. Or perhaps his face had merely gone paler. Something seemed to have stiffened within him. Rue Morgan thought it was wariness at being broached by another Thespian hopeful. She smiled and tilted her head inquiringly.

Rossford rose, a tall, straight figure delivering a lecture.

"I am not unfamiliar with your, er, father, Miss Morgan. Your family is good—"

"Is it?" she questioned sharply.

"Good in the only sense that matters in these times— wealthy, removed from the most lowering aspects of trade, even possessed of a certain colorfulness."

"I am as familiar with my father as you, Mr. Rossford. I trust you are not about to present him to me as a pillar of society whom I must not disgrace."

"No," he conceded, suddenly an actor whose partner's

talent for improvisation had deflated his stock role. "I, of all people, would not attempt to mislead you there."

He sat again, his face growing serious, an effect that tautened the lines around his eyes and, oddly enough, made him appear younger.

"You do not wish to tread the boards," he said persuasively. "These painted hussies with their latest fashions and pretty affectations of speech are little better than the women who drop their chemises for a few pence in the slums. Do I shock you? Then that is proper, for what you propose is most improper."

She flushed at what she knew was a crudity of expression he had deliberately flaunted before her, like a fond parent who produces bogeymen to keep children from imagined danger.

"Ah, no, you do not shock me. I fancy that I am about to shock you," returned Rue, folding her hands around the ebony walking stick upright before her and tilting it against her cheek at precisely the point the rose bow rested.

Rossford bit his lip.

"I wish to go upon the stage, Mr. Rossford, and I will do so. And I will be most obliged for your assistance. Most obliged."

"Damme, miss," the actor snapped, slapping his palm to the table again. His sharp eyes checked for her start, but she sat as calm and unruffled as a cat watching the scurryings of a particularly elusive mouse.

He leaned back against the table again and picked up a rougebox, turning it slowly between his long elegant fingers.

"And have you any facility in declamation, elocution . . . ?"

"I have not the slightest notion," Rue replied blithely.

"Then why this mad passion for the stage?"

"I have no deep fancy for the stage, sir. You mistake me. I require the . . . proper, improper setting . . . for a certain scheme of mine. I wish to make a spectacle of myself, Mr.

Rossford, and the stage strikes me as the most suitable arena. I suppose I could always attempt the circus, but I fear I am deplorably inept at horsemanship, having been town-reared, and I do not fancy tumbling from some thundering beast's back through a paper hoop in a toga up to my knees. Like you, I prefer dignity when making a display of myself. And to my observation, that makes me an actor."

The rougebox snapped to the tabletop.

"You make me a fool, Miss Morgan. Your father would never tolerate such nonsense—"

"There is little that my father has tolerated of me, Mr. Rossford, but I have left his house, and if he would have me back, he must be willing to tolerate a ball through the spleen. And if he should appeal to the magistrates, I promise I shall make quite a stir in the papers, so if you fret over scandal, I think it would be far wiser to find me a place on the boards. I do not require any lines, just a certain prominence of placement. I want a lover, you see, and he must be wealthy. I have no time to find one by conventional means, as my funds are somewhat limited. Do not the town's finest bloods congregate nightly to pay tribute to the ladies of the stage?"

Rossford ran a hand through his tied-back hair, distraction tracking his symmetrically lined forehead.

"I need not trouble your company long, sir," Rue went on consolingly. "I shall find someone suitable to support me and my retinue—which is humble, I assure you—within the month." Her tone became cajoling. "And I am not unaware that you must see some advantage in sponsoring my brief career. I will mistress you for the month, though I warn you I quite intend to pass on."

Rossford blanched. "You cannot mean this, this blasphemy! I am old, you are young, you—" he objected, his elegant diction reduced to a sputter of astonishment.

"An actor refusing a lady?" Rue's eyebrows elevated as elegantly as his own were wont when the situation called for it. "La, sir, then the stage's reputation is overstated and your argument loses force."

She considered the head of her cane, spinning it slowly in her gloved fingers.

"It is true, I confess, that you are a bit older than I had anticipated. Yet you cut a fine figure at fifty feet and in candlelight, sir." She smiled. "I fancy I can tolerate you nearer for merely a month. No, don't look so shocked. It quite distresses me to have shocked such a scandalous creature as an actor. It means that there may be no redemption for me." She sighed. "Am I not pretty? Surely you could take some consolation in me—"

"Stop! Impertinent chit. Have you no shame to so boldly usurp the lines from a past master of seduction?" He leaned forward, the ruffles of his stock stirring against his coat front. His voice dropped.

"But, confess, my dear would-be Messalina. You are young and chaste as Diana, and what bubbles from your lips is all bluff."

"I am young," conceded Rue, lowering her voice as well, "but no virgin to protect from yourself or any other man, including the most honorable of actors."

"You have truly shocked me then," said Quentin, his eyebrows drawing together.

"There are many lost innocences to mourn in these days, sir. And the innocence of the body is a trifle compared to the innocence of the soul. My father has taken my soul, Mr. Rossford. And I will have his in return. Will you aid me?"

The actor reared away from her, his troubled eyes disbelieving. One expressive hand reached out to her, fingers splayed as if he found her unreal and needed to touch her. Rue Morgan thought she read pity in that faded, handsome face. Pity and something deeper, something quite despairing.

"And what of your mother in all this?" the actor mused, his eyes lost in some distance only he saw. "What would she say—?"

"She is dead. And perhaps the better for it. So I am my own creature with naught to stop me but the timidities of others—"

"Yes, dead." The actor's blue gaze came back to the even more vivid eyes that had never left his face. He smiled sadly.

"So you are alone in the world, Rue Morgan, and you wish my aid. You shall have it then. We will make such a sensation of you that London will rise to its feet. On the stage I will put you. For a few weeks, at least, I can induce La Pericole to step aside. Lydia Languish it will be, in the revival of *The Rivals* I mount next month! Yes, a languishing Lydia you will make."

"Is that not rather a long part?" inquired Rue, alarmed.

"Indeed." The actor's eyes narrowed at her speculatively. "But perhaps there is an actress in you, after all. Certainly there is a will. And the way of the world is to give way before wills strong enough. Lift up your skirt."

"I beg your pardon, sir!"

"Up with it. If you balk at revealing an ankle, you will make no actress, much less a mistress." The blue eyes drilled her, almost as if hoping she would refuse. Rue lifted her chin with her hem, drawing the rose skirt and its now revealed border of white lace petticoats rapidly up to the ribboned garters that fluttered below her knees.

"Enough," entreated the actor. "You've a good turn of ankle, and many a man of my age hungers back for the years when a pretty foot was not hid beneath street-trailing skirts. You will wear costume for Lydia—polonaise and shepherdess skirts and," he eyed the swelling fichu with cold professionalism, ". . . and décolletage."

"Impossible," sputtered Rue. "Even Mrs. Siddons does not don costume, no matter what period the play. Actresses are noted for their adherence to Fashion. You would have me disgrace myself by dressing in clothes nearly as old as I! And what of the lover I require? I could no more attract such a one in hoop skirts than a bowl of vinegar could draw a bee—"

"You underestimate yourself and overestimate your prey, my dear. Fashion is not what attracts men. I have reason to know of what I speak, believe me. If you wish to throw away your reputation—"

"I care not a fig for reputation!"

"—if you are set upon it, there is no one who could guide you more expertly upon this course than I," said Rossford. "I have made an avocation of it," he added bitterly.

Rue paused and sat back. After all, he had granted her wishes. She studied him. Long in the tooth, but once a very handsome fang indeed. Yet such things did not matter. If he had been as homely as a pumpkin, she could have kept her bargain with him. Love mattered nothing to her anymore; she no longer believed in soaring emotions. That left only the compromises of the body, and they were really no more than realistic accommodation. Men had discovered that long ago—that is why there were so many rakes.

"I am grateful for your assistance," she said, meaning it. "You will be pleased with me."

"I fear not."

"But—"

"I will put you on the stage, but I will not put you between my sheets."

"I would trust you more if I knew you had something to gain."

"Perhaps."

Quentin Rossford smiled and leaned his face on an elegant hand. His elbow pinned the discarded prop cards to the dressing table, and he moved it to brush them aside.

"My dear Rue," he said languidly. "I do not doubt that your innocence has been lost and that you are a very unconventional young woman any more than I distrust my eyes' testimony that you are a very lovely one. I've no doubt you will set this wicked old London on its end. But there are some matters in which perhaps you might concede a slight naiveté. I will not make you my mistress, not even for a month, dearest child, because I, ah, have no inclination in that direction. If you follow me." The bland blue eyes rested on her in a jaded kind of amusement.

"Follow? No, I . . . That is to say, you—"

"Prefer masters," said Rossford suavely.

Rue's eyes widened. Then a bit of color dawned on her cheeks and darkened into twin crimson spots.

Rossford leaned forward impishly.

"Remind me to rouge you well, you look quite charming. And as for your vaunted wish to immerse yourself in the scandal of the theater, I must caution you, my sophisticated blusher, that many men who walk the boards are those least likely to disturb the reputation you seem so eager to throw away."

Rue's hands tightened on the walking stick, her eyes cast down at her black kid shoetips peeping from under her skirt.

"Pray excuse my . . . misapprehension, Mr. Rossford. I thought . . . But you have so many women admirers! I have heard—"

"And I admire many women," he replied smoothly. "With women, I am profligate with admiration."

"Still I had not thought . . ." Rue pondered, then raised her head again. "And why, then, would you aid me? What does it serve you?"

"I aid you because I . . . admire . . . women. Because I am prodigiously bored at the moment and this masquerade will divert me. Because you are excessively pretty, my dear, and may snag someone influential who may assist my career. And because I am cursed with a monumental sense of drama, and you appeal to it. Monumentally."

Rue stood.

"Then there is little more to say. When do you wish me to return?"

"I will send for you at—?"

"The Queue and Bottle Inn."

"—and we will begin rehearsals in a few days. It is no

easy task to dislodge a leading actress and replace her with an amateur, you know," he said, smiling thinly. "So prepare yourself for the battle till then. Farewell, *ma tragédienne.*"

"*Tragédienne?* But you said I was to play comedy, *The Rivals*—?"

"And isn't comedy always erected upon tragedy, Rue Morgan?" His smile grew even tighter. "Good day. I must wrestle a bit more with Congreve before I give up on reviving him."

He turned his back to her and drew some sheets over to study. Rue stared at the impassive mauve back for a moment, then shrugged and rustled out of the cluttered room, brushing a ghostly suit of clothes that hung from a folding screen.

But not only the clothes felt the brush of her going. Quentin Rossford's eyes were sharp upon her retreating figure in the mirror. As soon as she had gone, he pushed the script away and leaned intently toward the glass, studying his own face, which he had seen in the guise of countless characters but perhaps never his own.

She was so young, so lovely. So . . . tender. He had been tempted as he had seldom been tempted before. And now . . . Ah, old sins always come back to haunt one. Old sins and old enemies.

Quentin Rossford's eyes narrowed again at his visage in the mirror. He watched, fascinated, with an actor's objectivity, as rage suffused that face and turned it into a strained mask of naked emotion. Even then he recognized the paradox that the nudest emotion is always a pose of sorts. A self-deception.

She would learn that, the young Rue, and grow old like himself. But perhaps it was worth it, perhaps she had given him the means of some satisfaction finally after all these years, nearly twenty years gone . . .

The expressive hand tightened on a large powderpot, as if it had a much-longed-for neck in its grasp. Quentin

Rossford shut his eyes and let the past and all its painful denials rush over him in a blood-thundering tide.

"Damn you, Black Harry Morgan," he burst out in a stentorian voice and turned to hurl the pot across the cramped room. It struck the screen full on, and the painted parchment wobbled on its legs, powder fanning out to obscure the pastoral scene painted there.

The empty suit of clothes hanging at one end shuddered from the violence of the blow, then, like a hanged man on Tyburn Hill playing out his last role, it grew slowly, inevitably still.

Chapter Four

"Tighter, my admirable black beauty! You do your mistress no service if you leave her overmuch room to breathe and with a waist no man may set his hands around. And that is the point, *n'est-ce pas*, Rue?"

"Oh, thunderation, Quentin! Enough, Heliotrope!"

Rue set her hands akimbo and stared down at the actor.

He was fully dressed and quite splendidly, with black satin breeches over blue silk stockings and a dark striped frockcoat brightly buttoned in brass. His hair was unpowdered, and its salt-and-pepper streaks but matched the striping of his coat. He was seated on a stool, hands folded on a walking stick poised between his casually splayed legs.

Rue, on the other hand, stood.

Indeed, she had done very little but stand during the weeks since she had joined the Drury Lane company. She had stood on the stage for endless hours of rehearsal. And whenever the direction had called for her to momentarily alight, fate would have it that she was called to replay the previous scene and must stand again.

She had stood in the wings while Rossford drilled her in the subtleties of his art. Apparently sitting was not one of them. And now she stood, yet longer, while Heliotrope laced her into the abomination of faded fashion that Rossford had insisted she wear, a corset of nigh-solid whalebone.

Rue's irritation was diverted by the most arresting phenomenon. She glanced down to her own waist and saw her hands on her hips with the long second fingers meeting in her middle.

Rossford laughed at her expression.

"Most dainty, are we not? If she can pass through a key-hole, she's laced, Heliotrope."

Rue nodded and sighed, but not too deeply. Her hair was dressed high with formal curls cascading down her chemise-clad back, but was powdered cake-frosting white. Her dark hair was such a facet of her personality that she looked oddly quenched.

She turned to the scratched mirror to verify this conclusion.

"I'm not . . . insipid-looking now, am I, Quentin?"

Rossford's light eyes rolled ceilingward.

"Bless the child. Now, at the least, you won't frighten off half of the eligible gentlemen. You look quite demure, and no man wants a tempest for a mistress."

Heliotrope's full lips pursed at this casual discussion of her mistress's most improper plans, but she continued fluffing the lavishly flounced petticoats that fell to Rue's calves without comment.

Rue studied her reflection. This last round of lacing had pressed the stiff corset front so tightly to her body that her breasts now mounded impressively above the buckram. She adjusted the low, lace-trimmed neck of her chemise over the phenomenon. There should be no need to tug at fichus now, or anchor her intentions with pins. She would be fortunate if no pair of rosy suns rose over the horizon of her neckline. She glanced horrified to Rossford.

"I won't—?"

"Lud, no." He guessed her anxiety easily. "In forty years

no lady has yet slipped her bodice, though men who were no gentlemen might hope so."

Rue returned to self-contemplation. While Quentin Rossford had tutored her in every aspect of the actor's art, he had left her sentimental education utterly alone. She had totally accepted his romantic indifference, indeed, had found it strangely comforting and could see why men such as he made fine companions for women.

Only three weeks before she would have been uneasy thus ungowned in his presence; now she sensed that with whatever emotions he might regard her—and they varied from amusement to sternness to an odd kind of melancholy—he would never look upon her with lust.

"But you swear, Quentin, that this gown shall cause a stir?" she asked as Heliotrope dropped the series of skirts over her hips, then laced her into the bodice.

"You would do better to worry about your part, not your parts," he admonished. "You must remember to advance to the footlights when you speak your speeches."

"The theater is so large, tier upon tier in the balconies, and tonight it will be filled with people!"

"I devoutly hope so. It is my directorial debut."

"And I will not disappoint you? I will do well?"

He tilted his head to regard her, the smile on it reminiscent.

"Ah, I thought you were all absorbed in your ends and not your means. You will be a sensation, Rue, but never an actress."

Her rouged and powdered face fell; he rose and walked over to her, opening a small enameled box. A tiny black heart materialized on her chin where his finger touched it.

"You said your heart was not set on the stage," he began consolingly.

"I believe I said I had no heart," she answered stiffly, but her eyes were bright with a glazing of tears.

Quentin found another patch, a pendant-shaped one, and applied it to her right cheekbone.

"You shall not disgrace me. If you but remember your lines and speak them, 'twill be enough. To put an accomplished actress in the part of Lydia is a waste, at any rate. It merely detracts from the rest of the play. And a bad one can't ruin it."

"I am bad?"

"No, child, merely passable, and that has yet to stop an actor." He patted her cheek and handed her the patchbox. "I think you will find it advantageous to place one of these . . . er, there."

His elegant hand waved discreetly in the direction of her cleavage. Rue contemplated her swelling bosom, then dipped a finger into the box and positioned a star daringly low on her breast.

Heliotrope sighed pointedly, but Rossford merely nodded approval.

"La Pericole wore a cross-knotted fichu and a great feathered hat and carried a parasol as Voluminia last week," Rue continued in a last spasm of doubt. "And her Coriolanus wore a toga. You're certain—"

"*Regardez,*" said Rossford, spinning her out of Heliotrope's hands to face the mirror.

She did indeed look striking. The underskirt was black silk with an overskirt of magenta draped in purple satin at the hem. A white brocade pannier puffed at her hips on either side of the now abbreviated waist and was drawn up in the back with black satin bows. The gown's bodice was black and purple striped satin, with a wide triangular neck edged in an upstanding frill and full white lawn sleeves to the elbow.

The hem was well above her dainty pale-stockinged ankles and her feet shod in black satin shoes with diamond-studded heels and embroidered magenta tongues. Magenta bows circled her throat and one ankle.

"Do you not think that Monsieur Guillotine spared Mademoiselle Bertin only so that she could flee to London and dress Miss Rue Morgan for the Drury Lane?" Rossford asked. "She dressed the late Marie Antoinette, and she has done royally by you. It takes me back to my youth."

"Well, it takes my breath away," said Rue, her hands smoothing the narrow waist. "But if gentlemen in search of mistresses are drawn to a great quantity of bared bosom, I daresay I shall do quite well."

"I assure you they are."

"And how *you* would be expert in such matters, I cannot fathom," she retorted.

Something in his face remained very still, like a mask painted on.

"Oh, but Quentin, you have been very good to me," she said contritely, moving to him. "I cannot imagine why."

In glancing down at her, he caught the twinkle of a discordant blue at her neck. He picked up the sapphire on its narrow blue velvet ribbon hanging slightly below the magenta neckband.

"Out of shade, my Rue. Why do you wear it?"

"It is a gift. From my father."

"You loathe your father."

"Yes."

Rossford stared for a long time into the hard but honest blue eyes looking up at him. Even in the higher heels, she was a petite creature, hardly taller than a child. He let the jewel drop back to her neck.

"I have given you your heart's desire, Rue. Yes, I know you say that you have no heart. I have not asked if it were right or wrong, but I have given it to you." Rossford sighed. "Do you know what your heart's desire is? It is to have no heart, and you have not yet achieved it. But I hold out great hope for your eventual success."

"Why?" she whispered.

"Because I had one myself years ago, and I have managed to divest myself of it quite efficiently."

"All actors are liars," she challenged.

"Not when I tell you the curtain rises in not many minutes. You must take your place."

He turned to leave, but she caught his silk-faced lapel.

"Quentin . . . I'm afraid. It's so vast and dark out there. So many are waiting—"

His face hardened.

"Nonsense. The run is but three days. You have that long to find your . . . heart's desire. Would Black Harry Morgan pause at a trifling anxiety, a great darkened theater, merely because it stood between him and his goal?"

"No!" said Rue fiercely. "He would stop at nothing. And neither shall I."

She marched from the dressing room without another glance to Rossford, Heliotrope, or even the drowsing Piquant curled atop her everyday clothes, the little heels striking wooden flooring purposefully.

In moments, the candlelight from above and below the proscenium arch was falling squarely on her powdered hair and bosom, her shining satin gown, her jeweled little heels, her antique patches as lewd as a wink.

But Rue Morgan, as she launched into *The Rivals*'s "circulating library" scene, was aware only of the proper lines flowing in her clear voice into the dark, dimly lit house where vagrant jewels winked and arched tiers towered to a distant ceiling as remote as heaven.

Chapter Five

On the third and last night of *The Rivals*, Rue met Sir Nigel Pagett-Foxx.

Quentin Rossford had been a prophet who recognized the lay of his own land.

Rue Morgan had been the talk of the town. The audience had buzzed over her unconventional costuming—imagine, in style with the time at which the play was written rather than the moment!—and had applauded her loudly on curtain calls. The other actors had been most rude on the whole, and La Pericole gave even Piquant sullen looks when he waddled past.

But the great anonymous masses in the dark beyond the footlights adored her. She drew bachelors-about-town to her dressing room by the score. And while she would have chatted happily with them till dawn, both Rossford and Heliotrope would have no late-night lingering when she played the next day.

"But I will find no lover if you drive them out so early!" exploded Rue the first evening, when Rossford's stirring stage voice had declared her admirers' audience at an end and he had ushered them out personally.

"Well enough," said Heliotrope, unlacing her mistress with savage jerks of disapproval.

"Quentin, you said you'd abet me."

"And so I will. There's not a beau in the bunch in a position to maintain such as you, *ma petite.* These first-nighters are all Sir Shallows and Mr. Would-Wish-Its. We will do better tomorrow."

Once again he was right.

And by the second day, several of the gossip sheets that clogged London's many presses included extremely favorable paeans to the Drury Lane's charming new ingenue, though they tsked at the inappropriateness of her gowning.

Within another day, an answering salvo from *The Crier* in defense of the new realism began a small-type debate that would rage for weeks. Even Richard Brinsley Sheridan, intent upon a political career, would be drawn from governmental concerns into arbitrating on the depths of Rue's décolletage. He professed himself in favor. As indeed did most of London, with the possible exception of Black Harry Morgan, whose name popped up more frequently in theatrical discussions than it had been wont.

But by the third performance, Rue was despairing. The enormity of capturing a rich man-about-town willing to lend her his heart, house, and financial resources in the course of her brief hour backstage greeting admirers seemed remote.

Her gown from the French emigré dressmaker Bertin had cost a small fortune, her pounds had been lavished on such necessities as food and lodging, and it was clear that she dare not risk another run at Drury Lane, for the company would rebel.

So Rue chatted with her milling admirers on her last night, sick to the heart that she didn't have at the quandary of choosing one and drawing him inexorably to her. They all seemed the same, these fine polished gentlemen with the latest frockcoats and unpowdered hair and lavish bouquets and endless compliments as evidently empty as their intentions.

"My dear Rue, I'd like to introduce a most ardent admirer."

Quentin had dragged an unprepossessing fellow in an apple-green figured waistcoat over to her chair. At the moment he was bowing, and all Rue saw was the gilded top of his unpowdered hair. But a figured waistcoat, dear Lord!

"Sir Nigel Pagett-Foxx," said Quentin coolly, edging away again.

"You," said Sir Nigel, rising from his bow only halfway so his face was nearer hers, "you were marvelous!"

He thrust a heavily scented bouquet of roses at her, a nice enough thought, had not her head been whirling from overmany floral offerings.

"You are divine, Mrs. Morgan. Celestial. Ah, your eyes are blue. I sat through the entire second act last night wondering, and I was correct."

"Last night?" asked Rue, thrusting the flowers on the farthest edge of the dressing table behind her. "And I don't wish to shock you, Sir Nigel, but I am a Miss."

"Nothing about you could be amiss," he responded, his eyes sparkling at the wit of his reply. It was lukewarm wit, but Rue laughed at it nevertheless. That was one thing she had learned in her scant three days as a Sensation.

"But you say you saw the play last night? As well as tonight?"

"And the night previous, Miss Morgan." Sir Nigel glanced to his shoe tips, which were abominably embroidered in puce silk thread. "It has taken me three days to draw forth the courage to tell you how much you affected me in three hours."

Rue was aware of the crowd in her dressing room dispersing, primarily because of persistent nudgings from Rossford. She sat up a bit straighter and leaned forward in her chair, feeling her bosom press dangerously near the corset brim.

"You flatter me, Sir Nigel."

"Never. I have not world enough and time."

"Truly? You truly thought I did well?" She was vain enough about her performance for a touching trace of wistfulness to bedew her voice.

Sir Nigel, stunned by his goddess's need for reassurance, pulled up a stool and sat beside her.

"Most splendidly, my dear Miss Morgan. You shall have a compelling career on the stage."

Rue flashed a triumphant look to Rossford, but his back was turned.

"And are you an ardent devotee of the theater, Sir Nigel?" Rue reached back to break off one of his roses, strip its leaves, and plunge it into the center of her décolletage.

"I've only arrived in London," he answered dazedly, eyes glued to her neckline. "But shall you not scratch yourself?"

"Such a trifle would be well worth pleasing so ardent an admirer as you," said Rue sweetly, in fact finding the bloom rather nettlesome though she'd been most careful to strip off its obvious thorns.

Sir Nigel gulped. He brought his light eyes up to her face. "I could only wish to share such an honor with my rose."

Rue raised her silk fan and waved it agitatedly in front of her face. Her eyes sought Rossford's, and she found them dwelling significantly on her. The dressing room was nearly empty, thanks to Quentin's ushering, and Heliotrope waited unobtrusively on a stool to disrobe her.

Rue leaned back against the dressing table, her open fan pressed across her bosom. This barrier seemed but to draw Sir Nigel's attention more assiduously, much to his confusion if not hers.

"And why have you not come to London before, sir," she demanded, the fan flicking forward to tap his arm faster than a snake's tongue. "I would have met you sooner," she added in a lower tone.

"I—I had duties in Norfolk. Filial chiefly. My, er, mother had not been well, and I was required to be by her."

"Oh, I am most sorry for it! You must not believe me

critical of your absence from London. I think only of myself."

He blushed, not she.

"And your dear mother?"

"She . . . is . . . dead," he stuttered. "Both my parents are dead. I am my own man now, and I have come to London. I had always wanted to see it."

Ah, that explained the tiresome waistcoat and the infernal shoes. A country bumpkin, that is what Rossford had dredged up for her. A poor fellow tied to his mother's apron strings and now let loose enough to dream of corset strings instead. Not hers, Rue thought, she would not settle for such.

"Well, sir, I am most pleased that you approve my Thespian efforts." She swung around briskly to face the mirror, dropping the fan to the dressing table top. "Perhaps I shall meet you again."

"Perhaps. 'Perhaps' is such a lukewarm word. Could you not say, 'assuredly'?" His hand moved tentatively to her bare arm.

She turned her powdered head to regard it, the touch so undemanding yet such a violation of every convention. Rue Morgan took another assessment of Sir Nigel Pagett-Foxx.

He was in his thirties, a bit thick of form but not over-larded. His hair was cut abominably and lay about a rather square face. His brows were light, as were his eyes. None of his features was directly unpleasing. He was merely so unfinished, so awkward. And rich? Was he rich?

She swiveled back to her glass.

"And where do you stay while in London, Sir Nigel?"

"I have purchased a house. And grounds. In Grosvenor Square."

A house? And grounds? In Grosvenor, when land there was so dear? Wasn't her father buying up all Marylebone if he could, intending to develop it into neat squared and leased houses? Ah, he was fascinating, Sir Nigel.

She turned back to him.

"A townhouse. How splendid. I fear I must make my home at an inn."

"An inn?" The light eyebrows shot up, shocked.

"It is the theatrical life, my dear sir." This time her hand rested on his arm, and the fingers dug into the fabric seeking flesh beneath. "Who knows when I may tour the provinces? Perhaps, dear sir, if you will not stay in London, you may see me there."

"You're not leaving London?"

"My commitment here, alas, is over."

"But I cannot permit it! It would be criminal. To lose such a . . . a blossom as you to the provinces. My delightful Miss Morgan, I have spent too long in the counties myself to permit you to retreat to them."

She folded her fan and balanced her chin upon it.

"My dear Sir Nigel, your concern touches me, but my fate is at the direction of the managers. I fear my debut at Drury Lane has offended some—"

"Never!"

"But you admit you are new to these London jealousies." Her attention drifted to Heliotrope. "Ah, my dear, take my silly Piquant for an evening stroll. There's a love. Quentin will accompany you."

Heliotrope stood, rebellion in every line of her face. But Rossford picked up the slumbering Pekinese, drew its leash from off a hook, and silently presented the package to Heliotrope. She reluctantly collared the dog and went to the dressing room door, Rossford at her stiffly rustling skirts.

Rue looked past Sir Nigel's shoulder to the two people who had been her accomplices in an enterprise she had never suspected of failure. She must not fail now. She nodded farewell and stared for a last moment into Rossford's knowing eyes.

He was poised on the threshold, the door edge in his hand, every line of his body indicating uncertainty. She met his eyes again. He looked for a moment as if he might forestall her.

Then he turned on one high, elegant heel and left, shutting the door firmly behind him. She knew she could rely on him to see that no one opened it again before she was ready.

"You have perceived that I love the theater, Sir Nigel," she said, rising and trailing dramatically through the tiny room. "But it is a cruel . . . mistress, the theater. I fear I may have to contemplate giving it up."

He stood as well.

"Such a loss, my dear Miss Morgan. Perhaps I could see you elsewhere?"

"If I know where 'elsewhere' is to be. Here, a token for you." She flourished the rose from her breast, the gesture deliberately harsh. Some unplucked thorn left a crooked vein of red in its wake.

"But you've injured yourself!" Sir Nigel stepped dangerously near, his eyes transfixed.

"A trifle, as I told you, Sir Nigel, for the honor of meeting you." Her hands went to his shoulders, as though to hold him a distance away. Or as though to not.

"But you bleed." His fingertips trembled toward the valley between her breasts and paused but an inch away.

"Are there not country cures for such matters in Norfolk, Sir Nigel?"

His eyes met hers, shocked, hopeful.

"My nurse used to kiss small hurts away," he offered thickly.

"I could not quarrel with it," she said softly.

But he did not move, the great lummox. Rue slid her hands down to his arms and dug her fingers into the muscles she felt there. She closed her eyes.

"It would not do for an actress to scar," she said.

After a moment she heard a sudden rustle of cloth and felt his lips pressed to her flesh. Won, she'd won. Won a house in Grosvenor Square. Won the means to make her father's life the hell he made it for other people. Won the first move in the game. Her heart began beating triumphantly, pounding against her exposed breastbone in sweeping, powerful throbs.

"Your heart, I can hear it."

She glanced down at the fair head pressed to her breast.

"Yes, I am exceedingly happy to have met you, Sir Nigel. You cannot comprehend it."

"Promise me you will come home with me to Grosvenor Square," he murmured. "Promise me you'll not return to an inn. Tonight. Promise me, Rue."

"I promise. But you must let me collect myself. Please go for a moment . . ."

He started away, then emboldened, came back and clutched her in his arms, tight against the frightfully figured waistcoat. She felt the satin slippery upon her flesh. His mouth came to hers, pressed hard, remained there for a long time.

Ah, red. Red-sleeved arms around her, and the linnets calling over the hedge. High summer, and the grasses long for concealment's sake, and his mouth on hers, sweetly inquiring. Do you love me, Rue? Forever, her heart pounded. Forever.

She was standing alone, almost reeling on her feet, but an ecstatic Sir Nigel, already at the door, didn't see it.

"Until you send for me, love," he whispered, eyes shining. "Soon."

"Soon," she said with a tight little smile. But not forever.

She dimmed all but one candle in the room and undid her back laces as best she could. Her tortured lungs expanded with relief. In moments she heard the door open. Over her chemised shoulder, she saw that it was Quentin Rossford.

He came up behind her, his hands on her shoulders.

"I promised you your heart's desire, Rue Morgan," he said in his smooth actor's voice. "What will you do now that you have it?"

"Like Ophelia, I'll wear my rue with a difference," she said lightly. But the jest had touched on the real regret she felt for her cold-hearted course. The tears had brimmed to her eyes, and she was not yet actress enough to conceal the catch in her voice.

"Do not quote lines from Shakespeare at me, my little *tragedienne*. I have lines that could break your nonexistent heart. If you are ever in need of a cynic, come to me."

He left then, and shortly after Heliotrope returned to ungown her. Rue dressed, picked up Piquant, and walked out to the passage where Sir Nigel Pagett-Foxx and his house in Grosvenor Square waited.

Chapter Six

She had a suite of rooms, all airy Adams and white plastered ceilings with swags and urns. She had rooms full of Sheraton and Hepplewhite furniture on graceful, gazelle legs. And a Chippendale lady's writing desk-cum-fire screen, so her slippered feet would be warm of the winter while she corresponded with her friends. She had no friends.

Nigel said that she could have it all new if she wished.

She had six wardrobes full of new clothes, stitched by the pert French seamstresses expelled from Paris by the revolution. She had gowns from Mademoiselle Bertin in the latest of fashions, and it was no longer necessary to don antique corsets and crush her bosom to inviting heights.

She had a footman to attend Piquant, and could have had several personal maids, had she not preferred Heliotrope.

She had Nigel Pagett-Foxx, who came often to her royally testered bed and pressed her to the icy winter linens. Somehow they never seemed to warm, though the weave was very fine.

And she had no heart, although it crossed her mind to wonder how Quentin Rossford fared. Well, no doubt. She never wondered how Graham Winthrop fared. She had no heart.

And finally, when January winds howled across Marylebone's still partially untenanted fields, she began to think of revenge.

"There are a great many clubs in town, Nigel," she said one night after the fowl had been served, and they faced each other down the long mahogany table. She wished their bedrooms were as distant.

"Clubs, Rue? Ay, and a great deal of time wasted at such. I would prefer to spend my hours here with you."

"But these gentlemen's clubs, have you visited each one? Surely they would be eager of your membership?"

"And why should I join? To gamble?" he took a contented sip of port. "To wench?" A blond eyebrow raised confidently, and Rue prepared herself to evince a jealousy she did not feel. Would that he *would* amuse himself elsewhere. . . .

"Wenches! For shame, is this what they teach you in Norfolk, Nigel?"

"No, this is what you teach me in Grosvenor Square." He laughed.

She tautened, sure that tonight, once more, her bedcurtains would flutter and he would lurch into her lap, as eager for petting as Piquant and not nearly as silky. It was time he paid for his privileges.

"There is, of course, Brooks's for the gamesters," she pointed out. "And the Hell-Fire Club for the libertines. But I have heard an intriguing thing. Is there not a coffeehouse near Pall Mall where they meet to discuss matters of commerce—the Cockatrice Club, is it not?"

Nigel lowered his ruddy glass, and his heavy face grew heavier.

"My delight, I can guess what rumors you've heard. You must not pretend that it matters so little to you."

"What do you mean?"

"Rue, Rue . . . You've heard of the syndicate against your father."

"My father disowned me, Nigel, when I took to the boards. I have told you that."

"Ah, you have no communication with him, but I can see that you pine in your heart for something. I was very . . . attached to my parents, Rue, though they were monstrous overdevoted to me. Yes, 'tis true, there is a coffeehouse claque devoted to your poor father's downfall. The Basilisk Club it is, though either a cockatrice or a basilisk pretends to be able to freeze with a glance. I know but one who can truly accomplish such a feat."

He rose and moved to her chair, leaning close to her ear. His breath was hot and heavy when he spoke.

" 'Tis you, dear Rue. You with your icy azure eyes. I have sat up for hours sometimes, wondering why they chill me so when your lips murmur words of love."

"You have had overmuch port, Nigel, pray sit down."

He leaned further over her shoulder, and the scent of wine ruffled across her cheek.

"You had a wound once, of love. I would cure it." His hand pawed the frosty fichu at her breast.

"Nigel! You've overdone. Sit down, Nigel, or I shall be cross."

He straightened, suddenly contrite at the ice in her voice, and walked carefully back to his seat at the table's end.

Rue took a slow sip of her port.

"I have the headache, Nigel. I fear I should retire early."

He curled his fingers around his glass stem and said nothing.

They finished their meal and parted, speechless. But it had been so before, and then he would appear at her bedcurtains and would not be speechless at all. She decided to have Heliotrope sleep on the sofa in case she developed a migraine.

But he did not appear that night, and she slept better for it.

In the morning, she was contrite.

"My dear Nigel, I have been frightfully cross-tempered. I think I require a turn along the shops. May I take Heliotrope and go for the day?"

He gazed into her sparkling eyes.

"And have you pounds enough, love?" He reached for a bell.

"A great plenty, my profligate one! Never fear, I shall not spend your generosity on fripperies willy-nilly. And when I return, I shall be in better spirits, I promise you."

She wrapped her arms around his cravated neck and pressed her lips to his temple. "You will not deny me?"

"No, no!" He caught her arms when she would leave. A frown puckered his brow. "I am used to country life, my pretty city kitten. Perhaps I am a dull fellow—"

"No, no, sweet Nigel. I am content. And now I must hasten if I am to have the pick of the muslins."

She tripped away, leaving him still clutching the bell. Much later he rang for the port.

Heliotrope sat beside her in the well-sprung coach as they careened through Picadilly, then Thames-ward toward Brooks's and Pall Mall.

Heliotrope wore a fine new turban, wide enough to shade her shady features, and a soft, frilled fichu and gloves of white kid like her mistress's. Heliotrope said little nowadays, but there was nothing in her demeanor to criticize and Rue held her tongue. Sometimes the effort hurt.

The carriage jolted to a stop and rocked softly on silent springs. Rue thrust her wide-hatted head out the window, black curls catching the gleam of a bright winter morning.

"Ah, here at last. Heliotrope, wait for me in the coach."

"But it is most improper for you to enter alone—!"

"And it would be doubly improper for *two* women to broach the portals of the Basilisk Club! My stick, if you please. Hand it out."

The tall, beribboned staff followed Rue from the carriage.

She flounced down the steps and gave the footman a smile as dazzling as the sun flashing from snowbanks.

He tucked his tricorn under an arm, and his powdered head turned to follow her proudly, all the way into the masculine premises of the Basilisk Club.

There was only one group of men gathered around the scattered tables who were numerous enough to be deemed a "club."

Rue sailed directly for them, ignoring falling faces and rising voices at her unescorted presence.

There were six around the polished table, a patchwork of the waistcoated and the frockcoated, the bewigged, bald, hirsute, and unpowdered. Their combined age, Rue guessed, would amount to something over 360 years.

Behind her back, she heard the scandalized echoes rising incredulously, "Rue Morgan . . . Rue Morgan . . . Rue Morgan . . ."

She waited until the murmurs had reached her prey and smiled loftily down at them.

"Good day to you, gentlemen. I trust I address the distinguished members of the Basilisk Club."

Dazed, they stared up at her, then—realizing that she indeed addressed them—began standing in sequence, one by one, as if their feet beneath the table were linked by chains and someone had tugged, forcing the entire set to come lurching reluctantly upright.

"Good day."

"Most . . . pleased, Ma'am."

"How d'ye, d'ye, do-ye . . . *achoo!*"

"Most obliged."

"Ah, very fine to make your, ah, acquaintance."

"And what brings you, Miss Morgan, to our humble gathering?" said the last to rise and the only to give her a curt nod instead of a bow or, at least, a bob.

He wore a full white wig with a black-bowed queue and a stern frockcoat of the most severe cut. His face matched his attire, and his manner matched both.

"You are the spawn of Black Harry Morgan, and if you know of our club, then you know we've no reason to welcome you to it."

"Dr. Radclyffe, I take it," said Rue with unruffled accuracy. "I know not what you gentlemen may welcome, but I most assuredly would be grateful of a chair . . ."

Three of them scattered, despite the famous surgeon's disapproving eye. When Rue heard the appropriate scrapes behind her grind to a stop, she sank without looking onto the Windsor chair that materialized there, the walking stick tilted in her hand like a sceptre.

"Some coffee, perhaps?" suggested one.

"Or chocolate," urged another.

"I thank you, gentlemen, no. But I do crave an introduction." She smiled round the circle, and they began naming themselves as jerkily as they had risen.

"Sir Feverell Marshwine." Stout and bewigged.

"Addison Hookham, Esquire." Thin and foppish.

"Lemuel Humphries of Renfield Hall, Kent," snapped the third, whose flushed face looked choleric.

"M—m—merivale Fenton-Mews, if y—y—you please," said the fourth, staring fixedly at a cooling cup of coffee before him.

A fifth waved a snowy handkerchief, not for effect but for necessity. "Colonel Rutherford Trumbull, at your service," he hawked behind its airy offices.

Rue's eyes returned to the physician.

"You are the diagnostician among us, Dr. Radclyffe, perhaps you can tell the others why I am here."

"Diagnostician?" drawled Addison Hookham in a voice as thin as his frockcoated frame. "My dear Humphries, what can she mean?"

"Bright in the brain," snapped the red face surmounted by a snowy wig.

"I'm not accustomed to dispensing medical opinions for free, Miss Morgan," the physician said. "I'd say, for a start, you look a bit peaked and seek diversion."

"Peaked? Peaked? To the contrary, dear doctor, I've never seen such a bloom of a girl. No indeed, sir. Now I've a catarrh that gives me no rest. Perhaps you could bend your atten—ahhh—ahhh—ten—choon! . . . Your pardon on that." Colonel Trumbull buried his well-veined nose in a pinch of handkerchief and fell silent.

Rue glanced amused about the circle, including the slumped figure of Sir Feverell Marshwine sunk into his rumpled satin waistcoat, dozing serenely.

"And you call yourselves 'Basilisks,' sirs? If I recall my mythology, a basilisk is a great coiled snake of a beast that breaks from a cock's egg and slays with one poisonous glance." Rue assessed the watery eyes fastened upon her. "Fie, sirs, your stares conjoined would not make a bird blink. I offer you a Medusa for your arsenal."

They stared at her, as if turned to stone. And wasn't there something snaky about the way her dark locks writhed to her shoulders? Something frozen and fearsome in her expression?

Rue had worn a black redingote over a red-and-gray plaid taffeta skirt, a cataract of lacy white stock at her neck and a great yawning brim of a black hat shadowing her face with a crimson plume dipping flamelike to her shoulder. They noticed the pallor of her face, the distant glimmer of her blue eyes, and finally, there, pinned to her stock, a third eye in the shape of a sapphire teardrop. The members of the Basilisk Club sat speechless for once.

"Egad, sirs, I feel my blood stilling already," said Addison Hookham, retracting his head on his neck like a wary stork.

Rue laughed.

"No wonder my father flummoxed you, sirs. It's plain you're more ready for gout stools than for action."

Since three of the twelve legs under the table were elevated on precisely these appliances, a string of throat-clearings circled the table. Stout Colonel Trumbull pulled himself up pointedly and suppressed a yelp in so doing.

"Come now, Miss Morgan, you named me the diagnostician. Why do you trespass in these matters?" inquired Dr. Radclyffe.

"Because I am a tactician, sir, and must point out where your defenses need shoring up. Gentlemen, gentlemen, it is known in half the town that you all share something in common more than your gout stools. Each of you has been wronged by Black Harry Morgan. All of you would avenge yourselves upon him. This much is understandable. What is incomprehensible is that you have been so damned ineffective at doing it." Her stick rapped on the floor.

"D—damned, did you say, young woman? Did you say—oh, I cannot repeat it!" Colonel Trumbull cradled his long face in narrow hands and shook his head mournfully.

"Oh, Lud, Colonel Trumbull. If you quail at a word, you'll not go far against Black Harry Morgan."

"How can we be certain of your sincerity?" inquired Lemuel Humphries sourly. "You may be more Delilah than Medusa."

"No Delilah, I! Besides, none of you has hair to spare, so you'd hardly be worth the shearing." Rue assumed a more serious expression and, adapting Quentin Rossford's stage instructions, gazed round the group with queenly authority.

"Each of you has known, gentlemen, some outer discomfiture and a great deal of inner anguish at the hands of Black Harry Morgan. Each of you knows me for his daughter. Have you not thought that if he can so injure a stranger over a mere matter of finance, his wrongs to a daughter would make your injuries paltry by comparison?"

They considered it. They considered the hard, dead tone in her voice as she spoke. Each one, from his own private stock of recollections of Black Harry Morgan, imagined how he would turn these same qualities upon a daughter. And each of them shuddered.

"He is a devil!" burst out Sir Feverell, rousing from a doze and finding reality the nightmare. "He not only ruined my speculation in coal, but has arranged it so my own lands cannot accrue benefit to me from the canals now under construction."

"And I," chorused Humphries. "My best captains lured from a decent merchant trade into the high-paying blasphemy of the slave trade. My patrimony has shrunk to a third of its amount at my inheritance."

They each wailed out their wrongs in turn until the round came to Dr. Radclyffe, and there it stopped.

"I have more reason than most to believe your sincerity, Rue Morgan," that worthy said finally, spreading his thin-fingered hands on the mahogany and staring at them.

"At your mother's death he was most insistent that my attendance had hastened her departure. My own . . . diagnosis," he continued with a bow of his wigged head to Rue, "was that he had visited more grief upon her than she cared to survive."

Rue's hands twisted on the ebony stick.

"I fear that I was one of them, doctor."

The physician sighed. "I thought as much. There was quite some fuss among my practice at the time. I was not invited to tend a woman of good family at her confinement for some years hence. And such services do much to help a doctor call earls and prime ministers his patients. I am of middling origins. Doors once shut do not open easily again."

"Then you vouch for my appalling lack of filial devotion?"

"I alone of those here have seen the domestic side of Black Harry Morgan," the surgeon pointed out. "I concede your right to be among us."

"But what shall we do?"

"Do, Sir Feverell? We shall form a syndicate and forestall him at every twist of his black and serpentine mind. I have but recently come from his house, gentlemen. I have heard much of his plans. I will place what I know at your disposal. And I begin by telling you that his financial heart is set upon acquiring the land around Grosvenor and developing it as Morgan Crescent."

"Morgan Crescent? The upstart, the bloody villain—!" Humphries's ruddy face went scarlet.

"Morgan Crescent," mused Hookham. "What a parvenu he is. Usually such honors as bestowing one's name on a square or a crescent are reserved for peers of the realm. Or, at the least, the architects. Soon we shall have fishmongers christening corners after themselves!"

Colonel Trumbull's voice was thick from asthma, but he managed to produce a new frothy white handkerchief and wave it dramatically before another sneeze overtook him. *"Ah . . . chooo!"* was his only comment on this latest revelation.

"But, but, we should be . . . neighbors if he built near Grosvenor!" wailed Sir Feverell Marshwine, swinging his gouty leg from under the table and revealing it to be attired in swelling purple silk hose. "How revoltingly distasteful."

"He shall be more than our neighbor, gentlemen, if this speculation goes through. He shall be our even richer neighbor," pointed out Dr. Radclyffe calmly. " 'Tis a consummation devoutly to be avoided."

Dr. Radclyffe looked to Rue, who had absorbed the invective hurled at her absent father with a sort of surprised complacency.

"Gentlemen, you outdo even me. It warms the heart I have been told I do not have to hear my news raise such uproar among you. What do you propose to do with my information?"

"Use it, by God!"

Lemuel Humphries's fist curled and hit the table, setting coffee and chocolate cups dancing on their saucers like a troupe of leaping Russian rope dancers.

"Stirringly said," agreed the dandy Hookham languidly. "We still retain some means. Let us use them as well."

"Do I take it that a certain syndicate of gentlemen, loosely known as the Basilisk Club, will show a sudden interest in purchasing land for development?" Rue asked, cocking her head so the crimson feather drooped, then trembled eagerly over her coated shoulder.

"You may take it and wager your soul upon it, Miss Morgan," swore Colonel Trumbull nasally. "As do we . . . we . . . *ah, ah, ahhhhhh* . . . as do we all." His last sneeze did not fully emerge until a round of assent rose from the table's occupants.

"Then I bid you good day, gentlemen. I shall call next week to hear of your success."

Rue smiled regally, rose royally, and sailed forth into the street beyond while the Basilisk Club clattered to its feet as gracefully as it could and bowed anxiously at her departing back.

But their eyes as they sat again were grim with remembered affronteries, and their ill-assorted heads drew together while their voices lowered. Other coffeehouse patrons strained in vain to hear what the Basilisk Club would do after its odd visit from Rue Morgan. The scandalous actress, you know. Shocking. Bound to no good end. A disgrace to her family, her father. . . .

They would have whispered more if they had known what the Basilisk Club planned, and what stunning lack of success waited them.

Rue returned the following Friday, this time attired entirely in scarlet with an ermine muff and black fichu. Ermine swathed her shoulders and banded her wide, red velvet hat.

On this occasion, the heads around the table were not surprised by her entrance, and they bobbed up as soon as her footman had seen her across the threshold.

"Good day, Miss Morgan."

"A fine afternoon, Miss Morgan."

"W—w—well met."

Rue accepted their deep bows all round and sank onto the

chair sitting ready for her. She surveyed the fellow members.

"You wear winter faces, gentlemen, despite the warmth of your greeting. Do not tell me all has not gone well?"

"Well? Ah, it has more like gone down the well," replied Addison Hookham gloomily, resting his long chin upon pale mauve kid gloves.

"But it's not the worst," interrupted Sir Feverell Marshwine, lacing his fingers across a puce and yellow embroidered waistcoat swollen by forty-five years of overeating.

"N—n—no," smiled Sir Merivale, casting Rue a shy look from under a baby-bland forehead. "At least Black Harry has not won, if we have not either."

Rue absorbed and considered.

"When men are cryptic, women had better look to their rears. Enough shilly-shallying! Do you take me for an empty-headed Miss? Name your difficulty, gentlemen."

"Varian Temple!" growled Lemuel Humphries.

"The Earl of Argyle," snorted Colonel Trumbull, producing a contemptuous blow into his ever-present handkerchief.

Rue looked puzzled.

"And what do the Earl of Argyle and this, this, er, Dorian—"

"Varian."

"—Varian Temple have to do with my father and Grosvenor Square and the discomfiture of the Basilisk Club?"

"It is not Varian Temple *and* the Earl of Argyle," explained Addison Hookham condescendingly. "Varian Temple *is* the Earl of Argyle."

"And a damned nuisance to us, I warrant," said Humphries, taking a sour sip of chocolate.

"And what has the earl done to counter the stare of the dreaded Basilisk Club?" continued Rue.

"Bought the place up, right from under all interested

noses," explained Colonel Trumbull, so upset that he couldn't even produce a sneeze from his own.

"Is my father's proboscis one of those so defrauded?"

"Indeed, we all are left sniffing the wind and naught else," said Humphries.

"Well, then, I think we ought to congratulate His Lordship, not castigate him."

"You miss the point, Miss Morgan," came the cool, dry voice of Dr. Radclyffe, spreading a chill like iced champagne over the gathering huddled around steaming coffee and chocolate cups.

"Then instruct me, Dr. Diagnostician."

"If Varian Temple can buy, he can as easily sell. To your father rather than us."

"Would he do so?" Rue asked sharply.

"You're the blade among us, Hookham," suggested Lemuel Humphries. "Tell us, what kind of man is he?"

Hookham enjoyed the way every gaze swiveled to his own. He had not garnered so much attention since losing half of what he owned at Brooks's one dreadful evening long since. He swung his quizzing glass contemplatively by its black silk cord.

"Varian Temple . . . Yes, I've seen him across the green baize many a time." Hookham pursed his bloodless lips, then began a lazy recollection.

"Varian Temple. He's rich as Croesus, pardon the exhausted comparison, but there's no other way to describe it. First son of an ancient family and lucky enough to have survived the vicissitudes of childhood. Lost a sister along the way, I recall. A dazzler, too . . . There was some scandal, but Temple would have been only a boy then . . ."

"We care not for the man's personal history, Addison," interrupted Humphries testily. "You confounded aristocrats are all alike, eternally reciting your family lines into antiquity. What's the man's financial lineage, that's what I want to know," he demanded, rapping his knuckles on the table.

"Yes, Mr. Hookham," Rue said, "so far we ascertain, he's

rich, which we could have gathered from his recent invest-
ments. What other do you know of him?"

"He's a devil with the dice, Miss Morgan. Luck incarnate. And has money enough not to need luck even when
it's running against him. I've seen your father himself skulk
from the table when he's bet against Temple at hazard."

Rue sat to the rim of her chair, the sweeping red velvet
hat cocked interestedly.

"My father? He has played against my father? And
won?"

"Ay, and seemed to take no small satisfaction in it. He's
a well-bred fellow, you know, and doesn't like to see up-
starts naming crescents after themselves—no offense meant
to yourself."

Hookham elevated his glass to his eye and regarded her
minutely through it, concentrating especially on the unconventional black fichu.

"I'm sure there was," said Rue, laughing and returning
stare for stare. "So you think the Earl of Argyle might take
as great a pleasure in foiling my father as the esteemed
members of the Basilisk Club, however mixed their origins?"

"You are overoptimistic, Miss Morgan," objected Dr.
Radclyffe. "Even one of middling origins, such as myself,
knows that our first families are capricious nowadays. It is
not enough to hold the purse strings of great fortune, or
gamble it away, or tend to one's attire and oversee the marrying and the burying of one's kin and call yourself a Lord,
for keeping a warm seat in the House. There are too many
men like Black Harry Morgan making fortunes in the Indies
trade and gobbling up fortunes here at home. The Earl of
Argyle has invested in the Grosvenor land to make himself
richer, I'd warrant, and for no other reason. And if selling
it to Black Harry Morgan makes him richer still, he'll do it
with a high heart and tumble the dice out more prodigally.
I've seen enough of the world not to count on snobbery as
an ally when there's good English pounds involved."

A long silence greeted this unpleasant dose of realism.

"Can w—w—we not buy from him?" suggested Fenton-Mews timorously.

"Most certainly, an' he'll sell to us and not Morgan. But if Morgan offers more than we can—"

"Perhaps he does not care to sell at all," mused Rue, turning her cane of red Brazilian wood until the black ribbon near its golden ram's-head top twisted itself around the stem.

"What a tangle," she said, absently unbraiding it. " 'Tis but one thing to do—ascertain the intentions of Varian Temple on selling to my father."

"And if he should choose to do so?"

"Then, my dear sirs, he must be persuaded not to."

"And who will undertake this scheme?"

"I will. You have done your part, and through no fault of your own, you were forestalled. I shall beard the earl in his, er . . . temple and enlist him as an ally."

"His temple, Miss Morgan? Surely you do not refer to a place of gaming?"

"And where else may a dicemaster be found? And mastered. Or mistressed. Mr. Hookham, you have prattled a bit of the earl's wealth and his familial duties and naught of much else. Save his love for the tumble of the dice—"

"But none dare challenge him there!" objected Hookham.

"Precisely why I shall. I may not win at hazard, sirs—indeed, it is my intention not to—but there are other games for which I am more suited than you, you will grant. Is he married?"

"N—n—no, not that I've heard," began Sir Merivale.

"But he's mistressed, or has been," interjected Hookham. "I fear you'll find no vacancy there."

"I do not require a vacancy, gentlemen." Rue stretched her fingers like a cat its claws and drew the black kid gloves tight preparatory to departing. "I only require, as in the case of the Basilisk Club, an opportunity to introduce myself.

But I *shall* require an escort to Brooks's. Tomorrow evening, shall we say? I always feel lucky of a Saturday."

"To Brooks's? With you? Decidedly not!" Addison Hookham icily drew back against his Chippendale chair and would not participate in the discussion further.

"I'm not one for the cards or the dice at any rate," gruffly objected Lemuel Humphries. "I love neither tight gamesters nor loose women," he added, frowning significantly at Rue.

She smiled angelically.

"Gentlemen, when you pick up the gauntlet in the game of revenge, you must not quibble about its composition. Mr. Hookham, you would not do in any case. You would never be suspected of falling prey to me."

Whether she meant to salute Hookham's innate taste or her own was not clear, so he did not respond.

"And you, Mr. Humphries, would be an unlikely visitor to a gaming party, 'tis certain. Nor, Dr. Radclyffe, can it help your reputation to introduce me so scandalously, and your name has already been besmirched by a Morgan, so you are exempt from enlistment.

"Colonel Trumbull, you would cut a fine figure, but would sneeze a fitful beside me and thus distract the game, I fear. Sir Feverell, you are a dear fellow, and I would be most fond of your escort, but I believe that you are too well known at such establishments to go lightly against their customs.

"No, my escort must be an outsider, one whose innocence of intention is clearly written upon his face, one who *blunders* rather than challenges. One caught in the toils of a shameless hussy like myself, who can easily fade into the background when I require it . . ."

Rue knit her brows and allowed the members of the Basilisk Club to remark at what a charming facial trick it was, and how little a pair of tiny parallel furrows could roughen the alabaster perfection of her brow.

"Miss M—m—morgan."

Rue was so deep in thought that she didn't look up.

"M—m—m—miss Morg—g—gan. You haven't mentioned me?" The voice was timorous but slightly hurt.

Rue's red hat flashed up from its downcast position, revealing a pair of impishly satisfied eyes.

"So I haven't, Sir Merivale Fenton-Mews, most decidedly I haven't."

Fenton-Mews blushed, but his slight figure drew up in his brocaded chair. "I would be honored, Miss Morgan, if you would venture into the den of the gamesters with me. We will give them a run for't!"

"I would be honored, Sir Merivale. You may call for me at eight. At Sir Nigel Pagett-Foxx's townhouse. Naturally, Sir Nigel will not be accompanying me. Till then, my dear. Good day, gentlemen."

Rue nodded like a great velvet rose on a graceful stem and swept full-blown from the coffeehouse.

Fenton-Mews beamed, a few scattered drops of perspiration dewing his triumphant forehead. The other members of the Basilisk Club exchanged significant looks.

Finally Addison Hookham leaned forward, his chin resting again on the hands enfolded upon his canetop.

"I'd give my soul to be round the tables at Brooks's tomorrow night," he said mournfully.

"Then it's lucky that you haven't got one," snapped the doctor and dismissed the meeting.

Chapter Seven

.

Brooks's was ablaze that January night, for there is nothing like an Englishman for gaming.

And it never for a moment troubled the blooded aristocracy gathered under the dazzling chandeliers that blood as blue as theirs flowed down French gutters, and that Paris aristocrats were wont to watch the tumble of each other's titled heads into baskets rather than the roll of ivory dice on green baize.

His Lordship, the Earl of Argyle, was holding forth at his usual table, to the right of the mirrored fireplace wall, where he had a fine overview of all entrances and exits in Brooks's main gaming room.

Beside him, an ormolu-edged wooden bowl was heaped with rouleaux he had won in the course of the evening, cylindrical packets of gold coin, hard and ridged to the touch.

Whenever he left Brooks's after winning so publicly, His Lordship was wont to carry a pair of rouleaux in his greatcoat pockets. Gentlemen had ceased wearing dress swords only recently, but footpads had not desisted practicing their age-old profession one whit. The earl was prepared to defend his possessions with his fists if fashion forbade a blade, and a rouleau in each hand was marv'lous effective.

He knew this from experience, for a rogue or two had come away from robbing His Lordship with a broken jaw and no more.

Actually, the earl relished such encounters; the century was grown too tame for him. He'd be damned if he'd carry an umbrella instead of a cane, as so many gentlemen did nowadays. He had nothing to fear from rain.

His downcast eyes flicked to the great mirrors beside him. The room was filled to overflowing with gamesters, but he saw no familiar back that would offer him a challenge suitably piquant for his mood.

He had recently completed a headily successful piece of business, yet the erection of rowhouses for the middling classes around the soon-to-be-constructed Argyle Square did not uplift him. It smacked of trade, and these were trifling times when a gentleman had to go into trade in self-defense.

He sighed, and the man sitting next to him noted it.

"What, Varian, tired of winning? I'll gladly take over the role for you. Pass your luck to me." He held out a well-tended hand, palm up.

"Your hands and your purse are empty enough to have room for a bit of luck, Jonathan. But luck is not a title, alas. It cannot be passed on."

"No doubt yours is a gift from the devil, so I'm heaven-bound if I'm a pauper. I shall look down on you roasting, Varian, and smile."

"I imagine they smile more in hell, Flemming," said the earl, smiling. "The heaven-sent always struck me a rather sober-sided lot."

His Lordship stretched his legs under the table and idly examined the diamond buckles at his knee, which sparkled very handsomely against brown satin breeches and black silk stockings. The earl yawned behind a politely fanned hand and drummed his fingers on the baize tabletop.

A large, black-stoned ring twinkled there, for the earl was

nothing if not coordinated, thanks to an assiduous valet and his own rigorous taste. But his dress had a severity despite its richness, and an insensitive observer would at first glance assume him to be less expensively attired or of less rank than his fellows.

Yet his dark brown hair was cut into the latest cluster of curls at the brow and temple, and one could gather that the Earl of Argyle would rather face a firing squad than the world wearing an antiquely tied headdress or worse, powder. He was a modern man, though it bored him. And that fact, above all else, was what made him formidable.

His quick eye in the glass had caught an eruption of color at the opposite archway, floor to shoulder-height royal blue.

"Good God, Varian!" hissed Flemming at his elbow. "It's a woman!"

"Yes, I've seen the species before," murmured the earl, picking up a pale die and rolling it gently in his closed hand.

This conclusion as to the sex of the intruder was being voiced, softly and loudly, about the entire room. Glasses ceased clinking, canaries and wines lay becalmed against crystal, cards fell face up in disarray, and dice suddenly stopped chattering in their boxes.

"Good God," muttered Flemming, a worried young man of eight-and-twenty who dallied in London despite the fretting of his conservative parents.

"You repeat yourself, Flemming," observed the earl. "Next you will be informing me that it's a woman."

"Now I apprehend it—that Morgan woman! Did you see the Drury's latest *Rivals*? It's the Lydia, I know it, though she's not wearing powdered hair now."

"She is not wearing other attributes of the role either," observed the earl acidly, taking in the contemporary fichu which, though splendidly lavish, substituted its own lacy frills for the snowy bosom under it.

"You saw *The Rivals*?"

"The first night," conceded the earl languidly.

"And . . . you thought?"

"I have always fancied the play."

"But her?"

Varian Temple shrugged and let his die roll across the baize, landing with a single dot upward.

"I do not think her main talents lie in that direction."

"You're a savage, Varian," said Flemming, laughing. "Half the bloods of London had to physically restrain their pulses at her entrance. And most of them paid court in her dressing room."

"You?" The earl cocked one dark eyebrow.

Flemming colored a bit. "Yes, I. But I swear she never noticed me in the tumult. Rue Morgan, Black Harry Morgan's daughter."

"I know whose daughter she is."

"Morgan must not relish his daughter's new occupation."

"Why not?" The earl shrugged again and retrieved his lone die. "Morgan is a common enough fellow. It's not as though he bore a title . . ."

"Uncommonly rich, though, as she is uncommonly lovely. You are incorrigible, Varian. When you're broiling in hell, I'll wish you the lady for company and then see if you blow so cool."

Flemming grinned and caught up the other die while His Lordship ordered another round of port.

Across the room, Rue Morgan was lost amid a thickening circle of frockcoats. Their owners were too flattered by her attention to tell her in strict terms to be off. The lackeys had been swept aside at her entrance and henceforth were kept busy fetching drinks, for the gentlemen seemed to have developed a prodigious thirst of a sudden. Many of these new thirsts seemed contingent on Miss Morgan joining their table for a glass of ratafia.

"You flatter me till my head spins, gentlemen," objected Rue. "And if I drank at each of your invitations, I'd have a head spinning for certain. Please forgive me, I must decline you all, for fairness sake. Also I have come to game, sirs, and must keep all my wits about me in such skilled company as yours."

Rue's cheeks were flushed without the aid of spiritous liquors at any rate. She was still new to being the sole female in a masculine environment and while the flatteries of the dressing room had been pleasant enough, here she felt she trod on very uneven ground.

It would take but one dissenter, and Rue Morgan or not, she could find herself on the pavement outside, turned out like a strumpet who'd crossed Pall Mall and was promptly returned to the seedy byways of St. Giles.

"Sir Merivale has escorted me, and he may fetch me one small glass of ratafia, if none of you gentlemen quarrel with his right," said Rue, glancing around the circle.

None did. Fenton-Mews blushed with pleasure and ordered the libation, hovering like a mother hen until it arrived and then whisking it from the hand of the waiter to present it to her personally.

Rue sipped demurely and peered around the vast room. Pale ceilings decorated with raised plasterwork arched overhead. The paneling was painted white as well, and candles dripped everywhere. Rue had chosen well in her dress.

She wore vivid blue taffeta, sashed in night-black velvet. Her sleeves were full to the elbow where they ended in rows of black velvet bows. Across her shoulders lay a cameo-centered, deeply laced handkerchief from which her equally white neck and shoulders rose like the summit of a snow-covered mountain.

Her hair, tumbling halfway over her back and shoulders, was dressed with nodding blue plumes and a selection of pale silk bows and flowers. At her neck, the sapphire lay securely at the base of her throat on a black velvet ribbon. Her fingers were ringed with pearls, and so were her wrists. Her fan was ebony mounted with curling black plumes, and she waved it airily while sipping ratafia and glancing around the room.

She tilted her head to Sir Merivale attentively hovering

slightly to her rear, like a page to a queen, for Rue's admirers had already driven the gentle little man away from his prize.

"And which is he, this monster of good luck, my dear Sir Merivale?" she inquired under her breath and behind the shielding spread of the fan. Her breath made the feathers quiver, and Sir Merivale, detecting it, quivered with it.

" 'Tis so . . . bright and crowded this night," he began worriedly.

"Nonsense, you can do it. Name the man, sweet Judas, and I shall reward you with a kiss in the coach. I will not expect you to kiss the earl. Pointing him out will be sufficient."

Fenton-Mews blushed furiously, at which of her suggestions the more it was hard to determine.

"He is wont to sit over by—ah, ay, 'tis he indeed. And looking ready to depart. But mark him. There, seated next to the man in the frockcoat of green."

"I am looking, and I hope it is not some villain out of Mrs. Radcliffe's *Mysteries of Udolpho*, though that, I assure you, should not deter me now."

"He wears the plain brown with velvet lapels."

"Brown! Oh, dear me." Rue ran her glance casually over the far table until she had pinned her subject.

"A very good brown. You did not mention that, Sir Merivale. Ah, for the older days and a quizzing glass. Well, mine own naked eyes shall have to do. Come."

Rue rustled without warning across the room, not stopping until she had reached the indicated table and drawn up directly across from the lounging figure of the earl.

Flemming scrambled to his feet.

"Miss Morgan, I believe. I have admired your performance in Mr. Sheridan's *Rivals*."

"Yes, it was unrivaled," commented the earl, rising a bit more calmly.

"I trust we may see you in some new work—" said Flemming, nodding to a lackey to fetch her a chair.

"I fear not. My gifts, I have decided, lie in other directions."

Flemming stared at his friend, but the earl simply flicked a bit of nonexistent dust off his black velvet cuff and looked complacent.

Rue regarded the carved Sheraton chair the lackey brought.

"I think there, if you please," she said, indicating a place directly opposite the earl. Flemming looked crestfallen, but her blue eyes twinkled at him as she sat.

Fenton-Mews tumbled to another chair, and the earl nodded, his mere gesture automatically promising more wine for the party.

Rue folded her hands on the tabletop, ringed fingers entwining and bepearled wrists laying pale against the green, like a Renaissance madonna's ivory-painted limbs.

"I believe we have met before," she said to Flemming.

"I am gratified by your memory of it," the young man replied. "At the Drury. I am Jonathan Flemming. And my companion is—"

"Varian Temple," that gentleman cut in swiftly, omitting his title.

Rue inclined her head toward him with a little smile.

"Mr. Temple," she acknowledged. "It is kind of you gentlemen to allow me to join you, but I confess I had an ulterior motive."

Beside her, Fenton-Mews choked on his wine at this bald admission.

"Ah, you could never be ulterior, only superior," said Jonathan gallantly.

"You are an admirable beau, sir, but I am no belle for my head to be rung with empty compliments. It is gaming I am after. I see your dice still decorate the baize. Will you not have a hazard with me?"

"A woman gaming at Brooks's?" queried Flemming, not willing to refuse directly.

"We play for high stakes," interjected the earl softly.

"If that is your only objection . . ."

She lifted her reticule and pulled out a handful of rouleaux, homemade since no one at Brooks's would allow her to buy the sets of coins. Rue's were encased in black velvet matching her gown and rolled noiselessly across the table when she dropped them there.

"Impossible," began Flemming. "We could be expelled for such a breach—"

"Do you prefer that I cast, or you?" inquired the earl.

"You look like a gentleman of luck. I will set my wagers against your good fortune," said Rue even more calmly.

"I must warn you, Miss Morgan, he has prodigious fine luck. Your rouleaux are as good as spinning away from you now. Please, I must ask you to . . . Varian, only a dog would take advantage this way."

"I assure you, Jonathan, no one is taking advantage of Miss Morgan. She is Black Harry Morgan's daughter."

"Thank you, Your Lordship," returned Rue, nodding to Temple.

"You see, Jonathan, this is no lamb to the slaughter."

The earl herded the loose dice into the Florentine leather casting box and shook them gently against his covering palm.

They spilled out onto the green, coming up a one and a deuce.

"Three," noted the earl. "I shall not want to repeat that throw often," he added, referring to the "crabs" that instantly ended early play at hazard. "What shall we play for now that you've seen my capacity for rolling wrong?" he inquired of Rue.

"I am not one to prolong agony, Your Lordship," she said serenely. She thrust a number of cylinders forward. "Half."

"I do not roll 'crabs' often," the earl warned.

"I do not wager half often either, Your Lordship. I am being cautious. I am prone to wager all."

"All?" The earl's eyebrows shot up. "You see, my dear Flemming, I am the lamb now, throwing against the wolf.

All. The Morgans are greedy," observed the earl, shaking his dice and then turning them loose upon the table with the casual flick of one elegantly frilled hand.

Again his throw was low, a four, and he had to recast, as only a number between five and nine could serve to play on.

The dice chattered in his hand again, sprang free, and rolled until four spots and one lay upright.

"Five," announced Flemming. Rue nodded, and the earl reshook the dice for the next cast, which could win or lose the game.

He threw—a five and two came tumbling from the box.

Both the earl and his feminine watcher breathed sighs of relief.

The rules of English hazard were simple. One casts the dice, and one wagers on the caster's losing. After rolling a "main," the caster can throw certain numbers that instantly win or lose the game in relation to the main. Or the caster can be lucky enough to throw a neutral number. In that instance, the suspense continues.

If the caster throws his second, "chance" number before the original "main" comes up again, he wins. If he throws the "main" number first, he loses.

So the earl had only to coax the dice into turning up seven, instead of five, and he had won. Seven.

The earl shook his leather box until the gilt stamped upon it blurred into a streak of gold.

"I feel reckless," he commented, throwing the dice down violently. He came up with a reckless, but neutral, number. A six and a five. Eleven.

He gathered up the dice and cast again, more gently.

Seven.

Rue had thrust her rouleaux over to his side of the baize before he could draw back his winning dice.

"Again," she said, pushing the last of her rouleaux to the table's center.

The earl's hands stroked the black velvet cylinders, his fingertips tracing the ridges of hard gold coins within.

"This is a great quantity I have won of you already. Joined to my previous winnings, it makes more than I shall be able to carry home. I think we have gamed enough."

"Will a Morgan wager all and not an earl?" challenged Rue, her raven eyebrows arched in supercilious disbelief but her dark blue eyes blazing.

The earl scooped the dice into the box without replying and rolled them out.

"Two!" Jonathan said. "A deuce. I say, Varian. You've never rolled such unlucky low numbers before so early on, even if it doesn't count until you establish a main."

Jonathan Flemming drew his chair nearer the table and folded his arms on the baize. Sir Merivale nudged nearer also, his pale face flushed with excitement.

In the center of the playing space lay the matching piles of black-swathed rouleaux. His and hers. And beside them, the evil upturned eyes of the dice, each reading one.

The earl retrieved his dice and rolled again, once more drawing a main of five.

"I cast low tonight," he murmured, throwing again. Fenton-Mews and Flemming let out mutual breaths as a one—possible defeat—was joined by a tumbling five, certain chance.

It was now only a matter of the earl casting a six before a five rolled to the surface again.

He cast. A nine. Again—a four. Once more—a seven. He began reclaiming and throwing out the dice in a certain rhythmic pace, as if each throw were not a matter of winning or losing.

Again he cast. Rue bit her lower lip as a die rolled to a stop with three marks up and the second die still tumbled. Make it a two, her mind willed, and the game should be hers. Full fathom five, thy ill luck lies, Varian Temple. Cast a five, not a winning six.

The last die rolled over and slowed. A four on top.

His lips tightened slightly, as if he had read her mind, and he tossed again. Eleven. Once more. Nine. All neutral num-

bers, coming up as though neither the five nor the six would
dare show its spotted face.

A circle crowded the table. It was rare when hazard
played out so long without the deciding toss. And all those
muffled black rolls of gold at stake. . . .

The earl paused as he assessed the mounting interest
around him. Flemming laid his chin on folded forearms, his
eyes almost level with the tabletop playing field. Rue edged
forward slightly in her chair, the diaphanous fichu seemingly stirred by the invisible path of her breath.

The earl took a sip of port, then shook out his right wrist,
reclaimed his casting box, and threw again.

Another three, wobbling to a stop. To make a five? Or a
six? The second die came up four. Seven!

"Your lucky number," said Rue, her eyes flicking from
the table to the earl's.

She found his glance already crossing hers and realized
he had been watching her face rather than the roll. A murmur mounted above and around them.

Rue felt trapped around the table, her efforts hinging on
the tumble of an ivory cube. And the earl, the earl seemed
bored by it all and indifferent to winning or losing. He was
simply going through the motions. When the Earl of Argyle
played hazard, evidently that was enough.

He rolled again. Double fours. Eight. But not the five that
would see her win. She demanded a five. She required a
five. By God, he would cast a five! Her fists tightened on
the table edge, a gesture he acknowledged with a downward
flick of his dark lashes.

Rue no longer cared that her emotions showed. She
wanted to win. She no longer cared that she had assured the
Basilisk Club that winning would not be necessary. With
the Earl of Argyle, it obviously was. Cast again, you devil,
her mind urged. Cast a five!

He picked up the box, fanned his long fingers over the
open end, and rocked the die gently, softly, as a nurse does
a baby. They spilled out, tumbling cubes of off-white—a

three, three sweet dark spots in a row, and . . . another, another three!

"Ah, my elusive six." The earl's fingertips played across the forfeited rouleaux as if they were clavicord keys. He rolled them delicately to his side of the table and piled them high in his ormolu-edged rouleaux dish.

The earl pushed back his chair.

"A most entertaining game, Miss Morgan, but I fear your funds are exhausted and I am as well—"

"Wait!"

Her voice rang into the mounting congratulatory murmurs, its tone of command freezing the admiring hands clapping down on the earl's perfectly tailored shoulders.

"I have no more gold, but . . ."

She ripped the rings from her fingers, gold and pearl, and spun them like gaudy dice into the center of the baize.

The earl paused in his withdrawal. He spread his fingers across the cloth, his lone dark ring gleaming faintly.

"I have no great fancy for rings."

"Perhaps one you know does."

The earl shrugged and sat back to the table, picking up his box and casting carelessly. Out came an eight, five and three.

"Your main is eight," Flemming noted unnecessarily, his voice husky from not speaking.

The earl flashed his friend an amused look, then tossed again. Five. Again he had skirted the Scylla and Charybdis of win or lose and went on for the longer route. He cast. Each die tumbled to point a single cyclopean eye at the chandeliers high above them. Crabs! Had he cast them a turn ago, he would have lost. The earl threw them once more. Eleven.

Now Rue found herself hoping that he would not throw the winning five, when in the previous game it had been a five that would have defeated him.

He threw. A five.

Before the "ahs" of astonishment had faded, Rue's pearl bracelets were stripped off and cast onto the table.

"Again," she ordered.

The earl gave a small smile at her tone, but picked up the box and complied.

He threw a nine for his main.

Then he threw again and matched it.

"I win," he observed, flicking the dice into the pile with the abandoned pearls.

"No!"

"I am afraid so, my dear Miss Morgan. And you have nothing left to wager . . ." His eyes traveled the bare expanse of her wrists and fingers fisted on the green baize.

"Then I wager . . . I wager this!"

Her hands clawed at the center knot of her fichu, and she unpinned a great cameo that rode there. The cameo she threw to the table; the loosened fabric she spun round her shoulders and caught tight in one fist, like a handkerchief.

Her neckline was stripped down to the frill of her corset, the slash of unfichued blue cutting across the curve of her shoulders and very low across her breast, lower than had been commonplace within a decade.

A great silence from the hovering gentlemen greeted this sudden exposure. Eyes were drawn inexorably to her bodice; the great cameo rocked unnoticed on the piled pearls. The gentlemen standing behind Rue leaned inward and craned their necks downward.

But Rue's eyes were only for the earl. The fingers of one hand noiselessly drummed the baize, her eyes triumphant, her cheeks flushed, her freshly unveiled bosom heaving angrily against the meager rim of bodice containing it.

"Well?" she demanded.

The earl laughed the laugh of one who has been containing it for minutes, bursting forth unfettered.

"Black Rue Morgan, on my soul! One last hazard, and then I pray you stop. I have no use of garters."

He shook the leather box briskly and threw an eight for

a main. His second toss resulted in a seven for chance. He threw again, watching the brows opposite knit when a five came up.

He shook, threw, saw the dice roll out the winning seven in a six and one combination.

The earl regarded his penultimate roll and frowned slightly.

"You bring me ill luck, Miss Morgan, I have never cast so many ones. It takes but two at the same time to lose."

"At least I had half a chance of winning," said Rue, suddenly dampened. "Your luck is prodigious, Your Lordship. I cannot contest it any longer." She leaned forward to sweep her jewelry nearer to him, breasts curving milkily into her gown's foaming lace brim. The watching gentlemen leaned inward with her.

The earl cleared his throat and cast a significant glance around the gathered gamesters. Once again he was lucky in his throw; they scattered, leaving only the original quartet at the table.

"I could use a sip of ratafia, Sir Merivale," Rue said to the quiet man on her left. She shut her eyes briefly.

Flemming finally raised his head off his arms and caught the earl's eye.

"I think you should give Fenton-Mews a hand with the ratafia," said the earl smoothly.

Flemming bowed his way out of Rue's presence and, snagging Fenton-Mews, steered him to the room's other end.

The earl leaned forward, his lacy stock shifting, and pushed the pearls back toward their erstwhile owner.

Her eyes challenged him.

"I am not a jeweler," he explained. "Besides, I game for sport. I do not require your pearls. Or your cameo." His eyes fell to her unabashed neckline before he picked up the cameo in question. "It is of remarkably fine texture and color. Quite, quite lifelike," he noted with just a tinge of regret.

"Keep the cameo, at least," said Rue, her dark lashes lowered on flushed cheeks as she snapped on her bracelets and redonned her rings.

"Shall you not need it?"

"It is the least valuable of my things."

"Ah, you underestimate its services, Black Rue. I'll keep it then, since I have managed to retain my stock and you have not. You have little place left to pin it."

He turned to face the mirrored wall and jabbed the cameo through his ungemmed lace. The pale peachy tones complemented his frockcoat's rich brown perfectly.

Rue tilted her head at the earl's back.

"If it had not become you, you would not have kept it."

"Of course not," he agreed, spinning to face her again. "You want something of me, Rue Morgan, something more than a lesson in hazard or fashion."

"I want . . . your undivided attention."

"Then don your fichu," he suggested, gathering up his rouleaux.

"You can call upon me. Tomorrow noon."

"Assuredly I can," the earl agreed, "but I may not."

"You know of my father. I have something to say to you of him."

The earl paused slightly in his preparations to depart. "And you wish to say it in . . . private surroundings?"

"Yes."

"Very well, I will call. Where?"

"Grosvenor Square, number twenty-one."

The earl rose and paused again. "That is Pagett-Foxx's new city seat."

"Yes."

"Ah. Well, Miss Morgan, I shall see you on the morrow. I admit that you have stirred my curiosity abominably. How clever of you to know that curiosity, rather than greed, rules the gamester's heart. I trust you will sleep well."

He bowed, sauntered past the still buzzing groups of club members, and vanished through the great arched portal.

Sir Merivale Fenton-Mews returned at the earl's departure as if suddenly released from a leash. Indeed, Flemming had encountered great difficulty in restraining his charge from interrupting the earl's tête-à-tête with the scandalous Black Rue Morgan, as His Lordship had just christened her for all London.

"Your ratafia. A thousand pardons for my d—d— dawdling, dear Miss Morgan, but that foolish Flemming would not stop chattering and virtually held me prisoner."

Rue's fingers curled around the slender glass stem, then she raised the brew to her lips and drank it in one long draught.

"Well? How did we do?"

Rue stared at him unseeingly for a moment, then her hand went to the sapphire blazing midnight blue at her throat.

When she spoke, it was as if she had plunged back into the present time from a long distance away.

"You did splendidly, my gallant Sir Merivale! I did less well, although I think I have netted the earl's attention for a fleeting moment."

Rue gathered up her abandoned scarf and, trailing it airly, rustled through the room, nodding regally to every head that turned to regard her.

In the foyer as they paused for the lackeys to fetch their wraps, her face looked a bit pale and fretted. And she was uncommonly quiet as her black velvet cloak was slipped over her bare shoulders. Fenton-Mews received his great-coat and ushered her into the waiting carriage.

Halfway up the carriage steps she paused and turned to her escort, her face lit by the blazing flicker of Brooks's great torches.

"Do not think, my dear Sir Merivale," she said, leaning near so the footman couldn't hear, "that because I am some-what distracted in mood that I have forgotten what reward I promised you for accomplishing your mission."

She smiled, her face dancing in the flamelight, and ducked into the dark interior.

Fenton-Mews blushed furiously, praying the footmen would take it for fire heat, and scrambled in after her.

God help Varian Temple, he thought before turning his speculations utterly upon the promised delight that awaited him.

God help him.

Chapter Eight

The object of Sir Merivale's ardent concern presented himself at Grosvenor Square at one the following afternoon.

A lackey accepted His Lordship's clouded amber-headed cane carved in the semblance of a dragon, his high-crowned black felt hat with curly brim, and his plum wool greatcoat so weighted with layered short capes at the shoulders that the servant nearly sank to his knees when it had been conveyed into his charge.

The earl proffered his yellow kid gloves last and inquired politely of the house-steward after Sir Nigel. He was told the master was out. His Lordship then evinced some interest in the health and whereabouts of the, er . . . mistress.

The steward's sour face was impassive under his powdered wig.

"If Your Lordship would repair to the lady's sitting room," he suggested, bowing, then swiveling on his blackly disapproving heel. He led the earl up a curving staircase lined with innumerable lofty oils of rural scenes, dead hares, country hunts, and equally uninteresting portraiture. The earl followed calmly, evincing no interest in the impeccably classical interior architecture, although the lackey below was still studying His Lordship's impeccably understated attire.

This consisted of buff-yellow India nankeen breeches above black silk stockings striped in blacker velvet, a changeable plum-colored silk, cutaway frockcoat with an upstanding black velvet collar, and a supernaturally white stock. Plainish, the lackey concluded, and went to hang the anchor-heavy greatcoat.

The earl was led down a wide, Oriental-rugged passage to a white door surmounted by an interior Greek pediment. His eyes gave momentary upward tribute to the plasterer while the steward announced him, then he crossed the threshold.

"Good day, Your Lordship. It is a splendid day, is it not?" asked Rue, all good cheer, deployed at a vanity table in a dressing room midway between the bedchamber and outer room.

"If you find it so."

"Come, if the loser be in good spirits, it is criminal for the winner to be mopish. Pray seat yourself."

The earl looked at the light sidechair with its seat of apple-green striped silk as if it were an indiscretion committed by a visiting child. He flicked back his long plum coattail and sat, regarding his hostess.

Rue—swathed in a champagne-colored silk wrapper foaming with lace at the elbows, throat, and down its billowing, multi-bowed front—was arranged at a slender Sheraton dressing table while a white-capped black woman in striped dimity made forays at the artfully tempestuous assembly of dark trailing curls that was her hair.

At the moment this midnight attribute was drawn into a heavy chignon at the back of her head, with teasing tendrils tumbling around her face and down her silk-robed back. It would have taken such a quantity of hair to produce this luxurious effect that the earl suspected some of it of being false, save that adding hair was much harder now that powder had paled in fashion.

He could only conclude that in the matter of tresses, Black Rue Morgan was as admirably equipped as she was in seemingly every other conceivable area.

His hazel eyes flicked over the highly polished surface of the dressing table where a collection of spired bottletops made almost a cathedral of glass. Despite their number, they were still remarkably few for a lady of fashion's service.

He saw that most of them were colorless, intermixed with the standard bottle of Imperial Water—suitable for both external and internal consumption—and the frightfully costly Balm of Mecca that had been doing absolutely nothing for gentlemen's purses and ladies' complexions since the century's dawn.

The earl crossed one nankeen-clad knee over the other and examined the French cut-steel buckles that adorned his shoes. They matched the cut-steel buttons on his coat and were dearer than goldwork now that such daytime substitutes for diamonds had become the rage.

He noticed that Rue Morgan flouted the rules of gem-wearing as she did everything else. She still wore the sapphire, now shifting in the hollow of her throat like a baby in the womb. Such faceted stones were best saved for the flickering flattery of candlelight. Cameos or garnets would have done for day.

The earl's idle observations ended in his noticing a small cylindrical box covered in black velvet with designs picked out in gold thread on the dressing table end nearest him. Since his hostess seemed totally absorbed in the disposition of her curls, and since the earl was perfectly content to let her take the initiative, there was nothing better for him to do than idly pick it up.

"I have been practicing, Your Lordship," Rue said instantly, as if her eyes had been upon him all the while.

The earl tilted the box, and a pair of dice tumbled out, turning over each other. One stopped soon and came up a singlet. The other rolled beyond his easy reading, and he leaned forward to determine its number.

She scooped it quickly into her hand and held the closed fist before him.

"Fie, Your Lordship, you are here to discuss other matters than gaming. Suspend your . . . curiosity a while."

He leaned back into the chair, seemingly content, but Varian Temple was annoyed. By withholding the fall of the second die from him, Rue Morgan had brought him face-to-face with precisely how obsessed he was to know just such things. It would nag him all afternoon, that lost chance. He decided that she must learn he was not to be toyed with.

"A dish of chocolate, Your Lordship?"

He shook his head no.

"No wonder you own so many acres around Grosvenor; you are a man who is all business."

"Most gamesters prefer not to mix business and pleasure," he responded coolly. "And what do you want with my land?"

"I? I want nothing with land. I am merely interested in knowing if I can anticipate having Your Lordship for a neighbor."

She finally took her attention off the small looking glass on the dressing case before her and glanced to him, tilting her head, curls, expression as appealingly as a china shepherdess.

The earl uncrossed his legs and crossed his arms.

"I am a busy man, Miss Morgan," he announced. "I have an appointment with my tailor. Pray come to the point."

Rue instantly realized she had ceased to amuse him and was now dangerously near to being regarded as merely tiresome. She spun on the curved-legged little bench, leaving Heliotrope's fingers hovering over nothing. The maid would have fussed further, but Rue flashed her an impatient glance.

"Enough, Helia. You are a perfectionist, and we dwell in an imperfect world. His Lordship has no time to witness my toilette."

Rue ended by smiling dazzlingly at both her maid and the

earl, so neither would find fault with her mercurial change of tempo.

The earl unfolded his arms, aware suddenly that Rue Morgan's vanity was as arbitrary a characteristic as anything else about her. It disturbed him—a beautiful woman who was not vain at bottom was as dangerous as she was rare.

The black woman rustled into an adjoining room, through whose half-opened white door the earl glimpsed a rose damask Chippendale loveseat, a slice of Aubusson carpet, and the draped intricacies of outrageously extravagant rose damask bedcurtains.

From the same door there shortly trotted out a long, low, ambulatory muff of a creature, who minced up to the earl's chair and began licking steadily at his black satin shoes.

"Piquant! Our guest finds me troublesome enough without suffering footbaths from you. Away!"

The creature yawned, its short snout splitting to reveal a rose-lined mouth and sinuous tongue, then retreated to curl up under the dressing table. Rue's bare foot absently stroked the recumbent Pekinese as she regarded the earl with an alert, inquisitive eye.

"So. You will not take chocolate with me, nor will you have small talk from me. Business it shall be. I know that you have purchased most of the undeveloped lands around this square. There is nothing more to be bought between the Thames and Oxford Street. May I inquire your intentions towards this property?"

"You may inquire," said the earl pleasantly, leaning an elbow on the nearby dressing table and resting his chin upon his loosely folded fist.

He was remarkably clean-shaven for a dark-favored man. Rue guessed that his man applied the razor thrice daily to achieve this alabaster of jaw. It was just as well. Rue did not think she would fancy the earl in a beard, though of course, she did not fancy him at all.

"If you will tell me your interest in this land, I will tell you mine."

His Lordship nodded regally.

"I have some reason to know that my father is most intent on acquiring these lands. You know of Black Harry Morgan?"

Again the earl inclined his head without speaking, his hazel eyes half-shut with languid consideration, though Rue thought she detected a lurking green gleam in them that was far from asleep.

"My father has made many enemies in his career, as well as much money. If you are not among these detractors, you should know that I am."

This pronouncement of daughterly dereliction had not the slightest effect upon the earl's unruffled demeanor.

Rue rustled restlessly upon her little bench, then leaned nearer the earl, lowering her voice. Behind her, over the frilled citrus-colored shoulder, he saw the black maid moving to and fro in the room beyond.

"Your Lordship is a most . . . gracious listener," noted Rue dryly. "The matter at hand is simple. I, and certain of my associates, wish to ensure that you not gratify my father in his wish for land. We are willing to buy you out or, if you guarantee that you will not sell to my father, will rest happy with your assurance on that. It is, as I told you, a very simple matter."

She sat back on her stool and awaited his reply.

The earl sat still for a moment, then rose slowly. A round, gold timepiece hung from a brocaded ribband at his waist. He picked it up to study the time, then let it fall from his fingers as he took a stride or two about the room.

"Since this is a matter of business, I will be plain with you, Miss Morgan. Item: I will not commit myself to any party on the future disposition of my lands or anything that belongs to me. Item: I will not regard with favor any suit that is presented to me upon a petticoat. Let your syndicate come forward man to man. Item: I have no—" While the first part of his speech had been spat out rapidly, here the earl paused with his back to her, his hands clasped behind him. "—animosity toward Black Harry Morgan, so there is no reason to assume that I would support the vindictiveness of his daughter. Item: I do not believe you, Miss Morgan."

He spun and regarded her narrowly through eyes that were definitely of a lupine cast.

"You may be acting for or against your father, but in any case it means nothing to me. I do not believe you, Black Rue Morgan. You will find me far less an easy target than Pagett-Foxx."

Rue had risen, her cheeks flaming, suddenly as dark as the spots on a deuce of dice.

"Your Lordship," she began, the mockery and anger under the words like a lash to remind him that his abrupt rejection of her proposal was hardly gentlemanly. "I came to you in good faith, and if you think it odd that a woman be spokesman for an investment syndicate, recall that I left my father's house poundless and penniless, with little to bring to a joint venture in the way of capital. Except myself. With gentlemen, as you have made it plain, their word is their bond. Since I am no gentleman, as you have also made very plain, my bond is something . . . other. That is the proof of my sincerity, unless you judge me to be one who would be prodigal of myself with every loathsome specimen of humanity that fate tossed at me."

A smile suddenly twitched at the corner of the earl's mouth. "Are you saying that you offer yourself to me?"

"Perhaps."

"Because if you are, you seem to be reassuring me that it would take a very depraved sort of woman indeed to throw herself at me unless she intended to be honorable in the matter—"

"I would be!" Rue interrupted fiercely. "It is all I have to bargain with."

"And Pagett-Foxx?" the earl asked curiously.

Rue shook her black hair and made a dismissing flutter of her fingers. "It does not signify."

"You will remain with him in this house and yet seal a bargain with me with your body?"

"Yes!" blazed Rue.

The earl cradled an elbow on his palm and supported his chin on his hand while he tilted his head at her speculatively. The gesture once again drew Rue's attention to the dark ring he wore, a huge oval stone rimmed in pearls that covered his third finger from first to second knuckle.

The earl let his eyes run over her with a practiced assessment he was wont to apply to new coursers for his series of carriages. In this instance, the gesture was wasted, for Rue was swathed from neck to foot, though she betrayed a certain restiveness that would seem to indicate otherwise.

"And, my dear Miss Morgan, do you believe that such a bargain requires a single sealing? Or rather duplicate, triplicate, oh, scores of resignings?"

"As many as Your Lordship requires," answered Rue stiffly. "For myself, once would be sufficient."

"Ah, you sound like a bride," the earl said with a laugh, "as more than one bridegroom finds to his sorrow."

His changeable hazel eyes focused over her shoulder to the room beyond. Rue finally turned and saw her maid still busy there.

"Helia," she said flatly.

Heliotrope emerged, regarded them both, went calmly to the dressing table, and abstracted Piquant from beneath it. She finally, with great stateliness and not a glance backward, sailed out the door and closed it.

A sudden awkwardness descended between the room's remaining inhabitants.

"It is all hypothetical, of course," the earl offered gallantly.

"No!" Rue turned her back to him, but before her swirling skirts stopped their silken hiss, she spoke again.

"You say you never mix business and pleasure. What then of mixing pleasure with pleasure?" She moved near the dressing table and thus nearer to him. Her fingertips fanned on the polished surface, and her profile was tilted down. "It may be you do not care to acquire me at all, but if you do, our bargain is sealed, at least on my behalf."

Her eyes, dark blue as the sky at the sun's final dimming when only the last black entrance of the night is still to come, flashed up to his face.

"I have a pair of dice. Throw for me, Your Lordship. If you win . . . you win."

She had tilted her head back to regard him, her fine blue eyes shining through lash-rimmed slits, her mouth slightly parted with an emotion the earl knew well, gambler's fever. The same malady faintly painted her cheeks rose, and he could see a pulse throbbing in her throat.

"High or low?" the earl asked curtly.

She frowned briefly.

"Do I win throwing high? Or low?"

Rue Morgan laughed deep in her throat, softly.

"Low, I think, Your Lordship. Six or below. I am wont to play for high stakes. You will cast?" she asked eagerly, feeling that if he eluded her challenge now the Basilisks would never be certain of him, *she* would never be certain of him.

"Of course," he said casually and picked up the small velvet box in his right hand. His other hand went behind her back and he swept her to him, kissing her deep and hard on her startled mouth.

Suddenly swallowed in the earl's arms, Rue heard the dice chatter as if chuckling at her and then roll sharply across the wood. She levered herself away from the engulfing plum frockcoat to stare, shocked, into his eyes.

"You didn't even wait for the cast."

The earl's eyes—and they weren't anything so commonplace as hazel, but a mysteriously shifting mélange of brown and green and gold—never left her face.

"See for yourself," he said softly.

She glanced aside to the tabletop. The dice lay there. A singlet and a five.

"Six . . ." said Rue through stiff lips. "Six. The highest

winning number you could throw that rides the razor's edge of loss—and you knew! You *are* luck incarnate, you *are* the devil!"

He laughed, his eyes moving intently over all her features as though they were both about to be plunged into darkness and he must memorize them first.

"I am your lover now, Rue Morgan, and that is all about me you need to be concerned with," said the earl.

He pressed her back into his arms, the cut-steel buttons riveting through the negligee's flimsy folds and impressing the reality of Varian Temple to her body. He was a good deal taller than she, and though he bent his face to her mouth, her own head was angled far back upon her neck. He kissed her for a very long time, and Rue thought that being Varian Temple's mistress might be a very uncomfortable proposition.

His tongue breached her chapping lips and forced inward. She reared away, but he buried a hand in the curls massing at her neck and pulled her closer until their mouths were so blended Rue could not tell where hers ended and his began. Her heart was drumming against his encroaching body. Not with pleasure—fear. She, who had conquered the lamb and though it so easy, was about to lie down with the lion.

He abruptly pushed her away, his arm about her waist sufficient, it seemed, to hold her in his grasp. He glanced down her gown front and began unleashing the long rows of bows that joined it with ruthless mechanical gestures. Item: a bow. Item: another. Item: yet another. Item: the last.

Rue felt the material fluttering open down the length of her body and his eyes driving inward as inevitably as his tongue had established residency in her mouth. She was growing confused. She felt like a transaction, like so much fertile farmland to be acquired and ploughed under. Nigel wasn't—

He had picked her up, and the gown's opening curtain was temporarily delayed as the full folds lay slack but modestly across her body. He brought her directly to the rose damask bed in the adjoining room and laid her on it. Rue tautened in anticipation, but he stepped away to the bed's foot, half-visible behind a draped post. Rue clutched the wrapper across her breast and raised up experimentally on one elbow.

The earl was disrobing, neatly folding and laying his apparel on the bench at the bed's foot: his frockcoat, underwaistcoat of matching plum silk, silken white shirt, white undershirt . . . He came round the bedcurtain to sit and take off his shoes, peel off his stockings. Good heavens, Rue saw the cloud of dark hair gathered upon his chest like a storm—he was an ape! She half-sat in horror.

Nigel would come, it was true, in the dark of night with one candle, and that he would quickly extinguish. But Nigel would come swathed in a nightgown like hers, and cover her in tiresome wet kisses like Piquant's that never went deep, and then he would fall upon her and, and—it was over very quickly, at the worst. And tolerable, though unpleasant. Rue Morgan had the sudden insight that the Earl of Argyle was not Nigel.

But she was still Rue Morgan, and a bargain was a bargain.

She sat up completely and forced her tense fingers to loosen one by one on her gown front. The fabric parted softly, dropping away. She felt the room's cooler air draw a narrow path three inches wide down her breasts, over her stomach, between her folded legs. She put her hands to the embroidered counterpane and held them there, concentrating her will on feeling the texture of the cursive designs.

The earl stood and began unbuttoning his nankeen breeches. He was nearly naked now, and the light-colored breeches made him look nearer naked than not. Rue studied his pale flesh, watched the muscles of his upper arms shift with each motion. The breeches fell floorward, and there was only his drawers. She did not have to force herself to move her eyes to his face.

He looked up from his undressing soon after to see her

regarding him with the defiant cold stare of a cat. The gown was split open enough to provide a creamy landscape of undulating light and shadow that eradicated from his mind any other purpose he had for this encounter but one. He stepped toward her, their gazes locked still. Then a flash of color at her throat caught his attention. He stopped directly before her.

"That bauble, take it off."

"I always wear it," said Rue, dropping her eyes to the darkly furred chest before her with glimmers of moon-pale skin shining through.

Nigel always wore a nightshirt, Nigel only came and—this was not Nigel. And now this not-Nigel was telling her to remove the sapphire that had once sparkled from someone's watchfob. Someone long ago in fragrant grasses . . . His mouth had been grass-sweet, his arms red and embracing as a sunset. She remembered it then, a certain rhythmic rapture, a soft dwelling on a touch here, a tender pressing there—no, she had no memory but revenge, saw no red but blood, saw no sun rising for her but a pale lemon bird winging into inescapable death.

Rue reached back beneath her heavy coiling hair and undid the last bow on her person herself, the small black velvet bow that held the pendant sapphire fast at her throat. She laid it softly on the bedside table, watching the velvet curl round the stone like an ebony snake.

Before she could draw her eyes away from that, the Earl of Argyle's weight had carried her back upon the bed, the great naked length of him atop her in broad daylight, her gown wrenching open further . . . Her gown was gone, and she was as naked to the earl as he was to her.

His face loomed above hers. That was the sole part of him she had always seen naked, and now she did not know it. He pressed his greedy mouth to hers again, kissing, driving, roughening, wrenching, delving. His hands played down across her body, first tracing a chaste narrow line down her center, then roaming farther, scavenging around the base of her breasts, climbing them, possessing the summit, weaving again down the valley of her waist, traversing the slight swell of her stomach, verging on her lowest forest, and retreating to rampage upward again.

She twisted under him, but it simply aided the infinite variations of the movement his free hand made against her. He roamed her body like a wolf his immemorial acres, and the more she bucked at his lordly domination, the more she made herself his.

His hand honed itself finally between her thighs. She clamped them shut on it faster than thought. He withdrew his mouth from hers then, but not the hand. The wolfish eyes narrowed.

"Is there something the matter?"

She was surprised that his voice sounded quite human, though a husky half-whisper. She suspected he had been somewhere far away where voices are not required, only howls, and thus found it rusty to speak.

Rue tossed her head upon the pale pillow. "My hairdressing," she said finally.

"Be damned to it," said the earl, eyelids dropping over the disconcerting eyes as he bent back to her face.

"And, and—it is my monthly time."

This gave the earl pause.

"Would Rue Morgan, Black Rue Morgan, offer herself to a man when she was in no position to fulfill her bargain? You disappoint me, my dear."

"No," objected Rue. "I was not expecting it! But something has happened now . . . I can feel it starting."

The earl regarded her, as unblinking as an owl. "Are you in pain?" he asked finally.

"N—n—no," she confessed reluctantly.

A small smile crossed his lips. Rue wondered that they were not bruised, as her own felt.

"It is of no significance then," he said, entering her with such swiftness that her legs parted enough to admit him before she could think to close them. His mouth was over hers again, muffling protest, though it required the earl's arching his back like a longbow to keep it there.

Rue considered that lovemaking was a great deal of trouble, but at least in this instance the end was near. She welcomed his thrusts now, not because of any pleasure they brought her, but because she foresaw the blessed moment of withdrawal when the weight and the pawing lifted simultaneously and she was her own woman again.

But it was not-Nigel who rode her, and he did not seem inclined to spend himself quickly. Things went on a great bit longer than usual, no matter how passively she lay, and when he finally paused and pressed her deep into the linens while she felt his pleasure shake him, Rue was mystified beyond reassurance. He rolled off, pale and sweating. Indeed, it was one small comfort to know that even earls sweated.

Rue lay still, legs apart as they had been, hair tempest-tossed upon the pillow. The scent of sweat and other liquids mingled as they never seemed to when she had been taken by clothed lovers. Perhaps the earl was an eccentric.

After a moment he rolled over her again, balancing his weight on either side of her on long, muscled, white arms. Ape. Her legs snapped shut. The earl grinned at her and ducked his head to her face. He kissed her, pecked her really, lightly on the lips, and a good thing, for she was exceedingly sore there.

He was dressing now and would soon be gone. A diaphanous cloud came floating down on her, her wrapper hurled from wherever it had fallen or he had thrown it. She felt the fabric waft across her like a winding sheet. When she at last looked up, it was because she heard the rustle of plum silk.

He was dressed and looking quite civilized. Something in his hazel-green eyes made a sudden thought leap against her breastbone. Anxiety pounded her ribs. She sat up, clutching the wrapper to her bosom.

"You will promise then to keep my father from the land he wants? You will not sell to him?"

The earl considered it.

"Sir! It would be infamy to accept my bargain and then renege. Your Lordship means but to tease me. Well?"

The earl looked to her eyes.

"My dear Miss Morgan, no gentleman is bound by bargains made with one who is no lady. But that aside, I won you in a toss of the dice, not by any promises that tumbled from my mouth, if you will recall. You are a bold and clever hussy, but if you are determined to live in a world without honor, you must not expect any back for yourself. 'I'd no more play with a man that slighted his ill fortune than I'd make love to a woman who undervalued the loss of her reputation,' " the earl quoted. "Congreve. I have made an exception to this maxim, which I take for my own, in your case because you are an amusing wench and have promise—if not promises that are kept. Perhaps in future you will set a higher store upon yourself; it lends a certain savor to the game. Good day."

The earl turned and left, Rue staring at his disappearing plum back like one but lately raised from the dead and uncertain how to live again.

"You . . . devil!" she was able to hiss at the door only as it swung shut again.

She collapsed upon the bed, her negligee across her. She felt taken, used, sore about her mouth and at the mouth between her legs. She lowered the wrapper enough to examine the swell of one pearly breast, an abrasion of tiny points, like a half-moon of button.

All this, this storming, and still she had gotten nothing from him. Well, it was not over. Not even an earl had his way with her, and his rough, high-handed way with her on the throw of six.

The Earl of Argyle returned to his cavernous house on Cavendish Square late that night, closeted himself in his study, and proceeded to get slightly drunk on port wine.

His Lordship had had a very long day after leaving Grosvenor Square. He had visited his tailor, who had fussed at a certain carelessness in His Lordship's present attire, a fault he laid at the feet of the earl's absent valet. His Lordship did not correct him.

The earl then had visited his club where he had read the papers and taken the fine canary always kept there, had dined later with the Marquess of Lanceburry, and gamed at Brooks's until closing.

He had lost twice at hazard to Jonathan Flemming, a happening rare enough to elate that young man and cast the earl into a blue ruin totally unabetted by the gin that produced this lamentable condition in the lower classes.

Now he sat in the great brown leather Queen Anne chair whose surface was glove-soft from three generations' sitting. Beside him was a small piecrust table, slightly nicked, but warm-wooded from polish. The earl had imported an Irish cut-glass decanter to his side without calling upon the aid of a servant, and his hand returned frequently to its faceted stopper, which he swiveled, then withdrew and weighed in his palm, like a doorknob he debated turning.

In the end, he always poured another rich stream of red into the tapered French crystal glass at his fingertips.

The only other thing on the small table besides glass and decanter was a mother-of-pearl inlaid casting box containing the earl's favorite dice.

They were fashioned of bone and had a slightly macabre legend attached to their origin. He had won them from a mad German count at hazard early in his gaming career, but he never used them to play now, only for his own delectation.

The earl took a swallow of port and cradled the dice in his palm. His eyes roamed the room with slightly hazy satisfaction.

All palest jade-green-painted paneling, and a semicircular array of towering bookshelves. The bookshelves were properly divided by severe Attic columns and pedimented with a graceful Greek triangle above. All pale green, and then the rich russet, brown, and red leathers of the gold-tooled book bindings blazing within the classical architectural setting like a remote kind of fire.

The earl's feet rested on one of three richly figured, scarlet and ivory Oriental rugs that sprawled across polished parquet floors. Under the severely pillared shelter of a white marble mantel, a fire crackled at full blaze, courting the bright brass andirons with warm glances.

He threw the dice softly to the little table.

One and one makes two. He stared at the twin dark spots. Like eyes they were. Her eyes. She was very much like dice, Black Harry Morgan's daughter.

He picked one up and rubbed it softly between his fingers until the bone warmed and his senses could detect every smooth striation.

It was time he came to terms with his . . . what should he call it? Was it possible that the Earl of Argyle had developed a new addiction? She had intended to seduce him, he had known that all along. In the Morgan mind, anything was justified as long as it led to a satisfactory conclusion. Father and daughter had that much in common. She bargained with her body, as women had been doing since men had been willing to bargain for them. Since Adam.

But he had not intended to accept her so blatantly extended offer. And he had. That was unlike him.

His hand fisted on the single die until its cubed edges pressed into his flesh. He picked up its mate and cast them again. One came up a singlet once more. The other—two! Another unlucky toss. Three.

He glanced to the shadowed Greek pediment across from him. He was wont to study the incised figures gamboling there. They gave him a frozen statuary peace that he seldom found elsewhere.

Tonight his shadowed mind turned the pure Greek triangular pediment into the dark inverted pyramid at the junction of Rue Morgan's creamy thighs. Ah, of course, her coloring is what had claimed his infatuation. He, who had been fascinated by the play of dark spots on milky cubes, now had found a whole, warm, living body playing out the same color scheme.

And so unforgiving, too, she was. As were the dice. Turn her this way or that, on one throw she would land all smiles and sweet satisfaction. Another hazard, and her uncompromisingly hard, dark eyes would stare at the gamester uncomprehendingly.

She was her father's daughter. She was Black Rue Morgan, and he must not forget it. An alliance with her was an alliance with the forbidding face of the dice on their most vindictive throws. She bargained with her body and would cost a man his soul, like every temptress since man first needed temptresses to excuse his own rampaging lusts.

The earl laughed at himself in the empty room and dropped the dice into their container. There was so simple an explanation.

She was handsome—why was he not as susceptible to that as the next rogue? That was all. That was an answer he could shut his eyes upon at night. He desired her. Might do so again. Nothing was lost by it. Nothing. She was ruined already before he had met her. No innocent, she. Nor was he. They were well-mated.

On a whim he cast the dice again. They came up three. He stared at the lone spot, and thought of one other, one he had not thought of deeply for years, though she was never done haunting the back of his mind.

Whenever he allowed himself to think of her, she blossomed in his brain like a painful rose, a white rose shedding petals, full-blown. Full-blown away.

She was owed to the score of Black Harry Morgan, though the debt wound back through time almost as long as Morgan's daughter was old. Fifteen years ago, very nearly, and still painful; the root of his hatred drove straight and deep within him. He was only aware of it when he deliberately tugged upon it, as now, but he never pulled at the hatred to dislodge it. No, he nourished it, even as he put it aside in his mind for his sanity's sake.

Now the port wine drenched its deep-buried roots, and the farthest tendril of his hate greedily absorbed whatever fuel it could.

Varian Temple leaned his cool glass against his forehead, its contents tilted perilously. He pictured Black Harry Morgan's daughter spread white as linens beneath him and thought it only justice. Time exacts its penalities. He sipped from the finely edged glass, polished so smooth the port slid over it like a breath.

He thought of Rue Morgan's mouth, polished and brittle as glass. He paused with the liquid just tilted to his lips so the wine's spiritous tingle teased his lips.

This is what he would draw out of Rue Morgan, save he knew it wasn't there. There was no passion, no love in her, any more than there was something called "luck" in dice or in cards. No, a man found in anything only what he brought to it.

To Rue Morgan, Varian Temple brought an old hatred, a hidden purpose, and one fine, throbbing pulse of pure desire. Perhaps it was enough.

He cast the dice one last time that evening. A pair of ones. Deuce. Deuced unlucky. He stared at the hard, inexpressive eyes of the dice. He would order a decorative pair set with sapphires for her, to cool her rage. She gambled with her eyes at any rate. It would be amusing to watch her gamble with those he had given her.

Two. For eyes.

Varian Temple decided he was very drunk.

The Earl of Argyle rose contemplatively, drained the last glass of port, and went up to bed.

One of the objects of his ruminations remained awake.

Rue Morgan lay staring at the softly draped canopy above, while beside her Nigel slept to the rhythmic accompaniment of soft snores. She had not extinguished the single bedside candle and took some solace from its slow-dancing loyal burn.

She had stayed abed the remainder of that afternoon, earning no sympathy from the returning Heliotrope, who had taken one glance at her mistress and had gone to draw the curtains.

"I could have told you that one would be a high-stepper," said the maid between lips drawn I-told-you-so taut.

"There is nothing worse than a worldly wise virgin," Rue snapped back, but she was grateful when Helia came to plump the pillows and draw the covers up. "I shall need another dose of your wretched potion," she said, referring to the vile liquid that supposedly prevented unwanted consequences of certain, very natural acts.

She had not contracted her monthlies, as perhaps the earl had known better than she, and that too was unfortunate.

When Sir Nigel returned home at six and found her still abed, he had been moved to order dinner in her suite and then join her. She could not claim malaise as an excuse and, not being able to think of another rapidly enough, was forced to accede.

That night she had found even Nigel's puppyish squirmings overvigorous. It was but one more discomfort she could lay at the feet of the earl. She vowed to return his indignities upon her person threefold and then turned her restless mind upon her father. They still must ensure that he be blocked in his land speculations. But was there not some trifling disservice they could do him in the meantime?

Rue then remembered the rough men who sometimes came to Blackstone House's rear entrance, the men her father took coarse pleasure in showing to the library and offering his finest port—to the servant's dismay.

They were seafaring men, low, common sailors—not surprising since her father owned a merchant fleet. But there was something underhanded about their access to her father and his interest in them. Perhaps that was a tack that Morgan's fellow shipowner, Lemuel Humphries, could take. She must see the Basilisk Club soon and then perhaps enlist their aid on a small scheme she had in mind for the earl.

Black Rue indeed! He knew not the half of it, the Earl of Argyle. But he would. Oh, he would indeed.

For the first night in her life, Rue Morgan fell asleep not dreaming of revenge upon her father. But she still dreamt of revenge. And of other things.

Chapter Nine

"A dish of chocolate, Miss Morgan?"

Ever since he had escorted her to Brooks's, Sir Merivale Fenton-Mews had taken on the role of Rue's protector, escort, and general supplier of all comforts.

It was he, for instance, who had seen to it that a small embroidered stool be set ready for her dainty feet when she met with the Basilisk Club. Since contemporary shoes, even for daywear, were exceptionally fragile, Rue appreciated this foresight.

Since it was also an exceptionally dank March day, Rue appreciated even more that her chair had been drawn up before a blazing fire at the coffeehouse's rear, and the Basilisk Club herded around her like a group of dozing spaniels at a country house grate.

It had been nigh two months since Rue Morgan had so spectacularly joined their ranks. In that time, their only decisive action had been to report one of Black Harry's crimping houses to Bow Street. It had been closed, the English government officially taking the dimmest view of rapping English subjects on the head and shipping them out to service at sea until they dropped, died, or ran aport on a suitably foreign enough shore to ensure they never came home again to tell the tale.

Black Harry Morgan's backing of such an enterprise had caused a stir but no surprise. He had paid a heavy fine, the English government also taking the position that when it found one of its leading citizens in arrears of the law, the best way to treat such an offense was with a lavish assessment for the public tills.

That such monies rarely found their way back to the poorer citizens for whom they were ostensibly intended was another matter entirely.

And Black Harry Morgan was not totally without profit in the affair. Two days after his fining before the magistrate, a small jewel box had arrived at Blackstone House, and in it lay a single, round sapphire of exceptional fire and quality.

Black Harry could have chosen to regard it as a gauntlet from his errant daughter, but he was avaricious enough to simply consider it a foolishness on her part and an admirable addition to his possessions.

Heliotrope had been more upset by Rue's profligate ways with her mother's sapphires than she had been by Rue's lavishing her other, more personal attributes on the Earl of Argyle but two months before.

"You are mad," she had raged in her softly modulated voice, velvet even when its owner was rubbed against the nap. "Mistress Rue, I've grown with you, served you, ay, even thought we were friends—"

"Helia! You don't think else now?" Rue's hand reached out to quiet the one that flew in sewing some braid to Rue's newest redingote. "I've simply a purpose that goes beyond the worth of a paltry string of jewels. As he gave to me, so shall he be given back by me, from gemstones to justice," said Rue, her voice very hard, her hand tightening rigidly on Heliotrope's.

"But the set was complete! And all your mother left you. Have you no sentimental attachment to it for that reason?"

"No. It has passed to me through him and in that has lost

all meaning but the contempt with which he regarded the necklace, my mother, me . . . I only wish that I could be certain of returning all seventeen gems as tokens of each step of my revenge," continued Rue. "That would be worth anything!"

"Even . . . the earl? Again?" asked Helia shrewdly, her dark eyes glancing up sideways from her stitching.

Rue stared at her for a moment, then laughed.

"Ay, even the earl, if suit my purposes. But don't fret so, Helia. At the moment, the earl's chief interest for me is his disposal of the lands he has acquired. I suspect he is very parsimonious of his rouleaux and his lands, but if he even considers selling to my father—Well, Helia, then I fear you shall find much to tsk about," finished Rue heatedly, her blue eyes narrowing at the black velvet casting box atop her dressing table.

She overturned it, and a pair of pale dice obediently tumbled out, their spots inset with rows of tiny sapphires. The earl was as fond of gestures as herself, and as unsentimental.

It struck Rue with irony that as she sent sapphires to her father, so the earl sent sapphires to her. They had arrived a month before, and the workmanship was very fine. French—although it was likely some exiled Paris jeweler had executed them not far from the center of London.

Rue picked up the ivory dice and cast them. They came up doubles, three sapphires in a twinkling row on each surface. Six. Rue laughed and tossed them back in their box, dampening their sparkle in the room only half-lit by a dreary March day.

"Helia, you need another candle if you sew. I'll fetch it."

"You are most solicitous," noted the maid dryly.

"No, my love. Only I wish to wear that redingote to the Basilisk Club tomorrow," said Rue lightly.

And now here she sat, in Heliotrope's carefully stitched braid, the waist-length redingote buttoned up her corseted front and cutting away to a long coat in back. The red coat had a distinctly masculine, almost military cut that the addition of braid but abetted. Rue's waist was sashed in what was quickly becoming her colors, an answer to the red, white, and blue of the French tricolor that had briefly dominated even English fashion in the early '90s.

Rue's colors were red, black, and white. A striped sash of the stuff circled her waist and tied into a bustle of loops at her rear. The same material traveled in pert bows up her high-crowned, black felt hat and perched in a knot at the back of its tilted brim, laying against her tumbling jet curls.

An upstanding white frill circled her shoulders and bodice with almost Elizabethan stiffness, and inset against her neckline was a swelling white fichu of the newly transparent tulle affixed as low on her breast as recently liberated fashions allowed by a black intaglio onyx pin.

Rue kicked her slippered foot nearer the fire, causing a rustle of her black taffeta skirt that sounded like a flock of crows in flight. The gesture caught the joint attention of the Basilisk Club.

"I will have some chocolate, Sir Merivale," said Rue, accepting libation at their hands for the first time. "And, Mr. Humphries, the matter of the crimping house was well done. I think we may be pleased with ourselves."

Lemuel Humphries bowed, snowy wig eclipsing his florid face momentarily like a cloud in the sunset.

"But . . ."

They hung on her next words, though she forestalled them with a sip of the chocolate Fenton-Mews delivered almost to her lips when he presented it.

"I understand you fear that my father has contacted the Earl of Argyle about His Lordship's property adjoining Grosvenor Square."

Rue pulled up her crackling ebony skirts, exposing a delicate lace ruffle of petticoat and the slender arch of white-stockinged ankle, and thrust her feet nearer the blaze.

"Oh, you shall s—s—scorch!" objected Fenton-Mews in what was very near a squeal.

"Nonsense, my dear Sir Merivale! It is others who must 'ware of my scorching them, I assure you."

"The earl emerged remarkably uncharred," observed Addison Hookham, eyelids low over his eyes in his cavernous face. He wore a lemon and violet-striped, high-waisted frockcoat this day with a grass-green waistcoat peeping out from the area of his concave stomach. And pantaloons running down to feet clad in low-cut shoes as dainty as Rue's.

She regarded him with a cock of her head that set the bows on her high crown fluttering.

"Mr. Hookham, there are some of us who wear our sentiments less visibly than you. The lightest heart may be at times the heaviest. Be assured, I will deal with the earl again if you gentlemen think it prudent."

"We do."

That was Dr. Radclyffe injecting his magisterial accents into the circle. Radclyffe seldom spoke until matters had reached their heart, so Rue turned to him instantly, concern rippling across her features.

"How so, my dear doctor?"

Radclyffe leaned forward, his thumbs hooked in his old-fashioned waistcoat.

"Your father has been to call in Cavendish Square. And the day after, the earl visited his solicitors."

"Circumstantial, gentlemen." But she frowned.

"We agree that forestalling your father in the matter of developing his Morgan Crescent scheme is the heaviest blow we could deal him," said Colonel Trumbull bluffly, drawing out the handkerchief that accompanied his every speech. For when Colonel Trumbull talked, he would invariably sneeze. The members of the Basilisk Club drew subtly back, as was their custom.

"So my *ah*—" the Basilisk Club blanched as one "—dear, I believe it would be well to persuade the earl to desist from dealing with your father. If you do not wish to undertake the *ah, ah, ah ... chooooo!* ... that is, this commission, per- haps some other members can broach the earl—"

"No." Rue drew her feet abruptly from the grate. "Where I begin, I finish. It will be necessary to ascertain the earl's immediate movements—"

"Nothing simpler," interrupted Sir Feverell Marshwine, starting up from a doze. "I have a well-traveled footman in my employ who has served the earl. He retains acquaintance among His Lordship's servants, particularly the sister of one of the groomsmen."

"And?" demanded Rue. "We need to know more than af- fairs of the heart among the earl's retainers."

"He leaves for Tunbridge Wells tomorrow," replied Sir Feverell indignantly. This information had been his only contribution to the plotting thus far, and he was inordinately proud of it. "So I think we need fear nothing more from him for the fortnight at least," he concluded.

"Does he post down?" inquired Rue, referring to the cus- tom of changing horses at intermittent stops.

"Not damn likely," said Hookham. "He's won a pair of spanking fresh grays from the Midlands's best breeder at Brooks's and is eager to test 'em. He drives himself in his perch phaeton, you can wager on it."

"We do," said Rue coolly. "I thought the earl only played for rouleaux at hazard—why did he accept the horses?" she asked suspiciously.

"He does play only for coin unless the stakes be horses or women, as you might recall, or unless the poor fellow across from him has lost all his coin to the cards. And the game was faro, not hazard."

Rue nodded. "I stand corrected, Mr. Hookham. And," she said, standing in actuality this time, "I have a scheme. I shall require your aid, Mr. Hookham, and yours, Sir Feverell, and that of your inestimable informant in the earl's stables. We shall withdraw to discuss it, and report to the re- maining gentlemen on its success or failure later."

Rue swept out to her waiting carriage, the two men in her

wake, and invited them into the tufted depths within. There was much discussion in low tones, interrupted by a startled exclamation from Sir Feverell now and again and a low, admiring chuckle from Hookham.

The footmen stood at attention under their powdered wigs, admirably repressing any curiosity that might foam to their heads like a too-hastily-poured ale. They would speculate later, if they had a moment to remark upon it, and usually they were kept too busy for gossip . . . except perhaps the Earl of Argyle's second groomsman, whose sister Moll the underhousemaid had a certain sentimental attachment to Sir Feverell Marshwine's ubiquitous footman.

Rue Morgan was pleased to think that the Earl of Argyle could be underdone by an armorous footman. It was, she decided, poetic justice. When her two henchmen among the Basilisk Club bowed their way out of her presence, she drove back to Grosvenor Square and the ever-more-tiresome Nigel in high, good, gaming spirits. This time a throw of the dice should not be enough to extricate the earl from her purposes.

Not even a six of sapphires.

Chapter Ten

Only 800,000 souls inhabited the ten miles of London sprawling on either side of the Thames in the year 1795, but events led some observers to believe that fully half of them were footpads, cutpurses, thieves, and highwaymen.

Indeed, Piccadilly, sandwiched as it was between elegant Pall Mall and the outer residential areas of Grosvenor and Berkley Squares, was a no man's land after dark and considered quite unsafe for any sane man, woman, or child.

Observers then may have wondered at the sight of an unescorted perch phaeton drawn by matched grays with charcoal manes and tails, springing along Piccadilly's rough granite cobblestones as if running from the devil or driven by him.

Nor was this a mere pleasure run. A quantity of luggage was mounted on the four-wheeler's front transom and over the rear axletree as well, all anchored by leather straps. The vehicle's small, hooded body swung on a devilishly intricate arrangement of springs, straps, and leather braces, all geared to suspend the coach as high as possible above its smaller front wheels and as far forward as possible from its larger back wheels.

The rig was painted ivory and royal blue. Every so often a whip would flick from under the hood and lick lightly at the grays. They seemed to need no urging, though. Their pale hooves fairly flew over the clearing evening roads, not a covered dray-wagon or any other lumbering deterrent to speed in their way.

The phaeton turned south finally on Blackfriars Road and sped toward Blackfriars Bridge over the Thames, the body of the vehicle lurching wildly on the turn.

"Your Lordship, I vow that I have left my hat upon Fleet Street," objected one of the two persons who sat the high seat. He was not the driver.

"Then you shall have to see Tunbridge Wells hatless, Welles," returned the Earl of Argyle unsympathetically as Bridewell Prison's bulk flashed by on his left. The westering sun painted this enlightened institution for the idle and the vagabond ruddy.

The earl's tilted jockey hat showed no signs of leaving his head, nor did his eyes leave the rough city road. Things would be smoother once they cleared Southwark and came upon regular road. They were only bound to Camberton, where the earl and his valet would stay the night before making the final journey to Tunbridge Wells in the morning.

Undoubtedly, the earl could have postponed departure until the morrow, but he was devilishly eager to try out the newly won grays, not to mention the perilously sprung perch phaeton.

As he had hoped, they were matched to perfection, and there was little danger that the vehicle should meet its comeuppance in a ditch, as Welles so evidently feared. Upended perch phaetons were some of the metropolis's more entertaining everyday sights, for they were as oddly constructed as a waterbug and less stable in their element.

But when his departure had been delayed by first one annoyance, then another . . . well, the earl had fretted and paced, gracing the carriage house with his frock-coated presence while the second groomsman struggled to untangle the wonders of the grays' new harnesses. The man had taken damnably long about it as well, explaining himself with only stutters, his hanging head never quite daring to meet the earl's angry hazel eyes.

The earl did not like obstacles, and when the repairs were finally announced complete, he had collected Welles and driven off, despite all protests that it was darkening and dangerous to do so.

These protests had mostly come from Welles, and when the earl did not answer them, that most privileged of servants finally went silent.

Now Blackfriars Road unwound before them, pleasantly wide in token of its importance to the city, but gloriously deserted as well. In minutes, it seemed, the moon was up, casting very little light on the darkening countryside.

The earl's hands tightened slightly on the reins, and though his heart leapt with satisfaction to feel the responsive grays quicken to his gesture, he was glad Camberton lay but a mile or two distant, offering the comforts of stable to his coursers and of inn to himself and his man.

He had just slightly slowed the pair for a rather long curve when three horsemen emerged from a roadside grove and cut in front of him.

"You damnable fools!" he shouted, struggling mightily with the reins to stop the speeding grays from plunging into the party. "You ride the wrong side of the road."

The phaeton rolled to an abrupt stop, its well-oiled springs hardly creaking protest.

"Explain yourselves," the earl demanded imperially with all the authority of one who knows he is in the right—although he had taken the corner at a bit of a pace.

"Very well, sir," said one dark form. "Stand and deliver!"

In the waning light, the earl saw a pistol pulled from a sash and its long barrel leveled at himself. The earl sat silent, stunned, while Welles began sputtering indignantly at his side.

"Do you know who this is? The Earl of Argyle, you rogues! You'll be sent to the French to have your heads taken off if you persist in this madness. Desist, villains."

"Thank you for informing us of the value of our prey," said one of the highwaymen, urging his horse nearer.

Light from the carriage lamps at either side of the phaeton hood fell on this figure then. The earl saw he was a long, narrow man with a scarf tied around his lower face and a soft hat pulled down to his eyes.

The second highwayman, a lumpish stout fellow, stayed at the grays' heads and held the reins.

"Stand you have, sir," noted the third. "Now deliver."

"I will not stand for much," said the earl coldly, for the last voice had a youthful cast despite the muffling handkerchief, and he saw its owner's hand was uncertain on the reins.

"Here, take my purse," offered Welles, "and go!"

"No, my gallant servant, 'tis my purse they covet," said the earl, stopping Welles's gesture with a firm hand. His own purse, heavyweighted with coins, jingled into the lamps' glare, and he held it out.

The lean horseman spurred nearer to take it. He paused for a moment, as though considering his next words.

"Yours, too," he finally barked, nudging his pistol barrel at the valet.

Welles offered his own small purse, and the highwayman leaned over his mount's neck to accept it.

The earl sprang from his seat, one hand snaring the drooping reins, the other knocking the highwayman's pistol-holding arm askew.

Both men were on the ground almost simultaneously, the startled horses rearing from the earl's grasp, and the highwayman cursing and searching for his fallen pistol.

"To me, to me!" the highwayman shouted into the dark as the earl hurled himself upon him.

The man at the gray's head dismounted hastily and ran over, brandishing an equally long-barreled pistol. The third rider came over more slowly, boot heels urging mount to little avail.

"Stand and, stand and, and—be still!" ordered the second rogue as he surveyed the struggling figures. His voice was coming huff-and-puff, and the earl, turning from having subdued the first robber, regarded the pistol now thrust into his stomach with disbelief.

"Why, 'tis a comedy!" announced the earl. "Confide in me, rogues. You are turned out from Covent Garden or Drury Lane and must now rob instead of sing for your supper!"

The earl's fist curled into the thin man's coat collar, and he dredged up the fellow while regarding the plump man before him with further bemusement.

"It's Falstaff you play, confess it," the earl urged, prodding the fellow in his ample belly despite the pistol still aimed for his own middle. "And you, my attenuated fellow, 'tis Sir Andrew Aquecheek, as I live and breathe. And the lad on the horse, I'd wager he makes a pretty Viola."

If the earl felt the situation well in hand, a shocked Welles most certainly did not.

From his perch high above the three men on the ground, he saw only the lantern flick on the pistol's metal pressing very near the fine chamois vest into which he had buttoned his master but hours before. Perhaps now, while the earl was distracting the rogues . . .

Welles's fingers curled around the whip handle, and he lifted it to bring it down on the highwaymen.

The earl heard a quick motion behind him, saw the pistol rear up past him, and discharge, a puff of powder smoking by his ear. Welles whimpered and came crashing to earth.

"You cowardly dogs!"

The earl gathered both highwaymen in his maddened grasp, wrenching the pistol from the stout one, who fell like his victim to the road.

The slender one now sensed that something was at stake and wrestled more feverishly with his tilted adversary.

"Watch out!" warned the mounted youth as the earl swung out with the pistol butt and barely missed the kerchief-swathed jaw. "Watch out, Hook—er."

"Ay, say your names, rogues," urged the earl between his teeth, "but with 'em or without 'em, I'll see you hang at Newgate yard for this."

The fallen man had risen, and the earl turned on him with wolfish fury.

"Hooker, is it?" inquired the earl, his fist driving home into the fellow's stomach. The man doubled over, and the earl's attentions returned to the stout figure hanging onto one of his arms with amazing ineffectiveness.

"Sir Feverell! Be wary!" came the mounted voice again.

The earl whirled, struck by something familiar in not only the name but the voice, that voice—it couldn't be!

He glanced up to see the horse's belly at his back and a silhouetted figure looming above him with a full moon over its shoulder under the shelter of scudding night-bright clouds.

He saw the butt of a pistol hovering black against the lighter sky. It hung there for a long instant before it rushed toward him, and then the earl saw nothing at all.

"You've killed him!" cried the stout man.

"And what do you call what you did to his man, Sir Feverell?" asked the third highwayman, dismounting clumsily and joining the other two.

"He nearly half-killed *me*," objected the first highwayman, rising in the dark like a walking mountain.

"Addison, what do you think? Will he live?"

Rue had knelt by the unconscious earl, her fingers feeling for pooling blood. Addison Hookham tore the cloth off his face, took one of the phaeton's lanterns, and knelt by her.

"I'll never speak the same," he grumbled, rubbing his jaw.

"Never matter. It was the only thing I could think to do,"

Rue hissed to her companions. "He gave me the idea himself when he turned the pistol butt against you. Well? I only intended to stun him, but I've never done it before. Mayhap I've stunned him into eternity, and that's a predicament."

She pulled her own face cloth down and proceeded to bite her lips while the recovering Addison Hookham examined the earl.

"I'm no Dr. Radclyffe, that's for certain. Ahhh, and a fine royal goosebump you've given our peer. He'll do if his head's as hard as his fist. Ouch!"

"And what of the other?" asked Rue.

Sir Feverell scrambled with Hookham over to the prone figure of Welles.

"I saw him looming above like the Lord in his vengeance," he fretted. "What was I to do? The pistol discharged aforetime, I swear it. I meant no harm."

"Nor did we," said Rue, "but it may be beyond mending. How is he? Dead? Breathing? Tell me!"

The small circle of lanternlight roved over Welles's dark and still figure.

"A wound, all right," announced Hookham. "You surprise me, Marshwine. I'd have sworn your fingers would have gone to jelly with your knees if it came to firing."

"I wouldn't have fired! Save he loomed over me so. And we'd none of us be in this fix if you had not allowed the earl to overpower you at the onset."

"But how is the servant?" demanded Rue.

"Well enough," said Hookham. "He'll heal."

"Then Sir Feverell, you will convey your ... victim to your house, where you will tend him and see that he raises no outcry. You and I, Mr. Hookham—"

"Hooker," corrected that gentleman acidly.

"Very well, so I nearly betrayed your name. We are all at fault this night, save for the earl, who managed to combat us gallantly, and this poor brave man, who is worth all four of us combined. Take good care with him, Sir Feverell. And you and I, highwayman Hooker, will take the phaeton and its driver back to Grosvenor Square."

"I will have to drive," advised Hookham.

"Most certainly," said Rue, who had never been indulged in a gig and pair by her father.

"And the earl will have to ride in the seat beside me."

"Of course. But first we must bind his hands."

"Then where will you ride?" Hookham demanded in exasperation.

She turned her attention on the two-seater now waiting docilely in the road.

"Why, I shall ride here!" She circled to its rear. "Here, atop this trunk at the rear axle."

" 'Twill work, just." He bent to help Sir Feverell with Welles's inert body, taking it through the nearby grove to the conspirators' awaiting post chaise.

Rue unhooked the remaining lantern by half-clambering up the high wheel and came round to inspect the earl again. She squatted beside him in her borrowed men's clothes and let the lanternlight fall on his face.

He looked as white and as dead as a churchyard marble. And he was very nearly as heavy when she aided Hookham in lifting and pulling the inert form back into the phaeton.

Rue assumed her seat at the vehicle's rear and hung onto the frame struts as Hookham turned in the road and set the grays at a brisk pace for London.

Blackfriars Road unrolled behind her, an undulating moonlit ribbon still empty and lone.

She considered the night's occurrences as she jolted at road level between the high, spinning wheels. Her ultimate assessment agreed with the earl's.

"A comedy," she whispered to herself, shaking her slouch-hatted head. "A comedy."

She then remembered Quentin Rossford's assertion that all comedy was based on tragedy and crossed her fingers where they clung to the leather straps.

Chapter Eleven

The Earl of Argyle was in that blissful, foggy in-between where the awakening senses are wont to woolgather when they know only cold reality awaits on the everyday side of consciousness.

He was flying along in his perch phaeton, the grays a cloudy blur of pure speed ahead and Welles by his side, applying the whip frantically, shouting demonically for more speed.

The earl was curiously distracted, concentrating instead on casting a pair of dice on the phaeton's floorboards. No matter what the throw, the dice came up in only one pattern, a death's head.

He looked up and saw a spectre in a long black cloak beckoning to him from the side of the road. His head turned to follow the figure as it flashed past—a mistake, for a sudden pain set the entire landscape on its heels, spinning into one overriding gray blur of hooves and wheels and motion.

The earl groaned and awoke.

As some instinct had suspected, wakefulness was not an improvement.

For one thing, his head was pounding as if he had spent

the night in a gin mill. For another, there was the fact that his face was horizontal, his cheek resting on some linen many notches of quality below the silk bedsheets he was accustomed to reclining upon.

The third disagreeable realization was that when he moved to sit upright, he instantly sank down again. This he could attribute to the increased pitch of throbbing in his head and the fact that something heavy and iron seemed to be affixed to his wrists.

The earl, his eyes still shut, considered the possibilities of what could have transpired since his roadside encounter with the trio of highwaymen. He concluded that after he had been knocked unconscious, the authorities had happened on the scene, apprehended him for a criminal, and incarcerated him in Fleet Prison.

The earl smiled at this ridiculous fantasy and opened his eyes. They focused on subterranean stone walls, a close, deserted chamber occupied by a long rough trestle table, the cot he lay upon, a guttering candle, and a swag of black iron chain from the wall to his manacled wrists.

He shut his eyes again. They remained closed until the room's heavy wooden door creaked open and Rue Morgan passed through it.

The earl let out a low hiss of relief. He would never have guessed that relief would be the next emotion Rue Morgan would instill in him, but there it was.

The earl was too familiar with the limbo of England's penal institutions to be certain that even a peer of the realm, unidentified and purseless, couldn't fall into one and disappear forever. Black Rue, on the other hand, could only have a purpose for him that included making the most of his position and freedom.

"Awake, Your Lordship?" she inquired serenely.

"Conscious, I think," he replied, forcing himself upright, though his head throbbed abominably. "I would that you were fully conscious of what you've done. How is Welles?"

"In better circumstances than you, I warrant. He took a

ball through the shoulder, it's true, but evidently it was a clean stroke. He is being tended not far from here."

"And where is 'here'?" asked the earl, looking around and then sorry for it as his eyes detected moss upon the stones and his ears heard the trickle of what his nose told him was distressingly fetid water.

"In my cellar," said Rue. "An understoreroom to be exact."

"And these?" The earl toasted with his hands, holding manacled wrists together, though there was half a foot of chain between them.

"Striking, are they not? A mere precaution. Luckily one of my fellow conspirators is also on the prison board and thus had access to all sorts of ingenious inventions. These, we hope, will keep you quiet while your head heals."

The earl automatically raised a hand to that extremity, but found the chains too heavy going.

"You rapped me with your pistol butt, didn't you?" he asked, more attempting to recall than accuse.

"A mere love tap," said Rue, smiling. "My other conspirator assures me that your head is hard enough to survive it."

"And the phaeton and grays?"

Rue's smile broadened as she sat on the table edge.

"I have sent them as a token of your regard to the young squire from whom you won them. I'm sure a Midlands lad had no idea that he was gaming with the fatal Earl of Argyle."

His Lordship stood in such sudden outrage that the chains rattled and the pressure in his head carved a frown in his forehead. The earl blinked stalwartly.

"Damn your connivance! I want those grays."

The earl took note of his current condition and elected to sit again.

"We all of us want many things, Your Lordship," said Rue softly, "and having won them, as we think, lose them. I told you once that I wanted your attention. Now I have it, and by God, I shall use it. I will see you in the morning when your head has cleared somewhat, I trust. There is a necessaries closet behind the screen. I would offer you late supper, but I fear you would not stomach it."

Rue rose to collect the candle in its plain pewter holder.

" 'Good night, sweet prince, may angels . . .' Ah, out of temper for the bard, are we? I assure you, you will mellow by morning."

She drew the door shut, then popped her head through it again.

"I've two dim-headed but sturdy footmen stationed without, Your Lordship. Please do not try to join them."

The door shut again, latch and bar thudding into place, light vanishing utterly. The earl lay back and closed his eyes, determined that he would sleep, for clearly he would need it.

Being a fatalist as well as a Peer of the Realm, he did.

Morning, revealed only by his keeper's return with a fresh candle, also made clear to the earl that his fashionable frockcoat had been removed and folded neatly at his feet. He collected sufficient energy to raise a hand to his head and found some sort of cloth wrapped around it.

"Yes, you are a real beauty, Your Lordship," commented Rue, whisking out the door again in her voluminous wrapper.

It was as frail and expensive as the one she had worn on the occasion of their last meeting. The earl wondered that she should care to trail it over the damp floors.

She returned with a laughably decorative silver tray laden with wedges of cold meat pie, a few thick slices of bread, and a steaming pot of something. The earl eyed it hopefully.

"Shall you pour or I?" he inquired.

"I," she said, setting down the heavy tray with relief and bringing a cup of the stuff over to him. It was, as he had most fervently hoped, coffee.

He wondered why she was fetching and carrying herself. Possibly no one besides the guardian footmen were aware of his presence in the house. That was a fact to store up for future use.

"Now then, Miss Morgan," he said after three rapid sips in a row. "You appear to have disposed of my valet, my phaeton, and my steeds efficiently enough. How do you propose to dispose of me?"

"I'm hoping that won't be necessary," said Rue sweetly. "It seems that you did not think I was serious when I enlisted your aid against my father. I cannot see why anyone would refuse to forestall him, for he is a rather horrid man, if you have never met him—"

"I haven't," the earl interjected, "but if you resemble him, I take your word on his character."

"It is so simple then. Your cooperation loses you nothing and you foil a beastly man."

"Perhaps I would rather foil his daughter more," suggested the earl, still sipping.

"I think you have already," she answered coldly. Rue got up and swept a bit nearer her prisoner.

He was a pitiful sight, the lopsided bandage cocked over his dark hair, from which the careful curl had fallen. He looked an escapee from a coal bin, with a smudge of beard growth darkening his once marble jaw, and road dust spotting his slightly askew stock. But that unshaven jaw was set, and the eyes under the tousled hair were very undisheveled.

"Does your head still ache?" she asked abruptly, curious.

"I'd not remained seated in the presence of a lady, an' it did not," replied the earl deliberately.

"But that would have nothing to do with your posture in my presence, would it?" Rue retorted with a grin, recognizing the verbal sidestep. "It serves you right and proper, as the servants say, Your Lordship. You made more than my head ache, I fear."

" 'Hell hath no fury . . .' " quoted the earl, regarding the ceiling, no uplifting sight, for it was spider-webbed and distressingly crumbled.

"But that is the point!" Rue seized a plate of beef pie from the tray and clutched it fiercely as she advanced toward her victim. "You did not scorn *me*, only my very businesslike proposal. Here!"

She thrust the dish at him so violently the pie nearly slid off it.

The earl accepted it rapidly, being appallingly hungry, and considered the wisdom of dropping his breakfast, capturing his hostess, and demanding that the supposed footmen release him. If she had no footmen, however, such direct action would be useless.

He decided to try the pie, breaking it into pieces with his fingers and bringing it to his mouth despite the chains rattling against the plate.

"That's the finest china," Rue admonished.

The earl attempted to examine the dish his chains forced him to hold directly under his chin.

"So it is. Canton. And a favorite pattern of mine, too. Surely you could have found something shabbier, Miss Morgan, something more in keeping with the ambiance of your, er, subterranean guest room."

"Will you eat or talk?" snapped Rue. "Or shall I take it back?" She extended the flat of one imperious palm.

The earl looked up with narrowed green-gold eyes.

"I should caution you, Miss Morgan, that you stand too near even a chained man. A mere twist of the wrist and I could seize you, pull this length between my wrists across your throat, call your footmen to release me, and use you as a hostage. Or being vindictive, I could break your neck and starve happily beside your corpse. Or wait for your men to come in, then bribe them, and escape . . ."

He finished the pie and laid the empty plate very gently on her palm.

Rue jumped back as though bitten, retreating until she judged herself beyond the reach of his chains. The earl reclined on an elbow, hands prayerfully together, looking like a remarkably disheveled but angelic street urchin.

Rue hurled the remaining pieces of bread to his cot.

"I am most grateful for your advice," she said icily. "You may wager upon it that I shall not make the same mistake in the future, but shall stay well out of your reach."

"My sentiments precisely," said the earl dryly.

"Then all you need to do is agree to my terms— do not sell your land to my father."

"Is that all? Very well, I agree."

"I don't believe you."

"There is no pleasing you, Miss Morgan, something I imagine Sir Nigel meditates upon in the night. Fortunately, I no longer allow small distractions to affect my slumbers."

The earl lifted a booted leg and fixed it atop the cot, idly tearing the bread into edible morsels with his fingers. Save that he had to duck his head to eat the pieces, he looked as though he were upon a picnic.

"I know my father called upon you," accused Rue, eager to ruffle his aggravating calm.

The earl elevated a dark eyebrow until it vanished under his thatch of ruffled hair.

"I had no idea that you kept such a close watch upon my movements. Yes, he called upon me. Even you are free to do so, were I at home to receive you," he mentioned pointedly.

"To ask about the Marylebone land?"

"It is the only interest we have in common. I do not count you, of course, as I suspect that your father is as eager to be rid of his Rue as I am of mine."

She stamped her foot, forgetting her thin-soled slipper would come out the loser with the hard cellar floor. Rue set her lips to keep from hopping in discomfort and sat again on the table, swinging her burning extremity and incidentally revealing a good deal more ankle than was fashionable.

"You can't be as pleased with yourself as you pretend," she said finally. "I have kept you for a day in this most unpleasant of places, and though you appear to value fine china, I am certain that you do not fancy your manacles. It is not a game, I shall not let you throw for your freedom. You will satisfy me or pay for it!"

"Your hard-hearted attitude makes me considerably more wretched," he said, swinging his legs down and sitting once more. "And you are such a fragile little thing . . . Very well, I tell you on my honor that I refused to sell your father the lands in question and will continue to do so. I tire of your hospitality as much as you tire of me."

"But you saw your solicitor after!"

The earl sighed and looked down to the manacled wrists resting on his leather-breeched knees as if he sought inspiration there.

"Miss Morgan, my dear Miss Morgan. I assure you, contrary to your impression, I have business to transact that has nothing to do with Black Harry Morgan or his disagreeable daughter. Now then, if I may point out that your interference in my movements has nearly seen my man dead, myself knocked into Bedlam, my horses taking a fatal spill—I advise you to end this charade and free me."

Rue regarded him from under lowered brows. Everything he said was true; she had extracted all the assurance she could expect from him. The episode was ended, and the earl, being a prideful man, was unlikely to publicize it even to her discredit because it so patently made a fool of him as well.

She had his commitment that he would never sell to her father; it was all she could expect to gain. Rue realized only then that it was not enough.

"No." She stood. "I shall be out for the afternoon, but will bring you something to sup ere I leave for Ranelagh tonight."

The earl, incredulous, rustled forward on his narrow cot lip, but Rue had already slipped to the floor and sprinted for the door. It shut behind her hard, and he heard the familiar slam and fasten of the latch.

His expression of calm amusement dropped to the floor

with the breadcrumbs he tore between his fingers. He frowned.

If giving Rue Morgan what she purportedly wanted—which was in accordance with his wishes anyway—were not enough, what would be? The earl did not think he liked the answer that occurred to him.

Beyond the door, Rue paused, as if to listen for something within the chamber. But what was there to hear? Curses? Laughter? Howls? She would have to release him, that was clear, and fairly soon, or the game would become something no one dare ignore.

His concession; she had it. His word. It was no longer sufficient. What was then? She folded her hands together and found them chilled. She pressed her fists against the warmth of her breast and thought. She thought for a very long time. Then she turned abruptly, went through another door into a larger cellar, and pattered past the footmen on duty.

Nigel found her clattering up the rear stairs from the kitchen.

"Rue, my sweet! I never know where you will turn up these days. What were you doing in the pantry?"

His hands were on her elbows, and she had to answer.

"Not the pantry, the kitchen. I was fretting we'd not have enough for tea this afternoon if we're to dine at Ranelagh."

"Such domestic arrangements are nothing for you to worry about."

"But I do! And I have never been to Ranelagh. I am most excited."

"Silly girl. But I like catching you on the back stairs. I can pretend you're a bit of muslined housemaid—" Nigel pressed Rue to the wall and endowed her with a full and wet smack on the lips.

She wiggled free.

"Nigel! You're shameless. I must work with Heliotrope on my gown."

Rue rushed past him and up the remaining stairs, rounding choked little turns, and was soon out of sight. Once on the house's second story, she darted into her rooms, searching frantically until she found her maid stitching spangles onto a parchment fan.

"Helia!"

She whirled to shut the door behind her and sank to her knees beside the black woman.

"That, that potion you mentioned once. The gypsy Fenelia's. For sleep, deep sleep. I will need it, I think."

Heliotrope's eyes widened until her pupils were awash in surprise.

"The earl? You must drug him now?"

Rue Morgan's blue eyes suddenly twinkled.

"Oh, 'tis not the earl, Helia, not the earl at all."

But more she never said, her mood only changing for the better when the maid returned late that afternoon with some strange liquid in a misshapen amber glass bottle.

Rue was dressed and ready early. She instructed Helia to tell Sir Nigel she was still agowning and slipped once again down the narrow servant's stairs.

In the kitchen she instructed the startled maids to lay what food was prepared upon a tray—for she needed a bite before leaving—then ordered them out of the kitchen. They scattered like gray and white chickens.

Rue lifted the reticule that swung from a long satin cord on her wrist and laid its massive burden on the corner of the tray. A pistol, the same one in fact that had so recently seen duty as a bludgeon for His Lordship. She covered it with a fresh white napkin, picked up the heavy things, and quickly elbowed her way out the cellar door and down the ill-lit steps.

The footmen aided her once below and were at her back when she stepped triumphantly through the earl's prison door, the tray bearing a candelabrum that lit up her evening jewels and most particularly the sapphire at her throat.

"*Voilà!*" she announced, delighted to see his eyes narrow as he saw her twin footmen for himself.

She laid the tray beside that morning's one. Sir Nigel had a great quantity of trays; there was no reason to return them as their absence would never be noticed.

"I promised you supper, Your Lordship," said Rue merrily, "for I should not be able to dance my soles off at Ranelagh an' I knew you were starving here. See, roast beef and a fine asparagus soufflé, and mmmmmm, yes, a hasty pudding. But I'll fetch it to you."

The footmen faded into the outer area as Rue lifted the tray again and tripped over to the earl's cot, leaving the candelabrum wavering upon the table. By its light she observed that her prisoner had grown shaggier than ever and that the trace of a bad-tempered frown was etching itself into his brow.

She sat beside him, the tray between them, pushing the silver to his side of the salver.

"Pray do not refrain on my account. I will not regard it a rudeness if you begin alone."

She thrust the knife and fork at him. He reached slowly for them, suspicion hardening on his face, suspicion and perhaps a gambler's instinct to take what chance offered him. His hand closed over the fork and knife, nearly enveloping hers.

Rue flicked a napkin up from its place on the tray, revealing the pistol so near her other hand and pointing toward the earl.

"A serviette, Your Lordship?"

She would have thrust it into his stock, but she noticed that this piece of apparel was missing. Indeed his entire ruffled shirtfront sagged open, revealing a chest as hairy as his face was becoming. What was he up to?

He had noticed her puzzled stare and nodded brusquely to his wrists and their wide iron bracelets.

"Your, er, hospitality has an edge on it, Miss Morgan. I merely offset it."

She saw that his stock had been sacrificed to bandage his wrists from the chafe of the irons.

"Why did you not tell me?" she demanded. "I would not have hurt you for the world. It was not my intention to cause you any discomfort," she noted sarcastically.

He shrugged and attempted to lever knife and fork into position on the plate.

"I fear you had better give this to your loyal footmen," he said after a moment. "Prisoners drink gruel from bowls because they have not the freedom to mince beef into civilized portions." His gesture revealed the impossibility of carving meat with his hands anchored together.

"Why, fie, Your Lordship, I shall be happy to assist you," said Rue, picking up the utensils and attacking the beef. The pistol she moved to her lap where it sank to rest in the groove between her thighs.

The earl regarded her evening gown, a tissue-thin shift of finest white silk dropping sleeveless from her shoulders to her feet, save for the wide slash of a red sash high at her waist.

"You're not wearing that out?"

"Of course, but do not fret I shall spill upon it. I am very neat."

Rue brought up a forkful of beef and held it before his mouth. The earl weighed dignity and hunger, and found the latter more compelling. He accepted the morsel and chewed it methodically. Rue, prim as a nanny, but her eyes sparkling wickedly, proffered another forkful. The earl accepted it.

Rue decided her revenge upon the earl was progressing delightfully. There was something so rewarding about having him under her power, so thrilling about her secret guest in the cellar.

It reminded her of the ragged, battle-scarred tomcat she had chanced upon as a child, and hid and fed in the stables for weeks, careful not to let her father know of her new charge. It had been a wrangling, roaming beast, perhaps causing more trouble than it was worth. She had to confine it under a box to keep it from wandering off.

Then one day it had, and Rue had wept for it, though it never extended her even the slightest gesture of affection.

The earl shifted on his cot, and her free hand went to the polished wooden pistol butt. It had warmed against her body through the flimsy fabric. She suddenly feared it and turned the barrel off target. How dreadful if through some accident she should actually wound the man.

The earl, she discovered, had been watching her intently through ungrateful cat eyes, watching for the careless lift of the box, for her head turning too slowly . . . Except she didn't think he watched for that at all now.

No, he waited to pounce on the slightest flush of color to her cheeks, the tentativeness of a gesture, the catch of a breath too much or too soon.

Rue turned her stern glance to the plate and carved beef fiercely.

"I believe they're small enough now," observed the earl.

She looked at her work with her full attention and saw the roast beef squared into dice-sized cubes.

"Enough, yes . . ." said Rue breathlessly.

She drove the three-tined fork into several cubes in succession and thrust it at the earl's mouth, suddenly fascinated by the act of devouring, his unshaven jaws masticating slowly, his catlike eyes orange-yellow on her.

The earl's chain rattled as he brought the napkin up to his lips, but instead of lowering it again, his hands continued up and over and down behind her back.

She was prisoner of the earl, though no doubt if she wriggled to her knees and away, stood up, overturned the tray, fought him, ruined her gown, she could be free.

Was it possible that she did not wish to be free?

Rue glanced to the tray still between them.

"And the, the, ah . . . asparagus?"

"I do not care for asparagus," said the earl, quite seriously.

"It is . . . very fresh."

"I do not care for it," he repeated, his voice going lower, more intimate, until Rue wondered wildly what it was they truly discussed.

She had his attention now, as she had so determined she should have it. Wholly, intently, flatteringly. She could feel his indeterminately colored eyes etching glances into all the odd unconscious portions of herself that one only studies when one seeks to know the entirety.

His glance missed her eyes, for instance, and studied the swell of her cheekbone; ignored her mouth and meandered over the sweep of her chin; bypassed the sapphire in the hollow of her throat and dwelled on the slant of her shoulder between her neck and the rim of her gown.

His arms behind her hardly brushed her hair or her gown. She glanced slightly over her shoulder and saw the white-shirted bonds of his arms tightening. She leaned inward over the tray, and the things upon it tilted together.

Their faces tilted together.

"I think we understand one another," he said very precisely and very softly. "You go to Ranelagh tonight."

"I—I shall get the migraine."

"Only fair, my dear Rue," the earl said, chuckling, "that we share that, too."

"I shall come home early."

"And could your sterling footmen find me a suit of clothes, a bit of hot water, some place discreet?"

He had leaned so near his breath caressed her face, and shortly thereafter his lips pressed unmoving on her cheek and the side of her neck. All the while the earl's stray-cat eyes watched her as if she were some canary cast cageless into the world.

Rue sensed she was finally playing the ultimate game of hazard with the Earl of Argyle, the game as it was meant to be played—fast, hard, and with only one winner. She would cast upon it!

"I trust these stalwart fellows have a key . . . or have you hidden it somewhere clever, dear Rue?" His lips pressed firmly to the skin over her heart.

Rue interjected a hand between his lips and herself.

"I have the key—that is all you need know. Now may I leave?"

"Anything to hasten our reunion," assented the earl, his arms making a sweep that set her free.

Rue stood, retrieving her pistol and watching the gesture raise no alarm in his eyes. His attention was all on her, for her. She offered her hand. He caught it and drew it to his lips, smiling all the while, a hard and certain smile.

Rue snatched her hand away and rustled out of the room, leaving the candelabrum blazing behind her.

The Earl of Argyle locked his manacled fingers together, then leaned his unshaven chin upon them and smiled a very lean and wolfish smile that had nothing to do with kissing hands.

Chapter Twelve

It was no great matter for Rue to feign headache at Ranelagh that night. A stubborn little throb began ticking at the base of her head shortly after she and Sir Nigel left for the fabled pleasure emporium.

Once there, the brilliant flicker of lamps and candles both indoors and out, the reflections from many mirrors and jewels, the arpeggio of voices exploring the entire scale of shrill and unpleasant sound—including the celebrated Madame Mara whose operatic trills reminded Rue more of a celebrated cat fight—all joined to turn a faint pulsing at the back of her head into a crashing.

This was one of Ranelagh's scandalous masquerade evenings, with the more daring ladies gowned to make Rue's Drury Lane costume look chaste by comparison. Indeed, on one occasion not too many years past, a Miss Elizabeth Chudleigh had appeared so near to nude that posterity was still puzzled about precisely what she had and had not worn.

Rue and Nigel had made an obligatory pause in the great gilt Rotunda, which chauvinistic Londoners of the time compared to the Pantheon in Rome, and had explored the exotic intricacies of China House, an Oriental pavilion spanning a man-made canal like a waterspider a narrow stream.

Now, they promenaded in the circle around the Rotunda, a brilliantly lit alleyway of lantern- and flower-hung orange trees that tempted strollers off its formal paths and into invitingly dim glades and grottoes where night was allowed to lay on her shadows with a free hand, and many young gentlemen were equally free-handed with giddy young females.

No such forbidden fruits drew Sir Nigel Pagett-Foxx, and his mistress, Black Rue Morgan, into these bowers. And Sir Nigel could not complain, for Rue, uncostumed though masked, was such an attractive vision in the flattering warm ebb and flow of lanternlight that her escort for once thought it a shame to keep her to himself.

So Nigel, coaxed into a new frockcoat, strolled proudly beside Rue in the gardens. Whenever a passing party's attention focused on her, he absent-mindedly thrust his thumbs into the waistcoat pockets he was accustomed to cramming them in. Now his hands slid off the unpocketed coat, and the gesture came to look like the wing flapping of a chicken.

Rue sailed alongside him untroubled. She had added a long-fringed shawl to her gauzy white slip of a gown, for this May night was chill, not warmed even by the frequent, rainbowed explosion of fireworks overhead in the black sky.

These visual bursts echoed noiselessly in her throbbing head, and the slight wind off the river made her draw the rose and peacock blue wings of her shawl closer.

"Cold, my love?" asked Nigel solicitously. He leaned his face nearer, the eyes behind the plain black velvet mask light gray and concerned.

"Slightly chill, yes, Nigel. And I have the germ of a migraine, I fear. Perhaps we should return—?"

Rue turned her head to watch a Renaissance pope and Queen Elizabeth stroll hand-in-hand through the lanternlit alleyway of trees.

Her mask was white, crowned by an aigrette of ostrich

feathers. It changed her expression completely and, despite its innocent color, added something demonic to her lower face, the straight little nose slightly sharp, the firm chin, the lips defined so well without the assistance of paint.

Nigel recognized the set of those lips now; they would return, she had set her heart upon it. His thumbs took one last habitual jab at his now fashionably frockcoated sides.

"Very well, Rue. You've been teasing me for this evening out, but we shall take our evening in if you wish."

"Oh, my dear! You are very kind to me, especially when, as you point out, I have not been consistent," answered Rue contritely. "But I truly have a headache. Perhaps if we return home, you may find some country cure for it."

She linked her white-gloved arm over his dark sleeve and leaned inward on him, her unhooped skirts pressing against his hip.

Nigel thought he could detect every fragile layer of petticoat between himself and the treasure house of her body. And she had as good as promised him access tonight, she who had been so miserly of late. It was worth the wherry ride across the Thames, the truncated evening, yes, worth even the confounded frockcoat.

Sir Nigel pulled the short double-breasted coat front more firmly to his waist, took Rue's arm, and steered her for the river walk and home.

She was silent most of the way, a fact Sir Nigel attributed to the headache. He was suddenly repentant of his suspicion, his sense of being defrauded. She had been thrown from her father's house at a tender age, forced upon the stage, forced even perhaps to rely on a hen-brained country squire like himself for support.

He was blessed among men to have her. He reached out across the carriage to her. Her pale, gloved fingers curled into his hand like a child's. Sir Nigel Pagett-Foxx was content.

Indeed, the night seemed to be proceeding according to

his dearest wish. Once arrived at Grosvenor Square, Rue announced her headache cured from the night air.

She not only allowed him to accompany her upstairs, but suggested they retire to his rooms where a decanter of port wine always glowed ruby before a snapping yellow fire.

"Your head, my love, where is it?" he said, laughing. "You'll bring the migram back."

"Not tonight, Nigel," she promised, her face glowing behind the mask. She untied his own disguise and ran a light finger over the faint worry lines impressed at the edge of his eyes. "I may have wine tonight and not rue it, I promise you. You always come to my rooms. Let me visit in yours. Take me there."

She put out her kid-gloved hand. He caught the spirit of the game and led her laughing down the vacant passage, the portraits on either side staring impassively down upon them as though they were naughty children.

Sir Nigel heard her gown and petticoats rustling behind him. He turned back to find himself leading an exotic creature sheathed all in white, the plumes above her mask nodding regally at him. He felt he was accompanied by a stranger, a dangerous stranger, as rare and fey as a white unicorn . . .

And in his rooms even, the evening smacked of an underground prank, when the privileged young men of Cambridge or Oxford would smuggle town girls into their tiny chambers for a spell of candlelit roistering. He had never done it, of course, he'd merely heard.

"Your rooms are very fine, Nigel. Yes, rid yourself of that frockcoat. Exchange it for a dressing gown. I think both you and I shall like it better. No, don't ring for your valet. Let us have this night for just ourselves."

Sir Nigel wandered, dazed, into the adjoining bedchamber, his fingers trembling on the buttons as he shrugged off the hated frockcoat. He felt like a bridegroom. He would marry her, by God, he would. He was not one to sneeze at social customs, but his first instinct on seeing her had been to whisk her away from the licentious stage and into his own care.

With his mother and father dead, there was none to quarrel with his choice of a slightly scandalous bride. He would marry her! But now she waited him without. The dressing gown swished over his shoulders, and he struggled into it, buttoning it awry and never noticing.

"Ah, Nigel! I poured myself. Here, have a glass."

Rue stood before the marble fireplace, white as one of its supporting caryatids, those frozen marble maidens the Greeks so loved. There was no color on her, for the shawl had fallen into a run-together pool of color on the figured carpet.

She was all white, save for the hard blue glitter at her throat—which he saw on her always and now seemed as much a part of her as her sparkling blue eyes—the crimson sash, and the gleam of blood-red port in its crystal glass. She held one glass at her breast. The other was extended to him, lifted high as for a jubilant toast.

"Port, my dear, is a heady drink for a woman," he cautioned, nevertheless moving to take his glass from the white fingers curled around it.

"A toast, then," she said, "to success in all our enterprises."

"Enterprises?" he questioned between fevered sips of what seemed a love potion rather than the finest of French ports. No wonder the amorous Parisians drank of wine so heavily. "What enterprises do you sponsor, my dear Rue?" His blond brows shot up heavily, attempting lightness and only managing to convey ponderous surprise.

"My schemes . . . of an empire of fashionable new gowns. My plottings . . . for an entire armada of hats. My hazard . . . upon the entire season of merrymaking. What other enterprises could I have, dear Nigel? Save perhaps, my conquest . . . of you."

She had come nearer on each sentence, closer until her eyes, shadowed by the mask to a blue as dark as the jewel

she always wore, were driving into his. Sir Nigel found his
rooms of a sudden hot.

"I'll take your glass," she said.

He looked to see the empty bowl tilting in his fingers as
if it had grown suddenly heavy and drew itself inexorably to
the floor. He felt himself swelling like it, growing bloated,
leaden, drawn ruthlessly downward to the floor, the carpet.

"Why, sit. You look a bit pale. Perhaps you have the
headache as well."

Rue, growing ghostly and shadowed by a twin of herself,
pushed him once gently. He found himself seated loosely in
the fireside chair, a great gilt affair with a tapestried stiffness he had always found uncomfortable. Now he could not
seem to move, it was as if he had melted into the chair
frame.

Before his eyes, which he could no longer lift to the two
Rues—though that was a lovely sight, two of her—before
his fading eyes the firelight jigged a mad pattern on his pupils, on his eyelids now, his very heavy eyelids. On only
black night, the firelight danced. The night skies at
Ranelagh and the Chinese fireworks spiraling into dragons
across them. He was there with his love, and they stood and
watched the spectacle together. . . .

Rue hung over his askew face, every line of it sagged
into unconsciousness. Three drops of the brown fluid and
Sir Nigel should slumber till morn. That should be long
enough for Rue Morgan to rouse her below-stairs guest and
bring her enterprise to its most satisfactory conclusion.

Rue slipped out of Nigel's chambers, more fearful of at-
tracting the servants' attention than rousing her victim.
Down the deserted passage she fluttered again, the candela-
bra flames whipping wildly at her progress, the painted eyes
in sober faces looking down painted noses at her.

Rue slipped through the door leading directly to her bedchamber where the linens were turned down and the fire
was banked for ready blazing upon her retiring. Heliotrope

was there, drawing a thick-toothed comb through a dozing Piquant.

"Helia, is all ready? Hush, Piquant—yes, yes, you are a most sublime creature, but I have no time to pamper you now. You were able to accomplish your mission discreetly?"

It was not the capering dog she addressed, but the distinctly subdued maid.

"Oh, it was accomplished all right. Getting him upstairs unseen was no problem, and to the French guest room. But he took exception at my aiding him in his bath—"

"My Lord of Argyle shy?" interrupted Rue in a tone that conveyed lifted eyebrows, had not the mask been there to hide them.

"—though seeing him after a day or two untended in the cellar, I was not overeager to assist him," finished Heliotrope, unruffled. "Nor was he pleased that I aid him with the razor. He commented that since my ancestors were cannibals and my mistress a savage, he could rest easier cutting his own throat."

"Oh, I do not think the earl will ever have to stoop to such work himself. There are plenty would do it for him, I swear. Where is he?"

Heliotrope gestured to the other room.

"Then take Piquant with you, Helia, for the night. And go."

"Mistress Rue," she answered, dark fingers fanned on her white-aproned hips, "first my ancestors' eating habits are impugned, then I am told I must sleep with . . . this one. He wheezes, you know. I think we were better situated in your father's house."

"No! Anything is better than my father's house. And I remind you that if you find your sleeping partner repugnant, pray consider that I am to sleep with the wicked Earl of Argyle, gamester and rake and lately of the cellar."

Rue dipped to peer in the dressing table mirror and patted at the tendrils the evening had disarranged. She centered the pearl-twined coil of hair down her back, ensured that her pearl earrings still dangled from her lobes, and turned the sapphire aright on its ribbon.

Behind her, she could see the arm-folded form of Heliotrope, for once not swift to obey.

"I think you misestimate the earl. I do not think the lay of anyone's linens is enough to sway his judgement."

"Nonsense, he is a man! The impulses of the body are one of the few honest urges I have found among the species. How else can I trust him and know that he has reason to play fair with me? I knew the earl had escaped too lightly before. He thought to teach me a lesson! But this time I have him, I feel it. Don't look so grim, Helia, for there is no lion more delightful when tamed than a peer of the realm. Now out! If you did not wish to see His Lordship bathing, you certainly will not wish to see His Lordship when I have done with him."

Rue pushed the slow-paced Heliotrope into the passage, then glanced down it for the footmen she had assigned to her doors. They came with the punctuality and alacrity of the well-bribed and stationed themselves at each door of the suite.

They would melt away by morning to their accustomed duties, but by then the earl, too, would have vanished like mist. And Rue Morgan would have firmly entoiled an ally as weighty as iron in the balance.

She withdrew behind her chamber door again, rustled to her dressing room table to dab cologne upon her wrists, then opened the communicating door to her sitting room and entered it, feeling oddly like a stranger come to call.

A fire beat impatiently in the grate, whipping against the blackened brick to be free. Candles lit the collection of porcelain figures atop the mantel. Candles illuminated Rue Morgan's reflection in the pedimented gilt-framed mirror towering above the fireplace.

The room glistened with late-night excitement, the curve of cabriole legs reflecting crescents of light in white smiles, the window hangings richly shadowed in their folds, night's opaque cloak pressing against the mullions from without. Rue saw herself reflected in the window panes across the room with all that chamber's richness of fabric and furnishings laid out between her and the windows like a painting. But there was something absent.

The Earl of Argyle.

She stood frozen in the room's center. Helia had been on guard, then the footmen, he couldn't—A clink of glass at her right. She looked. The Earl of Argyle stood by a narrow console, pouring something amber from a decanter. He stepped into the center of the room.

"Ah, my delightful liberatress. A true daughter of Liberty—they would be prodigious fond of you in France. I was simply pouring some brandy," he explained, as Rue regarded the overblown glass in his hand with amazement.

"But, I keep claret here. Not brandy. Brandy is—"

"Below, in the study. Yes, I know, where do you think I obtained it?"

"When? You were not seen—?"

"I wasn't," said the earl shortly, cosseting the glass in his palm while he circled the liquor in the bowl. He looked up with eyes ever-so-slightly tinged green.

"You have rapped me upon the head, which I grant you is hard but not impervious, and you have kept me prisoner in your cellar for at least two days as I reckon it. Claret is not sufficient restorative for such an ordeal. Only brandy, as Mr. Johnson said, is fit for heroes."

He lifted his glass, sipped from it, nodded gravely.

"Pagett-Foxx's taste in spirituous liquors is better than his preference in clothing, among other things." He fetched a second glass. "And brandy, for heroines."

Rue took it and sipped from it as he did again. It was strong, fiery stuff, not syrupy like wine, but thin and lethal fluid. More like the drug she had given Nigel. She regarded it suspiciously.

The earl laughed.

"It's good French brandy, my dear, rest easy on it. It's not the potion you likely lavished on your gullible bedmate, believe me. Why would I drug you when my intentions toward you require all of your senses be alert?" he asked quite civilly, cocking his head for an answer to this unavoidable logic.

"I . . . was not certain that our alliance was to be . . . consummated."

Again the earl laughed.

"What a way you have with words! I congratulate you, Black Rue Morgan, on your cool heart and your hot head and your impeccably warm wit."

He went to sit in the fireside armchair, stretching his slippered feet toward the blaze. Rue had been foresighted enough to refrain from forwarding the earl's luggage to the unlucky owner of the grays. His transformation from prisoner to bedchamber intimate had been accomplished in part thanks to his own emerald brocade dressing gown and the fresh lacy stock and shirt he had intended to wear in Tunbridge Wells.

His hair was uncurled, but clustered a bit, still damp, at his neck. He was finally clean-shaven again, and a great difference it made. But Rue noticed a bit of sticking plaster here and there and reflected that bringing an earl to the point of performing his own personal grooming was no mean achievement.

She would have liked to have seen him in Heliotrope's firm hands; that would have been a battle of wills worth paying to observe.

Rue sat opposite him on a little embroidered footstool. She was nearer the fire, so the flames reflected on her pale gown and skin, flashed richly from the sapphire. Rue tucked her white satin slippers under her hem and cosseted her own brandy glass on her knees.

"Well, I shall have to let you go at any rate," she said meditatively. "Perhaps I am wrong. I had thought you desirous of doing business with me."

"I am always ready to talk business," said the earl, leaning forward, a tight smile on his face. "But you do not believe in business unless it is accompanied by other bargains, do you?"

"The difficulty is, Your Lordship," said Rue, contemplating the coffee-dark depths of her glass, "that you have no weaknesses."

"I have myriads of weaknesses! To say other is to accuse me of having wasted eight-and-twenty years of the most lavish catering to the aristocratic eccentricities that are my birthright. I have a weakness for hazard, for horses, for . . . whores."

Rue looked up.

"Those you can buy, but I—"

"You prefer to bargain. I know."

The earl set his glass down on the marble hearth at his feet. He leaned forward and took Rue's, which she had hardly tasted, and put it beside his. He then reached out and took her hand, drawing her off the stool so she knelt before him. His hands molded themselves lightly to either side of her face.

"Take off your mask, Rue Morgan, for you do not need it with me," he said, reaching to undo its ties. He laid the frippery beside the two glasses, one almost full, the other emptied to a pale film of brandy at the bottom.

Rue stared unabashedly into his eyes. She had not needed the mask. Masks were fine theatrical props for the easily impressed, like Sir Nigel Pagett-Foxx. With the earl, it was far better to play a dangerous, bare-faced game.

All she required of him was his surrender. His honest infatuation with her, one instant of unadulterated passion, and he would be hers, just as Nigel was hers so much more cheaply. But she had exerted every ploy in her hand, every power of her will, her wit, and she had gained nothing that she could depend upon.

He was the only man she had met who she felt was capable of refusing her—with the exception of Quentin Rossford, and he didn't signify for he was immune from women. Had not the earl already bedded her, she might have suspected him of the same malady.

It was not natural to be so invulnerable, to have no heart. Unless you were Rue Morgan.

The fireplace heat was warming her cheeks, or perhaps the earl's hands were. He drew her slowly nearer, leaning nearer himself, pulling her nearer.

She saw the firelight reflected in his eyes, saw herself there, tried to keep staring at these externals rather than into the intense depths of his expression. But his eyes drew her to him and only him. They were very probing. She felt her own lashes flutter while his remained statue still. She steadied then and met his gaze, waiting, waiting. . . .

The slightest smile curved her lips, for she saw his certainty deep in his eyes, and his will and also the faintest of questions and a tiny quiver of—pain? So she curved her lips slightly, and his eyes hardened, as she had known they would, and he finally dropped his lashes over them. Then she could see them no more because her own had fluttered shut and his mouth was pressed to hers more deeply, more desirously than she had ever dreamed, ever imagined it could be.

Triumph welled up in her and rushed to her lips to kiss him back, harder than Rue Morgan would ever have. Victory pulsed at her every pore. She pushed nearer and nearer him. Somehow she had gotten from the floor to his lap, her face above his and impressed there. His hands had shifted from her face to her shoulders to her waist, as if seeking the most satisfying place upon her body to rest and never quite finding it.

Their mouths remained locked, as their eyes had, save there was a kind of violence, a contention in the very physicalness of their contact, as if each vied to kiss the other with more passion, pressure, innovation. Rue was no longer worried about bruising. She sought to bruise.

Somehow the earl had risen to his feet and was holding her so hard to him that she felt molded to the muscles of his body. She felt one particular muscle of his body almost entering her by sheer pressure from without.

The earl suddenly pushed her away, as if she were an attacker. Rue stood panting, feeling she had run a race, aware of a mindless drumming in her blood impelling her to hurl herself upon him again, even though her brain told her that would be a mistake, not clever. . . .

He was staring at her as if he'd never seen her before. Then he reached down and took her hand quite calmly.

"Come, my dear Rue, to bed," he said, leading her to the mantel where he blew out a candle, then kissed her.

He blew out the next and then kissed her, always watching her face in the gradually dimming room. Rue stuttered backward before him as before an unstoppable force. She began laughing at the idiocy of the game, even as something in it excited her. It took two breaths to blow out one candle, two kisses were required to quiet her mouth after.

He smiled as he saw her savoring the suspense. The candelabrum at the opposite mantel end awaited them.

Rue retreated from him, her eyes mischievous. Perhaps she would flee, and he would not get his reward for each snuffed candle.

He blew, and another undulating flame died. His mouth claimed hers, and it was warm and softly waxen as the pooling beeswax around the smoking black wick. He was laughing now as well, softly, and growing out of breath, for the last candle shivered wildly, but flared up at three not-too-carefully aimed breaths.

Rue giggled, put her fingers across his mouth, pouted her lips, and blew softly, slowly across the candle top. The flame bowed out, and the earl was obligated to devote an excessive amount of time and invention on the lips she offered him wordlessly, triumphantly.

He finally released her, but her head turned restlessly until she spied the candelabrum on the console table near the decanter. Rue tripped over to it, red sash ends fluttering behind her. She paused by the table, ready to spin and fly to another part of the room, but the earl anticipated her and instead of following her came up before her as an emerald barrier.

She laughed with all the childish fear and exultation of a game of hide-and-seek she had never had as a child in her black-tempered father's house. The earl caught her and held her—a simple task, for her fear was as mock as her flight.

He licked his thumb and forefinger and pinched a candle out. Rue watched, her eyes wide until he kissed her, then they dropped instantly shut. Again, he pinched the living flame. Rue could hear the hiss even as she felt that dying smolder transfer itself from his lips to hers.

He reached for the third flame.

"You'll burn yourself!"

He paused another moment and, without wetting his fingertips again and his eyes half on her, reached out and extinguished the third flutter of fire.

Rue studied his face for any flinching and saw only his eyes dwelling on her. She brought her own fingers to her lips, then struck out blindly for the last flicker of candlelight.

It winked out. The earl captured her wrist an instant after and brought her hand up to his face. In the dim light, he examined her fingertips.

"You are set on playing with fire, aren't you, my dear Rue?" he asked finally.

"No more than you." She broke away and ran through her dressing room to the candelabrum blazing on her nightside table. He followed her.

"Not those," he said. "And you haven't paid for the candle you cheated me of."

It is one thing to be kissed, another to kiss. Rue Morgan teetered for a moment on the brink of decision.

He aided her not one bit. He did not tilt his face down toward her, shut his eyes, reach for her. He merely waited.

Rue's hands climbed the black moiré lapels of the emerald dressing gown. She drew nearer, leaned up on tiptoe, kissed him very softly on the mouth. His hands pinioned her wrists as if she were an adder entwining him.

"Black Rue Morgan," he said, though he would not say why.

She was bewildered. "If I may not have my candles, where is my brandy?" she said finally, laughing.

He went and fetched it calmly enough, the brandy warmed from the beating of flames upon it. She cradled it in both hands and brought it to her lips, laughing at him over its crystal rim.

The earl narrowed his eyes and watched her, taking pleasure in her posing as one would the antics of a kitten. She was not intoxicated, far from it. But something bubbling and dangerous and heady, a champagne of the senses, had effervesced in her.

He let her have one or two sips on the brandy before he took it away and set it next to the unquenched candles. She watched him, unchallenging, her eyes large and dark, of no color in the shadow-haunted chamber.

"Your pendant," he said and said no more.

Rue reached back without demur and undid it. She turned to place it by the brandy snifter. Then turned back to him.

"Your bargain," she said, her voice dusky.

He drew her to him again, knowing she was as molten as candlewax to his fingers. One pull turned the sash into a scarlet river flowing toward her feet. A few laces drawn in the semidarkness, and her gown, a white and silken pool, was ebbing over her shoulders. It was sufficient only that it was loosened. He let it drift lower upon her shoulders and then stall.

His hands were now utterly occupied with positioning her face to his, drinking deep of the brandy of her being, that elusive human elixir so seldom tasted no matter how ardently it is searched for.

She was immersed in a sea of surrender. His hands dropped away from her, but she remained as welded to him as ever. He tore loose his own stock, the tie of his robe, felt the clothing brush away, felt Rue Morgan press nearer in its stead.

He took her head in his hands, wrested her mouth from his, and pressed her face to his bare breast. She was utterly still at the foreigness of the terrain, her lips frozen and soft upon his skin, upon the nipple hardening beneath them.

She was never one to wager half, Rue Morgan. She committed herself, her mouth suddenly as mindless as before upon his flesh, her attention concentrated upon whatever of himself he chose to give her.

He finally caught her face between his hands and pulled her head back a bit, tilting it up. He bent and kissed her, then deliberately moved her mouth to his other side. This time there was not a pause. Rue pushed what remained of the dressing gown aside, and her fingers twined in the coiled hair of his chest.

Rue herself was not aware of any threshold of mind or body being crossed. It was all Rubicon to her, all confused, storming intoxication of the senses. She felt only what she reached for, what seemed so distant but desirable. She felt finally his hands on her shoulders, pressing there with equal insistence so her entire body sank slowly, slowly past his flesh, down, down, down. . . .

She came face-to-face with his wishes and this time recoiled. No. One of his hands was tangled in her hair, curved to the back of her skull, pressing her forward. The other hand rested, fingertips splayed on her bare shoulder. Around her, the loosened gown slid slowly to her knees.

Rue shut her eyes. Surely, no other woman in the world would do this. No other. If she did this, she would have won, won where no other woman in the world could win because no other woman was so determined, so daring as Rue Morgan. His hands held her still, not forcing her to anything against her will, but not allowing the easy escape of a careless shift away, a moment lost, a gesture half-accomplished and forgotten.

She brought her lips where he wished.

After a while, he pulled her to her feet again and picked up the brandy glass and tilted it to her mouth. She drank a bit and felt her head clear. He pulled her finally down to the bed, pressed her there and pressed himself into her as she had expected all this time, him thrusting deep within her until the motion was almost pleasant, until their movements were as melded as their mouths, their tongues, their scents, their sweat, until—

She felt as if she had been wrenched back from the brink of a cliff. That faint pale thing wafting gently left and right all the way to the bottom, that could have been her. It wasn't. She was the limpid flesh that lay passive under the Earl of Argyle, the flesh that lay wet, worn, and somehow content under the weight of so much bone and muscle and unhappily placed limb digging in here or there.

He levered himself away and collapsed beside her. He pulled her heavy hair from beneath her to fan it off her face and neck where it had festered moistly.

"Well?" Rue Morgan turned her head slowly to his. "Now will you be my ally?"

The earl curled a lock of her hair around his forefinger, as if it were a black satin bandage.

"My dear Rue," he said, smiling. "You are prodigious prodigal with your body. Perhaps it is because your heart's not in it. Bargains are sealed with flesh and blood. You have only flesh to offer. It is almost enough."

Rue half-sat, dazed. "Lucifer," she hissed.

He unwound from beside her, fished up her fallen petticoats, and tore a ruffle from the hem of one. It was a moment's work to pinion her wrists and wrap them soundly in the fabric. The long trailing white end he tied tightly around the bottom bedpost.

He reached under the bed and withdrew a bundle of clothing from the luggage he had concealed there— breeches, stockings, shoes. He began to dress, rapidly but efficiently, wasting no motion.

"I shall call my footmen!"

"Yes, your infernal footmen. I am well aware of them. Call them, I pray you. I am not possessive of my pleasures—even footmen deserve the honor of seeing Rue Morgan unclothed. You see, we English can be as democratic as the Americans and the French."

"Diable! Démon!" she accused in that language of lovers, bucking frantically at the end of her bonds.

But Rue's petticoats were constructed of the finest lawn, sheer and soft as a breath, as strong as steel. Her thrashings only drew the knots tighter.

"I shouldn't advise that," said the earl. "It's rather hard on the wrists," he added, drawing his shirt ruffles over the bruises still braceleting his own wrists.

Rue could feel the cloth burns tingling already and calmed. The earl, dressed though frockcoatless, reached down for his abandoned dressing gown and draped it over her shoulders. She moved to shrug it off, but his hands held it in place.

"The fire will die by morning," he pointed out. "You are unmatched in methods of amputating your nose to spite your face, but I beg you keep it."

The earl smiled at her quite politely, as if they were at a Montagu House tea and he had just extended her some gentlemanly courtesy.

"Your Lordship," she said, her voice as lightly remote as his own. "You could have left when Helia brought you upstairs. Why did you not?"

He pulled the gown more snugly about her shoulders, as if he were tucking a child away for the night.

"You could have released me upon my assurance that I had always intended to do as you wished and keep my lands from your father," he answered. "Why did you not?"

Rue looked down to her white-tied wrists.

"I wanted to . . . seal the bargain. It was the only way I knew—"

"You do not know very much," he interrupted gently.

"And, and I . . . I wanted another game of hazard with the Earl of Argyle."

"And so you have had, my dear," he said, moving away.

"And I wanted to win!"

It was commonly said that angry women's eyes blazed; Rue Morgan's did. The earl paused to admire their fire. He smiled and stepped back to the bedside table and retrieved her signature jewel. She was as still and dangerous as an untrained horse to the bridle when he fastened it around her neck again. But she kept her head and her flaming blue eyes down, as though she didn't trust herself to move while he touched her.

The earl stepped away and regarded the room like a thief taking care to leave no traces.

Rue watched his last survey calmly.

"You cannot leave yet, Your Lordship. Pray recall my infernal footmen. They are not to retire until dawn."

"You think I would stick at knocking heads together now? But you are right, I loathe a domestic fracas. I will leave by another method."

He went to the window and swung open the casement.

"But 'tis two stories!" The first inrush of night chill reached Rue, and she shivered under the dressing gown.

The earl straddled the windowsill and examined the drop.

"Ah, a convenient drainpipe. Most ladies' chambers, you see, are situated near such necessities. All architects have hearts."

"You'll have to walk home!" objected Rue, threateningly. An earl afoot struck her as the greatest of indignities.

"I fear not even that awaits me. The hackney drivers prowl the better neighborhoods in search of aristocratic fares."

"You have no money!"

"I shall simply sway, drunk as a Lord—my title forgive me—and the driver will convey me home and collect a fine fee there."

He swung his other leg over the edge and sat on the sill for another moment.

Rue rose to her knees on the bed, the gown clinging to her shoulders like folded emerald wings. The earl glanced back to her half-draped form, as white and remote as a Greek torso. A captive Trojan maiden.

"Why have you done this to me?" she asked finally, her last question what should have been her first.

The earl eyed the length of the leap to the drainpipe and answered abstractedly.

"For my valet, my lost grays, my cracked head, and your own good, Rue Morgan." He glanced over his pale-shirted shoulder. "We have hazarded together again and drawn deuce. We are too well-matched to cast other than losing numbers to each other. I suggest we withdraw from the game. Adieu, Black Rue."

He vanished as swiftly as a sill-sitting bird.

Rue lunged at the window only to fall prone across the counterpane. She thrashed to the bed's other side. The sole things available to her there were the burning candles and the almost empty brandy glass. The glass was all she could reach.

She picked it up, ready to hurl it at the grinning fireplace with its witnessing caryatids' pale marble faces smirking at her and the flames tsking in the grate. She paused and carefully put it down again.

The breeze from the window invaded the earl's dressing gown, wrapped chilly fingers around her, toyed with her until she shivered as if waiting for a lover.

"Démon!" she hissed at the window, at the vanished Earl, and at his accomplice, the wind, that he had let take her after him.

She burrowed into the coverlet under the dressing gown and wept angry, icy tears. Perhaps he had fallen, Devil take him, perhaps even now he lay dead on the pavement.... Rue jerked at her leash and found it held. She couldn't even go to the window to gaze after her lover, her enemy.

After a long while, when the candles were guttering and the fire had faded to a red-hot landscape of embers, Rue rose and faced her nightstand again. She tried to stretch the cloth bonds to the sputtering flames, but the lawn would not reach.

Finally she picked up the brandy snifter by its stem, awkwardly. The earl was right about the difficulty of doing ordinary things with one's hands bound, that earl who was so adept at doing extraordinary things with his hands unbound.

She gathered herself, then smashed the brandy bowl across the nightstand's marble-topped edge. Glass, shattering loud enough to wake the dead. Rue waited, and when only the wind came to sniff invisibly at the spilled drops of brandy, she examined the ruins. Ah, one large, triangular piece on the carpet, still trembling slightly on its curved outer surface.

Damnation! Even hanging over the bed on her stomach, the tie was too short for her hands to reach it. Rue worked herself over the bed's edge and finally thumped to the floor. She waited again. No footmen. Evidently footmen expected to hear thumps and shattered glass when their mistress entertained an earl. Well enough.

Rue laid herself down ever so gently over the glass shards until her desired piece was directly before her face. She drew back her lips in what would have been a smile were it not a baring of teeth. Delicately she closed her teeth upon one jagged edge of the glass and drew back and up, slowly levering herself to her knees by pressing her bound hands into the glass-strewn carpet.

Sweat streamed down her face by the time she was sitting up again. And the heels of her hands were impressed by a dozen sharp edges, a hundred tiny slivers of pain. But she had her glass. Her teeth released it gently into her cupped palms, and then her long fingers manipulated it between their tips, and she began sawing awkwardly on the nearest strip of cloth.

The candles burned themselves out before she was done.

The fire went gray to ashes, and some prelude of light softened the black windows. Rue sawed methodically at her
bonds, her brow frowning and sometimes deepening into
furrows when the glass slipped or dug too hard at her skin.

She remembered then how vulnerable the wrists were to
a self-inflicted slash, and that it was a dangerous thing she
did. Her face set but harder. And while her stiff fingers performed the tedious, nigh impossible task, her mind flew outside her ajar casement and surveyed the earl's bent and
broken form on the stones.

No, it came back to the bed, and there lay Rue Morgan,
pale and naked and dead upon the brightly figured carpet,
surrounded by a pool of red velvet blood—a pool, why, an
ocean of it!

And the Earl of Argyle in the dock for murder, his hands
manacled before the magistrates, and all London sitting silent and shaking their heads. Ah, no. He was in Fleet
Prison, grown even more disreputable-looking than when he
had been in her cellar. He was in a filthy cell and in swept
Rue Morgan, pale it is true, but noble-looking with her
wrists neatly tied in lace.

Then the earl, wearing a powdered wig, most incongruous
atop the black, weeks' worth of beard upon his chin, the
chained earl sank to his knees and meekly begged mercy,
kissing the hem of her gown, which for some reason lacked
a ruffle, kissing her feet, her fingertips while over his shoulder through a barred window she saw Madame Guillotine
raised and at the ready.

The great steel-blue blade shivered along its sharp,
slanted edge and then in the space of a breath slashed downward and through. A great fountain of red, and—

Rue watched the lash shred of lawn snap at the dull saw
of the glass. Her wrists sprang apart with the sudden release
of force strained against. She was free! Rue dropped her
tool and stood, knees stiff and unwilling to support her. But
she donned the green dressing gown drooping over the coverlet and rushed first to the window.

Yes, a far faint glow over the garden and the chimney-populated rooftops of the nearest neighbors. And nothing below but the last shadows of night and the still of a deserted terrace. She drew back and shut the window.

Then she untied the lawn from the bedpost and stirred the fire ashes to raise a dormant ember. She fed it the strip of cloth slowly until it caught and burned brightly. Then she returned to the bedside and collected every last splinter of glass, depositing it in the grate for the servants to sweep out.

Only when all traces of the night's events had been banished did Rue turn to her wrists. She looked as if she had been toying with a kitten; sharp little scratches ran every which way across them. She bathed the cuts in stinging cologne and bound her wrists in handkerchiefs.

The green robe she bundled into a ball and thrust deep at the back of her wardrobe under a fallen pile of petticoats. Rue fished her most luxuriously laced wrapper from another cupboard and donned it. The ruffles fell easily to her knuckles and hid her bandaged wrists if she kept her hands down. And that she would do until every mark of her ordeal had vanished, like the earl out the window.

Rue finally threw herself back into her bed, exhausted, and drifted to sleep just as the birds' early morning chirps were gearing to concert pitch outside the fastly closed windows.

Chapter Thirteen

"And Varian Temple?"

Rue regarded her interrogator blankly.

"The Earl of Argyle," the voice said impatiently.

Rue had forgotten he had a Christian name. To her he was only a titled force.

"And the earl?"

Rue Morgan's hands rested, as was her wont, atop the ivory-headed handle of a delicate walking stick. She twirled the stick in her fingers, as also was her wont, while she framed a reply. This motion did not dislodge the saffron lace that cobwebbed her hands to the knuckles in the length of sleeve that was the rage.

"The earl will not sell his lands to my father. I have his word on it," she finally said quite haughtily, as if she resented being questioned upon the success of her enterprise even by her fellow members of the Basilisk Club.

"Well done!" Lemuel Humphries smiled broadly around the table. He leaned against his spindle-backed Windsor chair. "I think we do not give the lady enough credit. 'Twas a formidable chore."

"Yes, formidable," drawled Addison Hookham, sitting

forward in his chair. "Had I witnessed your achievement of this miracle, perhaps we could patent it."

"Mr. Hookham! I do not care for your tone," interjected Sir Feverell testily. "We owe much to this lady, an' if she achieves our ends, I think no gentleman among us would question her means."

Rue inclined her head silently to Marshwine and accepted what had become a ritual "dish of chocolate" from Sir Merivale.

"Sir Feverell," she inquired after a sip so studiously accomplished that not a ruffle ebbed past her thumb knuckle. "Sir Feverell, I trust you were gentle with His Lordship's valet?"

"My dear Miss Morgan, not a King of France has been so luxuriously tended. He ate the first of my board and reclined upon my finest linens. Dr. Radclyffe attended him daily and bled him frequently. I even, ah, overlooked the fact that the, er, upstairs wench was found lingering in the vicinity of his, er, chamber . . . that is, late in the . . . ahem, day. Why, when I received your message to release the fellow, I'll be damned if he wanted to go! Of course, I supplied him amply with coin in recompense for his inconvenience at my pistol. Do you suppose the earl will make a fuss of it?"

"I assure you, the earl may not have been treated so liberally at my hands, but he was well-satisfied. Depend upon it, we shall hear no more from him if he hears no more from us," said Rue, turning her cane even faster in her gloveless hands.

May had somehow fluttered into June and the height of the London season. The Earl of Argyle would be occupied with assemblies and teas and dinners and gaming and driving. . . .

"Er, Miss Morgan," said Sir Feverell timidly. "One thing. Was not His Lordship a bit peeved at your disposition of the grays and perch phaeton?"

Rue turned her airily turbaned head to regard her questioner. The walking stick hung dangerously still.

"He thought it a rare jest, Sir Feverell, as do we all. Even an earl can savor a jest."

"Ay," responded Hookham, "he took it so well that within a day of his release he was seen upon the Strand in an even more disasterously constructed perch phaeton drawn by a pair of coal-black steeds." Hookham leaned across the table to lower his voice to Rue. "With a set of red, black, and white ribbands in their flying tails. Now what do you think of that?"

"I think His Lordship is overfond of speed," answered Rue, unperturbed.

" 'Tis said he won 'em his first night free in a game of hazard with Lord Castlemere. He's a deuced fortunate fellow," said Humphries.

"Hmmm, yes," agreed Hookham, dropping his eyelids and ebbing back into his chair. "Perhaps more fortunate than Miss Morgan is telling us."

"Enough preening ourselves on past triumphs, gentlemen," said Rue sharply. Her small fist rapped the table until the ruffles danced atop her white knuckles and every member of the Basilisk Club sat upright.

"I have been defrauded of sending my father a sapphire too long. We must fashion another scheme. Surely there is some other enterprise in which we could diddle my esteemed sire?"

Their heads bent together, and they drew their vagrant thoughts out like dice on the table. Addison Hookham hung back for a moment or two, watching Rue Morgan digest each offered suggestion with narrowed eyes and firmly set lips. Then he pushed his own unvoiced questions to the back of his shallow mind and leaned inward and joined the conspirators at their entertaining occupation.

Only when he was firmly netted into the group's concerns did Rue Morgan's blue eyes flick toward him and then away, probing and well-satisfied.

* * *

"Oh, m'Lord, I am most relieved to find you so fit. I feared the worst, you know, every moment," said Welles, fastening the double buttons on a smartly cut jade green frockcoat and fluffing the white frill across its low-cut lapels.

"I was evidently in no worse straits than yourself, Welles," said the earl dryly, for he had read between his valet's copious lines about his own incarceration and detected the truth of it.

"Oh, it was terrible, m'Lord, terrible. To be so helpless, so totally at the mercy of blackguards, however soft-spoken they be."

"I was in the hands of a lady, Welles, so no doubt my sentence was gentler than yours."

Welles flushed, and the little man stepped back from the earl's impeccably attired form to survey his handiwork.

"I cannot claim that I was not thankful for the, ummm, rest, Your Lordship."

The earl laughed then and clapped Welles upon the shoulder so robustly that the valet started.

"You were a gallant ally on Blackfriars Road, my dear Welles. Had a cowardly ball not ended your new-born career as a man of action, I warrant you'd have done a deal of damage."

"But Your Lordship has taken wounds of your own." The valet's fingers fanned the earl's wrist laces. "We should have the villains hauled into court, if we but knew their identities."

"Enough, Welles. It was but a prank at the hands of some disgruntled gamesters. I do not wish to pursue the matter," he concluded coldly enough to stifle the valet's Tom Thumb brand of courage and outrage. "We shall forget the matter, Welles."

"If it pleases Your Lordship," said the valet meekly, whisking a brush across the earl's broad shoulders.

The earl narrowed his eyes at his severely tailored reflection in the long glass.

"It does not please me, Welles," he remarked softly, "but

I fear it is the only sensible course. My ancestors did not endure so long for hurling themselves into the very teeth of lunacy, even if she wore a fair face."

The earl shook his lace over his wrists and pulled his frockcoat sleeves sharply to the proper length. And then he smiled.

"I returned the brandy decanter to the study," announced Heliotrope when Rue returned from her meeting with the Basilisk Club. "I do not think it has been missed. Sir Nigel prefers the port."

"That is a house servant's task, Helia, not a body servant's," objected Rue. "You should have left it for them."

"It did not get here by their offices. I thought it would cause less comment if it returned without them."

"How do you know *how* it got there?"

"You do not drink brandy," said the maid, folding away Rue's sapphire taffeta redingote, "but I can guess who does."

That was Heliotrope's first and only comment on the night three days past. She had not even taken verbal note of the fact that Rue seemed inclined to do most of her dressing herself. Nor that she had taken triple doses of the potion guaranteed by the gypsy Fenelia to ban offspring.

Rue sat at the dressing table in the room between her bedchamber and sitting room.

Ahead, if she looked, was a corner of the mantel with the frozen-faced caryatid just visible and an unlit candelabrum on the snowy architrave above. Behind her, if she swiveled, was the draping of her bed. Of course now she could not see the bedchamber fireplace, which decorated the wall at her back.

She could not see the classical features of its pair of maidenly supporting statues either, nor the candelabrum which sat atop that mantel and burned phantomly in memory of another occasion.

Rue Morgan caught Heliotrope's black eye falling upon

her grimly as the maid passed behind her. Rue Morgan leaned into the tilted tabletop glass and inspected the unblemished skin of her cheek. How contrite Nigel had been when she finally woke late that morning and he had blundered in, apologizing for the fault of falling asleep when her evening had just begun.

Rue Morgan had been magnanimous and reached out with her lace-dripping hands and pulled him dressed into the linens with her. Then she had applied her new lessons to undoing the intricacies of his dress and other things that had him stammering with delight and babbling of marrying her.

But she had made up to him whatever sore head the drug had given him. She wished the earl had been there to see how she kept a bargain. She wished the earl—Rue Morgan leaned nearer her reflection so Helia could not see it and smiled.

The Earl of Argyle alighted from his new red and black perch phaeton and idly patted the damp blacks in passing.

He kept the driving whip in one leather-gloved hand, the long trailing tail neatly folded back upon itself. He advanced over the hay-strewn stable floor until he found his second groomsman.

"I want a word with you in the tack room."

The man dropped the bridle he was mending and looked up into the earl's set face. His Lordship was lightly striking the whip butt against his leather-clad legs, and one booted heel tapped noiselessly in the straw.

In the tack room, the earl was brusque.

"I have found your work at the harnesses unsatisfactory—well, what is your name?"

"Brown, Yer Lordship."

"Brown." The earl savored the lowliness of the name. "Your . . . clumsiness nearly lost me my grays, Brown. I will not have incompetence among my servants, Brown. I pay you a fair wage. I will not accept disloyalty in exchange for coin of the realm."

Brown quavered.

"I could not help myself, Yer Lordship. She was most insistent upon it, she—"

"She?" thundered the earl, uncoiling the whip in one flick of a well-laced wrist.

Brown went white.

"Ay, me sister Moll, Yer Lordship. She's frantic taken wi' a footman o'er Grosvenor Square. Sir Feverell Marshwine's establishment. She's 'alf-mad for 'im, and 'im a whey-faced fellow in powdered wig and mincing steps. I warned 'er, I did, I said—"

"Sir Feverell Marshwine . . ."

The earl digested the name and let it ring in his head as it had once sounded just before a descending pistol butt had set other things reverberating in his brain besides names.

"I see it now." He frowned fiercely at Brown. "Fetch her!"

"Fetch 'oo, sir?" quavered the terrified servant.

"Your sister, the lovelorn—what does she do here?"

"Underhousemaid, Yer Lordship."

"Then go to the house and fetch her here," ordered the earl between his teeth.

Brown scrambled away half on his knees, and the earl paced the tiny room shadowed from the sun, but ripe with the smells of leather polish and hay.

In moments she was there, curtsying on the threshold, her eyes still blinking from the courtyard's strong sunlight.

"Well, and your name is Molly?"

"Ay, an' Yer Lordship please."

Her handkerchief was crossed tightly on her bosom, but it was a swelling one for all that. She was a pale city creature, washed away by a life indoors scrubbing steps and making beds. Despite it, her figure had a winsome grace, and her feet, crudely shod beneath an anklelength calico hem, were not overlarge.

Brown, cringing behind his sister, watched the earl survey her minutely. He stepped forward.

"She's a good, obedient girl, m'Lord. 'Tis true she 'as a fondness for some liveried fop from yonder, but she's obedient and eager to please, if Yer Lordship follow. Perhaps, Yer Lordship might care to 'ave trial of 'er?"

He shoved the girl forward, though everything in her face and posture fell at his words. She stumbled to her knees before the earl.

"Oh, no, m'Lord, no! I'm not that sort. 'Tis true, I'm, I'm wi' child"—she glanced wildly to her brother—"but James Frankson and me plan to marry, an' his master permit it. I'm sorry I done wrong. I should never've talked Matthew into foolin' with Yer Lordship's 'arnesses. But it seemed only a little prankish sort of thing one gentleman might play on another, and James was certain Sir Feverell 'ad 'is 'eart set upon it."

Here she broke into choking sobs.

"Sir Feverell what?" demanded the earl, incredulous.

" 'Ad," she hiccoughed, " 'is . . . 'eart," again a hiccough, "set upon delayin' Yer Lordship that night. I thought little 'arm could come of it, and now I'm to be dis'onored on me back and thrown out to the streets to starve. Oh, please don't take me, sir. I'm a good girl!"

The earl's face grew sterner.

"Do you mean to imply, my remarkable young woman, that lying with an earl is greater disgrace than growing balloon-stomached by an ordinary footman?"

"Oh, 'e's a splendid fellow, m'Lord, not ordinary at all. It'll be a fine day when St. Mary Le Bow's bells ring for the weddin'."

Her brother recovered from his astonishment and lurched over to catch Moll by the ear and drag her to her feet.

"There'll be no bells for you, Moll, now you've got us both fair parboiled in 'ot water. An' ye'll do the earl's wishes and keep your mouth shut upon it!"

"Yes, she will, Brown, and you may release her now or my whip will have to encourage you to it," said the earl in overeven tones. "Hush your bawling, girl. I'm not accustomed to having calves in my stable."

He took one turn about the tack room while a wet pair of eyes followed him hopefully and another pair simply clung to his movements.

"You're both out of my service," he announced finally. "I've not space to bed and board traitors. And whether you starve upon the streets or are put away in Bridewell is no affair of mine, you'll agree."

The girl's head slowly hung, and she put her trembling hands across her aproned stomach. Her brother's eyes deadened at the reality of what waited for them on London's teeming, heartless streets. He went and put his arm about her shoulders.

" 'Ere, Moll, there's no way out of this one. I'm sorry for it . . ."

"And I am, too," said the earl. "I advise you to take yourselves to Grosvenor Square, Sir Nigel Pagett-Foxx's residence, and present yourselves to a Miss Rue Morgan there. You may tell her your sad plight and by what actions of your own you have brought it on. Tell her you are in lieu of the grays and I expect her to pay her debts."

In the dim light, the whites of two pair of eyes glimmered thankful. The earl saluted with his whip, turned, and left the room. Moll Brown dissolved in smothered sobs and hid her face on her brother's shoulder.

And so Sir Nigel found himself with the services of an additional groomsman, and Rue Morgan found herself on a mission to arrange the nuptials between a maid and footman.

Sir Feverell Marshwine was not so pleased to add two more mouths to his household, including one which would not work for at least seven years, but he acceded to Rue's pointing out that it was the least he could do in view of the nearly fatal accident to Welles.

Moll Brown and her footman were delighted.

* * *

"Varian, you rogue! We've missed you across the green baize."

"Thank you, Flemming. It is good to know that a winner is as welcome as a loser at Brooks's." The earl looked up from his throw to smile warmly at his friend and nod to an adjacent chair.

"How did you find Tunbridge Wells?" asked Jonathan, flicking back his coattails to sit.

"Rather, er, confining," confessed the earl.

"You are a city cat, Varian, no country mouse. I could have told you that. Was there much gaming?"

"A bit," said the earl, throwing idly and rolling a six. "I'm afraid I applied myself to the study of the white baize rather than the green."

"The white—? Ah, I see, a lady." Flemming laced his fingers together and, with elbows at the table rim, supported his chin on them.

"She cannot have been as splendid as the lady who gamed with us here," he noted morosely.

The earl considered the matter.

"I would say . . . her equal."

"Surely not!"

"In every respect," grinned the earl, "including some you have not yet thought of, I assure you."

"Varian, you grow cryptic. It cannot be healthy. And I have heard that upon returning you were seen gaming at Boodle's!"

"I did."

"But Boodle's is Tory through and through!"

"It is."

"And you are a thoroughgoing Whig, as are all of us at Brooks's. I'm surprised they did not horsewhip you forth at Boodle's."

"It would look ill to be so rough-tempered with a winner," said the earl, tossing the dice idly again. "Even for a Tory."

"But why did you go?"

"My dear Flemming, I cannot let politics interfere with my acquisition of a good pair. I wanted Lord Castlemere's vaunted blacks."

"But you had just won those splendid grays here, from that dull-witted squire."

"I found them ... elusive, Jonathan. Flighty. My new blacks are much more solid-steppers. In horses, as in women, it is good not to settle too soon on a choice."

Jonathan Flemming stood.

"I do not understand you, Varian. You have a perfectly fine pair of grays and discard them for another. A divinely handsome woman comes to Brooks's and practically throws her fichu at your feet—God knows what else would have followed—and you must off to Tunbridge Wells to consort with some mysterious female. I am ordering the port, and after you have consumed three bottles or so, I will question you again and see if I can find some sense in your answers."

The earl laughed and swept the dice back into their box.

"I am not one to object to wine, my good inquisitor, but I have told you nothing but the truth, and all the port at Brooks's shall not float anything other out of me."

The earl shook the box vigorously and cast. The dice tumbled out. Deuce.

Flemming leaned over and picked up a die, turning over the single dot to reveal the six opposite.

"The truth, Varian, always has two sides. Perhaps someday you will show me the reverse of yours."

The earl smiled and accepted the die as it dropped into his waiting palm.

"Perhaps someday I shall know it myself."

Chapter Fourteen

 "But I was planning on taking you to see the British Museum myself."

"Dearest Nigel, don't fuss. Surely you are not jealous. Dr. Radclyffe is very old, I assure you. He delivered my mother of me and is a kind of ... godfather."

"That was only nineteen years ago. He could have been a stripling at the time," remarked Sir Nigel glumly, sitting on the apple-green upholstered chair by Rue's dressing table.

"He wasn't," said Rue firmly as Heliotrope lowered a sweeping summer straw onto her tangling curls. "They are cutting hair quite short now, perhaps I should—" suggested Rue, turning her majestic head from side to side in the mirror.

"Most certainly not! I forbid it. Rue, you are mad." Nigel had started from his chair like a mechanical toy.

Rue laughed and patted his gesticulating hands.

"Very well, Nigel, have your way on the hair. But I must have mine on Dr. Radclyffe and the British Museum. Adieu, I will see you at dinner."

Rue swept out, a violet silk parasol in her hand matching the satin sash that waisted her.

Nigel stared after her departing pale blue muslin skirts and sank back onto the chair, his face in his hands and his elbow overturning a black velvet dice box on the dressing table edge.

Out rolled a six in twinkling sapphires, but Sir Nigel Pagett-Foxx neither noticed nor cared.

The British Museum was only six-and-thirty years old the day Rue Morgan first strolled its cluttered corridors in Montagu House on Russell Street, Bloomsbury.

Yet it was crowded already with curiosities and antiquities. The least of these latter was Dr. Radclyffe himself, who would have been most incensed at Rue's descriptions of his infirmities and great age to the jealous Nigel. Dr. Radclyffe was young enough to savor the stares his entrance with such a vision upon his arm earned them both.

"This is quite kind of you, doctor," said Rue, as oblivious to the attention she drew as a queen is to a curtsy. "You must have ordered the tickets weeks ago."

"I have, uh, had this little visit in mind for some time," he admitted, steering her up the great broad staircase to where a pair of enormous giraffes, quite stuffed, awaited them.

"How bizarre. These creatures are as spotted in attire as one of these new republican Frenchmen, these *incroyables*. I am glad Nigel did not escort me. He would straightaway dash out and order spotted breeches. Good Lord, what a neck!"

"I'm glad you entertain yourself, my dear," said the doctor, steering her downstairs to the exhibit rooms below. "But I asked you here to discuss business."

"Of course, doctor, how could I suspect you of other? You are as near to a true father as I have, I suppose."

Dr. Radclyffe stammered his thanks for this signal honor and led her through a room wherein rested the fabled split cane hat of the patriarch of China.

"Most odd," said Rue, staring. "And why could we not discuss this business at the Basilisk Club?"

"It is . . . rather indelicate. I thought first to present it to you alone. You had asked, I believe, for some scheme to truly discomfort your father. I think I have it, but I warn you, it savors of the, er, crude."

Rue stared at the assembled bleached bones of what was labeled a "Roman elephant." No doubt Hannibal himself had ridden it. She did not turn to Dr. Radclyffe.

"Pray do not underestimate me, doctor. You say you alone of the Basilisk Club observed my father's domestic methods. They, too, were crude."

"Precisely my point. There is within the situation something to exploit, if we wish to."

"What?"

Dr. Radclyffe escorted her to a pair of chairs from which they could contemplate the disjointed pachyderm.

"There is a tendency in men of a certain age," began the physician, "to, er, lose certain characteristics of youthful vitality, the virile attributes that make a man a, er, man."

"My dear doctor," Rue said calmly, "you need not be so roundabout when I sit here studying this great pile of bones. I apprehend your meaning quite well. You speak of my father!"

Dr. Radclyffe cleared his throat repeatedly before speaking again.

"You have it, dear Miss Morgan. What an admirable midwife you would have made."

"But I sit here to contradict it! And further, if this condition existed at my birth, why should it still maintain?"

"Time does not heal that kind of wound," answered the doctor. "As for yourself, the condition may not have been chronic then. But whatever our supposition, I warrant that Black Harry Morgan would be interested in a cure for impotency, both for its financial potential and its personal, er, potency."

Rue turned and narrowly regarded Dr. Radclyffe's rather prim face, studying the aquiline nose, the pursed lips, the pale eyes under well-wrinkled lids.

"You fox! You have such a cure?"

Dr. Radclyffe stared straight ahead at the white bones erected into a semblance of their original configuration.

"Elephant bone is a major ingredient. You can see why by the size of this fellow. And, of course, that most clever trunk. It is a mystery that no one conceived of it before. Ground elephant bone. Miraculously effective. The formula is most secret, of course. I would only part with it for a great price. To the proper party."

Rue and the doctor exchanged glances, then smiles.

"To Black Harry Morgan! A brilliant ploy, Dr. Radclyffe. But, but it doesn't actually work, do you suppose?"

Dr. Radclyffe's watery eyes slid to hers.

"My dear Miss Morgan, I devoutly hope not. It is not my intention to play Priapus to half of London. The wives would never forgive me."

"Ah, yet think, dear doctor, how grateful the whores would be! But how do we convince my father that your, er, formula, this potion, this—"

"Aphrodisiac," offered the doctor.

"No, my dear sir. 'Afridisiac.' Remember the elephant and his origins. But how shall we prove it to him?"

"We must have a subject, a scientific demonstration of the formula's efficacy. I've thought of recruiting some Bridewell debtor, or even of Bedlam, but—"

"No! Your scheme requires nothing so unreliable as a pauper or a madman, but a man of many parts—an actor!"

"But what actor would play such a role? What actor can we trust?"

"I know one, dear doctor, who might essay the role for me, though it go much against his conscience. He must be shown to my father aged, weak, uninterested in anything below his waist save his bowels. And then each day, with the administration of Dr. Radclyffe's miraculous potion, he grows younger, more vigorous, straighter in every respect, a veritable satyr whose appetites are unbounded. Oh, what a comedy! 'Tis better than highway robbery. We will do it. You must take me directly to the Drury. Goodbye, old elephant, a blessing upon your bones."

Rue had risen and was leading Dr. Radclyffe out, leaning upon his elderly arm and whispering refinements of the plot into his slightly deaf ear.

The other museum visitors shook their heads and gossiped and said that Black Rue Morgan, as the Earl of Argyle had so aptly named her, had developed but more scandalous tendencies.

Rue Morgan stared nostalgically around the dressing room. It was dim and crammed with unused props, populated with pieces of former costumes. It was a place for ghosts, and she almost felt one herself.

Quentin Rossford was no spirit, though. He was busy at the glass rearranging the more material alterations he had made to his handsome face for a recently performed pantomime.

"White lead and red cheek spots! Who would have thought it of the age's finest Romeo? But the public demands entertainment, and mere plays are not enough. They must have mimes and acrobats and soon, I imagine, capering gibbons instead of actors. Ah, my wasted diction. Well, my dear Rue, your scheme has its drawbacks, but is sufficiently challenging to tempt me. 'Twould be a triumph, though for an audience of one. A reversal of the seven ages of man in the bard. I would start two-legged, as it were, and grow a third."

"Don't underestimate my father, Quentin. Black Harry Morgan is no fool to be taken in by hocus-pocus and flummery."

Rossford turned from the mirror, a perfect rouged circle

on one cheek giving him an oddly rakish, though effeminate, air.

"There's nothing, ah, dangerous in the good doctor's powder, I hope? It would be damned hard convincing your father if I lost use of my, er, supporting cast."

Rue blushed. She always felt a bit apologetic for her wicked, worldly ways when with the actor. Perhaps it was because he had been her first mentor and knew her before she had gone up in the world via bed linens. Or perhaps it was because he was the only man ever to refuse her.

"Quentin, I swear, Dr. Radclyffe has promised his potion shall be harmless as wig powder. You must chase a chambermaid or two to convince my father of your intentions and ability."

Rossford straightened indignantly.

"I am a good actor, my dear. If necessary, I can play any role to the hilt."

"Well, then . . ." Rue smiled and bit her lip. "Dr. Radclyffe feels you must reside at Blackstone House so my father can keep an eye on your rising good health."

"Of course." The actor nodded, turning to sponge off the rest of his paint.

"I'm very grateful that you will do this, Quentin. We may be wrong about my father's personal interest in this potion, but he's bound to see the commercial potential."

"On the other hand," said Rossford, swiveling back to regard her, "you may be right. Your mother is not here to tell the tale, that's for certain. Poor woman, if Dr. Radclyffe was correct, she had a bitter lot of it."

"Perhaps," said Rue, "she found solace elsewhere. I think if I were wed to Black Harry Morgan, I should prefer his virility to be minimal. There must be nothing worse than to bed with a man one loathes but whose carnal appetites are monstrous!" Rue shuddered.

"How goes it with young Pagett-Foxx? He's not over-bumptious?" asked the actor shrewdly, his eyes narrowed.

"Nigel? Oh, no, dear Quentin. You picked him for a lamb, and he is one. Really, don't look at me like that. I must reassure you that he is no trouble to me, save he slobber a bit on my fingertips—and my feet, would I let him. He is exemplarily devouted." Rue sighed.

"But you do not find a lap dog challenging?" asked Quentin, smiling. "Is that the trouble?"

"Oh, a portion of it, I imagine." Rue pleated the folds of her flowered summer frock. "Quentin, you shepherded Nigel to me precisely because he was such a shearling, didn't you? There were, are other sorts of men I could have found to support me, men that—"

"Men that you cannot play Bo-Peep to," he finished abruptly. "I may be a disreputable old roué, but I am not brutal."

"A roué and a Rue. We make a good pair." Rue extended her hand, and he took it. "I am truly grateful, Quentin, for your aid."

Rossford looked down at the fingers he held fast, white and ringless. He gave them a playful, almost chiding shake.

"You have met with more than lambs since I last saw you, my Rue."

"Oh, with veritable wolves, dear shepherd," she mocked.

"May I know the name of this wolf?" he asked quietly, his vocal timbre vibrant even in low tone.

Rue withdrew her hand.

"No. All wolves are nameless. And I have my own claws."

Quentin Rossford shook his graying head. "A kitten's," he said contemptuously. "Well, you must become a cat in your own way."

Rue stood. "Quentin, enough talk of menageries. Besides," she added, "I do not think he is a wolf. He is more a lion."

Rossford's eyebrows rose and stayed there.

"Then you shall have to learn to be a lion tamer," he suggested.

"Ah, this beast won't tame, there's the rub. But see you keep my father well within whip range, Quentin. I think he is a more dangerous species than a wolf or a lion or even an actor. Good fortune with your masquerade," she finished, smiling and drawing on her white gloves.

Rossford escorted her to the dressing-room door. His hand lay lightly across her muslined shoulder.

"Good fortune with yours, Rue Morgan," he wished her. "And with your lion. I fear more than playacting will be required in your case."

"For me, there is nothing more than that. You forget that I have no heart."

"Just see that *you* do not forget that," he advised, shutting the door behind her.

He leaned against it for a moment, his fine face troubled. Then he straightened as if shrugging off a burden that was not his to carry.

He returned to the looking glass and inspected his features closely, already planning the timetable of his transformation from aged impotent to veritable tower of virility. Rossford grinned at himself in the mirror.

"Defend thyself, Black Harry Morgan," he declaimed in mock villainous tones, "for Quentin Rossford comes to thee with the intention of making a fool of thyself under thine own roof, blackguard of old, defiler of daughters and of wives!"

Rossford leaned back to regard himself and cast the makeup sponge to the tabletop.

"And know, Black Harry Morgan, that Justice is the author of this farce," he said more softly.

Black Harry Morgan let the vial of powder tip toward his palm, pouring a fine white stream into a mounting pyramid in his hand.

"Elephant bone, you say ... And anything other?" He looked up from under brows as veiling as shrubbery.

Dr. Radclyffe leaned back in the easychair, balancing his port glass on one upholstered arm.

"My dear Morgan, 'tis a secret formula."

"And it will be my secret?"

"If you pay for the privilege."

Morgan funneled his hand and let the powder sift back into the narrow glass tube. He was careless, and several grains fell free. Dr. Radclyffe fidgeted nervously in his chair.

"My dear Morgan, a bit more care if you please. I am not spraying drops of your best port about the carpet."

"This stuff's as flighty as a filly. And that is not my best port, doctor," Morgan said gruffly. "But you swear it works, and safely?"

"It is as safe as anything that stirs the venereal capacities to their fullest efforts. That is to say, it may ruin reputations, destroy marriages, exhaust masculine constitutions and female ones as well, but it is guaranteed to cause not the slightest bit of direct bodily harm."

"And you call it an ... 'aphrodisiac'?"

"Afridisiac, my dear sir, in tribute to the elephant. But aphrodisiac is the proper term, or improper one, depending on your point of view."

"Depending on you having anything to point, eh, doctor?" interjected Black Harry, laughing bawdily.

"Precisely," concurred the doctor.

"And you promise a method to prove the, eh, efficacy of the stuff?"

"Not precisely, my dear Morgan. What I have found is Mr. Bartholomew Fayre. Now he isn't pretty, and he's lost the use of more organs than one, I warrant, from his brain to his liver. 'Tis terrible what the gin shops'll do. But if my powder can resurrect the capacities of the good Bartholomew, I swear it could resuscitate a chair leg, sir!"

Dr. Radclyffe, exhausted by this effort of oration, sat back and took a long draught of his port.

"Well, have him in then," ordered Black Harry. "See to it." He frowned at a lackey loitering in the hall.

The gentlemen sipped port in silence, enjoying their separate anticipations of the events to come. Black Harry's savoring smile grew broad and lewd. The physician's grew only tighter and more sly.

Into the selfcongratulatory haze finally was ushered a bent, ragged, cringing, limping shadow of a man. This creature lurched uncertainly toward the doctor where it executed a bob rather than a bow and waited as expectantly as a well-trained spaniel.

"Doctor Radclyffe, this is the person to whom you expect me to open my bed and board while the experiment transpires? I said a sorry fellow would prove the powder's power more, but this specimen is more ready for the charnel than the carnal house."

"The perfect subject then, you'll agree. That's right, Bartholomew, would you like some proper food and a bit o' rest in this gentleman's care?"

The wretched man turned his head toward Black Harry Morgan, belatedly doffing the grimy fabric that masqueraded as a cap. His stringy gray-brown hair hung tangled to his shoulders.

He began absently fanning himself with the cap, as if exhausted from the effort of mere locomotion. A strong odor wafted into the hairy nostrils of Black Harry Morgan.

"Look here, man, how old are you?" asked Morgan, checking his magisterial lean forward in favor of his sense of smell.

A tongue popped out a grimy cheek so it looked carbuncled. The visitor considered with cocked head.

"Well, sir, I be six-and-, and-, and- . . . fifty! That's it. Right well done, Bartholomew, right well done—there's a clever fellow. Have'ee got a penny for old Bartholomew Fayre, sirs?"

Black Harry regarded the lean-fingered hand cupped before him with some disgust.

"Here," interrupted the doctor. "You'll get many pretty pennies if you do as we say. You'll get fine beefsteak to eat and good port—"

"Country wine'll do, doctor!"

"A nice, robust country wine then. And all you'll have to do is take this powder but once a day as I've explained. You can manage that, eh, Bartholomew?"

Bartholomew didn't answer, but considered the matter with narrowed eyes, gaping mouth, and eternally cocked head.

"Look here, fellow." This time Black Harry leaned forward. "We'll sweeten the bargain. How'd you like a bit of petticoat, eh? Damn, what's the words for it in the sewer this rascal has crawled from? A nice fresh young lady in your sheets to do your biddin' and your beddin'."

The elderly face screwed into as many cracks as line a rain-thirsty road. Bartholomew Fayre turned his ragged headgear in his clawlike hands and stared first at Morgan's feet, then at the wall, back to the doctor, and finally at the floor.

"Wench, you idiot! A female in your bed. Surely you can't have forgotten that?"

The seamed face regarded Morgan intently. Then slowly, with a dawning that rivaled the moving of mountains for ponderousness, a sort of smile began on the homely visage until the filthy skin cracked to reveal a lolling tongue and the few blackened teeth remaining to portcullis it.

"Ay, sirs, I 'member somewhat o' that. A wench, says you. An' more wenches than one, I remember . ..." The smile faded as interminably as it had dawned. "But 'twas a bit ago, sir—yes, 'twas. I was but a lad then, if you know what I mean. Quite a lad I was then. Then I was. Yes, indeed, sirs. A wench, that's what it was, a wench."

He subsided, nodding sagely and vacantly all the while.

Black Harry Morgan turned a significant eye on Dr. Radclyffe. "We could not find a more ideal candidate unless we dug him up."

"And then rigor mortis might cloud the issue," suggested the physician dryly. "Yes, our Bartholomew will do nicely."

The man was as alert to the intonation of his name as a dog. "Do? Ay, sir, I'll do as you say, all ye say and anything you say. Hav'ee a penny for old Bartholomew?"

"I believe a first round of powder is necessary. Mr. Morgan sir, the port."

" 'Tis a middling port, that's true, but . . ." Black Harry indignantly eyed the empty crystal glass in his hand.

The doctor's imperious gesture was uncompromising. Morgan handed over the glass and watched dourly while the physician filled it with ruddy liquid, then poured the vial's contents into it like snow into blood. He shivered slightly.

Mr. Bartholomew Fayre smacked his lips and seized the proffered glass, its rim toasting his few remaining teeth. Black Harry flinched. The old man drained the vessel in one long gesture of upturned head and returned it, pausing to carefully wipe the lip on the skirt of his filthy coat.

Both men seemed loath to take the glass. Bartholomew shrugged and crammed it into his bulging pockets to no one's objections. "Ay, sirs, and I think I'll like it 'ere well enough. Right fine gentlemen you be," he pronounced. "Have'ee a penny?"

Evidently, Dr. Radclyffe's miraculous Afridisiac powder for the restoration of the venereal capacities first had to resurrect the other physical capabilities.

During his residency in Blackstone House, old Bartholomew showed an enormous appetite for continual quantities of beefsteak, for instance. Black Harry balked at first, but the doctor pointed out that the beefsteak in question had been requested rare, and that this was an encouraging sign.

Then there was the matter of old Barty's prodigious appetite for spiritous liquors. Furthermore, as the days went by, his demands would only be satisfied by increasingly fine vintages.

Black Harry Morgan glumly paced the lower rooms while

servants paraded upstairs almost hourly with trays bearing the best of his pantry and wine cellar. The doctor advised forbearance: a true test of the organ's condition would rest upon the well-being of the entire organism.

"Quackery," snarled Black Harry. "We must test the powder, though you claim 'tis disastrously premature."

Morgan thundered up the staircase and found a bit of skirt protruding from the depths of the linen room. He summarily extracted its owner.

"You look a sturdy sort, girl. Into the fellow's chamber wi' you."

The maid paled and drew back, but women servants in Black Harry Morgan's establishment were selected for reasons other than a virtuous upbringing. She went, her wail of objection more directed to the object of her attentions than the fact of them. Both men entered the bedchamber with her.

On the testered and draped bed, surrounded by orange peels, bread crusts and many less identifiable substances, Bartholomew Fayre sprawled like a sultan. One of Morgan's own dressing gowns—the fine scarlet damask—gaped open across a scabrous chest decorated with matted coils of grizzled hair. A tipsy nightcap crowned the dull gray strands of what only a charitable observer could term hair. Barty's bare feet, callused to hard yellow horns, lay askew on the embroidered coverlet.

"Me benefactors!" this vision screeched, rising to his knees on the mattress. "God bless you both for yer generosity."

He would have raved on, a half-drained decanter of wine beside him spurring his enthusiasm, but Black Harry interrupted him.

"Thank us more. Look what we've brought you, fellow." He shoved the housemaid forward.

Old Bartholomew's face beamed as if he had seen a Christmas pudding, his greasy hands clawing the sides of the robe. Unfortunately, that article of clothing was so dirty

that it was debatable whether he was attempting to wipe his
hands, or begrime them further.

"Oh, ay, sir, 'tis a pretty, cheeky country wench—"

Everything in his face gleamed, from his rolling eyes to
his spittle-daubed lips. The girl quailed.

"See what you can do with her," Black Harry ordered,
"and be quick about it."

He caught the doctor's sleeve to pull him from the room.
In the passage beyond, both men paused to press their ears
against the painted wood. They heard nothing for a time,
then a bound of bedsprings, a high feminine shriek, some
senile chuckling, and a very long silence.

Suddenly, the door withdrew from their inward-leaning
faces. The maid exited between them, face flushed and lips
set.

"Well?" demanded Black Harry.

She regarded him before shaking her head fiercely.

"Nothing happened?"

"Ay, and I'm pleased o' it. That stinking, slobbering creature doubtless carries the pox. He's limp as an eel under the
overlapping robe, and as chill belike. 'Twas only pinching
and patting he wanted," she declared, rubbing her skirt-
swathed rear.

Black Harry let her ebb from his grasp as he glowered at
the doctor.

That gentleman sighed, but kept a cheerful face. "Why,
that fellow wouldn't have pinched a chicken, much less
fairer game, five scant days ago. We must give him more
time."

"And more powder," agreed Morgan. "This loitering with
our ears pressed to doors is undignified; I'll have peepholes
drilled."

He turned and marched down the passage to his own bedchamber.

"Peepholes, is it?" the doctor warned softly through the
still-ajar door. "What think you of that, old Bartholomew,
eh?"

"That I shall bestir myself to greater efforts, for an actor likes nothing better than an audience," sang back the sotto voce baritone of Quentin Rossford.

A moment later Bartholomew Fayre's disreputable old face peeped out the crack in the door, and winked.

Treatment progressed with applications of aphrodisiac thrice daily in wine, and a great deal of victuals passing both in, and out, the meager frame of Bartholomew Fayre. Soon the housecats showed a fondness for lingering about his door and had to be driven away by broom-bearing maids.

"Rats," mumbled Morgan in despair, envisioning the next invasion Fayre's presence in his house might cause. Yet he said little more, and the reason why was strange and wonderful.

For, slowly, old Bartholomew was growing straighter, smoother, sharper. His hair was recovering its original mousy brown and thickness, and his manner grew increasingly jaunty.

Even old Bartholomew sensed this, calling for a barber, and, by God, getting one. He demanded a proper suit of clothes. When Black Harry ordered an underfootman to give up his own, the doctor persuaded him to treat his guest as royally as he expected his guest to perform for him subsequently.

Morgan surrendered another personal article of clothing. This one Bartholomew took some care with, even calling for lavender water. At this, Black Harry cried for quarter.

"Now, Morgan," the doctor urged, "humor the creature, and we'll know the truth of the powder for once and all. You must admit that he's grown uncommon vigorous of late."

This conversation in the downstairs library was interrupted by a shriek from above. Both men charged the stairs to find the upstairs maids herded into the linen room, fending off the windmilling hands of Bartholomew Fayre.

"Oh, you little chickadees, run from old Barty, will 'ee? Here's a pretty birdie, give me a peck now—" He caught one young woman and smacked her resoundingly on the lips.

"Doctor Radclyffe, I care not what you say, 'tis time," Black Harry announced.

"Ay." The physician nodded slowly. "Time it is."

Black Harry confronted the crowd in the linen closet. "You, sir! Back to your chamber, but first choose one for your entertainment."

The faces under the white caps grew suspenseful, and some actually looked hopeful.

"Why, all of 'em, good sir, if you permit it," old Bartholomew suggested. "All of these neat little wenches at once, an' I have a plate of beefsteak first."

"All?" demanded the doctor, his eyes drilling Bartholomew's. "Don't be piggish, man. You may, er, injure yourself."

" 'Tis all or nuthin'," the creature asserted truculently, his long arms drawing three maids under his protective wings. " 'Twouldn't be Fayre otherwise, would it? To choose might leave somebody out."

The maids giggled.

Black Harry and Dr. Radclyffe took their eyes from the astonishing scene before them only long enough to exchange a swift, unanimous look.

"By all means, man," Morgan bellowed in a tone he took for genial agreement. "Take as many as you like, as many as you can."

"And me beefsteak?" demanded the lascivious old creature.

"It's coming." Black Harry sighed and rushed below to order, galloping upstairs again for fear of missing something.

He needn't have worried; Bartholomew Fayre meant to present no show until he'd had his promised treat. Morgan and the doctor were forced to watch, fidgeting, while old

Barty gummed down the rare meat that finally came. Evidently, Dr. Radclyffe's miraculous powder could not strengthen blackened teeth. The maids gathered around likewise, by now as awe-stricken by this enterprise as anyone.

Bartholomew chewed happily, his greedy eyes inspecting the maids, who herded together like geese, hiding reddening faces in their uplifted aprons.

"Me hands be weak," he complained. "I've got to save meself, sirs." He dropped the knife and fork, his barber-shaven jaws still masticating doggedly.

A maid timidly stepped forth, sitting the edge of Bartholomew's bed while she cut the remaining meat into smaller pieces. In a moment she was proffering him the food while he winked broadly all round and pinched whatever of the girl came within reach. In another moment, she had fallen back in giggles upon the bed, and what came within reach was a great deal.

"Enough of this mummery," Morgan ordered in a fever of impatience. "Away with the damned beefsteak! You'll get down to business directly, man," he instructed old Bartholomew. " 'Tis not a demonstration of your pinching abilities we're after."

Old Bartholomew sat up to regard his keepers with haughty dignity. "I must have me privacy, sirs. Then we'll see if a pinch is as good as, as . . . other matters," he promised.

The gentlemen withdrew, Black Harry glancing toward the doctor.

"Three," he whispered, "three wenches. The fellow is all beefsteak and buffoonery! His eyes are bigger than his other parts. Even if he be remarkably restored, and I grant your potion that, he'd be lucky to swive one sufficiently to make her toes curl, much less three."

"My powder makes no claims for toe-curling," answered the doctor serenely. "Its action is more in the way of straightening. But let us adjourn to the front row seats of our small domestic drama; I confess myself mightily curious to see how our subject handles himself."

"Again, Doctor, 'tis not the handling of himself that matters," said Black Harry dourly. "But my housemaids be a lusty lot, from what the lackeys tell me, an' he tumbles but one effectively, I'll pay your elephantine price and set about selling it to Londoners wishing to become more upright citizens than previous."

They repaired to the next chamber in unseemly haste, nearly jamming themselves in the doorway by rushing through at once, and took their designated posts. Black Harry's peephole had been drilled at sitting height; a cabriole-legged chair was drawn up at the ready.

The doctor, however, had to stand, and his observation post was set just beneath a sconce on the wall's other side, so a graceful curve of brass played bifocal to his view of the scene.

Only chaos could be witnessed, at any rate. The inventive Bartholomew had invited the maids onto the tangled bedlinens and was amusing himself by popping strawberries into the mouth of one while a second massaged his now amazingly firm and hairless chest, and the third pouted on the fringes.

"Ay, a lovely set of wenches," he finally announced, leaping up to set the strawberry-eater deftly on her back and drawing the remaining two his each side, where he began essaying remarkable forays into the nature of their dress and what lay beneath it.

"I'm damned . . . he's engaging all three," hissed Black Harry, pressing against the paneling so his eye could center upon the primitively drilled hole as through a monocle.

"And most efficiently," murmured the doctor, watching aprons fly, petticoats froth and neat, stripped skirts collapse into bedside piles like deflated balloons.

In mere moments the maids had been reduced to corseted expanses of pasty flesh, flailing limbs and flushed faces. In their midst, old Bartholomew was smacking and spinning and turning like a circus contortionist, his borrowed scarlet robe whirling about his spare frame. That finally slipped off to reveal the lean, muscular body of an amazingly fit man of, say, forty years. It also revealed other obvious attributes of the rejuvenated Bartholomew Fayre.

"Migawd, Radclyffe," croaked Black Harry Morgan, clawing a hairy hand into the doctor's shoulder above him. "Did you, er, take measurements previous to the experiment to verify the powder's effect?"

The doctor abstracted his face from his peephole as though the wood were hot. "Why, ah . . . no. I didn't view the experiment in terms of taking, er, measurements. In fact, I think we need not stoop to snoopery much longer—"

Once again Morgan's hand clamped the doctor's shoulder. "The Devil take him! Now what's the fellow's up to—?"

The good doctor shut his eyes from further temptation, his powdered head rearing away from the ever-more-outrageous scene. "With your pardon, I will wait in the passage."

"Wait where you like," Morgan said, never unfastening his eye from the peephole. "You can wait at the anteroom of Hell, for all I care. But you'll have your ten thousand pounds, man; that's another thing your devilishly effective powder can take credit for raising."

The doctor allowed a tight smile to touch his lips as he stepped into the passage. Dr. Radclyffe sank—slowly—onto the gilt Chinese Chippendale chair, which squatted opposite its mate like a foo dog guarding its territory. He waited. He waited for a very long time. Finally the peep-chamber door opened and Black Harry emerged, mopping his bewigged brow.

"Prodigious. Miraculous. We'll give the old devil an extra pound for his labors, but then out with him. I want him gone and gin-soaked soon after, so he'll not tell the tale, nor even recall it. My aphrodisiac will not be wasted henceforth on louts like Fayre who cannot, in any event, afford it. And give me the proper formula, doctor, or I'll have something more appropriate than your head for it."

Black Harry's threats were interrupted by a cracking of Bartholomew's chamber door. Out popped a flushed, mob-cap-topped face, then the entire maid, in the process of tying her apron on askew.

Black Harry moved to block her exit. "Well?"

"Ay, sir; and twice with Nelly. Just finishin' up Fiona, but she's a stolid sort and takes her time."

"Back to your duties, then! I'll not have my maids lolling about." Black Harry smacked her retreating skirts, and she spurted away in a burst of giggles.

Morgan paced, impatiently, soon rewarded by the emerging Nelly.

"Twice, girl?"

"Ay, and right royal it was."

"Get on with you." Another roguish smack from the master.

The laggardly Fiona finally came out, with head high and shining, shy eyes. Away from the others, it was obvious that her skin was the color of a haggis, and pocked besides. She struggled to fashion an acceptable apron bow around a cumbersome waist.

"*You* as well?" Black Harry asked in amazement.

Fiona looked up, bright eyes casting sunshine on the plain landscape of her features, and nodded. "He said he had saved the best lass for last," she confided to the floor, still struggling with the delinquent apron ends. "So gentlemanly he was, a most handsome gentleman. 'Twas as if he knew I'd never—"

The apron tied, Fiona's feelings unraveled in a rush as she fled down the hall, half-sobbing and half-laughing.

"My God." Morgan stared after her. "If he can swive *that* ugly wench, your powder's a marvel that may sell better to wives than their husbands. And the girl's utterly stupid, besides: 'handsome, gentlemanly' indeed! Go bestir the scrofulous old devil and send him on his way. I'll see you below presently."

Doctor Radclyffe bowed acquiescence with a straight face. The moment Morgan's aggressive heel taps had become an echo on the stairs, he turned to confront lecherous old Bartholomew Fayre.

The doctor stood stunned in the bedchamber doorway. A red-robed figure still reclined upon the chaotic linens enjoying the last of the strawberries.

"Ah, doctor. Alone at length. I warrant I could use some of solitude soon. I'm not as young as I used to be, a sad commentary on the waning spirit of our century."

Quentin Rossford yawned, lazily stretched his scarlet arms wide, and grinned at the doctor. "Well, dear and glorious physician, did I 'saw a passion to tatters'? Or, rather, did you view the tatters of my passion to good effect? It adds gusto to know that one's labors are being appreciated from afar as well as from near at hand."

"Don't be disgusting, Rossford," hissed the doctor. "I left the adjacent chamber as soon as it became apparent that your part . . . that is, that your role in this masquerade went according to plan."

"Black Harry did not bow out so early, I wager." Quentin laughed, stretching like a cat that has risen from one nap only to move a few paces to take another. "I could feel his greedy black eyes upon me all the while."

"Oh, he'll pay dearly for the powder. I hope we haven't done him a favor; mere belief in a medicine may be what makes it work."

"I assure you, doctor; your powder's excellent offices owe their sole effectiveness to my Thespian abilities and, of course, my jaded youth. I enjoyed this enormously, good doctor, and, I warrant, so did the maids. If Black Harry Morgan gleaned a wee warming of his privy parts in the affair as well, I can gladly exchange that for knowing we've severely chilled his pocketbook and will turn his own wealth against him further. I am content."

"I must admit the lasses came out cooing and dimpling, even the last, so I suppose you've done no harm a gentleman might not care to admit to—"

Rossford frowned. Even with Bartholomew's unkempt brows spirit-gummed to his forehead, he was now handsome enough for the doctor to see how the slow-witted Fiona had made her mistake.

"The last one was a tricky bit o' work," the actor admitted. "No woman needs more delicate handling than a Scottish virgin."

"You deflowered her, man?"

"There was no help for it, the display had to be convincing."

The doctor pondered his role in this ruination of virgins, a species one would not expect to encounter in Black Harry Morgan's household—not even, perhaps, his daughter.

"Damme, we have done a great wrong here today. At least she went out of here declaring you the King of France, or as good as. Well, our—"

"—'revels here are ended,' Doctor, and like mischievous Puck I must make my airy exit. Arise, Sir Bartholomew Fayre, take up thy bawd and walk."

Rossford bounded off the mattress, arms wide as if taking a bow, then instantly shriveled into the grizzled likeness of old Barty.

"I thank'ee, doctor, for your kind attendance in my recent recovery," he quavered in the old beggar's voice. "I couldn't stay another night, I suppose—? No. Very well, I be gathering up me fine new suit of clothes and leaving this most generous establishment. But, 'fore I go, I've a last question for you, doctor. Have'ee a penny?"

Palm out, head cocked, eyes screwed avariciously half-shut, Bartholomew Fayre exited Blackstone House on the same whining note as he had entered it. The doctor couldn't help bursting into triumphant laughter.

So did the Basilisk Club, when—two days later—a magnificently clad Quentin Rossford (for he had been well paid) sallied into the Basilisk Club and regaled the gathered gentlemen with the entire tale.

Rue Morgan, of course, had not been present to hear the tale. The episode was deemed unfit for ladylike ears, even if the lady were Black Harry Morgan's daughter and had helped to conceive the entire charade.

Rue did not mind being left out of her drama's denouement. She ached to concoct another scheme, something more public than the Afridisiac affair, that would make Black Harry Morgan's name ripple through every London gathering like a piece of scum-ridden flotsam caught in an inevitable, shoreward-drawn tide.

She did not tell the Basilisks of her plans. This time, she feared, what she was likely to invent would be too daring and risqué even for her dear gentlemen friends of the Basilisk Club.

Chapter Fifteen

 Rue found the innocent means to the daring scandal she sought at one of the most brilliantly lit and attended of the London Ton's affairs.

"You do not care for the piano?" Nigel asked anxiously that night and unwittingly started it.

They were gathered, along with a great quantity of splendidly gowned and coated men and women, around a ladylike prodigy of sixteen who played most delicately upon a marquetry inlaid spinet in a music room on Bloomsbury Square.

"It is not the piano that distresses me, Nigel," said Rue, idly shaking out her fan, "but the presence of all these barristers. I swear, the law is a profession that makes dullards of us all."

"There are some very eminent men present," returned Nigel a bit stiffly since their host happened to be his own attorney and since the practice of the law had never been one to bar its members from rubbing wigs with the land's first persons. "And I think the young woman at the piano is most skilled, as well as quite amiable."

Rue let her escort's sharpness slice past her like an ill-aimed dagger.

"If you care for it, dear Nigel. I leave you to enjoy it without my carping presence. I will take a turn about the drawing room, an' you permit it."

Nigel only nodded curtly, his face setting more stubbornly. Rue studied the slight frown on his pale brows and the harsh lines of his mouth. He was becoming as boring as a barrister, her Nigel. At least these demi-tiffs kept him from rattling her bedside curtains at night.

She sailed away, dressed in a high summer gown of palest lilac-figured tissue sashed in silver gauze. Her velvet ribbon had been exchanged for a lavender silk one, but the sapphire still glittered darkly at her throat, as persistent as a scab, a hard, blue-blooded scab. Save her blood was quite common, whatever her mother's genteel country connections, for she was the spawn of Black Harry Morgan and must never forget it.

"Fetch up a minute! Miss Morgan . . ."

It never took Rue's admirers long to determine when she was detached from the glowering Nigel. One came tottering after her now on gem-studded heels, his impeccably curled and shorn hair not disarrayed a bit by his haste, so well laquered was it.

Rue was amused by these London dandies. She found them alert and percipient despite their airs, always oozing the latest gossip, knowing the correct milliner, the moment's most highly esteemed poet or artist.

"I thought I would never find you free of your watchdog," this particular fop confessed a bit breathlessly. "I've An Eminence who confesses himself most anxious to meet you."

"He has heard of me?" inquired Rue serenely.

"No, never. He has seen you tonight and must see more of you. It is Romney, the great portraitist, and believe me, my dear Miss Morgan, it is a signal honor to stick in his eye. He has been painting that lumpish Lady Hamilton to eternity. We thought no other female form or face could intrigue him. But evidently yours have, O, admirable Rue. But hasten—he is old, and his fancies shift with the wind of reason through his brain."

Rue was shepherded to a farther wall where a row of sidechairs had been drawn up for the more infirm of the guests, a white-haired line of the age's first citizens under the reign of George II. Among them was a plump-faced gentleman of rather morose demeanor.

Rue curtsied to him with unerring accuracy.

"Mr. Romney, a pleasure, sir. I have long admired your paintings. It is a double honor to be given opportunity to admire the person who executed them."

"Ah, she talks, too," barked this gentleman dourly. "An excellent thing in a woman, be she young, pretty, and short-sentenced."

Rue inclined her head mischievously without answering.

"What, girl, have I robbed you of your tongue?"

"Should one speak before a painter? It is a silent art to practice and deserves the reverence of silence in return," she answered demurely.

Romney laughed and reached out to capture her wrist, being sixty years of age and exempt from some of the manners polite society decreed.

"Let's see you in the candlelight better, my silver-tongued Miss Morgan. You've an interesting face upon you. Ay, it looks more the conception of some painter than the Creator. You have been on the stage?"

"Briefly."

"That is long enough. Too much artifice jades a woman. I will paint you," he concluded abruptly, so abruptly that Rue bridled, though half of fashionable London besieged Romney weekly and was turned away unpainted.

"You will come to my house in Cavendish Square to sit for me—though God knows how many years I have left, and I may not finish your likeness," he concluded gloomily.

His eyes, dark under his powdered, curled hair, looked shrewdly at her.

"I wish to work large. I feel that you will do for a subject, Rue Morgan. I sense that you wish to work large as well."

"Cavendish Square?" asked Rue. The name tasted familiar on her tongue. It had a bittersweet flavor.

"Yes, number twenty-four. The artist Cotes had it 'fore me. Now my neighbors include Lord Bessborough and the Earl of Argyle, not to omit the lovely Mrs. Nelson here."

The painter turned to the rather plainly attired woman beside him, for whom he was obviously escort of the evening. She smiled and reassured Rue, as he no doubt wished.

"It is most respectable, I promise you, Miss Morgan. A great many ladies clamor to sit for Mr. Romney, as well they should. He is the first portraitist in the land. I myself have been assured of the honor, but I must wait for the return of my husband, who is on naval duty in the Mediterranean."

"In the present wars against France, you mean?" asked Rue. "How noble—he must be a very brave man."

"He was ship captain at four-and-twenty," returned his wife proudly. "But he'd been retired from active duty until a few years past when France tired of lopping off its aristocracy's heads and declared war on us. And Horatio would not seem a brave man to you, though he is. He is very frail, his health. I fret for him so."

Her hand tightened on Romney's arm, and he patted it, his artist's broad spatulate fingers very noticeable.

"Now, my dear, he'll come home a hero, mark me. And you can drop by and watch my sitting with Miss Morgan commence. Before you know it, you'll have an oil of your own self as well."

"I'd rather have one of Horatio," she said firmly.

"My dear Mrs. Nelson, you have no vanity," said Rue, laughing. "Alas, I do. And my vanity is much polished by your interest, Mr. Romney. When would you like me to call?"

"Tuesday next? At one? I begin at my easel at eight of a morning, but I cannot ask a lady of fashion to rise before noon."

"Indeed, I am so devilishly intrigued that I might rise at midnight to see you, Mr. Romney," said Rue warmly. "I trust my sentences shall never be overlong. Good night."

She sank into a girlish demi-curtsy and swept away, having attracted a train made up of, among others, two cohorts from the Basilisk Club who had gathered around during her interview with the artist.

"A portrait by Romney, oh, you will be shamelessly famous now, Rue Morgan," drawled Addison Hookham.

"And j—j—justly so," said Sir Merivale, detecting a tang of mockery in his fellow member's voice.

"Just so," said Rue, stopping and confronting her admirers. "What think you, gentlemen? Can it do any harm?"

"No," conceded Hookham, "if Romney understand that you're not a proper married lady."

"She is not m—m—m—m—arried, but proper she will always be!" argued Fenton-Mews indignantly. "You see, Miss Morgan, you make even the hailed Emma Hamilton pale to p—p—pastel when you come on the scene. It will be a great triumph."

"Yes," said Hookham, adjusting the icy fall of his cravat. "He will undoubtably show his new subject at the Royal Academy, and your name will become as common on London streets as the call of 'crayfish'!"

"Must you always be so disagreeable, Addison?" Rue smiled, but her voice did not. "My notoriety is no concern of yours."

"No. Save I recall another project that nearly went awry."

"This one will go 'a-Rue,' I promise you, Addison. I have a plan, and I will not rely upon you gentlemen for accomplices, as you are so critical of the last time."

"Oh, please, Miss Morgan, you can rely upon me. 'Tis n—n—nothing I wouldn't do for you."

"Then keep yourself still about this sitting with Romney," said Rue, pressing her forefinger lightly to Fenton-Mews's lips.

He whitened, then reddened as she sailed away. And oddly enough, he was not heard to stutter for a full hour after that.

Addison Hookham, noting this sourly, considered to himself that the Basilisk Club could more profitably make a powder of Rue Morgan and peddle it to all London itself.

Nigel naturally did not object to Rue's appointment with George Romney. The man was third only to Gainsborough and Reynolds in popular respect, and he had the advantage of still being alive.

Sixty years old, Romney had abandoned wife and children in the country to come to town to make his fortune, although that dereliction had long since been painted over by the skilled strokes of his brush.

"In addition," said Nigel, overexplaining himself and thus becoming even more tiresome, "he is utterly, almost senilely infatuated with that Hamilton woman. He's done fully dozens of portraits of her in every conceivable fashion. What Sir William thinks of his wife's painted face staring out from every wall of the Royal Academy is beyond me.

"But one portrait shan't ruin you, Rue," he added, smiling a bit. "And I shall buy it, can Romney bear to part with it."

"Thank you, Nigel," said Rue, extending him the rare gratitude of an unbegged kiss. "I will be as good as gold, I promise you."

Alas, gold has never been known for goodness, nor for eliciting that virtue in humankind, though to be fair to Rue Morgan, her intentions were very vague and undoubtably harmless when she called at the new stone house in Cavendish Square that was number twenty-four.

There were far grander abodes on the square, she noted as she gazed across the central garden surrounded by an iron railing with the gilt equestrian statue of "Butcher" Cumberland in its center.

This rather forbidding gentleman, the lead-based Duke of Cumberland who'd massacred the Scots at Colloden Moor, faced directly toward numbers three and five, either of which was a very grand house and either of which could belong to the Earl of Argyle.

Her footman soon elicited an answer at the door, and Rue passed under George Romney's graceful fanlight into a world different from any she had ever experienced.

Romney was as formally attired as he would be for an afternoon at a coffeehouse with his fellows—black sateen waistcoat, breeches, buckled shoes, and a somewhat full, old-fashioned coat of copper brocade.

"Come along, Miss Morgan. The oils have been flowing splendidly all morning, and I am anxious to begin selecting a pose. My studio is above," he explained a bit awkwardly, "you will see why when we arrive. I assure you I am not leading you up to a gentleman's chambers. But here. What think you?"

"In short sentences, Mr. Romney? Ah, I fear I cannot please your ear and answer your question both. It would take paragraphs to adequately describe this room. May I take a turn?"

"Of course, of course. I will study your coloration as you stroll."

He picked up a palette and began mixing the colors thereon, his eyes darting from her face to the oils.

Rue rightfully ignored this painterly scrutiny and studied the chamber. It was huge, perhaps two rooms made into one. A great skylight had been cut into the roof. Rue stood under its brilliant shower of pure light and looked up.

"Two artists have lived here, hence the place is twice as suited for a studio," explained Romney. "North light, of course, facing away from the square. If the daylight is not true, the portrait will lie by candlelight. I strive to paint portraits that do not allow their subjects to lie about themselves."

Rue looked at him and smiled, but moved out of the brilliant unfiltered light from above. The room was traditionally furnished for the most part, ringed with bookshelves surmounted by white marble busts.

There was, of course, Romney's easel and a raised platform with a chair for the subject to either sit upon or lean against. Rue wandered over to acquaint herself with her setting.

"A full portrait, I think, Miss Morgan. You are not a tall woman; I can convey this better if I work in full-length."

Rue nodded. She turned to regard his finished and unfinished portraits lying about. Good gracious, a great many of the odious Hamilton indeed. Rue had never fancied that faded coloring. And her features would coarsen with age, it was already evident. Mr. Romney did indeed paint true. It was a pity he did not realize it more himself.

There were other canvases—vast, gloomy things representing the outpourings of a darkening mind, a curdling view of the milk of human kindness. And there were innumerable miniature representations of classical sculpture, including the famous Venus de Milo with her truncated arms and softly draped lower limbs only emphasizing the sweet twist of her torso.

"Yes, a pose like that," suggested Romney, "trailing a shawl perhaps to account for the movement. If you could hold it."

Rue had spun instantly into a facsimile of the posture and looked at the artist for approval. He smiled and nodded.

"Ah, you are a most tractable creature. I thought it might be so. Try this for a drape."

Rue swirled the multicolored India cloth over her shoulders, letting it swag below the snowy foothills of her fichu.

"There is a great taste for things classical now, is there not, Mr. Romney?"

"Yes, you are right. A great taste."

The artist was fussing around her attire like Heliotrope, pulling folds even here, fluffing lace there, fanning fringe more pleasingly.

"I was considering . . . Perhaps you could paint me as a classical subject."

"But, my dear Miss Morgan, what makes a subject classical is the ancient dress."

"Precisely. Why could I not wear, oh, some sort of drapery? Like a Roman matron?"

"Or Greek. There is something Greek in your hair, your facial shape."

"You see! It is a grand idea. Surely you have a suitable cloth?"

Romney dug among his many suitable cloths and finally waved forth a great length of scarlet silk.

"Precisely the thing, Mr. Romney. I shall dash behind this screen and be out in a thrice."

Several thrices elapsed before she reappeared. Romney's mouth fell quite openly open. Rue had managed to drape the fabric into graceful, body-clinging folds that met atop one shoulder and left her other arm and shoulder quite bare. That one covered shoulder was only kept so by her fingers pinching the fabric together.

"A pin! My kingdom for a pin—ah, thank you, Mr. Romney. Now have you a looking glass? What do you think?"

Rue turned slowly in the sober-framed glass Romney silently indicated across the room, one hand holding half her black curls high atop her head while the rest snaked against her shoulders.

"You look quite, quite . . . antique," agreed Romney, very quietly and very slowly. "You have an aura of the exotic that is not quite Oriental but certainly is . . ."

He stopped talking and fell into deep thought.

"I have wanted to work large," he said finally. "Perhaps on the horizontal. We will seat you on a sofa like an old Roman, that is the answer."

Within moments he had wrestled a low sofa halfway across the room to the platform under the skylight. He draped it with a rapid, expert selection of rich, solid-color silks—royal blue, plum, gold—then took Rue's hand and led her to it.

"A pillow, I think, for my back," she suggested, still adhering to admirably short sentences.

He found one, and she arranged it under the rainbow of fabrics beneath her and assumed a languorous pose. Romney stepped to his easel and assessed the effect.

"Yes, excellent, most dramatic, Miss Morgan. A bit unconventional, but then you strike me as a rather unconventional young woman. You will not mind undraping your shoulder to all London?" he asked, smiling a bit. "Or perhaps I should ask if you mind undraping your shoulder to me to begin with?"

"No, Mr. Romney, I am quite aware that your interest is purely professional as a portraitist. But I think, and you must attribute it to my unconventionality if I take overlong to say this, I think I should like my portrait to be . . . totally undraped."

"Undraped? Totally? You can't mean—"

"Nude, do we not call it in art? Though the country folk call it naked. Why do you not paint me nude?"

Romney appeared to be incapable of responding.

"Naked."

Again even short words had deserted him.

"As my Creator made me, so shall Mr. Romney remake me. It is a suitably 'large' enough commission, is it not?"

Romney carefully put down his palette on a delicate teatable.

"Miss Morgan, I have—very naturally—painted from, er, life, as we painters call it. I must know the foundations of my subjects. And it is true, a great many, ah, nude—as you say—paintings are being done today. But the models are unknown—models by profession, and often much worse by profession—for only one kind of woman drops her chemise even for the noble intention of portraying a Diana or a Venus of mythology. It is unheard of that an ordinary respectable woman should do it. I cannot permit it. I forbid it!"

He turned his back on her and stalked to his palette, picking it up and continuing to mix the ardent red, though the wood shook slightly in its balance across his forearm.

"I am not an ordinary respectable woman," said Rue quietly.

"Perhaps not." Romney's piercing eyes drilled into hers. "But the shoulder is sufficient." He resolutely glanced back down to his paints.

"I beg to differ, Mr. Romney," she returned calmly. "I really must insist on my opinion in this case. Your painting will be infinitely superior undraped."

He looked up again to argue and froze, all the color in his face oozing downward to the oils on his arm. She had undone the shoulder pin and let the red silk flow away. It lay about her in natural rumples, the bright daylight highlighting every careless fold.

Against all the colored silks, Rue's white body was lush and sensuously rounded as a calla lily, caressed by shadows no sun ever cast, liquid as milk but warmer, perfect as some excavated Greek treasure of statuary, full, high breasts, even narrower waist, firm, sleek thighs. . . .

"No," said Romney, but his voice cracked.

"Your sentences have been overlong of late, Mr. Romney," Rue teased. "That last was better, but I do not like its sense. Paint me as I am, Mr. Romney. You will not be sorry for it."

"It will cause a scandal."

"Perhaps I wish a scandal."

"It will make you notorious."

"Excellent."

"It may be blamed on me—"

"I will accept all the blame."

Romney stared quietly at his palette for a few moments,

then glanced up at Rue. She was watching him as idly and composedly as if she had been cloaked from nose to toe.

"If we are to paint you thus, you should wear nothing from your neck to your toes. That jewel—take it off."

"I always wear it," objected Rue, showing discomposure for the first time.

"It does not belong on your neck. Remove it," said Romney.

She did so reluctantly.

"But see, I can tie it around my forehead, so, and you can say it is Messalina or some other debauched Roman empress you paint. That will ease the scandal—"

"Not much."

"But will it not look well here?" insisted Rue, tilting her head at him.

The ribband across her temples did lend a kind of Medici decadence to her wicked little features, and the sapphire shone in the middle of her forehead like a Mason's third eye.

Romney nodded agreement, and Rue suddenly wriggled herself more deeply into the fabrics, tossing an arm half-folded above her head and turning her calm gaze upon him.

"You must not look directly at me or the viewer," lectured Romney.

"Why not?"

"It is improper."

Rue stared at him for a long moment. Then she broke into cascades of laughter, her gemless throat thrown back on the pillows and her merriment pealing up to make the skylight ring with the echo of it.

"Improper! Oh, Mr. Romney, you are so droll. I pray you paint me better than you argue with me."

Captain Horatio Nelson's marooned lady, needless to say, never was invited to sit in on Rue's sessions with Romney. Nor was Lady Hamilton. They worked in the artist's studio for many days, Romney often continuing after she had gone, totally converted to the vision of the project that now obsessed him.

As outrageous as Rue Morgan was, so she was beautiful. He had never had a model from life into whom he had attempted to instill the same reading of character that he put into his clothed subjects. She was fascinating clothed, he had sensed that instantly. Yet reluctantly Romney had to confess to himself that she was even more fascinating unclothed.

This was not a matter of lust. At sixty he had not entirely renounced that aspect of life, although he had subdued it for years to the demands of his profession.

No, beyond the initial shock, the artist found his involvement with the play of light across Rue Morgan, the specific swells and hollows of Rue Morgan akin to what he imagined the great artists of the Renaissance had found in their nude subjects, a reverence combined with castrated intensity of artistic interest. In her he could blend responses of mankind to a larger-than-life mythology of body and soul.

The incredible part was that whatever he chose to call his subject matter, it still remained Rue Morgan and a damned good likeness, perhaps the finest portrait he'd ever done.

He named it *Jezabel*.

"Perhaps I should not show it at the academy," he noted one day as he struggled again with the peculiar, foreboding blue of her eyes. Deep blue, strong as an angry ocean.

"I insist you show it. Apart from being the subject, I find it magnificent. Though you have flattered me."

"Ah, you think so." Romney smiled tightly.

Rue kept her glance on the distance he had instructed her to view, although she would have given much at that moment to see his expression.

"Do not play games with me, Mr. Romney. I shall move."

"It does not signify. I am finished."

"No!" Rue sat up, stood up, started over, forgetting to drape herself.

It didn't matter. Romney's eyes were totally on the massive canvas before him, his full bottom lip stretched taut with triumph, grim triumph, the victory of the exhausted.

Rue, finally decently swathed in the red silk she had lolled upon for so many weeks, rushed over. She saw herself, minutely observed until the landscape of her flesh was reproduced as emotionally as the last scene ever witnessed from the memory of a blind man.

Her face was dramatic, the sapphire and ribbon lending it a demonically ancient cast. But the likeness was perfect, even to the slight asymmetrical twist of the channel between her nose and upper lip.

Romney had diplomatically drifted a nonexistent veil between her legs, but it was transparent stuff masterfully executed, and the deep play of shadows there hinted at other, more natural shadows. It was at once revealing and concealing, realistic and romantic, disturbing and peaceful.

The red ran in a pool around the painting's pale fleshy center like some cool flame banked but ready to leap up and devour its recumbent guest.

She glanced to the artist, but he was looking only at her painted self, his eyes consuming the image with the hungry love of the creator.

Rue Morgan suddenly realized that she had given herself to Romney, that she had driven another bargain with her body, though the exchange was not so physical, so personal as was usual.

He had taken her, transferred her to the eternity of his canvas, his artistry. For the first time, Rue Morgan blushed, and she blushed until her face and chest felt scarlet-hot and she had to rustle away behind the screen and dress before she subdued that sudden onslaught of shame.

"I'm ready to leave, Mr. Romney," she said finally, gowned and hatted at the door.

But the painter was too busy possessing his image of Rue Morgan to say more than a preemptory farewell to the real Rue Morgan. She nodded to his gruff goodbye and extracted his promise to inform her when the painting should show at the Royal Academy.

Rue saw herself out for the last time, suddenly aware both that she should miss the quiet afternoons under the often overcast skies of Cavendish Square and that she was glad to be rid of them.

Perhaps *she* was the mock-life, the illusion, Rue thought, nodding absently at the lackey who let her out the front door. She paused on the steps and looked out across the formal gardens, past the statued Duke of Cumberland, across the square.

A carriage had just pulled up at number three. Two men got out and strolled into the three-story house with its central Greek pediment. But she was too distant to determine who it was.

Rue pattered down the steps and into her own carriage, up the set of stairs the footman so promptly placed before her. And then took away.

Perhaps all life was walking on steps that were whisked away the instant you had trod on them. The great trick, then, was to not look back.

Chapter Sixteen

"But what will Sir Nigel say when he sees it?"

Rue Morgan stared into the brown velvet pools hardening before her and sighed. She had kept nothing from Heliotrope, but she was beginning to be sorry. Helia did nothing of late but ask questions that Rue chose to refrain from asking herself.

"I cannot predict, Helia. He ought to be pleased."

Heliotrope sniffed almost as loudly as Piquant was prone to snort.

"Well, at the worst we shall be on our own again, Helia. And I promise you, after Romney's portrait is unveiled, we will not have to shift for ourselves for long. Next time I will not settle for some misplaced country squire dredged up by an actor growing too old to judge male flesh anymore."

"One thing I credit Rossford with—he brought you a tame enough puppy. I shudder to think of what would have happened had you settled on the likes of the earl."

It was not necessary to inquire which earl Heliotrope meant.

"Nonsense. The earl is a cub, an' he's properly handled."

"That you'll never do," said Helia. "You can't even

housebreak a puppy. Mind me, Sir Nigel will be in a tearing rage to see you bare as a bodkin in front of all London.''

'' 'Tis not I—it's a mere conglomeration of oil paint.''

"Tell that to Sir Nigel, or the earl, or any of the town bloods bleeding lust at the sight of it, Rue Morgan. You're a greater fool than your father, and that is indeed a prodigious task.''

Heliotrope finished setting a virginal arrangement of strung pearls and white ribbands in her mistress's ebony hair and stepped back from the dressing table. She shook her white-capped head.

"A lamb to the slaughter. And for once, I do not refer to Sir Nigel Paggett-Foxx!''

It must be admitted that Rue Morgan was unpleasantly visited by a flock of butterflies in the region of her midriff that September morning—such a glorious day, a London for once ballooned over by a great clear blue sky.

The crowds were out in fine fettle, strolling or riding or confined in carriages. They thronged the crowded streets and made the daily cacophony of transportation, the grind of iron wheels and creak and uproar, seem trebled this day.

Rue Morgan felt a pulse in her throat under the hanging sapphire, beating in time to the din outside Nigel's carriage. Even if her face weren't instantly recognizable thanks to Romney's artistry, the stone, her trademark, should give her away. And properly so.

Everyone would know that Black Rue Morgan, Black Harry Morgan's daughter, had stripped herself of the last vestige of respectability for the world to wonder at. How they would gossip! How her father with his secret lust for acceptance would chafe at the callus of being father to shocking, scandalous, wanton Rue Morgan.

"My dear?''

Nigel had caught one of her white-gloved hands that was working itself into a fist and held it still.

"You fret about the portrait? But you have seen it. And you said you were pleased?''

"It is an excellent likeness," Rue confessed, her eyes cast down to her hand in his. "But, Nigel, it is . . . somewhat unconventional, and I am anxious for the reaction of the town."

Thus, when the carriage drew up at the arched colonnade of Sommerset House in the Strand, Rue kept her hand in Nigel's for once and allowed him to shepherd her to the cobblestones as if she were her fragile Great Aunt Ninevah and not an agile young woman.

Crowds, predominantly subdivided into couples, were feeding into the stately stone facade, many of the women surmounted by tiny silk sunshades. Rue had thought of carrying one, but feared she would hide behind it.

Bare-faced was better, she thought, and then smiled at the expression. Rue Morgan, bare-faced and a good deal else.

She and Nigel funneled into the mobs streaming into the academy's annual exhibition. How well she had timed her sittings with Romney, how well he had timed his finished painting. . . .

The great exhibition hall was as crowded with artworks as it was people, which was saying a great deal. Under the light filtering through paned half-moons of window at the top of the lofty room with its elaborately figured plaster cornice, fully hundreds of paintings lined the towering walls willy-nilly.

Contemporary portraits stood quite literally on the heads of diaphanous nymphs riding sea horses. Soldiers on rearing chargers pointed the way to country still lifes and scenes of horses and dogs in pastoral serenity. Some paintings were tall, some squat, all were gilt framed, and these elaborate, bright perimeters jousted each other for room and attention against the solidly decked walls.

The people gathered to witness this outpouring of the fine arts were equally jammed together. Tiers in the gallery's center were occupied by folk of all description, including children who, tired, cross, and confused, simply sat there and stared up at the paintings piled upon paintings.

Around them milled the unfortunate many who had found no seat—the men's tricorn hats nodding and bowing in conversation and obstructing the paintings on lower levels across the way, the women turbaned and beplumed like some of the painted chargers depicted above them.

Rue was no less frantic than the other connoisseurs at studying the gathered works. But no autumn blaze of red flamed from the walls in quite the conflagration she had seen on Romney's great easel. No lanquid white body reclined on the overpopulated perimeters. No *Jezabel*, no Rue, no Romney.

Finally she spied on the far wall a huge horizontal blank space halfway up. She dragged Nigel over forthwith.

"Sirs! Can you tell me what hung there?" she demanded, snagging the nearest frockcoat sleeve.

The gentleman turned an annoyed face, then softened to pudding.

"Why, no, Miss. And my companions and I were here from the first. Whatever hung there appears to have been removed more recently than the general hanging, but not as recently as the exhibition opening to the public. It is a great mystery."

"Rue, calm yourself. Perhaps Romney decided not to exhibit it."

Nigel's advice rang all too true. Rue tore herself away and threaded through the crowd until she found a familiar face.

"Mr. Romney! My painting—what has happened? Is it damaged?"

"No such tragedy," said Romney, drawing her aside.

"Then it was here? There rather, where the white paneled wall gazes through as smug as a sphinx? Oh, Mr. Romney, you cannot imagine how I was counting upon that painting."

He eyed her oddly.

"No, perhaps I can't, and perhaps that's just as well. But I'm afraid you'll not see it exhibited here. I sold it."

"Sold it! You were enamored of it," accused Rue. "You

worshipped it. Why would you sell it? And before it had been shown? I cannot believe you."

Her voice had risen to combat the tumult of the crowd. Romney pulled her nearer so his next words would have a semblance of privacy.

"My dear Miss Morgan, it was mine to do with what I pleased. I can tell you I did not intend to sell it. That's why I hung it here. But a gentleman, a gentleman who insists on remaining anonymous, approached me before the exhibit opened and bought it. For a very great sum indeed, a very great sum. One I could not in reason resist. And his conditions were that it was not to be exhibited and his name was never to be mentioned in connection with it. An odd request, but he was much taken with the work, I could see that."

"Mr. Romney! You disappoint me. It was not your painting alone. I had . . . risked . . . much for it. I never dreamed you would simply sell it—"

"Ah, but, my dear Miss Morgan, this is so much better for you. It is in the hands of a private collector. Most likely he will place it where only his eyes may see it. You did not truly wish to make a spectacle of yourself for all London?"

"Yes," she replied, almost frantic with frustration. "That is precisely what I wished. Good day to you, Mr. Romney. May your paints turn to powder!"

She turned on her heel and shortly after ran directly into Nigel's arms.

"Oh, Nigel, *you* have bought it! That is it, you said you would. You approached Mr. Romney shortly after I was finished sitting and bought it as a surprise, is that not so?"

"Rue, what are you talking about?"

"My painting! My *Jezebel*. Say you have done it, Nigel, it must be you. It has to be you, or else—"

"Rue, my darling girl, you are distraught. I have bought no painting—"

"Then I must go."

"Go where?"

"To, to . . . Cavendish Square."

"To see Romney?"

"Yes, that's it. I have not been able to find Mr. Romney here to ask for an explanation. Pray stay and look for him. I will go to Cavendish Square and speak to him if he's there."

"Rue, wait," begged Nigel as she turned and dove determinedly into the mob. "Why would Romney be there? He's other paintings to exhibit here besides yours. Rue!"

But her dark head decorated with white had vanished into a blend of blond, brown, and black heads similarly tricked out.

Nigel sighed and would have put his hands on his hips in frustration, save there was no room. He would have thrust his thumbs into his waistcoat pockets, save he wore an overbuttoned frockcoat.

There were a great many other things Sir Nigel Pagett-Foxx would have done, save the Royal Academy of the Arts was not the place for plain Norfolk talk.

It was six o'clock by the time Rue had found her way past the engulfing crowds, located Sir Nigel's coach, and finally arrived at Cavendish Square. She bid the coachman stop at number three, then sat awhile inside while she contemplated her folly.

He may not be at home.

This may not even be his home.

He may not have purchased her portrait, though Rue considered this last supposition the unlikeliest of the three.

She finally allowed her footman to see her out of the carriage and up the grand marble steps to Three Cavendish Square.

"Is the earl at home?" she asked the stately lackey who answered.

"Come in, Miss Morgan," he invited, bowing aside so she could step into the cool of a marble-tiled foyer where a tall-case clock ticked against the pale paneling.

The lackey showed her down the first-floor hall, a lengthy area with several pediment-topped doors opening off it, to one near the end of the passage. The curtains had already been drawn in this room in preparation for evening. Lamps glowed on polished mahogany and marble-topped side tables.

Rue was aware of being surrounded by a Greek temple facade of book-lined walls, soft green between their expanses of gilt-stamped leather. She was aware of artificially early evening shadows and of flames flickering in lamps atop candleholders.

She was ultimately aware of the Earl of Argyle seated in a brown leather wingback chair. He appeared to be waiting for her.

"Come in, Miss Morgan," he said, and only then was Rue aware that she had stalled upon the room's threshold as if its floor were a morass she might sink into.

Rue Morgan crossed the floor, her soles sharp on the parquet, noiseless once they met the thick Oriental carpets.

"A seat?"

She would have stood, yet she felt suddenly exhausted and sank onto the offered red leather club chair, but only on the very edge of it.

The earl was dressed for an evening at home—stock and cravat billowing over the black satin edges of a mahogany-colored dressing gown, his pantaloon-clad knees crossed, and his feet encased in plain black slippers.

Beside him stood a little table, and all that was on it was an inlaid mother-of-pearl dice box, a ruby-red decanter, and two empty glasses of French crystal. Rue could not tell if one had been drunk from already this day, evening. . . .

"You look a bit ruffled. Some wine?"

Rue extended a gloved hand for the glass and sipped from it while the earl poured a vermilion stream into his own glass. He did not drink from his. Instead he tumbled the dice upon the tiny tabletop.

"A six. You once said seven was my lucky number."

"Did I? I don't recall."

He scooped the dice back into their box and offered it to her. Rue shook it methodically, then turned it out upon the rug at her feet. The pale cubes tumbled into vanishing on the figured carpet.

"You have a three," noted the earl, "and a . . . I fear you've lost the other one."

"I don't care!" said Rue. "You have my painting."

The earl set his elbows on the arms of his chair and tented his fingers before his spotless stock.

"And what if I do?"

"You don't deny it?" asked Rue, astounded.

"If you don't," said the earl, grinning. It was altogether too clear that he had most certainly seen the painting.

Rue stood, furious.

"Pray do not move. I must find the other die. The pair is my favorite. I'm sure it's a grand gesture for you to go tossing them to the winds and something an actor like Rossford would find commendable, but I must insist upon my die."

The Earl of Argyle proceeded to drop to his aristocratic knees and search for the missing cube.

Rue watched, only more amazed.

"Oh, damn your die!" she exclaimed, dropping to her own knees and feeling over the carpet with her white-gloved hands. "Your Lordship is insane, if I may say so, and I don't intend to leave until I have ascertained what you've done with my painting. And here's your bloody die, so now will you answer?"

The earl crawled over to inspect her find.

"Yes, 'tis it indeed," he noted amiably, rising and leaving Rue to shift to her feet for herself. He dropped it into the box with its fellow and turned to face her.

"I have it above. If you would care to see it . . ."

"I have seen it already," said Rue between her teeth. "I care to acquire it."

"Come up then, and we will discuss it. And take your

wine. Certain things go well together, and fine art and wine are two of them."

Rue did as he said only because the afternoon's agitation had left her temper frayed almost beyond speaking.

No servants lurked about; it was as if they had all been ordered to be unobtrusive. He led her up an impressive, wrought-iron-balustraded staircase to the second floor and down a passage as wide as a room. He finally ushered her into another deserted, lamplit chamber, walked to yet another door and paused before it apologetically.

"My dressing room. That is where it hangs."

Rue marched stiffly up to the door, waited until it swung inward, and followed close on the waning wood's arc.

The earl's dressing room was as large as her own bed-chamber and furnished much like an ordinary room. On the wall facing her, about six feet from the floor, hung Romney's *Jezabel*.

It was a great relief to see it. She realized only then that she had feared he would destroy it and that it mattered more to her than that. It was most imposing hung; she hardly identified with it at all.

Save when she thought of it in the hands of the Earl of Argyle, and then she would have wished it destroyed. Rue was confused and sipped from the wineglass clutched in her hand.

"How?" she finally asked without turning. "How did you know—guess of it?"

"My dear Miss Morgan," said the earl, coming up behind her, taking her by the shoulders, and turning her to face in the opposite direction.

"My dear Rue," he said, his lips very near her ear, "my house faces across the square directly onto Romney's. I saw a great deal of your comings and goings and guessed that he was painting you. You should have selected Thomas Lawrence for a portraitist; he resides elsewhere."

The shoulders under his hands had begun heaving, but he did not release them.

"But, but how did you guess that the painting, that the painting would be . . . Oh, why did you bother with it? You cannot have known how much I wished to confound my father, the town—why could you not have left it alone?"

"Perhaps because you could not leave me alone," suggested the earl even more softly.

He reached round her and took the wineglass from her hand, setting it atop a small marble-topped table laid out with barbering utensils. His other arm slipped across her collarbone to grasp her opposite shoulder so she should not escape, fall over. . . .

Rue Morgan hung her head, regarded the floor, and felt bitter and defeated and dead, more dead even than when she had bowed her head and looked down into an ivory moiré jewel box and seen something dark blue and tear-shaped sparkling there.

She looked up to the painting, seeing herself through a distortion glass of tears, seeing herself white, remote, and naked on a blood-red ground.

"Do you . . . like the painting?" she asked.

"I think," he answered, "that your talents lie in other directions."

His breath was warm and rifling on her cheek. His arm still held her, half-imprisoning, half-caressing. Rue Morgan stared at the portrait, and her hand groped behind her to—it fell on a sharp pair of shears atop the bureau.

Instantly recognizing them for what they were, her fingers closed upon the scissors. She wrested suddenly free and hurled herself at a console table on the opposite wall, up atop it, and then reaching for the heart of the painting, herself, to stab the sharp shut tips inward.

He was hard behind her and dragging her down by the waist even as she kicked and flailed out with her arms, with the scissors. They finally fell harmless to the carpet below, the dark red carpet with the shears lying silver and agape upon it, two blades now, not one, ready to cut.

The earl kept hold of her wrist and bent down to close

and retrieve the fallen blades. He put the shears down firmly on the marble tabletop behind him and leaned against the fluted rim so she had to pass him to regain her weapon.

"We play for the disposition of the painting, not its destruction," he said quietly. "You can't do that to Romney."

Rue massaged her released wrist distractedly, then gathered her thoughts and began pacing. Her steps never took her farther than four paces in either direction. It was as if her attention, her body were leashed to the earl's immobile figure by an invisible lead and she dare not allow herself to test its strength.

She stopped abruptly before him.

"Nigel will buy it for me. He will pay twice what you paid."

The earl smiled. "Do you know what I paid?"

"A great sum," she answered stiffly, quoting Romney.

"Yet I think you could coax twice it from Pagett-Foxx. But be reasonable, Rue Morgan. How shall you explain your, ah, rather thorough *déshabillé* to that devoted young man? He is jealous, is he not? No, you cannot use Pagett-Foxx to buy you out of this affair. Besides, you overlook the matter of cajoling the seller. I do not wish Sir Nigel Pagett-Foxx to have the painting."

The earl folded his brocaded arms stubbornly, white hands carelessly fanned against the rich fabric, his one black-souled ring regarding Rue as coldly as his eyes.

"What possible use can it have for you?" Rue demanded in exasperation.

"Ah, there is where we differ. To you, everything is a tool, every person a key to turn to this or that employment. Some things, Miss Morgan, exist for themselves alone and have an unshakable integrity."

"But you do not like the painting!"

"Because Romney gave it its integrity, not you. It is an admirable work, though the title be arbitrary. I would have called it . . . *Red Rue.*"

Rue paled, then resumed pacing, this time her hands

wringing unconsciously before her so she resembled nothing so much as Lady Macbeth in an amateur theatrical.

She came to a stop before him again.

"You have ruined me," she announced tragically.

"Some would say you played a role in that yourself," the earl noted, "but I am not one to cavil. And how, may I inquire, can I have 'ruined' you by withdrawing from the public eye a painting that puts you in a most revealing light? I would be forced to argue that I have saved you from ruining yourself."

"But I *wanted* the scandal!" she raged, hurling herself into fevered pacing again. "It was my weapon against my father. I *wanted* the name of Morgan on every lip in London. The name we share is all I have to turn against him. I hazarded all to do so, and now you have undone me, ruined me, made my humiliation pointless."

"If you will instruct me as to why it is more humiliating to have an unclothed portrait of yourself hanging in a single gentleman's dressing room than bathed in the windowlight of Sommerset House for all the world to see, I shall be grateful."

Rue's hands rose to the sides of her head, frantic, white, unfurled fans to hold her chaotic thoughts in.

"Because there my humiliation would have accomplished something, here it is simply humiliation. It was not meant for you to see, to have. You have made it something other than I intended it, you—"

She shook her head slightly, covered her mouth with one hand, and resumed pacing.

"I could have seen it daily for the trouble of obtaining a ticket to the Royal Academy," the earl pointed out.

"That price I was willing to pay, as I was willing to wager you my cameo before the gentlemen at Brooks's. It is all in the game. But you have stolen my painting and exhibit it here as a trophy of my losing throw. That is not gentlemanly of you, Your Lordship," said Rue, pausing before him again and dropping her agitated hands to her sides.

"No," he agreed. "You do not bring out the gentleman in me, Rue Morgan."

Having calmed a good deal, she sighed and began talking again in a contemplative manner, as if she in reality stood very far from the Earl of Argyle indeed.

"I imagine you do not feel very kindly toward me," she hazarded.

The earl smiled at her dropped dark head, the blue eyes peering meekly through contrite lashes.

"I was wrong about your talents for the stage; they are incomparable. But you are right. You have kept me three days in your undercellar, a prisoner in chains. It was not a pleasant experience in any respect."

"None?" she asked, coloring.

"Oh, after—" he answered casually, "but such things do not assuage what went before."

"I thought you had . . . satisfied yourself upon me by your escape."

"So did I. Until I saw *Red Rue*."

His eyes flashed upward over her head an instant. Rue's hands tightened into fists. She knew what rankled her about the earl's possession of the painting as well as he did. It gave a part of her into his perpetual keeping, a part she had wanted to dole out herself. It was the only power she recognized herself as having.

His eyes returned to her face, fresh with a sight of her in a role she never wished to play with him again, never. The painting was a weapon for him as well. It neutralized forever the lure of her body for him. It reminded them both that a lure was all her body was to her, to him.

Rue Morgan finally smiled into the Earl of Argyle's vigilant eyes.

"The earl is possessive of his pleasures," she murmured.

The earl's eyes narrowed further, smoky brown-green marshpools in a face as uncommitted as fog.

"Yes," he said calmly.

As always, he had admitted nothing but the obvious. Rue

sighed again and took a slow pace away from him. She must fall back on her shield, the truth, since her sword had failed her.

"I see I have been very wrong, Your Lordship," Rue began resignedly. "I was wrong to attempt to bargain with you, with the flesh or any other commodity. You have no use for pearls, and it has been obvious from the start that you have no use for me, even in the most traditional of manners. I have drawn you into a contest you had no wish to enter, so you have played to win. And have."

She came up to him again, very near, as if she no longer had anything to fear from such proximity, as if the game had ended and he was truly of no more use to her.

"You have spoken of integrity. I have none except in one respect, and I think you do not understand it. I hate my father. I will destroy him at any cost, do anything, use anyone. I do not wish to be diverted from this paramount objective by side struggles with you. Release me from this pointless contest with yourself, and I will tell you the truth."

The earl stared at her for a long time.

"You are asking me to hazard upon you again, Rue Morgan," he said softly.

"The terms are not the same. I will not bargain with my body with the Earl of Argyle again, I swear it. It has always been my only weapon—I table it. There is nothing remaining but the truth."

"I think you are mistaken about that," he said, "but I never had any objection to listening to you plead your case in a civilized fashion," he added dryly. "Come, Miss Morgan, here is your wine. Let us sit by the fire, and you can see if you can persuade me to see your side by the purely vocal talents of your tongue, rather than otherwise."

Rue nearly let that tongue make a tart comment upon peers of the realm who insist on a clean gaming board, then bring up past plays, but she contained herself.

The fire was banked low but welcome, for September

nights grow coolish in London's great rambling townhouses. The earl's was no exception.

Rue turned the port glass between her fingers and stared into its soothing garnet gleam. She brought it to her lips, sipped, settled her gaze upon the glowing embers on the hearth, and began.

"I told you that I hated my father. Perhaps this is not a unique condition. I only know that I have hated him from the moment I was old enough to recognize him. Fortunately this dates from after my earliest memories; Black Harry Morgan was never one to moon about the nursery."

She smiled bitterly, her eyes glancing up to the earl's but not really taking notice of him other than as her token listener.

"It has been, it has seemed, as if my father existed only to foil my every wish—for trinkets, friends, anything that might be dear to me. I cannot tell you how many times I have developed a fondness for a thing only to have it . . . plucked away from me as by a great circling black hawk."

Rue shivered slightly, though she did not know it. A silken rustle on the edge of her consciousness barely impinged on her reminiscences. The earl doffed his dressing gown and very quietly rose from his chair to lay it across her muslined shoulders.

Her hands unthinkingly drew it around her, even as the port glass tilted automatically to her lips. But her eyes were only on the embers and the hatred she bore for Black Harry Morgan.

"It continued thus, with me set upon having something, anything I could call my own and keep, though I had grown quite clever at concealing precisely what was the object of my interest."

The earl leaned his white-shirted elbows on his knees and rested his chin on his fisted hands, listening intently, his face masklike in the soft firelight.

"Helia was one of my triumphs," she said, her face softening. "And Piquant—" Her eyes flashed to the earl's, momentarily startled to find him leaning nearer than previously. Rue returned to regarding the hearth. "Piquant. Poor triumph that he was, lazy and pampered . . . And, and a certain captain in His Majesty's Seventeenth Lancers. I thought him mine, too."

She shifted back against the chair, drawing the dressing gown so close about her that only her hand holding the giant cabochon of ruby port protruded.

"Of course, my father found out. And he forbid our marrying. It was almost as if he wished to compel events . . . I was frantic. He, my captain, was the only thing outside the environs of Blackstone House I could call my own. I would not give him up; further, I determined to make sure that he should not give me up, ever . . ."

Rue came to herself and looked coldly into the waiting eyes of the Earl of Argyle.

"Nigel was not my first lover, Your Lordship," she explained simply.

The face before her registered no shock. She would not have cared if it did. She was testifying to someone, something other than the man who shared the fire warmth with her. Perhaps it was herself.

"We were lovers then, my captain and I, even if only fleetingly. We determined to announce our forthcoming nuptials at my eighteenth birthday celebration when my father assembled all his acquaintances and dependents to display his overbearing generosity to his daughter. These."

She plucked the sapphire from her throat and held it up to the earl as if he had never noticed it before and must be shown the obvious. She was being careful, Rue Morgan. She would be as meticulous in her truth as in her deceit.

The earl leaned farther forward and took the stone in his fingers. It was warm from her body. He dropped it back and adjusted it into place with his fingertip.

Rue waited until his rustlings subsided as he resumed his listener's position. She continued, very carefully choosing her words, stringing them like sapphires in her memory, linking her past and present with each facet of her recall prodded scrupulously into place.

"The sapphires are from a necklace of my late mother's, and this pendant is the keystone. Father doled them out to me each birthday, since I was three, so I should never know anything whole, but only in pieces won from him. The center stone came on my tenth birthday, for father is methodical and didn't consider how more exquisite would be the torture if he withheld it till last. I gave it to, to . . . my captain. For his watchfob. And waited for my next three birthdays, when the final three stones would come and I would have the set complete. And my freedom, I think. Somehow I always linked my freedom with the complete necklace. Silly of me, wasn't it?

"But I couldn't wait two years until my twentieth birthday. My captain was impatient. My eighteenth birthday loomed on All Saints' Eve last. We would announce our intentions publicly then, and let my father rage. He could not stop us. We met on the eve of my birthday for a final rendezvous."

Rue Morgan looked again to the earl, straight into the eyes, until his feet shifted restlessly on the carpet as if he would be off. She set the wineglass on a table.

"I saw this stone on his watchfob that night, that night when he kissed me and told me all would be well. I told him I would love him forever."

Her blue eyes looked black in the dim light, and they burned into the earl's. They dropped, those intent lupine eyes of his. Finally, for the first time, the earl dropped his eyes from those of Rue Morgan.

She neither noticed nor cared.

"He did not come, my captain, the next night. He did not come ever again. And my father was most generous at my birthday festivities. Oh, it was a grand night; all candlelit and gay. I remember being quite gay. My father gave me the traditional jewel box. I opened it,"—her hands let the gown slip while she pantomimed her actions—"looked. All the remaining sapphires, three at one throw. A third, always that unlucky third. And a fourth. This stone, this!" She yanked the pendant away from her neck again as if there were some confusion as to which gem she meant, as if someone could have failed to notice the sapphire she wore daily, nightly.

"His."

Rue's hands dropped, falling slack across her chair arms. The earl's brown brocade dressing gown slid carelessly off her shoulders in slow stages that no one moved to halt.

"I have never seen him again," said Rue, looking up from the glowing logs to the earl's lowered eyelids. There was a taut, controlled note in her voice as if her throat were being stretched on a gibbet of her own internal erection. "And never will. I did not love him forever, after all. But I think I will hate my father forever. I have my sapphires, and my freedom, and my hatred. They are a formidable combination, you will agree, Your Lordship."

The earl waited for her to break the growing silence, and when she did not, sighed, moved his chin upon his fists, and finally looked up. His eyes rose no higher than the sapphire.

"What do you think happened to your captain?"

"It does not matter," said Rue in a voice as dead as her dark-pupiled eyes. "He did not come that night. He gave up my token. It does not signify how or when or where or why. It was accomplished. And so, you see, Your Lordship, why I have no heart and why I turn what I do have left—my brain, my will, my body—to the undoing of Black Harry Morgan.

"Yet every time I had composed a devastating scheme, I turned around and there were you. Buying land, buying paintings. You cannot blame me for attempting to disarm you. I had misjudged my quarry, my weapons—this is my only fault. I do pray your forgiveness. Now let me go and be about my father's business," she finished, irony twisting her voice into something far more brittle than it had been during her recital.

"And you've never sought to discover what became of your captain?" asked the earl doggedly.

Rue shook her head violently, as if answering would be too traumatic.

"Aren't you poor-spirited in that? If you had poured half of the energies you've dissipated in your schemes of revenge into finding the fellow or what became of him—"

Rue shut her eyes, and the earl, observing it, paused.

"It doesn't signify! If he's dead, it only means that my father will not stick at anything to win over me. If he's alive and was bribed or forced ... it only means that my father will stick at nothing to foil me and that my dearest friends are my worst foes, or capable of it. Which view of the situation would you have me know, which?"

The earl let his fisted hands drop between his knees and lace together.

"I don't know, Rue Morgan, which can you live better on tomorrow?"

"Neither! But that is my rue, not yours."

The earl stood, looking a bit ghostlike in the lampflicker, white silk shirt glowing eerily ivory, his hands on his buff-trousered hips.

"And if I gave you back your painting?"

She looked up, as white a figure in her summer muslin amid the ebbed circle of his dressing gown as Romney had painted her on the vibrant red.

"I do not think it signifies any longer, no more than my captain does. You have taught me again the same lesson that my father did. That all my schemes are hollow, my dreams dust. Keep what Romney painted of me, Your Lordship. I think it is more of me than anyone will ever have, even myself."

The earl reached down to capture the pendant again, letting the dark sparkle twist in his fingertips.

"No wonder I never cared for this. I always sensed it was from a bargain with the Devil. What," he asked softly, still turning the stone in his hand, "was his name?"

"The Devil?" asked Rue lightly, but her voice was low and very taut.

"Your captain."

It was the hardest thing he had ever asked of her. But she had promised the truth, the entire truth and nothing but the truth.

"Graham. Graham Winthrop."

The name fairly creaked from her lips. She already felt she spoke from the Eden of her existence, and that what she dwelled in now was as distant from that time as she was from her mother Eve.

Her questioner seemed reluctant to release the sapphire, the pull of it in his fingers strained against the back of her neck. Without thinking, she rose, and he drew the gemstone nearer his scrutiny. He finally looked to her eyes, his mouth a grim line and his eyes, his eyes something very different than they had ever been before.

"I will be your ally, Rue Morgan, because you have told the truth and because, as I have told the truth before, you are a bold and promising wench. But I do not like this trinket, and you need not wear it with me."

He lifted the hair at the nape of her neck and slowly leaned around her, pressing his lips to the bow riding there before he untied it with one pull and caught the sapphire in his other palm as it plunged toward her breasts.

Rue went hot, then cold, then something in between that was neither. She felt more exposed than she was in her portrait.

"But you said that was done between us, that we would fence no more with our bodies, that you would not accept my bargains any longer," objected Rue, her words not stopping the earl at all as he bent to retrieve the dressing gown from the chair behind her and drape it over her shoulders so caressingly that she felt he was taking it away rather than the opposite.

He used the garment to draw her nearer.

"This is no bargain," he said. "You must learn the difference."

"But I would never have told you what I did, had I thought we were to continue as we began. I have disarmed myself utterly because I thought you uninterested in continuing any . . . contest between us. I have nothing left that is mine!"

"Then you must become mine," he said, drawing her face to his and kissing her once lightly, briefly on the mouth. "Continue your arguments, my dear Rue. I would not be accused of gagging you," said the earl, dropping his lips to her neck and making a soft circlet of kisses around it.

The earl continued necklacing her with kisses as if to compensate for her bitter sapphires, as if to replace cold stone with warm flesh and somehow melt the stone that was her heart.

Rue let her head fall back and her eyes rest on the pale, plastered ceiling. There was no rune written there; no ruin either. The earl's attentions were oddly unimpassioned, soft, insistent, meticulously mapped across her skin as if he intended to lay siege to every inch of her and was in no haste to make the tour.

Perhaps he means only to kiss me to death, thought Rue, as his incursions marched up the side of her neck to her cheek, and her sideways glance saw only the close dark horizontal lines of his brows, lashes, and the straight, strong diagonal of his nose, his face so near her own. He meant a platonic partnership, the earl, all gallantry and no. . . .

His lips found her ear, his lips and then his tongue, plunging suddenly, filling her utterly with the warmth of his possession, telling her more forcefully than words what he wished of her, where he wished it of her, how. . . .

Rue sagged against the earl's shirtfront, her heart pounding so fitfully she felt it wished to leap into the chest she was pressed against, her weight hinging on the bar of his arm across her back. She felt already sated, as if their climax had been reached, not merely begun.

His lips remained at her ear, moving against it, so she thought she felt, rather than heard, his words.

"Dear Rue, I'll have to take you through my dressing room. Close your eyes if you wish."

She was not even aware of being hoisted horizontal into his arms, but there she was. She laid her head on his shoulder, shut her eyes, and felt herself ride to his motion like a ship. Passing through, passing—no.

She, like Psyche, would look. What a cold, haughty creature she was, the painted Rue. All Olympian white, a Venus of marble. Rue was astonished at the distance she felt from the layered, lifelike oils that were her facsimile.

He caught her peeking and stopped to regard the painting himself.

"An admirable likeness in many respects. My man, Welles, must have thought so as well. He nicked me thrice this afternoon," the earl said, laughing down at her.

She only brought her palm up to his face and stroked it lightly—hardly a passionate gesture, but the earl must have read something wonderful in it, for his face grew serious and soft simultaneously.

He walked on into the next room, not looking at her again until he had let her gently to her feet. She leaned against him while his fingers found and pulled out the laces at her back. He suddenly realized that her hands were still gloved, and made her sit on the bed's edge while he went on one knee before her and worked the long, tight kid sheaths off her arms, finger by finger.

Then he kissed her bare fingers and her wrists, her arms, like an attendant enamored of a tiny charge in the nursery, a gentle, thorough kind of doting that would have been ludicrous had his eyes not been so serious when they rested on her face, had the heart she did not have not ached at each new touch or at each interval between each touch. Rue Morgan did not know what she felt anymore, excess or absence, or a more tantalizing blend of the two.

He pulled her to her feet again to let her lean against him

while his determined fingers undid the efficiencies of Heliotrope, and he worked her loosened gown and corset and petticoats slowly to her feet.

Rue felt the passive revelation of her skin press first, shoulders and breasts, against the thin silken barrier of his shirt, then naked hip pressed against rougher breeches, calf brushing hose-sheened calf.

Barely had the final fold of her gown rustled to rest at her feet than he caught her close, almost lifting her off her feet, and kissed her on the mouth. Rue kicked her low-heeled slippers off in turn as her weight hung suspended from his shoulders, his lips, his tongue. She felt like a clapper in a great bell hanging in the heavens, being rung until the vibration of it pulsed throughout her body.

She was as naked to him as her portrait, barer than she had been before Romney himself, and she was not afraid, though she could not say why. It was as if in throwing everything to the winds, she rode them. Or they her. She pressed nearer, wanting the warmth, throb, solidity of him, her fingers roaming his shirted chest for what she had once forced herself to and now recalled and longed for, the dark geography of his body hair, the island of a nipple rising in her mouth. . . .

He pushed her away and sat her again on the bed, bending to pull off her knee-length white hose, the only article of clothing that remained to her. Then he knelt before her and would not lift his mouth or eyes above the level of her throat. He bent to her breasts until his mouth had raised hard gemstones at the summit of each in turn, then refined his discovery with his mouth, always warm and wet, sometimes piercingly sharp. His hands pushed her back while his head traveled to her waist where his tongue whispered warmly to her navel and extended many promissory demonstrations of an adeptness he would display in other parts with other things.

Rue tossed upon the waves of her own surrender. There was no longer a question of pride or purpose at stake, only the earl's inescapable intention to make love to her until she died of bliss. She had decided she was very nearly there when his mouth kissed its way across her taut belly to the soft, dark Vandyke of hair between her legs.

Those legs clamped shut; she felt the same awkward, puzzling dampness as she had on the last occasion with him. She had to hide it, or it would ruin everything. She felt embarrassed by her body, its eternal leaking at the wrong moment, like oils that would never dry.

He looked up. She saw his dark hair and lighter eyes, the lower half of his face flat against her. To see him at all she had to traverse the horizontal white lines of her own body, had to see where he had been with his eyes, mouth, hands, had to know she had become his because he was willing to give so much of himself to her.

The earl lowered his eyes, his face to her. Rue threw her head back against the linens and let her lips part in pleasure while all the promised warmth and wetness and probing flesh that was the earl entered her. Her hips became as eager to claim his mouth as her face had been. She felt his tongue make good the promise to her ear by driving into her and, if not getting far, repeating the procedure again and again.

Rue writhed on the linens, half-senseless, and paused startled to find his face parallel to her own, his mouth honing on her abandoned, aching lips. Yet still, elsewhere . . . She frowned and lazily traced the long white line of his arm down her body to where it vanished between her thighs. She felt her flesh tighten soft and warm upon something hard and long of his, and was content. She brought her glance back to his face and waiting eyes.

Her hands began untying his stock, pulling free his shirt, slipping off the subtle buttons of his breeches now pulled so taut it was doubly difficult to undo them and she had to wrestle with the fabric. She smiled, and his eyelids dipped in pleasure as he pressed his mouth to hers and probed luxuriously with his tongue. Rue felt silk wash away before her inventive hands. She felt the wolfish fur of his chest, the hard, deep warmth of him, aggressive nipples hungry for hands if her mouth was occupied elsewhere as he should know it was. She tugged at the buttons, exaggerating the motions so what they guarded should grow harder, more impatient. Below, his fingers strummed a pizzicato tune, and Rue, awash in exterior and interior warmth, felt herself strung taut in expectation of the crescendo of her lover's body.

Suddenly everything withdrew from her, everywhere at once. Beached, Rue gasped, her eyes flying open into the face hanging mere inches away from her own. His face was blazing, but his eyes were dreamy, gentle, his mouth permanently blurred to accommodate some secret part of her.

His fingers had returned from their deep exploration of her boundaries and teased lightly across her face very near her mouth.

She felt empty, deserted, defrauded, ready to shatter at the withdrawal of all his various parts that one might call himself. His eyes on her seemed to guess this, and his fingers circled lightly ever nearer her lips.

"Rue Morgan," he whispered, "Rue Morgan. Black Rue, Red Rue ..."

Her eyes questioned him desperately, her body beginning to shiver from the removal of an intoxicant so near still, so puzzlingly near but absent.

"Say my name," he said, his glance lowered to watch her mouth and her mouth only.

His forefinger had found a sensitive path along her upper lip from the center bow to the corner, and this he traced as lightly as a butterfly's wing fanning quite slowly again and again.

"My name," he insisted, quite coldly, quite cruelly.

She writhed under his single caress and hoped he would capitulate to her obvious excitement and smother her with his body again. But the finger persisted in its rhythmic, tortuous strokes, a pendulum of flesh swinging eternally to the rhythm of her balked desire.

"The Earl of Argyle wishes to be possessed by his pleasures," she finally said softly against his finger, wishing its motion would become forward rather than unceasingly lateral.

The motion stopped, his face hovered nearer. Then the finger swung even more lightly, more delicately, more lovingly along the line of her lip as if he were painting her on the most dainty of chinas.

"My name," he breathed.

Her eyes shut. She felt attached to the world only by his single irritatingly maddening touch. All her senses, her tensions were suspended at fever pitch, even now she could feel them begin to ebb away, leaving more and more of her islanded, alone.

She knew it, had always known it, could not even claim to herself that it had ever lingered at the back of her mind. It had always been on the tip of her tongue, though it was hard to say, very very arduous to articulate.

Her lips moved slightly, voicelessly. His eyes focused on them again, but she watched only the shadow of his lashes on his very sharp cheekbones.

"Varian," she said, each latter syllable falling as reluctantly as the first from her stiff lips, her frozen, painted lips that he would look at and not touch.

His eyes flew to hers for the merest instant, then his mouth was on hers. His body had breached her below, hard and fast, and she rocked in the whirlwind of his being, having, wanting, winning, tumbling, like the dice down an endless corridor of time, her die-mate rolling with her, grinding into her, overturning madly. She could finally begin to distinguish sensation again, separate the strands of his possession one from another. He drove at her from two directions, above and below. He was as bilingual in an active sense as she was in a passive one. His two tongues tunneled her, spread in her until she felt they should meet in her middle. Each thrust from below drove deeper, nearer to contact with its companion probe from above. She was a circle, as he was, and they whirled round and round, melting into one another until, until—Rue tautened, recognizing a precipice she had visited once before with him, only it was many times higher now and she was confused, caught as she was in the pressure, heat, and swirl that was him, her, them.

She tautened on every part of him within her, without her, and then plunged. This time was no matter of wafting slowly down, limpid as a leaf. This time was unbridled plummet, her stomach churning with dizzying sensations, her mouth jerking spasmodically away from his at last so she could throw her head back and howl into the place, the remote, faraway place where she ruled all she felt, so she could cry his name as she spiraled into sweet, drenching oblivion, into the possession of pleasure that was all hers because it was all his.

Rue Morgan came to herself to find that naked, helpless self in Varian Temple's arms. He was rocking her and laughing and saying her name over and over. And she was laughing, she thought, crying against his warm and fuzzy chest, and whispering his name as if it were the most fascinating set of syllables in the entire British empire.

Black Rue Morgan, for the first and only time in her young life, had finally taken a lover.

Chapter Seventeen

The Earl of Argyle did not contact her the next day. Nor did he attempt to call upon her, write her, or by any other means communicate with her the following day.

Nor the third.

Rue Morgan paced her rooms in Grosvenor Square, refusing food, refusing Nigel, pausing only every once in a while to stoop, throw her arms around the dozing Piquant, cradle her cheek on the rippling blond fur, and stare black-pupiled into the distance.

Her state was very different from what it had been when she had returned alone from her jaunt to the Royal Academy exhibition.

"Well?" demanded Heliotrope, for she knew what was at stake and that Sir Nigel had arrived at home alone hours before and gone directly to the port decanter in the library. Heliotrope had taken the liberty of bringing him a fresh bottle, amply dosed with the brown liquid.

"My painting was not exhibited," said Rue absently, sitting at her dressing table and pulling the ribbands out of her rumpled black locks. She leaned nearer her image and studied it fondly, her blue eyes unfocused and dreamy.

"You act as if you had a magic mirror and saw your future in it. I've not gone to the trouble of drugging Sir Nigel to get so little information out of you. What happened?"

"I told you, my painting was purchased."

"By whom?"

"His Lordship, the Earl of Argyle."

"Him again," noted Helia grimly. "No doubt you are most displeased about it, but it cannot be helped. I beg you put an end to this and leave it be."

"But of course I shall, Helia. I would not dream of interfering with His Lordship's tastes in the fine arts. I am most honored that the earl should wish to hang me in his dressing room."

"This is an out-of-key tune for you," said Helia suspiciously. "And how do you know *where* it hangs?"

"Because I have seen it. Because he desires it. Because he desires me, and I have seen that, too," said Rue in a veritable fountain of confidences, cheeks glowing, eyes shining brighter than the sapphire once again outposted on her neck.

Heliotrope drew back, shocked. She slowly sank beside her mistress on the dressing-table stool.

"The earl? You have become enamored of the earl?"

"His name is Var-i-an, Varian Temple," said Rue dotingly. "And he is as enamored of me as I of him—mark it, Helia." She caught up the maid's hands, threw herself upon the kerchiefed neck, and hung there a long while, part laughing, part crying.

Helia patted the muslined back awkwardly at this unprecedented display of affection.

"And a most forward example he sets you," the maid finally observed. "But you are sure of this? You have played hard with him before; he is not one to roll over easily."

"Ah, it was me he was more interested in having roll over, Helia. Don't scowl, I am jaded, I admit. But I have been taught by a master." She untied her sapphire.

"Here, put this in a box with its fellows, I have tired of it."

Heliotrope, who had never approved of Rue's obsession with her two-edged token, let it fall to her pink palm, speechless. This new indifference was even more dangerous than the former insistence. But she put away the gem and came back to disrobe her mistress.

Rue waved her away. It was as though she were still oversensitive from a lover's touch and would have no hands but his or her own drawing off her clothing.

Helia left, shaking her curlicued black head and inserting a worried ridge between her brows for the first time in her unrippled life.

After she'd gone, Rue left her bed to fetch Piquant, an exception to a long-standing rule. While the aging Pekinese snored loudly at Rue's feet, its mistress tossed upon her innocent linens and peopled her bed with an entire roomful of Varian Temples, each of them engaged in a thrilling but forbidden tender assault upon Black Rue Morgan, and each of them as welcome as their original.

It was, therefore, disaster when Varian Temple didn't pursue Rue Morgan in person.

The first day she was euphoric till noon. Then she expected some token, a billet-doux.

It never came.

By nightfall she was so anxious she retired early, only to pace her bedchamber in tight circles of four steps one way, four another. No one leaned against a marble-topped table to watch her, and her pacings grew longer.

Heliotrope danced in front of Nigel at the bedchamber door and pled illness on behalf of her mistress while his worried eyes darted over the restraining arm to Rue.

"Is it the damned painting, my love? Romney was there, after all. I found him, and he says he sold it to an anonymous collector."

If comfort these words were, they only caused Rue Morgan to pause and direct a venomous look at her hapless squire.

"Anonymous! You know what that means, Rue?" continued Nigel over Helia's shoulder, trying to put a good countenance on it. "It's probably the Prince of Wales himself! Who else would conceal his interest in a portrait of someone else's lady?"

Here Rue hurled herself face first across the bed.

"I'll see you in the morning, Rue," promised Nigel, only drawing more despair from Rue's huddled form.

Heliotrope came over to curl her hands around the hunched shoulders.

"It was only last evening. It is too soon."

"Yes, of course. He would not wish to stir suspicion," said Rue, raising a face already alarmingly wet. "He is most considerate in those matters."

But the earl appeared not to be most considerate at all. The next day no word came, nor the next.

Rue had stopped eating the second day and took up the hobby again the third, her demeanor all frozen over into the old ice, her eyes frigid, her expectations as arctic as her aspect.

Now Heliotrope's assurances fell on cold ears.

"Hush. I do not wish to hear of it. Nor of the earl. And keep Nigel from me, Helia, I beg you. I could not . . . bear it."

When Heliotrope stopped by Rue's sitting room for the eighth time that day, even as London's foggy twilight dampened all the rolling fields and fastidious gardens beyond Grosvenor Square, Rue lifted dry blue eyes and simply shook her head before the woman could speak.

"But—"

"Say nothing. Nothing. I wish you had never heard me speak such fairy tales."

Rue had taken out her sapphires and was engaged in laying them out on the dressing tabletop like cards. Four were missing, tokens for Black Harry Morgan. Two for the dismantling of his crimping house, two for his ready buying of the "Afridisiac," a totally worthless substance he was now manufacturing in mammoth quantities in what he believed to be a secret factory in Southwark. Rue was profligate in her vengeance.

And the center stone. Rue picked it up, rubbed it between her fingers until she smudged the refractive surface. She cleaned the clouded facets on the hem of her wrapper a moment later; she had determined not to wear it again. Now, now it didn't matter. She had no one to not wear it for.

Helia's hands had come to rest on her shoulders, wordlessly requiring attention. Rue looked up wearily to her maid's eyes in the tilted mirror. From such an angle, Helia appeared vaguely sinister, a remote black force staring haughtily down at her.

"He's here," said Helia. "That is what I've been trying to tell you."

Rue started. "He? Who?"

"Your late earl," continued Helia very calmly as if her matter-of-factness could stifle any hysteria on Rue's part.

Rue turned, stunned. "Where?"

"Below. Pacing the hall in his muddy boots under the watch of the house-steward. It appears the earl feels it is as unnecessary to dress when calling upon you as it is to forewarn you of his coming."

"Helia, stop!"

Rue considered, her hand at her forehead fanned over her eyes as if some light burned around her that was too bright to regard.

Yesterday his silence would not have mattered; the day before it meant nothing. Today it meant everything. Three days without word, three days which said more succinctly than any words: You do not signify to me, are worth not even the flick of my quill, the merest passing of a commemorative gesture through my mind. And still Rue stood pale and distracted.

"Quick, Helia. Nigel. The sleeping potion. Dose his chocolate. And show up the earl instantly. Instantly I tell you!"

Rue paced back and forth until her filmy gown flowed in swirls of motion that met themselves coming and going as she turned in tighter and tighter circles.

Fetching the earl was a task that took little time. He was at her sitting-room door in moments, Helia behind him, muddy-booted indeed. Rue paused, and all her draperies drifted into statuesque stillness around her.

She observed his brown leather breeches, dusted to buff from the roads, and his handsome, high-collared frockcoat, equally powdered. The wind had carved his features into his face, had barbered his hair. The Earl of Argyle looked as though he had spent the past three days in the hands of a demon barber mad for powder, dusting it about with a liberal hand.

"Your Lordship," she said, aware that the polite phrase had never been less descriptive.

He didn't waste time on preliminaries.

"I have found Graham Winthrop," he said sharply, watching Rue seem to freeze even more than she already had.

"Oh, God," she said, and the earl stepped forward and had her by the elbow even as she appeared to be wavering into the insubstantiality of her gown, all limp trembling stuff pooling on the floor.

He pushed her onto the nearest chair, a slender side seat near the door that with its mate bracketed a narrow, marble-topped table.

"I think some wine," he said over his distressingly dusty shoulder to Helia.

Heliotrope had a brimming goblet of red at the table in an instant. The earl handed it to Rue and watched to see her hold it securely in both hands and sip from it. His glance left her long enough to cross Helia's.

The woman extended a second glass to him, and the earl let a smile quirk the corners of his mouth.

"You are a treasure of intuition, Heliotrope," he said, taking the glass and draining it. He set it down sharply on the marble; it had served and was no more to be savored.

"How? Where?" said Rue, leaning her head against the painted paneling behind her.

Now the earl paced in front of her with long, abrupt steps that jolted the dust off his knee-high boots and his breeches.

"Shropshire. It was his family seat."

"Yes, I know. He often spoke of being suited for a gentleman farmer and no more. But his late parents had fancied him in military red, and once the war with France was on—"

"He is no longer with the Seventeenth Lancers. That is the first place I looked. He evidently left London as hastily as you left your father's house."

Rue shut her eyes. She heard the rustle of the earl's frockcoat, but knew he had not moved nearer her. She considered whether she were curious enough to open her eyes and decided not. After a long while, though, she did.

A full moon of gold hung before her on a chain. A battered moon, its countenance shadowed, creased, bruised. The earl let the trinket sway before her as if he were a mesmerist. He let every scar and ridge upon the shining surface crease itself into her brain, her eyes.

"Your captain, he was handsome?" he asked.

Rue finally tore her eyes away from the shattered timepiece. She finally let them rest full on the earl's own round, foggy green eyes, dark and mysterious as bogs somehow. Marsh-eyes. Dangerous. Painful.

"Was—? Yes, he was—all that."

The earl swung the timepiece nearer. She finally put the wineglass on the table and took it in her palms, her fingers exploring the minute valleys in the engraved gold.

"He's no longer with the Seventeenth Lancers."

The earl paced a long stride away, thought better of it, and drew up beside her. He glanced to Heliotrope loitering a few feet away.

"Your father had him beaten to a pulp, Rue," he began in

the coldly mechanical voice in which he had once dismissed her suit for his alliance. Item, item, item, it came again, the revelations of his discoveries.

"He had him beaten by two of his crimping house bullies and dumped on the barrack's steps after." Item: "Graham Winthrop could not attend your birthday celebration—he was half-dead." Item: "He had lost more than your token, Rue. He lost the sight of one eye, and his face . . . his face is as seamed as his timepiece there. He lives in Shropshire and no longer smokes a pipe because his broken ribs punctured his lung and the doctors very nearly despaired of him. Even now they do not expect him to live very long. I do not think Graham Winthrop cares about even that any longer. He gave me that watch as a token for you in return for the one of yours he had surrendered. He says his time is worth nothing to him any more. He trusts it may mean more to you."

Rue Morgan brought her hands to her mouth, clenched fingers through which could be glimpsed the phantom glitter of gold. She bowed her face to her hands and then both to the adjacent marble, laying herself flat along its cold, clean gray surface and letting her hard, deep sobs break against it.

She stretched one fist out far along the table, the earl had to quickly snatch her glass away lest she overturn it. Graham Winthrop's pocket watch was clutched tight in her palm. It seemed she sought to thrust it as far away from herself as possible, yet could not release it, could never release its hold upon her.

The earl put his hand to her hair. "Weep," he said, sounding like a physician offering a remedy, "weep all you can for Graham Winthrop."

The earl sighed and looked abruptly to Helia. They stared at each other a long moment, and something in the dark woman's eyes finally softened. She picked up the earl's empty glass, refilled it, and brought it to him wordlessly.

Helia was a servant who served only if she wished. The earl acknowledged her good will with an almost imperceptible nod, then sat on the light chair at the other table end from Rue, stretching his legs slackly on carpet and letting his own head roll back against the supporting paneling.

He waited, every so often bringing the wine to his lips and sipping, every so often glancing to Heliotrope, who had seated herself on a nearby settee, keeping watch with him.

Rue's sobs continued for a long while. The earl's glass was again empty, and he occupied himself with spinning the Venetian stem between his fingers. She was finally silent, but her head remained buried on her arm folded across the table. Helia rose, fetched a handkerchief, and thrust it into Rue's loosely curled fist, then sat again.

After a long while, Rue turned her face out toward the room, her cheek flat upon the marble slick with her tears. She raised her head a bit to see the long grayish slab of marble, like a tombstone stretching before her, and an empty goblet at its end catching the room's candlelight, and a rather disheveled earl still sitting across from her, profile tilted upward to the ceiling, his eyelids lowered, his face as distant and beautiful as a cameo's.

"Varian," she said, her voice thick and unlovely, as swollen as Colonel Trumbull's when he'd endured a sneezing fit. "Varian, is that where you've been? To find Graham for me?"

He turned his head, very slowly rolling it against the paneling. "And for myself."

There was a long pause while they regarded each other, and during it, Helia rose with a stately satisfied rustle, like a bedside watcher who has seen a fever broken, and left the room, shutting the door to the passage behind her very softly and carefully.

"Why did you not t—t—tell me?" said Rue, feeling tears flooding again, angry at sounding like Fenton-Mews at his most bashful. "Or leave word . . . ?"

"I didn't know what I would find. Or whether I would tell you of it if I did discover anything."

Rue sat up and applied the lace-edged lawn between her fingers to her cheeks.

"You have taken great liberties with my life, Your Lordship."

"Yes," he said.

She attempted to open the watch and found the mechanism operative, if rusty. She studied the time to which the hands as narrow as a hair pointed. Noon. Or midnight. Twelve of the clock. Mid-anything. Perhaps even mid-future.

"What made you decide to bring me this news?"

"It is necessary to mourn," he said, his voice expressionless.

He stretched his own arm across the table, his right arm, the dark brown frockcoat material brocaded with dust.

"You have driven far."

"And fast," he admitted. "I also took the liberty of having your groomsmen rub down my blacks."

"In a perch phaeton?" Rue asked, smiling a bit wanly. "I trust you encountered no highwaymen."

"Only of the heart," he said, spreading his fingers on the marble. "You may have noticed my token. You are not the only one to hide old wounds with new gems, Rue Morgan."

She studied the great dark oval on his third finger. Of course, she had never thought it before! A mourning ring. She brought a fingertip hovering above it to touch it, her eyes flicking to his for permission.

He was impassive, and she finally let her finger trace the ridge of bordering pearls as regular as a rouleau around the large oval. Then her finger moved inward and found the intaglio, a Grecian urn with a spray of black flowers, all engraved from shiny black onyx.

And below it, a motto, a legend. She leaned forward to read it as if it were a particularly teasing roll of the dice. "Anno Domini 1780." No, not "Anno." "Anne."

She looked up to the earl, alarm pounding in her breast,

knowing suddenly why he had torn across half the length of England to chase the will-o'-the-wisp of a name.

"Anne," she said, no inquiry implied in her tone, but her eyes all question.

His hand balled into a fist on the marble, whitening and drawing the stone but darker across it by contrast.

"Anne. My sister."

He looked up then, and she saw him feed on the relief in her eyes and knew that if they had not been discussing such painful memories, the Earl of Argyle would not be too fatigued from his exertions to engage in other, more rewarding efforts.

"My sister Anne." His fingertip traced the intaglio as men sometimes do the scars of wounds from past wars.

"She was seven years older than I. My lucky number you called it once. Seven. When a boy is twelve and his only sister is nineteen, that is a significant difference. She was a great beauty, like you, only I was too young to see it. She was my sister, and her eyes were gray as the mist above the Welsh valley, her hair as yellow as mustard in Farmer Smith's field. Fair, she was fair, though she powdered her hair white as was the fashion then. A dazzler, they called her in London. I didn't know, I had not been there, and was to tour the Continent before I was finally to become acquainted with my own capital city with its pleasures and vices and dices . . .

"Our parents died early, and since the children born between us had been carried off by one disease or another, we relied a great deal on each other, Anne and I. But then she turned eighteen, and various of my well-intentioned aunts—it is marvelous how elder relatives have a way of living on, and one's own generation fades away like the dandelion at the summer's end—my generous aunts had to have her in wicked London town for a Season, and then another.

"The object was to marry her off well since she had no

parents to accomplish it. Somehow while here, she met and became enamored of your father."

Rue stood, her disbelief so patent it hit him in an almost physical wave.

The earl laughed softly, bitterly and rolled his head to face the ceiling.

"I know. Sometimes I think the part of my sister Anne that I have most lost is that which would allow her to entertain such an uncharacteristic passion. Perhaps he was younger then, Black Harry. Perhaps he could muster a certain crude charm with the ladies. I don't know. I have asked myself a hundred times, a thousand." His eyes rolled again to her. "As I must now spend the rest of my life asking myself how such a man could have spawned you, Rue Morgan, and how I could find myself so taken with the product of his poisonous loins."

She bowed her head, for that was a question that she found hard to live with herself. He was her father and she hated him, and so turned the sharp edge of her loathing inevitably upon herself.

"Anne somehow then found herself under Morgan's spell. She capitulated to it, as you did to your captain, only to find herself with child by him. That, at least, is what the physicians surmise. For she killed herself, took laudanum until her mind peeled away from her in one foggy layer after another. She died young, as I think a part of me did."

Rue came and stood by him so he could look at her without moving his head, which seemed to be more and more heavily anchored on the paneling, the wood buoying him up as water sometimes seems to so play with a drowning man.

"You say your nursery days were free of your father," he said, taking one of her hands. "Mine were not. You would have been only the smallest child then, but I was a lad of twelve. We have a country house in Lancashire, we Earls of Argyle, did you know that? It is a very lovely place. My late father had Capability Brown design the landscape—all artificial cascades and hidden valleys and Chinese bridges with white marble orangeries rising from groves around crumbling gothic ruins and shell-lined pavilions. Anne haunted every ruin, and I spent months with my father's sword and my uncle Hammond's pistol, slashing the boughs off the yews, blasting bark from the elms, in short, hacking away at fifty years' of the most carefully constructed natural chaos to practice wreaking my vengeance on Black Harry Morgan."

"But you never—?"

"No. My well-meaning aunts again intervened and sent me on the grand tour. I agreed only because I wished to study fencing in Italy from the master Ceravelli. And I did that, and saw the great ruins of antiquity and withheld myself from taking practice shots at them with my Paris pistols, then returned to find that the age of duels had passed into the age of umbrellas, that powder and poltroonry were equally out of fashion, and that I was the sixth Earl of Argyle and had obligations other than blowing off the head or skewering the heart of a rather insignificant upstart called Black Harry Morgan."

He held his hand before his face, fingers fanned. "I had it made in Florence, this ring, possibly because by then I realized that I needed a momento of a woman who had died before her time, and of a man who has lived past his own.

"So I contented myself with driving your father before the stinging whip of my unconquerable luck whenever I spied him at a gaming table. It was no accident I bought his wished-for lands; that, too, I did deliberately, knowing it would checkmate his greed. But I also did it because it was a good investment for the sixth Earl of Argyle and would bring enough returns to keep the gardens at Hallowmere House in fine repair from the onslaughts of that boy of twelve.

"I think your father always guessed my enmity; perhaps I overestimate him or myself. At any rate, when his ravenhaired daughter appeared at Brooks's and flourished her fichu at me, I was not inclined to take her at face value—"

"You did," said Rue, smiling suddenly. "You took great advantage of her great folly. Was that, too, revenge upon her father?"

"No," he said simply, "it was revenge upon Rue Morgan."

He stood, caught her shoulders, and stared a long while into her face, which paralleled itself to his as if magnetized.

"Varian," said Rue, using his name like a token because she knew that no oiled simulacrum of herself could lessen one whit her own power over him now that she had recognized his power over her. "Varian, we will have one last, joint hazard against my father. We have reason, God knows, now that I know of your sister, and you know what became of Graham."

"I discovered that for you, Rue," he objected, "not only myself. To give you peace so you could forgive—"

"Forgive? I do not forgive easily. The wrong rides as deep. Graham Winthrop may only see the world with one eye now, but I still see it with two. I still see him winking out from my life like a base-formed candle . . ."

" 'Tis not the man's fault," Varian said. "If you had seen him as I—He had no conception the world raised such vipers as your father to human height. He has lost more than you by this. Pity him."

"I cannot!" Rue stepped away and paced to the dressing-room door. "But I thank him for allowing his misery to rekindle my plans against my father. You will have your fatal run at him, Varian, through me."

"You have thought of something?"

"Yes. There is one source of my father's wealth that is greater than all others, except his income from the Barbados plantation. His ships, his merchant fleet. Half the sailors in it are crimping-house wretches aboard unwilling. It is a great weakness to rely so upon those who hate one. We must find a chink in his scales, Varian. And this time we do not need the offices of the Basilisk Club."

"You are set upon another tilt at your father?"

"Yes."

The earl rubbed his jaw, dark and prickly from three untended days on the roads. He stepped over to Rue Morgan.

"Very well. Nothing simpler. I've contacts in Paris. We need merely determine through the list at Lloyd's Coffee House where your father's ships sail and when, and pass on this information to the French. They will pluck off your father's armada like ducks oil-bound to the reeds. The sailors will not spill British blood for your father, even if it means a French prison. And the French will be grateful of the cargo, though it will do little to advance their hostilities against us. It will be what is judged a moral victory, which means that it does great harm to no one and inflates the Frenchies' already high-risen opinions of themselves."

"It is a brilliant plan, Varian. Why have you not thought of it before?" Rue curled her hands into the lapels of his frockcoat, then brushed lightly at the dust.

"I did not need to extract my revenge on a grand scale before I met you," he replied. "Madame Admiral."

"Is there nothing else you have learned to commit to on a grand scale since meeting me?" Rue asked, tilting her face up at him.

Her eyes were still red, but that only made the blue of her irises more extraordinarily azure. Her lower lashes were yet dewy from her tears; he drew his finger across one and collected the glitter on its tip.

Her eyes suddenly shut, and silent tears came sliding out of the corners—whether of sadness or joy he didn't ask. He bent to kiss them away, a noble impossibility, and then surrendered to her surrender and kissed her lips.

Rue savored her own salt on his mouth and thought how Varian Temple always brought back the most of herself to herself, her best and worst. She felt again that odd conviction of their utter, endless circling of motion and emotion, inner and outer, undeniably physical, indelibly spiritual, until these supposed poles no longer existed.

She pulled away only to stare up at him and then murmur against his temporarily dormant lips, "Take me to bed, Varian. Oh, take me to bed."

His eyes narrowed in a resurgence of the cool irony he had so often dealt her.

"We are both fatigued." Item. Rue simply hung from his neck, undenied.

"We have grand designs of revenge to set in motion." Item. Her arms tightened around his velvet-collared neck.

"This is another man's house, Rue Morgan, another man's bed. Would you have me betray it so lightly?" Item. Item. Item.

She despaired of his cooperation and rose on tiptoes and began to press kisses along his rough jaw under his ear.

The earl laughed, pulled her away, and pinioned her wrists to his chest.

"I am fresh from the worst of this island's country roads and even perhaps less presentable than I was from your cellar. Have your tastes become completely abandoned?"

"Completely, they always were," confessed Rue Morgan. "Varian." This time she spoke his name on a slight demanding complaint. "To bed and be done with it," she whispered.

He laughed again and caught her as roughly in his arms as she was evidently so desirous of.

"I have driven three days to save your soul, Black Rue Morgan, and now I see you are more than ever likely to cost me mine. Very well, hussy, to bed, and do not complain of it after."

He brought his mouth to hers, which had been hovering only an inch or two away with lips parted already, and kissed her as thoroughly as he was capable, which is to say, very thoroughly indeed.

Rue only murmured incoherently against his lips and pressed herself even harder into his embrace than he was drawing her, allowing his tongue repeated bombardment of her mouth. She retaliated in kind with such fervor that she quite surprised him. He was too drawn into their erotic advance and retreat to hear the door to the dressing room creak open ever so slightly while an unseen presence lingered there.

"Varian, to bed," Rue half-ordered, half-begged when he finally declared a momentary truce.

He picked her up again and stepped quickly through the dressing room. He did not look about, and neither did she, but it appeared quite deserted, save for a slightly longer than usual shadow cast by the open door against the wall.

"You appear quite fond of carting me about," noted Rue with great content into the ear so convenient to her.

"It is the only way I can be sure of you, elusive Rue," he answered, sitting her down and shrugging out of his sadly abused frockcoat.

The motion raised clouds of dust, and they both coughed until they laughed and laughed, then stopped and hung on each other's eyes and kissed again until standing beside a bed kissing seemed to be the most logical and only necessary union for them.

The earl finally pushed her gently away, but not far.

"Rue. You must come home with me to Cavendish Square. You can't stay on here with Pagett-Foxx. Not now. You can't allow him with you any longer. I've overlooked these past three days, though the thought rode me like the Devil, but I had to track down your own demon—"

"Varian. He hasn't been near me for days, weeks."

"Come back with me to my house. My *Red Rue* desires Black Rue for company and so do I."

"Varian." Her fingers stopped his lips, then traced their shape as she talked. "I cannot. Not until this last scheme upon my father is done. He might recognize our alliance and be forewarned. How long will it take you to alert the French?"

"Not long. But a week or two. How long can you keep Pagett-Foxx on a leash?"

"As long as necessary. He is a simple man, not devious at all. Not as Varian Temple is," she noted, aware that he had subtly undone the fastenings of her wrapper and was drawing it down over her shoulders.

They murmured together, and it was likely that it was not plotting they spoke, as the earl concentrated his attention on that which was still partially concealed by the waning wrapper while Rue laughed softly and held his dark head to her body.

The earl broke away again, sitting shirt-clad on the bed before her; Rue was half-turned from the dressing room so all one could see from that angle was her riotous black hair and her gleaming bare shoulders and back and the soft fold of fabric still swagged at the curve of her hips.

The earl's hands, large on the delicate shape of her body, came round her waist and pressed into her half-draped lower back and pulled her toward him on a sweet, reciprocating curve.

"Varian," she rebuked playfully, though, of course, had there been anyone in the dressing room, he—she—would have been most curious to know just what the Earl of Argyle was engaged upon to elicit that teasing response.

But there was no one in the dressing room, nothing, just the empty apple-green upholstered chair, and the little stool pulled diagonally away from the dressing table as if Rue Morgan had just risen from it, and a number of bottles winking glassily in the unguttered candlelight, and the deep dark shadow behind the door. And the black velvet dice box, still unthrown on the same edge of the dressing table as it had once sat long before when Piquant had dozed beneath the shining mahogany legs.

Now not even Piquant was in the dressing room, and what was there had no eyes, so it could not have seen Rue kneel before the earl or see every one of his ten fingers curl into her head as she pleasured him in the way in which he had once asked her and now would never have to ask her again.

Her face was between his hands again, and he was leaning nearer, staring into her eyes, saying quite intensely, "You cannot stay here now! I cannot tolerate it."

She pressed nearer and said again what she was always saying, as the furniture in the dressing room would have thought, had it been sentient and could it think.

"Varian," she said softly, so softly that even the dressing room furniture could have barely heard, had it ears.

"Varian, you mustn't be jealous. From now forward, whenever I walk in the Strand and an April wind brushes my hair against my face, it will be whispering 'Var-i-an' as it passes. When my corsets draw tight and embrace me, they will be saying 'Varian' and will draw but tighter around me. And if Nigel Pagett-Foxx comes to my bed, despite my disfavor, and puts his hands and eyes and mouth upon me, he will be 'Varian' in whatever he does upon or within my body. No one will be more possessive of the earl's pleasure than I."

He grasped her by the elbows and pulled her down upon the linens beside him, and it would have been very clear to anyone eavesdropping from the dressing room that he had not answered her, but that he was demonstrating his response in certain, inescapable ways.

Rue Morgan and Varian Temple were pale figures lost on the pale linens.

The dark shadow behind the dressing room door detached itself from the room shadow and remained dark as it quietly moved back into the sitting room, then most carefully out the door into the central passage.

It slipped meticulously along the muffling Oriental runner down the passage to another door and through that into a bedchamber as well-lit as Rue's, a room somewhat expectant of her presence.

He went to the bedside table, that piece of Grosvenor Square furniture with ears, Sir Nigel Pagett-Foxx. Those ears—and they were perfectly acceptably shaped—were flaming red now against his limp cropped hair. A cup of cold chocolate sat on the table, quite full.

Nigel stared into its gray-brown depths until his glance seemed to make it colder. Then he drew the chamber pot from beneath his bed and emptied the liquid into it. The chambermaid would wonder at it, but she had no suspicions about chocolate, as he did, and would not mention it to Heliotrope or her mistress, Rue Morgan, Black Rue Morgan.

"Take me to bed, Varian, to bed," the teasing sentence chased its tail through Nigel's brain like a mad dog. *He* had never been so invited. No, it was, "I've the migraine, Nigel, later." "Take me to Ranelagh, Nigel, take me to the Royal Academy, Nigel." Never simply, "Take me, Nigel."

He sat on the bed, his well-tailored frockcoat heavy on his shoulders. For her he had given up waistcoats and figured stockings, for her he was left with no place to hook his thumbs. And she welcomed a muddy and road-dusted lout of an earl to her sheets and performed inventions upon him that made Nigel's throat close up to think of....

His mind wanted to call her a thousand vile names, but only one came to its forefront, only one. Rue. Rue Morgan. Nigel knew that there was nothing in her he would not find admirable if it were turned upon him.

He felt pity for Black Harry Morgan. The man must have been diddled by her since her birth, poor blackguard, poor misunderstood, unappreciated Black Harry Morgan.

Well, there was something even a simple Norfolk squire could do about it. Turning good English ships over to the frogs, the deceitful French known for their fashionable ways, their damned frockcoats, and facile tongues that were as dangerous when not speaking as speaking. French-tongued she was, and no, she would not waste her lingual dexterity on Norfolk.

Nigel paced the night until he heard a distant door click shut and, if he strained, the low voices of Heliotrope and her mistress in consultation, laughing consultation. They stayed up a good while longer, and so did Sir Nigel Pagett-Foxx until the house was utterly dark and still.

Then Nigel finally went to the port decanter, twisted out the stopper, and stood for a long time with the cut-glass belly in his hand.

He ultimately returned the port to its tray and restoppered it. He had better things to do than swill port wine and sit by the fire until Rue Morgan should choose to come home, should choose to favor him with her attention.

He had a patriotic duty to accomplish.

Rue Morgan would have to wait.

He had an assignation with Black Harry Morgan.

Rue Morgan. Black Rue Morgan.

Black Rue.

Chapter Eighteen

"You'll wear that still?"

"Until I can send it to my father after our last coup against him. Then I will rest my vengeance. I've promised Varian."

"And then you will have only the thirteen matched sapphires you had on the eve of your eighteenth birthday. I think you go backward, Rue Morgan."

"Heliotrope! And who goes forward these days? As long as I drive my father backwards, I shall be content."

Rue adjusted the sapphire again at her throat. Now it hung on a mauve ribband that matched the lilac muslin of her gown and frothy white fichu—Rebecca Bartle's lace, as it happened, but both Rue and Heliotrope had forgotten that. Faint blue shadows underlined Rue's eyes; they only emphasized her coloring and testified to three worrisome days of waiting . . . and perhaps more to a long, exceedingly unwearying night of reunion.

"You go to the Basilisk Club today?" asked Heliotrope dubiously, smothering a yawn. She had remained up as late as her mistress, though of course she had not been so taxed.

"My father is still a villain. We have all manner of pretty, petty plans to lay against him. Dr. Radclyffe tells me that my father introduced a few of his nearest friends to the wonders of the elephant bone powder, and that they meet weekly at one of the bawdy houses to test it. Dr. Radclyffe has named it The Pachyderm Club!'"

Rue dissolved into teary laughter, but Heliotrope considered the matter.

"When your father discovers the worthlessness of his so dearly bought powder, will he not go galloping after the good doctor for a spot of vengeance of his own? Have you thought of that, Rue Morgan? You and your Basilisks and your earl?"

"Helia! You overfret." Rue swiveled on her dressing stool to regard her servant seriously.

"Father would never dare retaliate on Dr. Radclyffe because he is too well-known; besides, too many Basilisks know of the Afridisiac enterprise. I fear Black Harry Morgan would have to wipe them out at one blow to still the secret, and even he is not daring enough for that. He prefers his foes one by one, like Graham Winthrop in the stables. No, he will do nothing. Nothing. Except acquire my sapphires until he sickens of the very sight of them."

"And you'll give him that"—Heliotrope pointed to the signet stone on her mistress's neck—"when this last venture is done?"

"Yes, I'll give him my rue and be free to go on and make my own instead of wearing the chains he forged for me long ago. Oh, I know you have not approved me in this and in many things of late, Helia, but it will be over soon. And you will like me better when I am Varian Temple's mistress than when I must lady it over Sir Nigel Pagett-Foxx, I promise," said Rue, her eyes sparkling as lethally as the sapphire.

"We shall see," said Heliotrope, unbending the crimp from a carelessly stored Italian leghorn hat. "At any rate, your fox has been remarkably absent from his vixen and his burrow as of late. I would seek for a secondary exit."

"Lud, Helia! When the descendants of cannibals speak in

metaphors, and animal metaphors at that, 'tis time I settled into staid domestic life on Cavendish Square."

"Hmmph, staid indeed," retorted Heliotrope. "Not with His Lordship, I'll warrant. You plan to wear this?" She elevated the cartwheel of a hat on one hand.

"Of course, though my spirits are buoyant enough to raise me off the ground like a trans-Channel balloon without its aid. We'll have the coachman set us down on Pall Mall so that we may enjoy a stroll."

" 'Tis overcast and may rain," noted Helia darkly, her neck craned at the leaden sky outside the bedchamber window.

"Not soon, I warrant," said Rue blithely.

"The street dust will grime your hat and your fine French muslin gown and your Flemish-laced petticoats and—"

"And my new linen drawers even, no doubt," said Rue, laughing and rising to spin in the room's center until her airy skirts flew almost high enough to reveal this latest necessity of female fashion now that outer clothing grew ever more scandalously sheer.

"Nonsense, Helia! 'Tis my day and nothing can happen to me on it. But where, oh, where is my blue silk parasol?"

"There is no sun!" objected Heliotrope, staring at her mistress.

"I beg to differ, my good Helia," said Rue, shaking out her dark curls and lowering the sweep of hat brim over them. "Oh, I most ardently beg to differ."

She laughed again, collected the delicate sunshade Heliotrope held out unbelievingly, and left the room with its dressing disarray and eternally observing caryatids at the mantel, their pupilless marble eyes not sliding to watch Rue Morgan go.

As desired, Rue Morgan and Heliotrope were deposited to the street in Pall Mall and strolled along the pavement. Rue set the pace with the folded parasol as a walking stick, bowing graciously to anyone who bowed to her.

Obviously, Rue Morgan was a formidable weather fore-caster. At least, she brought her own sunshine with her, for her progress along the street gathered a great deal of attention, not the least from a corner sweeper who bowed hastily as she and Heliotrope approached, then stooped to his labor of brushing the cruder flotsam of London's West End away from Rue's delicately shod feet.

Rue paused to nod regally as this office was performed.

"We shall have to ride shank's mare more often on our Friday afternoon visits to the Basilisk Club," she murmured to Heliotrope. "I confess that I find a stroll through London most exhilarating," she added as a dashing gig clattered by on the cobblestones and an exquisitely attired dandy bowed profoundly to her in passing.

"His Lordship won't like *that*," predicted the unmoved Heliotrope. "And I don't care for the soot and smoke that hangs about the upper air. 'Tis bound to be wiping its invisible feet on us. Three hours I spent bleaching and pressing that fichu so it would be snowy enough for Black Rue Morgan!"

"Ah, you call me that, too? Then attend to tipping the sweeper and keep your proper paces behind me, turncoat," ordered Rue in mock rage, sweeping across the street to leave Heliotrope groping in her reticule.

Even then Rue Morgan did not sweep unattended far. A carriage careened around the corner, its clatter looming out of the general uproar, and its four hard-hooved coursers sharply pulling up, barely missing the lone pedestrian in mid-street.

Rue started and looked up indignantly for any markings on the offending vehicle, but it was a plain hackney carriage. A footman descended instantly and caught her by the elbow.

"Apologies will not suffice, my man," Rue began indignantly. "This is Pall Mall, not a race track—"

The footman swept open the carriage door and, without the intervention of steps, grasped Rue around the waist and thrust her inside. The parasol slid from her hand and went crashing to the cobblestones while Rue felt herself pushed farther into the strange coach. The door slammed shut on her heels.

She had fallen on hands and knees on the vehicle's dusty floor. The coach interior was dim and growing dimmer, for she heard the windows' light-quenching shades being pulled to.

Immediately she began tossing around like a die in a dice box as the carriage started off with a jerk and accelerated to a bone-cracking pace, turning several corners in succession, Rue falling from one side to the other.

She finally landed upon a pair of stockinged legs, her chin bouncing roughly on the foot dangling at the end of one crossed calf. Rue grasped the coach seat opposite this figure and drew herself up on the leather.

The face opposite her was part of the shaded interior, but the shape, posture, and silence all belonged to only one man. Black Harry Morgan.

Rue arranged what she knew were now begrimed skirts and settled back against the tufting as impassively as her father, her fingers spread across the seat on either side to support her as the coach swayed madly from side to side.

Her father kept himself stable by virtue of a heavy walking stick impaled on the carriage floor between his now splayed legs. His heavy upper torso swung rhythmically from side to side over this perpendicular support; Rue could only think of Graham Winthrop's battered gold watch swinging as hypnotically before her not many evenings past. She felt anger embody itself within her and rise up, stiffening her actual physical self.

"If you'd wanted to speak to me, you could have called at Grosvenor Square," she finally said icily.

"Speak to you!" barked her father. "I never want to see you again, you scheming strumpet, and I'm man enough to see my wishes carried through."

"You've never been man enough for anything—" began

Rue, but from the shadow an arm struck out, and Black Harry Morgan put a period to her sentence with one stinging slap.

"You'll listen to me, girl. And listen well, for it'll be the pleasantest voice you'll hear for the rest of your life."

He leaned across the gulf between them, his heavy hand curled into Rue's muslined shoulder, Black Harry Morgan's fingers crushing the thin fabric, her flesh, bone.

"I know about your conspiracies with the Basilisk Club. Know all about your filthy schemes to turn my ships over to the French. Break me, would you, wench? I'll teach you what breaking is, I'll—"

Rue managed to wrench her shoulder away, though her skin burned with pain. "Break you, yes! I would break you after what you've done to me, to my mother likely—"

"Your mother. A pale yellow strumpet of the same ilk. Like me, they always said you were. Black Harry's black daughter." He laughed harshly. "I'll make you like me—if you survive what I've planned for you. Then and only then can you deserve to call yourself Black Harry Morgan's daughter. And you won't. I've seen to that."

He lurched back against the cushions, waiting like a bloated, smug spider for his fly to dance toward him along the long, trembling strand he'd just woven.

"What do you intend? You can't—"

"There's little I can't do, as you should know by now, you treacherous vixen. Well, your grand plan won't work. My ships shall sail unimpeded, and you shall be anchored somewhere so dark and so deep that even the ghouls won't find you."

"You'd kill me?"

Rue's throat went dry with sudden comprehension of what losing her life at the very moment of her finding it would mean. She did not want to die, would not die, could not die. Not now.

"What? A father lay a hand upon his own daughter?" mocked Morgan.

He leaned forward to pull her to the seat beside him, his rough hands closing on her breasts. Rue sucked in her breath at the perversity of this assault, this demonstration that Black Harry Morgan was prepared to perform the unthinkable.

He pinioned her flailing wrists with one manacling hand while his other hand rummaged beneath her fichu. His dim face leaned close to hers, and he began speaking in a coarse whisper, telling her of certain practices of the ancients in matters sexual.

"Your elephant powder was more effective than you or that mincing idiot Radclyffe dreamed, my darling daughter," he taunted, heavy lips at her ear, rampaging hand more crushing than caressing her breasts.

"I'm a new man, a better man than I was when your bitch of a mother led me around by more than my nose. Delicate she was, disgusted she was, didn't like this or that. But you're not such a one, are you, daughter? Your puppy Nigel told me what you like—and where! Had him half-mad for the seeing of it, didn't you? Half-mad!"

He hurled her across the coach from him. Rue simply huddled there, trembling. A bit of saliva had fallen on her cheek from his last hissed words; she feared that he was mad.

"You're lucky I don't cart you back for the entertainment of my lusty members of the Royal Order of the Elephant Trunk. We meet twice weekly to overturn wine casks and women with equal fervor. And invention. I'm sure the sight of Black Harry Morgan performing wonders of virility upon Black Rue Morgan would flog their flagging appetite—"

"You're insane! Insane, you—"

"No, my daughter. 'Tis you that's mad. And that's where you're bound, to a private lunatic asylum where they'll chain you to the wall and forget you as long as I see the pounds for your keep coming. 'Tis a safer place to hold you silent than the environs of the Royal Order of the Elephant

Trunk. We meet in your former bedchamber, though it has been, er, rearranged since you last slept there."

"I've friends; they won't allow it."

"They won't know it."

"I'm not mad, no matter how many unnatural proposals you hurl at my head. I am not mad. They'll not keep me there."

Black Harry laughed.

"There are fewer madmen in the private asylums than there are in the House of Commons. Madness has nothing to do with it, foolish girl. It's a matter of who has the pounds to pay to keep whom shut up. You'll soon go mad there anyway, I'm told, so whether you live or die you'll never threaten me again."

Rue was silent while she considered this. She inadvertantly sucked on her mouth, cut from his slap, swallowing the sweet, salty red of her own blood, though she was hardly aware of anything other than the rage exploding in her head and the fear pacing, pacing like a barely caged beast through every corridor of her body.

"Nigel . . ." she said finally. "He knew of the plan, came to you, betrayed me?"

"Not until you had betrayed him first with your sluttish ways," returned her father. "A poor-spined creature he was. Required an entire bottle of my best port before he could stutter out your perfidy toward him, toward myself. Then he grew most talkative, most. But the coach slows, I think we arrive. Arrange your fichu, it would not do for Black Harry Morgan's beloved daughter to enter even a madhouse looking like a street trull. And this—"

He leaned forward and wrenched off the sapphire barely glimmering at her throat.

"You'll not need this here. I do you a favor, sweet slut; the inmates might paw you to pieces for lust of it. If you still be living November next, I've a special present in mind for your birthday and will send it. Do not fear, daughter," he added as the coach swayed to a stop, "I'll not forget you."

Graham Winthrop flashed through her brain then. Red-coated Graham Winthrop, lying in his own red blood, his blind eye staring at her unseeingly, remorselessly like a conscience. Poor Graham, was this how he had felt, caught in the gears of some pitiless machine, slowly ground to nothingness in the maw of the walking obscenity that was Black Harry Morgan?

He had stopped her, stopped Graham, stopped her fine plan of revenge—but Varian! Varian would see it through—and find her if he had to turn Bridewell and Bedlam and every house in London upside down. Varian. Varian Temple. He would find her.

Her father shifted to leave the carriage, but Rue threw herself in front of him. He had leaned forward so a slit of light fell upon his heavy features. The same light glistened on her own eye whites and the wet film of blood across her lips.

"You forget, I have allies," she challenged breathlessly, jubilantly.

Black Harry Morgan sat back heavily against the leather, which creaked from his weight. He thrust Rue into her seat with the head of his cane sharply to her stomach, and she fell away gasping for breath, for words, for a way out.

"Allies! Your only allies are lice and cockroaches and gaol fever now, Black Rue Morgan. It might be fine torment to let your pretty head dream of your earl searching every alley for you by lanternlight, but I think the truth will gnaw on you more nicely in the next weeks. I've disposed of your earl, your peer of the realm, just as I've drawn your stinger. He has hated me from of old, but stayed at the fringe of my loathing. Now he has learned what it is to enter the ring with Black Harry Morgan. Don't fret—he will not pine for you, search for you. I've done with your earl and so have you."

"Father! What have you, what could you—? He is wealthy, well-known, a man of great influence, you can't, you couldn't have—"

"There is nothing that I can't do when I've been wronged," he growled, catching her to him again, his fingers bruising the soft flesh of her arms.

"How did Graham Winthrop wrong you?" she demanded. "By loving me?"

"Yes, my fine little slut. He did me the favor of deflowering you, then followed it with the disservice of hanging about to moon and murmur of marriage. I wed him to the fists of my crimping-house men."

"You . . . wanted him to woo me, then abandon me; take my maidenhead, then break my heart," said Rue very softly, sanely, understanding dawning for all past cruelties. "You wanted to . . . break me. Always."

"Yes! And yes and yes and yes. Like *me!*" Black Harry snorted, shaking her until her head slapped against the tufting. "You're nothing like me. You're soft, and I'll see you melt like candlewax, Black Rue, as I always wanted to see you vanish."

"Have you . . . no . . . natural feelings of a father?" she asked wonderingly, whisperingly, as if Black Harry Morgan were a phenomenon she finally saw whole and could not believe existed, as great a curiosity as the stuffed giraffe in the Royal Society staircase.

"No natural feelings whatsoever, wench," he retorted, kissing her hard and wet and revoltingly on her bloody mouth. Rue quite literally gagged against his lips, and he pushed her away.

"Pretty, aren't we? We'll get over that here, my girl. And don't stare so, like some damned pale-faced fallen angel from heaven. I'm not your father!"

"Not?"

" 'Not?' " he mimicked, though the mingled disbelief and relief that underlay Rue's voice was not in his. "Never was and always knew it, and had your harlot a mother lived long enough after your birth, she would have known I knew it and known it to her sorrow every day 'twixt then and now. But I am a poor widower and have but my dear only daughter to comfort me in my old age. Out with you, wench, to the pavement and your keepers and your new home."

He leaned over to swing wide the coach door, like a man cutting a melon. Daylight flooded in, bright and juicy.

Morgan caught Rue by the arms again and thrust her toward the square leading to the world without. Her fingers curled into the coach frame, and her soft-shod feet dug into the floor.

"Whatever you are, what have you done with Varian Temple? What have you done?"

"I've done for him, that's all you'll need know. Now out."

He prodded her stomach brutally with his engraved metal canehead. Rue hung on doggedly, allowing her body to curve out from the door frame, but still clinging to the painted wood.

"What have you done with Varian Temple?" she demanded, no pleading in her tone, only raw, naked demand, something Black Harry Morgan should recognize well.

He scraped at her clinging fingers, finally rapping them with the canehead. Rue dropped to the hard stones, but rose up on her feet without feeling the impact. She clung to the carriage floor even while hands from behind caught at her arms, her legs, and Black Harry Morgan settled back in his seat while the coach door slammed shut, and rapped twice on the ceiling to signal the coachman to drive on.

"What have you done with him?" she screeched at the top of her voice to the profile of her erstwhile father as it drove forever out of view. "What?"

The carriage was a black, wheeled square rolling away from her like a dark die, like one of the Devil's dice, every instant an irreparable throw away from freedom, hope, love.

The invisible arms behind her started dragging her backward. Rue realized she faced onto a modest street of gabled three-story houses, that decent-capped heads hung out from second-story windows and shook sadly from side to side while some were openly thrown back on long necks as their owners gawked with merriment at the sight of Rue Morgan, Black Rue Morgan, her gown filthy, her face bloodstained, her snowy white fichu disarranged from obvious pawing, her arms bruised, her knees bleeding, her spirit broken—no, her spirit bridled, not broken.

And they did not know her here. She was no longer a Morgan. She no longer had any need to be Black Rue in imitation of an indifferent father.

She was no longer a name, or a force, but only a question, one screaming question that feared its answer. Still the question echoed in her mind as the asylum men dragged her feet first up the stairs into their dark and dreadful house. Every blow, knock, scrape of that frightful entry into a place of the living dead was numbed by the question that burned redly, madly in her brain. What have you done with Varian Temple?

For Black Rue Morgan, as for most of the two dozen inhabitants of that nameless house on that nameless street, there was no answer.

Chapter Nineteen

The Basilisk Club sat complacent around their traditional table. An empty chair and footstool were drawn up beside them, and they waited with what but few of them yet recognized as anticipation.

She was late and had never been so before.

Lemuel Humphries fidgeted and moved his gout-ridden leg on his under-table stool. Sir Merivale Fenton-Mews twiddled his thumbs and cleared his throat. Dr. Radclyffe sipped coffee in Olympian disregard. Colonel Trumbull honked nervously into his eternal handkerchief in the vain hope that his hawking would be done by the time their newest member appeared. Sir Feverell Marshwine repeatedly pulled his waistcoat down over his corpulent stomach in the even vainer hope that clothing would make the man appear less fleshy than he was. Addison Hookham cynically watched his fellow members' impatience and hid his own by sipping a rather strong punch.

Finally the door to the coffeehouse swung open. A kerchiefed, turbaned figure stood limned against the vivid daylight. It advanced, growing into a darker silhouette the nearer it came.

"Good God!" Colonel Trumbull shifted his bulk enough to get a closer squint at the newcomer. "It's an Ethiope, a blackamoor!"

The vision thus heralded paused, but said nothing until every eye present was fixed on her coffee-dark visage.

"My name is Heliotrope. I serve Rue Morgan," she announced abruptly, "and she's gone."

"Gone? Is the woman mad? What's this, Miss Morgan's latest prank? A test of our perceptions, gentlemen?" asked Humphries gruffly.

"I've chased the carriage that bore her off down Pall Mall and St. James Street and quite far toward the river. She's gone, taken, kidnapped. I thought the Basilisks should know."

The woman turned to leave, silence heavy in her wake.

"No, wait . . . er, young woman."

Heliotrope turned her head only enough to regard Colonel Trumbull's chubby hand clenched in her skirts. Under her coffee-bitter gaze his fingers slowly uncoiled.

"I b—b—beg you, wait!" Sir Merivale rose and tripped after the departing black woman. "Pray, sit you here," he offered, leading her to Rue's vacant chair. "And tell us what you mean. P—p—please."

Heliotrope allowed Fenton-Mews to guide her into the midst of the Basilisk Club and sat calmly while the members leaned inward to frankly look her up and down and backwards and forwards.

"The woman is winded," pronounced Addison Hookham abruptly. "We must fetch her some chocolate."

The dark head shook no.

"Coffee?"

No.

"Wine would do better, gentlemen. Or brandy," said Dr. Radclyffe astutely, his eyes narrowing on the rough rise and fall of Heliotrope's white fichu, the flare of her already flared nostrils. "She's run a great way, as she said."

Heliotrope turned her head to the doctor.

"Yes," she said, "but I could not run far enough nor fast enough to keep up. I fear her father's taken her."

"Morgan? Taken our Rue? But why? Where?" Dr. Radclyffe was unaware of his proprietary tone, but Helia marked it and suddenly relaxed.

"He swept round the corner in a high, dark carriage and swept her into it while I was still trying to pay the corner-sweeper. We were on our way here"—the brandy arrived, and Heliotrope took a great swig of it, her face finally crumpling into the anguish she felt. "She was walking ahead, as happy as morning, and then, then . . ."

Heliotrope paused and simply shook her head silently.

"There, there." Sir Merivale patted the white linen shoulders and glanced around the table worriedly from under his baby-broad forehead.

"Now tell us, Hyacinth—"

"Heliotrope."

"Er, Heliotrope. Tell us what you believe occurred and for what purpose," said the physician calmly.

"We were on our way here. My mistress had evolved a plan in conspiracy with the Earl of Argyle"—here several glances crossed significantly—"to betray her father's shipping routes to the French."

Silence prevailed while the Basilisk Club considered this news.

"Capital!" finally remarked Humphries.

"A coup," agreed Colonel Trumbull, for once not sneezing but sounding as though he did anyway.

"Not an unworthy scheme," adjudged Hookham.

"B—b—brilliant," declared Fenton-Mews.

"Why did she not share this idea with the Basilisk Club?" inquired Dr. Radclyffe sternly. He was an inveterate club-man and saw no reason for such alliances unless they be thorough.

Heliotrope took another sip of brandy.

"She had formed a more intimate alliance with the Earl of Argyle. It was their scheme of personal vengeance."

Again silence hung over the round table, thicker than the hazy smoke from assorted pipes. Fenton-Mews blushed, and having blushed, hung his head and blushed more deeply.

"It was, er, is a good plan," said the doctor. "We can support it," he offered magnanimously.

"But Miss Morgan, wh—wh—where is she? Who took her?"

"Black Harry, of course." Sir Feverell Marshwine struck the tabletop with his plump hand, a gesture so uncharacteristic that several Basilisks started. "Someone betrayed the plan. Who, I demand to know, who?"

"I fancy," said Heliotrope in a dead and weary voice, "it was Sir Nigel. He has become more addicted of my mistress, and less satisfied, thus more addicted of the ruby port. She made no secret of her attachment for the earl."

"Ah, no. No, she would not make a secret of it, Rue Morgan," agreed Dr. Radclyffe, clearing his throat almost as nervously as Sir Merivale.

"What could he do, her father?" asked that gentleman, his voice very quiet and for once quite firm.

"A good deal of ill, I fear," said Dr. Radclyffe. "Well, gentlemen, it is incumbent upon us to find her and prevent whatever we imagine the worst to be. You, Hookham, locate the earl at Brooks's or his other clubs. Sir Merivale, you will try Cavendish Square. I warrant we'll do better in our search with His Lordship informed. Does he, er, return Miss Morgan's regard?" the doctor inquired of the stoic Heliotrope.

"Fervently," returned the maid, rising.

"Where do you go?"

"To Grosvenor Square to collect my mistress's pet and some of her more treasured things. I will not stop another night under Sir Nigel's roof," said Heliotrope, passion shaking her voice so suddenly that the Basilisk Club knew to a man that the black woman's composure hid an agitation even greater than their own.

"Grosvenor. I see." Sir Feverell's small lips pouted consideringly. "You may as well remove to my house, my good woman. Miss Morgan will want a familiar environment if she returns to our hands."

"When," growled Colonel Trumbull and blew his nose threateningly.

"When. This, er, pet. It's not a monkey, is it?"

Heliotrope smiled wanly, her well-strung teeth as mocking as a keyboard somehow in the sober circle.

"A dog, Sir Feverell, that is all, but one that is most elderly, stout, toothless, and of a choleric disposition."

Since her words could serve as equally to describe the Basilisk Club's members, several pair of eyes fell at this verbal riposte. They asked no more questions of Heliotrope. Sir Feverell ushered her out, prepared to escort her to Grosvenor Square and induct an entire menagerie into his house if it would guarantee the return of Rue Morgan.

"You had better accompany Sir Feverell," the doctor, now diagnostician in a very real battle, instructed Colonel Trumbull. "Pagett-Foxx might be present and turn nasty."

They scattered, the bewigged and bebandaged, the out of fashion and the dandy, the waistcoated and the fashionably pantalooned. And if anyone chose to call them a ninny-aping band of old tomcats, why, he was welcome to. Yet the resolve of a lion drowsed under the housecat facades of the Basilisk Club, and its members knew they had finally crossed swords in a deadly combat with Black Harry Morgan.

"What of Morgan himself?" asked Hookham under his breath of the doctor when the two had paused on the curb outside the coffeehouse.

"No, I fear that to confront him would only warn him of our intent. We'd best do this on our own. Thank God we've the force of the earl's title and means behind us. I think matters have turned grave, Addison. Very grave indeed. Fatal perhaps."

Hookham nodded grimly, his long face growing longer. The physician regarded him strangely.

"I thought you of us all was least taken by our Miss Morgan?"

"Ay, for she reminded me of her cursed father. Now she reminds me of myself."

"But her straits are dire!"

"Exactly, my dear doctor," said the dandy lightly. "She told me once that a heavy heart will often wear a light exterior. She knew me better than myself. I most resisted her because I most needed to believe in her. My fortune's gone, thanks to my gambling and Black Harry Morgan's financial forays against me. I am a confirmed wastrel, dear doctor, who must bilk my friends to keep me in silk handkerchiefs. But I will not let Morgan win this hand. We'll get her back."

"Be a realist, man! He could have taken her anywhere, shipped her anywhere. Slain her and drowned her in the Thames, buried her in Moorfields—"

"You are a physician, my friend, and uncommon crude," said Hookham, paling a bit. "We will find her, or we have all lost."

"I am not sanguine," insisted the doctor dourly.

"Nor I," admitted Hookham, resting a thin, elegant hand on the physician's stooped shoulder. "But it would not do to tell our brethren of the Basilisk Club this. A hopeless quest requires a high heart."

"By God, Addison, your pessimism but makes me paw the ground like an old war horse. Bedamned to the odds— we'll find Rue Morgan, and then, by Hades, we'll make Black Harry pay!"

The doctor frowned, spun gamely, and limped away on his goutish leg, leaving Hookham smiling serenely after him, well-pleased with himself for lighting a fire under the group's natural and key leader.

Black Harry Morgan stood in front of his dressing mirror on the second story of Blackstone House. He wore breeches and a broad, piratical, scarlet sash with a ceremonial dagger riding under it. His coat was brass-buttoned, epauleted, and embroidered in gold and silver thread.

Morgan abstracted a pinch or two of powder from a large glass bottle and dropped it in a wineglass that accompanied him in his movements about the chamber, resting always on the tabletop nearest his right hand. He drank Dr. Radclyffe's elephant bone powder and could feel the stirrings of his recent triumph and the potion's miraculous restorative powers working upon each other, exciting each other as feverish lovers do.

They would be arriving soon, the blackest and bawdiest old rakes that London town could call her own. He had gathered them together when searching for subjects for the powder and had found them ripe for a reconvening of the Hell-Fire Club that had caused such a scandal at the century's other end. He also had found them full of subtlety and improvisations of the sexual sort necessary to tease his always arbitrary body to greater responsiveness.

The female servants of his house had formed the first brigade of the newly organized Royal Order of the Elephant Trunk, but the men had soon graduated to exotic trollops imported from St. Giles and other degenerate sections of the metropolis.

Black Harry donned his ritual mask, a gray velvet appliance that covered his upper face. It featured ear-sized flaps at the side and a stuffed and stiffened trunk over his nose. He smiled at his thick-set grotesquery of appearance in the looking glass and half-drew the gemmed dagger from his sash. A pendant blue sapphire swung from the chain around its gold-worked hilt. He jabbed the weapon back into place, his fingers tightening on the haft.

In his wine-drenched stupors, Black Harry had confessed something of his unnatural daughter and of the hatred he bore her who had been borne as his by an unfaithful wife. They had heard of her, his jaded new friends, and teased at him to bring her to one of their meetings. It was dangerous, he could not . . . Yet perhaps if she lived a while, she could be imported on special occasions once the lunatic asylum had broken her . . . It might be amusing. Perhaps her birthday. . . .

Black Harry Morgan surveyed himself in the mirror and realized that his hatred of her who was known as Black Rue Morgan had, like his supposed daughter, finally come of age. The thought quite excited him.

"He's gone."

"What? Explain yourself, man. You can't mean it?"

"Nowhere to be found, I tell you, doctor," said Hookham. At noon on the following day, he had found Radclyffe alone at the coffeehouse table.

"Gone? As well?"

"Exactly. It is a double blow, and well-planned. Servants, friends know nothing. As best as we can ascertain, the earl vanished the night previous to our Rue. And as utterly."

The physician nodded to a serving girl and ordered brandy when she arrived.

"You'll swell one of the few sound legs left to our number beyond usefulness," cautioned Hookham.

"I'd like to see Morgan's throat swelling so under my hands," said the doctor, sipping generously from the glass. He sighed. "What's to be done, man? I confess I am most anxious. And I fear we've no time. Or damned little."

"We search. The prisons, hospitals, morgues . . . Passenger lists of outgoing ships. Humphries can help us there."

"And anything other?"

"We throw gold at the crimping-house bullies Morgan employs. Enough guineas should loosen some tongue somewhere."

They rose in concert.

"And Bedlam," said the doctor suddenly. "We should search there."

"He could not send her—or him—there. The public can observe the inmates for the price of a shilling or two. I know, I have done it with half the fashionable folk in London for company. Our quarry would be recognized."

"Not for long," pointed out the doctor. "I, too, have seen Bedlam, and the private asylums, which are a good deal worse, I promise you. But you are right—he wouldn't have sent either of them to Bedlam, more likely out of the city . . ."

They left, the doctor's brandy forgotten half-full upon the shining mahogany.

Rue Morgan sat rocking in a corner of the room. The half-paneled wall was dull oak; the house had once been respectable, but was now unrepaired and sank into deeper and deeper gloom.

The room was small, unfurnished. Here Rue had been thrust, kicking, flailing, and screaming when first taken into the madhouse.

She had been left untended, unfed, and unchained with only a straw mat to lie upon and that riddled with vermin, for sitting there now, she had found herself scratching herself bloody.

So now she sat in the littered corner against the hard wood, a few feet from the mousehole. Or perhaps it was a rathole. There she sat, the great black hole of the question that occupied her mind smothering her like a blanket. She had told Varian Temple once that not knowing what had happened to Graham Winthrop made his loss easier to bear. This was not true of her fears about Varian Temple himself— Varian, who had presented her the whole, unflinching truth about Graham and his punctured lungs and his broken face and his blind eye. And now she must play mental hazard with her image of Varian.

Throw the dice of the mind's eye.

Varian Temple drowned and floating face-down in the Thames. And a good thing, too, for now a night watchman fishes him shoreward with a pike and turns him over under the light of a lantern—all livid, swollen flesh, fish-eaten. . . .

No. No image for her to cling to. She must think better, or she would truly go mad.

Then a farmer in his field, the patient horse plodding forward, carving up the furrow of earth. And there, a pale hand uncovered with one lone dark ring upon it, and, and—green lichen, moss falling across the wrist like a morbid frill.

The farmer bending and brushing away more of the concealing earth, and long thin lines of white revealed—bones! And a skull, white as a die, the spots on it three. Two for eyes, one for nose. Crabs! A losing roll and no other.

Rue wailed and sent her cry snaking up the wall to the damp ceiling above her. It continued across the moldy surface and down the room's opposite side and came back to wind around her, a sort of sapphire sound that tentacled her throat and pulled tighter and tighter so her cries rose even shriller.

The door opposite creaked open. Rue was silent, panting with silence, like the room.

A cup and saucer levitated through the door and hung there, seemingly unsupported. Rue shook her head until her tumbling hair obstructed her eyes. She drew this veil away and looked again.

Now a scrawny hand, an incredibly veined and wrinkled hand came through, the saucer pinched by one edge in its clawlike fingers.

"A new mouse, is it? A new mouse in the old woodwork. I'll put out a bit of tea for the mouse," announced the newcomer.

A reed-thin woman in a ragged shift came edging sideways through the door, shutting it quickly behind her. Her eyes were huge in an overbony face. They shifted constantly, to the small casement high in one wall from which a bit of light leaked, to the vacant straw mat, and finally to Rue Morgan in her corner.

"Some tea, dear mousie? 'Tis all I can give. I'm Mad Agnes, and I'm allowed the run of the place since I'm the sanest of the lot. Mad Agnes am I, and fond of mouses."

The creature came and crouched before Rue, dropping into her squat with the agility of long custom. A true tea smell wafted to Rue's nostrils, hiding for once the sour, scatological reek that had pressed itself up against Rue's face, unwelcome as an alley cat, from the moment she had entered the place.

Rue took the cup, though it was almost black from the unwashed scum of previous teas brewed in it. But the brew was hot.

"Thank you," she muttered into the cup lip. "Are you a keeper here?"

The woman cackled her amusement at this misapprehension.

"An' I were a keeper, you'd not be sitting talking to me nice and mouselike, but climbing yonder wall with your fingernails. I'm Mad Agnes. I feed the mousies when I may. They're my pets. Pretty mousie."

The woman's claw raked through Rue's disheveled locks. "Don't run away, pretty mouse. You'll need a combing, or you'll get like old Mad Agnes here, who wears a bramble-bush for a headdress."

The woman began clawing at her own matted and grizzled hair with both hands, rocking on her heels and crooning some old-fashioned air to herself.

Rue recognized the rock she herself had just settled into and rose abruptly, still carrying the precious teacup. She paced. She would not rock with the rest of them, though she could understand the need to play mother to one's own self at a place like this. She would not slip into the rock and the forgetfulness of it. This mouse would avoid the bait and the clatter of the spring. She would walk, pace, think.

"What be your name?"

"Rue."

Pace, turn, in a tiny room. Who paced? Not mice. Cats, the great cats in their cages in the Tower zoo. Prison. Many heads fallen. Not Rue's. Not Rue Morgan's head. Rue's head still thought. It was just beginning, the horror. And at

the end of it, at the end of every day's survival lay the horror of contemplating what may have happened to Varian
Temple. May. Only may. Perhaps her—what did she call
that walking venom now?—perhaps *he* had lied to make her
lot more miserable. Not dead, no. Simply not here with her.
That was bearable. Yes.

"You're a great pacer, Rue. I'll call you Pacing Rue. I always like to name my pets. You're a lively one, though. I
think I shall like you. They let me wander. If you're good
and do as they say, they'll let you wander, too. Only you
must be wary of the tomcats, little mousie. They have ways
of pouncing! Like that! Scared you, did I?"

The old woman cackled and rocked on her heels, her eyes
following Rue's pacing, her thin lips splitting widely now to
reveal a toothless mouth.

"Are there many like you here?" Rue finally asked, pausing to crouch before the creature.

"No. I'm the only sane one," she announced proudly.
"Now."

Rue's eyes must have registered a disbelief that even a
madwoman could read more clearly than tea leaves.

"Sane. Yes, I am. I always was. Never mad a moment.
Then my husband, he tired of me. I was still quite young,
but not young enough. Not like you, Pacing Rue. He had me
brought here. It was to be an outing, you see, and then they
dragged me in—oh, yes, I raised such an uproar and the
neighbors all watched and laughed as they did for you—but
they dragged me in, and I've never been out since. Now
they call me Mad Agnes, and the best part of it is that I've
forgotten my husband's face and sometimes even his name.
And almost my own. That is the pity with forgetting; it is
not very selective."

"You seem an . . . educated woman."

The creature cocked her tangled head.

"Oh, pretty well we are, yes, Mad Agnes is no fool. I
wrote a pretty hand and did watercolors that were quite the
envy of my set. And at the minuet, none was so dainty at

her curtsies . . . We don't curtsy much here. Let's see your leaves—oh, very bad. Very bad indeed. I've never seen a worse fortune. There's something in it, you know. The tea. They put it in so you can join us in the common room without trouble. Can't let you have a room to yourself for long, like the Queen of England or the Princess Royal. No, indeed. Ah, a Pacing Rue you are. It will be nice to have something to watch."

"Something? In the tea? What, a drug? Yes, a drug . . . Was it a brown liquid, I wonder? Three drops and goodnight Sweet Nigel till morning!"

Rue paused in her frenzied march to and fro. Her senses were dulling, her feet not feeling as solid upon the wide-boarded floor. Up didn't seem quite so clearly up, down not so obviously down. She sank again to her knees beside the old woman.

"Mad Agnes, I'm glad you like mouses. Tell me, tell this mouse, how long have you been here?"

The thin lips pouted outward, drawing a fence of parallel lines along the shrunken upper lip.

"A long time, Pacing Rue. I was . . . sixty . . . no, six-and-twenty, that was it, when I came."

Rue stared. "But the king then would have been, have been—"

"George II. Some things I remember quite well. What kind of Englishwoman would I be if I forgot king and country as easily as my husband? German George he was. George II. Why look so strange? Is there another now?"

"Yes, Mad Agnes, George III. And between us lunatics, I must tell you that he is as insane as we, only he is king and they cannot lock him away as readily," said Rue, her eyes drawn off Mad Agnes to watch a white fog slither under the door and over to her feet.

It began swallowing her, the fog, and its name was oblivion. She fought it bitterly with her only weapon, a name. A name she would remember even if she had to attach it to shriveled flesh and splintered bone, and then only wind and dust prowling the tunnels of her memory. Varian.

"Oh, dearie, now don't drop the cup. There's a girl, Mad Agnes'll take it. Sleep, little mouse. Such a pretty mouse, the cats will be licking their whiskers. But not for long, no, we shan't be pretty for long. Sleep, mouse. Don't dream. It is best not to dream."

The woman uncorkscrewed herself and left Rue fallen unconscious near the mat of moldy straw. She tiptoed elaborately out of the room, closed the door as softly as a breath, and vanished.

But Rue Morgan did dream. She dreamed she was falling down an endless tunnel of blackness, turning over and over like a die, shouting something that the rate of her fall always brushed beyond her own hearing. The distorted faces of the Basilisk Club rushed past, all urging painted china cups of coffee, tea, and chocolate at her. And one shadowy figure behind them, a pale hand extending a blood-red goblet of wine. She forgot his name, but she thought it was important. . . .

Varian Temple shut his eyes and felt the meridian sun pouring down upon him. He tried to concentrate on that hot, honeyed bath from the blue sky arching above.

His hands were stretched above him, tied to the rigging. He felt the sun on every centimeter of his skin, burning the white, unweathered surfaces—eyelids, hands, bare arms, shoulders, back. But sunburn was better than that other, that other coiling even now over his shoulder.

The cat-o'-nine-tails fell, split into a thousand howling comets of pain, and clawed him caressingly around the ribs as it withdrew.

He had ceased counting, although that device had helped him bear the first occasion. Now it was all beyond bearing, though he did not scream as some of the other impressed sailors had. He grunted and sagged against the rhythm of it. Again. And then the balm of the sun. He could almost feel the celestial cyclops burning into the back of his head, burning out his eyes, perhaps his memories.

Something else was helping him survive the lash. The thought, the nagging slice of thought more hurtful than any number of welts from the braided leather, that she—the burn slicing across, this time he should not survive it—that she (Name her, you fool, name her), Rue Morgan, may have betrayed him as he suspected all along. As he knew better than—ah, it worsened.

Every blow now seemed to worsen, sweat and blood running down his arms, his brow, his back, my God, his bloody back—he must look a bleeding redcoat now. Winthrop had paid for his Rue, and now Varian Temple must pay his turn at the pillory she invariably put her men to. Agony, pure, almost aesthetic agony. And Rue Morgan. Did she, had she—?

Finally sagging now, unconsciousness pulling him down to the deck, the smell of the calking and tar stronger finally than his own sweat, his own blood. The sun snuffed out by a considerate hand. It was Rue's, Rue Morgan's high up in the sky, he saw it, saw it reach down and press something damp on his brow.

How could he have doubted? He was in his hell as Jonathan Flemming had predicted, and here was Rue Morgan sent down to comfort him. Ah, he was not so cool to her now.

"Easy, man. 'Tis a wicked world, and thou has seen a wickeder part than most. Don't move."

Varian lifted his head in the dark. He was on his belly in the dark belly of a wooden leviathan. A ship. Bound away from England. Bound away from Rue Morgan. Someone had laid a blanket of fire across his back, arms, brain, heart.

"Jonathan was right—they do not smile in hell," he murmured through stiff lips, caked with his own salt.

"No, my son, alas, it is not hell, but merely the hell men make for other men."

The speaker removed something from Varian's forehead;

Varian realized a cold compress had been applied there.
Odd, he felt nothing cold, only heat and not cold, save for
the icy splinter of doubt impaling his heart. Rue, Rue Morgan.

Some monster of cruelty was skating across his lacerated
back. He wondered if this imp wore red velvet and ermine
and the name of Morgan.

"Just a salve. It has helped the others."

"Are you a . . . parson, a physician?" Varian finally asked
the voice, aware that its owner was tending him.

"No. I am what the Church of England chooses to call a
Dissenter and bar from voting or holding office, though I do
not seem to be exempt from the press gangs. I am a poor
sinner and a sufferer like yourself, brother."

The man coughed softly, the chronic, deep cough of the
consumptive. Varian felt each of the man's fingers scathe
his back lash-sharp as he gently laid on the ointment. It was
a wicked world indeed when so much gentleness as he
sensed in this man could still rub raw against that world's
wounds.

"Lean nearer, that I may see your face."

"My name is Matthew," the man volunteered, bringing a
worry-writ visage near Varian's own pain-etched face. "I do
what I can to tend the wounded in body and spirit here.
And they let me in the belief that they will get more worth
from them. Thou has taken many savage blows, brother. I
fear thou has a contentious spirit."

Varian turned his face forward again and did not answer.
Yes, he had brought a good part of his durance upon himself. But when one had spent almost thirty years as an earl
of England, one did not leap into the role of lowly impressed sailor with the enthusiasm the boatswains required.
This was his third turn at the lash in a week; he guessed that
not many more in quick succession would be fatal.

"I think they wish to keep thee alive for the entire voyage, though," meditated the Quaker. "Strange are the wick-
ednesses of man. And strange the mercies of the Lord. I

believe thou are their prize prisoner, and that will save thee when others of us must be swept early into the arms of the Lord."

"Yourself?" asked Varian, wincing as the salve lay heavy on his wounds.

"I have the cough; this work is not conducive to it," Matthew answered simply. "I will do for thee what I can while I may. Here, a lime. Thou will have need of all thy strength, brother."

Varian took the small fruit, weighed it a moment in his hand. He bit into it savagely, routinely. The bitter juice flooded his mouth, stung its rawness, washed over him in an acid tide. He thought he knew its name.

Despite Matthew's tending, Varian's wounds became infected. His outward fires grew hotter as his inward inferno raged all the more. The fever, at least, saved him from deck duty, and Varian began to believe that some special overlooking power preserved his life. Unlike Matthew, Varian did not believe this power was heavenly. It smacked of revenge and Black Harry Morgan. And perhaps—ah, lash of the spirit—perhaps his daughter, Black Rue Morgan, who had intended this all along.

Varian would debate Rue's complicity endlessly, alternately using her image as a placebo to soothe his fevered mind and body, and as a goad to prod it to survival.

In his delirium, with the low murmur of Brother Matthew's soft voice praying over him, Varian Temple would press himself into the rough canvas upon which he lay and imagine it the soft and silken body of Rue Morgan, white and rippling with a thousand sweet satisfactions. And sometimes he would murmur her name, "Rue, Rue . . ."

A hand would rest upon his fevered head, and Matthew's voice would come laden with the bovine reassurance of the believer. "Yes, my son, thou has reason to rue of thy lot. Trust in the Lord and thou shall be delivered."

And Varian Temple—gambler, cynic, peer of the realm,

lover of women and of one in particular—would laugh wearily internally, curse his luck, and feel such a bizarre gratitude to the mad deluded fool who tended him that the tears would course down his face and rest upon his lips as bitter as the limes that Matthew brought him, as bitter as the traitorous lips of Rue Morgan, whom he then invoked and burned into the memory of his flesh out of sheer stubborn perversity.

Even Pacing Rue had to cease pacing.

Such occasions were usually only in the deepest dark when even the frenetic mad had paused. And then sometimes, if she sat and stared at the farther dark, sometimes very occasionally *she* would come. Anne Temple. A faint, pale figure in antique powdered hair and hooped gown. But the powdered hair was sheer glittering gold, a kind of halo.

"Is he there? With you?" Rue would beg mentally.

The vague figure would shake its head mournfully, whether answering her question or bewailing its own fate, Rue Morgan would never know, and Pacing Rue would never remember.

The figure would ebb, grow as evasive as a firefly. What was left of Rue Morgan's mind would call after it, "Is he there? With you?"

There was never a clear answer, just as there was never a day or night without the constant biting of the vermin, the badgering of the mad, and the lascivious glimmering of the keepers' eyes at what they saw of Pacing Rue's flesh through her tattered gown.

She paced back and forth, over and over, again and again.

In time, Varian recovered enough to be hauled into the light of day and made to haul upon a line, every motion tearing loose the scabs upon his welt-jeweled back.

He saw Matthew come and go on deck, hard-driven because his absences below to tend the wounded had convinced the taskmasters that he had not done his share. The man's consumptive cough heralded his presence; it lay as heavy upon Varian Temple's ears as the lash had upon his back.

And one wave-ridden night, when even from across the deck by the ship's lanternlight Varian could read the fever-rouge on Matthew's cheeks, the second mate prodded the Quaker aloft, though the man was already reeling on the boards.

Matthew climbed the thick wooden timber; almost every man on deck paused in his labor to watch, recognizing a strength goaded beyond endurance. Matthew, a meek and vanishing figure amid the billowing sail and the flailing ropes. Matthew at the cross-timber now. Matthew past it, and every man breathing somehow easier. Matthew pausing. Matthew plummeting past them quickly, soundlessly into the waves' watery throat, and the great haughty ship sailing on, bound for Africa and its barren western coast where it had cargo to take on. Ebony. Human ebony bound for the West Indies.

Varian Temple vowed that he would survive.

It was Rue Morgan's birthday.

She did not recall this, although if anyone had bothered to shake the dice box that was her mind, she would have recalled quite clearly her last assignation with Graham Winthrop. She could even erect, on Varian Temple's retelling of it, what had happened in the stable after her leaving, what had happened to Graham.

But not knowing that this was early November and thus her birthday, Rue Morgan did not construct these painful memories into the tortured edifice that she felt gave her a kind of architectural sanity—an up, down, left, right, real, actual orientation.

Rue still paced, Mad Agnes often at her heels as a pseudo-Piquant. Rue's fevered activity had kept the other, truly mad inhabitants of the place away. She appeared to be capable of erupting in any direction at will, no matter how thin she grew on the scum-ridden gruel, moldy bread, and three pints of beer a week she survived upon.

Rue's fabled black hair was a tangled grimy mop now, dull and greasy at once. Her beauty had whittled away to blazing blue eyes in a waxen, wizened face. Her gown was more rag than not, her shoes gone, stolen during a laudanum trance. For it was tincture of opium they fed her to keep her docile and quiet.

Rue Morgan was only docile when unconscious. And though an impartial observer could not quite call her mad, she frightened the truly mad more than if she had been as they, for a kind of mad sanity clung to her, and it was a lethal thing. She would kill if she could, Rue Morgan, and the mad usually sense that sort of thing.

"Pacing Rue, you've speed upon you today. What do you think when you run so?"

Mad Agnes tilted her matted white head nearer the dark one. Rue paused.

"I do not think, that is why I pace. I recommend it."

And she resumed pacing.

"What do you think, my mouse? I am so glad to have a companion mouse. You must not hate me for it," the woman whined, catching one of Rue's skeletal hands in her own.

Rue's mad smile tightened, and she paced. It was a mad smile only if one had seen Rue Morgan outside the madhouse. To the inmates, it was the sanest smile about, and they feared it and its possessor.

Rue paused and dug her hands into her snarled hair, scratching frantically at the vermin ensconced therein. Her arms, face, and body were marked by the tracks of these tiny tormentors; so were the limbs of every inmate. But thus far she had not contracted the dreaded gaol fever that carried off patients by the twos and threes.

The two women were the only inmates moving in the icy stench of the common room. Most had sunk into apathy. Not Pacing Rue and her shadow, Mad Agnes.

The door opened. Both women froze and cowered. Only these postures were safe when the keepers came.

The burly man stuck his head in the chamber, alert for danger from its half-starved, drugged inhabitants, then entered the room.

"Pacing Rue," he spat. Well he should, for a scar ran across his face where she'd got him with a shard of pottery once when she'd been fresh-arrived and still desirable and he had tried to take her in the solitary chamber.

Rue's eyes, still blue, sweet celestial blue in a face white and ridged as crusted snow drifts, looked up from her passive place on the muck-strewn hay. She reeked now, like the rest of them, and was best left alone.

"Here, my appetizing pacer."

The man hurled a pale box at her. Over and over it tumbled in the air, like a die, a memory. Rue's hands forked from the wrists as if they were manacled and closed prayerfully on the tumbling box.

"It's your birthday, I hear, Pacing Rue. There's them as pays enough to see you get this to make it not worth my while to steal it from you. Many happy returns."

The attendant sneered and left the room. Eyes glittering under crusted lids watched. Rue pried at the odd white moiré box, hands and mind unused to such complexities as finding the place opposite the hinge, cracking open the manmade shell to disgorge the meat inside.

The box yawned open, lazily ajar on her palms. The madmen around her gasped. Inside lay a ring, a great gold and ebony ring, pearl encircled.

This was All Saints' Day, and her former father, who was all-Devil, had offered her the latest in a series of sadistic birthday gifts.

Rue lifted the ring from the box, held it before her face, pressed it to her lips, and shut her eyes while a curtain of water cascaded down her face. She rocked on her knees, Rue Morgan, and paced no more. She finally heard a mass rustle of straw and opened red-rimmed eyes to see a circle of similarly red eyes round her, glimmering madly with possession, with theft.

She lurched to her knees, the ring folded in her hands, her hands folded on her breast. Weary she was, wearier than it was possible to be. But she paced, and her motion drove the ring of the mad back from her. She hurled herself into her movements, cast herself from wall to wall, paced and smiled and pressed the token to her mouth until they thought she would swallow it.

Eventually night came. They wearied of watching her, though the restless crackle of her pacing disturbed their troubled sleep.

In the dark so black no one could see anything and even Rue Morgan could not view her future or her past, she fell again to her knees. Rue took Varian Temple's ring and tied it into a strand of matted hair at the back of her head, very close to her skull.

Dead, dead, dead. Is that why *he*'d sent it, saved it until this most piercing of all moments? How else would *he* have it, how else? The bones tumbled in her fevered mind. Varian Temple, gamester, reduced to a thousand tiny macabre cubes . . . She finally fell asleep, the deep undrugged sleep of pure exhaustion.

In the morning when Rue awoke, she knew from the disarray of what was left of her clothes that they'd crawled over in the night, the mad, and searched her for the trinket in a thousand, maddening ways.

She turned against the wall and worked her narrow fingers against the thick mat of hair at her neck. It was still there, his ring, and perhaps so might he be.

Rue Morgan dragged herself to her feet and resumed pacing.

The *Ivory Queen* she was called, the ship that bore Varian Temple from England to Africa, the ship that had served for Matthew the Quaker's funeral barge.

It was not ivory she took on in Africa, but ebony—living,

breathing, bleeding ebony. Only when the slave ship assumed its human cargo did Varian discover the calculated cruelty of Black Harry Morgan's revenge.

No longer was he expected to serve as a common sailor above and below decks, hour after weary hour until his hands were rawer than his back had once been.

No, off the coast of Africa, Varian was chained in sequence with the naked black bodies herded aboard and prodded below decks into the steaming, stench-thick purgatory of the hold. Not mere impressment did Black Harry Morgan have in mind, but enslavement.

Of the horrors of the middle passage, little remains to be said. Fully an eighth of the black cargo perished in those six weeks of wafting across the blue Atlantic to a New World. Many dove off the ship's gunwale when taken on deck for the infrequent exercise periods. Exercise periods became even more infrequent. Then it was necessary to send sailors below to cart the dead from the body-crammed hold.

Varian Temple was the only white man below. He was hardly recognizable as such, for the topside sun had baked him brown, and his own dark hair had grown into a tangled thatch and beard. But he was whiter than the slaves with whom he rubbed manacles.

Though they ate the same swill, sweated the same salt, and bled the same rich royal red, they were other than he, and Varian was alone beyond any conception he'd ever had of such a condition.

He was alone when their wails and cries rose up to the swollen boards above them and bounced back. Alone when the stick-thin young girl to his right finally lay her dark head on his shoulder and died. Alone with her even through the long, heavy night and into the day when the sailors finally unchained her to cast her overboard.

He was alone when the strange syllables of their crooning erupted here and there, and he could not join in, could not be comforted by their alien comfort.

Once he had burst into mad song himself, the only thing

that popped into his overheated brain, Ben Jonson's "Drink to me only with thine eyes . . ."

A few hundred glistening eye whites had riveted upon him as he had fallen silent, laughing bitterly to himself until they had looked away and he felt secure in his aloneness once more.

Sometimes when they gathered together the energy to sing their repetitive choruses, he would join in under his breath, singing the one syllable that would not stand out from their own.

"Rue," he intoned, rocking unwilling in their chains with them, "Rue . . ."

Chapter Twenty

"My God! Rue, Rue Morgan!"

Pacing Rue stopped on her eternal rounds. The common-room door stood open, and a crowd of quite sane people posed in it. Quite sane, that is, save for the bent, cocked-head figure at their fore, a most disreputable old fellow who immediately sprang into the room and began sniffing about.

"Very fine, me lads, 'twill serve for old Uncle Barty. Ah, here's an able wench, a rollicking Lydia of a girl she be."

This figure paused before Rue and encouragingly pinched her thin cheeks.

"Smile for Bartholomew Fayre, my girl, that's right. Now, gentlemen, you've found a fine place for me, I admit it, and I'll be sworn these keepers look a gentle lot," he added, dancing up to the brutal form of the one conducting the tour. Old Barty outstretched a thin palm. "Have'ee a penny?" he whined.

The keeper's face froze with anticipation of what he'd deal Old Barty once the gentlemen who'd committed him were satisfied of their tour and on their way. There were a great many of them this time, these "interested relations" who were most interested in ridding themselves of a troublesome, senile old uncle, so they said.

The keeper didn't care if it were the awkward terms of a will or an unwilling bride or any such circumstance that brought him his charges. He cared only for the pounds to be made and the fun to be had at his victims' expense. Have'ee a penny indeed! He'd soon have the old fool whining something other than that.

In the meantime there was the stern, straight figure of the physician to satisfy, the fellow who had called out that odd name—Prue Morgan. No Prue here, although a quite handsome serving wench up the lane was so named, and the keeper had licked his lips at the thought of her for some time.

The keeper found himself elbowed out of the way as all seven gentlemen rushed willy-nilly into the madhouse.

"It's Rue, it is!"

"If it is indeed she, we'll have that villain's skin for this."

"Oh, Miss Morgan, dear Miss Morgan. Say you recognize us, do. We've searched for so long—"

The keeper fell back against the doorjamb as yet another figure darted in after the original onslaught. A blackamoor yet! The keeper rubbed his eyes and thought of a bitter pint at the crossroads where the tempting, buxom Prue presided.

Rue, Pacing Rue, stopped moving and backed away from these refugees from a sane and simple world, these clean, unclouded figures from a picture book.

She threw up her hands before her face and retreated to the nearest untenanted corner, her thumb and forefinger moving behind her neck where they fingered a lump in her hair there, what had become a compulsive gesture with her all these weeks, months.

"Mistress Rue!"

The dark woman fell to her knees beside her. Even the mad dropped their jaws at this clear insanity of calling the starved, wretched, ragged creature in the corner mistress of anything other than her own madness.

But that pathetic bundle of rags and bone and blazing blue eyes—always she had kept the blue and the blaze—looked up finally, dropping her hands a bit as if she peeked at the world.

"H—Helia? Is it . . . Helia?"

"Oh, yes, yes!" laughed Helia, gathering Rue, straw that she sat on and all, into her cloak-draped arms.

Heliotrope was still cold from the January weather without. Rue felt that chill enfold her and draw out the fever of the last months. She felt a sudden cold sting clearing her most foggy head and looked around more perceptively.

The faces ringed her, like the jolly painted faces on a set of Straffordshire mugs. Their hair was mostly white, their cheeks were red, and they appeared to be all beaming at her, though here and there a scarlet nose dripped, and some ran from the eyes, and one seemed to be overcome by a sneezing attack.

Rue looked to one ruddy, plump face.

"S—s—sir Feverell . . . Marshwine?"

A nod as vigorous as a puppet's.

She put out a thin hand to another circling face, this one as unlined as a child's.

"Sir Meriv—v—vale?"

"M—m—myself. And you've acquired my affliction, dear Rue." He caught her hand to his stock, but her eyes moved on.

"Why Dr. Radclyffe. How goes the elephant powder? You'll have all London at your window clamoring for it."

Her eyes moved on again, more feverishly than they had in weeks. They fastened on a morose, self-contained face hanging back from the circle.

"Highwayman Hooker!" she said, laughing, tears starting in her eyes.

A series of sneezes punctuated this remark. Rue's head spun to the other side of the circle.

"And Colonel Trumbull, dear Colonel Trumbull, how

marvelous to h—h—hear you sneeze . . . How marvelous to see you, hear you all—oh, Mr. Humphries, pray do not feel left out."

Her hands went around and around the circle as maniacally as once she had paced, touching them, grasping hands, her ruinous head sunk against Helia's cloaked shoulder.

One hovering face finally stymied her blossoming recall: a wizened, canny face frozen in suspense at the moment, unmindful of anything but her. It reminded her of something, the way the eyes were fastened upon her, the blue eyes under the shrubbery brows.

"Who—? Gentlemen, who . . . ?"

Her own vivid blue eyes sought theirs, the question in them as painful as daylight, for the old Rue Morgan would have known instantly, would have guessed even though she'd never seen her mentor in the guise of Bartholomew Fayre, beggar and satyr extraordinaire.

But this last, unrecognized face was melting before her eyes. Its owner was tearing at it, plucking out the unruly brows, peeling away the sad wrinkles. He grew younger, more familiar, dearer . . . For the first time, Rue Morgan began to wonder if she were going mad.

Unlike her own, his tangled, shoulder-length hair could be doffed like a cap; neatly trimmed salt-and-pepper black sprang into its place. He was smiling at her and tearing pieces of his face away, this strange man who was so very familiar, her first conquest, her only failure, it was. . . .

"Quentin! Quentin Rossford!"

"My dear, dear child," he said, the blue of his eyes glittering through quite genuine tears as he bent forward and caught her close in his arms.

"Quentin!" said Rue Morgan wrapping her arms around his neck and recalling her last, hideous moments in Black Harry Morgan's carriage.

Sanity reclaimed her, and with it intuition.

Her hands tightened on Rossford's neck as her own tears

streamed to the edges of her upturned face like something being left behind with supernatural speed.

The smiling happy faces reeled around her. Her grasp clamped even harder on Rossford's neck.

"Father?" she said softly. "Father?"

Quentin Rossford's arms only tightened about her the more.

Chapter Twenty-one

"I shall never be able to call you 'Father' again, Quentin. I have hated that word overlong."

"I assure you, dear Rue, that it has never been one of my life's ambitions to be so called. 'Quentin' will do nicely," reassured the actor, patting the emaciated hand that lay limp across the counterpane.

Sir Feverell Marshwine's Grosvenor Square establishment was very like Sir Nigel's, save these furnishings were older, leaning to walnut and Queen Anne cabriole legs rather than the straight-legged trio who now dominated interior fashions: Hepplewhite, Chippendale, and the upstart Sheraton.

But other than this more substantial atmosphere, Sir Feverell's house was so like Rue's former residence that she felt quite at home. This impression was furthered by the addition of a soundly sleeping Piquant outstretched against her hip. The dog's insistence on taking his traditionally forbidden bedtop post much nearer her patting hand was the only sign that the canine had been aware of her absence. For the gargantuanly self-involved Piquant, however, this change of habit was extremely touching; Rue reciprocated by running her fingers lightly through the flowing golden hair fanned across the coverlet.

"How did you find me?" she asked for perhaps the twentieth time in the day since she'd been taken from the madhouse.

Quentin Rossford recognized that a certain amount of repetition was necessary to one shut up from reality so long. He launched into his customary speech on the subject.

"We finally found the hired coachman, who recalled conveying a 'black-haired banshee' to a madhouse in London. Since there were only a few dozen of these appalling establishments, it was merely a matter of inspecting them all on the pretext of finding lodging for mad uncle Barty Fayre—a role, I might add, I had learned to perfection when enacting the great Elephant Bone Scheme of Blackstone House."

Rue shuddered.

"Yes, we all thought it a great prank to play with . . . *that man's* flagging virility, but I fear we inadvertently resurrected some very ugly tendencies in the creature. I can't tell you what he proposed in the carriage."

"My dear Rue, I'm sure that you could tell me, but it isn't necessary. I can guess."

Rossford leaned over to pull the linens more snugly under her arms, a totally unnecessary gesture that had anyone represented to him as "fatherly," he would have rejected the notion violently.

He regarded her with what he would have described as a purely avuncular expression. They had fed and washed her until the asylum's grime and reek had vanished. These services had only revealed the shrunkenness of her frame, the fungoid paleness of her once creamily vibrant complexion, the angry red march of vermin bites over every exposed portion of skin. And her hair, the fine raven locks that had tossed to the despair of some of the hardest hearts in London, had clouded into a great smoky tangle above her pale face, snarled as high as a court headdress, and only lacking the artifice that made the exaggeration attractive.

"You're frowning, Father Quentin."

"You promised not to call me by that sickeningly sentimental title. Adding my Christian name only makes me sound a priest."

He smiled and leaned back in the bedside chair, meaning merely to watch, not to tire her by talking. But words were what she wanted.

"You knew of me always then, Quentin? Why didn't you tell me?"

He leaned forward with a well-tailored silken rustle and caught up her hand.

"You mustn't hark back to the beginning of old tales when you are living their end," he urged. "I'll tell you again what I can only say: that I am an unprincipled rogue of a dissembler, an actor who's spent his life erecting imaginary characters on the boards, and who has taken advantage of that glamour in his life off the stage. I'd had many affairs of the heart by the time I met your mother, Rue, and was true to each in turn. For a while. Your mother was perhaps the saddest woman I have ever loved. A wiser man would have stayed clear of her." He sighed. "But, like the Moor, I loved more well than wisely on that occasion. Naturally a child came of it. You. I knew it, as did she, for her husband had run hot and cold with her and mostly cold, preferring to browbeat rather than to bed her."

"I hope she knew at least that peace at the end."

"She did, for Black Harry was disgusted by the generative process once it had passed beyond the point of his own pleasure." Quentin's hand tightened on her own. "We agreed, she and I, that we would end our affair; she would devote herself to rearing you. Neither of us guessed, of course, that she would die so soon after your birth. I was an itinerant actor, Rue, with no claim to the motherless babe that was you, nor any reason to think that Morgan suspected—knew—the truth. And I was not cast to be a devoted parent. I thought it best to leave you to your heritage, and frankly thought little more of it over the years. Until you came to my dressing room that day with your astonishing flair and rather incestuous proposal."

She laughed, coloring.

"Then your pose of a man who loves men was merely to excuse your quite natural refusal of me?"

Rossford crossed his graceful hands upon his cravat as one dead and regarded her wickedly through half-lidded eyes.

"My dear, on my funeral bier they shall have to guard me so I don't leap up and swive all of the lady mourners in a row. There would be many, I assure you. No, that was another reason why I would have done more harm than good serving as guardian to an impressionable young female. Though I must admit, my admirable Rue, you have managed to follow in the footsteps of your reprehensible pater quite astoundingly."

Her face clouded, as stormy for a moment as her hair.

"Ah, Quentin, I have made a great mess of it, and—"

Heliotrope swept into the bedchamber then, crossing the muting carpet, face frozen as an axe blade. She bent and whispered something to Rossford, who suddenly sat to the edge of his chair.

"And what mayn't I know now?" demanded Rue, the childish quaver in her voice reminiscent of the madhouse. "No secrets. I've had enough of secrets, please—"

Rossford turned to her instantly.

"Pagett-Foxx is below, wishing to see you."

Rue's hand paused in its rhythmic stroking of Piquant; otherwise, she was utterly calm.

Rossford turned back to Heliotrope.

"Tell the vermin to be gone; she's had enough of crawling things that bite."

"Quentin! Do I detect a tinge of parental outrage?" Rue smiled and put her hand on his frockcoated arm. "I'll see him, Helia, if you can lead him up without glowering like a cannibal. And, Quentin, you'll stay?"

"Try to eject me," he promised, assuming a most menacing frown.

So Sir Nigel Pagett-Foxx came one last time to Rue Morgan's bed to find her sheet-pale and ravaged on the linens, but her dark, snarl-crowned head still regal upon the pillows so carefully piled by Heliotrope.

Nigel was not so skilled as Rossford at concealing his shock at Rue's appearance. He stopped five feet from the bed and simply stared.

"I am pale, but I am not a ghost," she finally said. "Have you come to speak or gawk? You would find better game at Bedlam for that."

The old imperiousness rekindled his sense of injury. Pagett-Foxx jerked his head toward Rossford questioningly.

"Must he sit with us, your newest swain, no doubt?"

"He is my father, Nigel," she said quickly, as Rossford uncoiled more menacingly than a springing panther.

"You're seeing her on her own assent, not mine," said the actor very softly. "My notion of an ideal interview with you would be from your gibbet, sir—"

"Your father? Then, then Morgan is—"

"Not my father. Quite true, Nigel, though neither you nor I knew it. Black Harry did, though. He regaled me with some rather unfatherly proposals on my way to the madhouse."

"Good God."

Nigel sank into Quentin's vacated chair, lifting his hands to his face. He paused and spread the fingers, watching them shake with an undisguised self-contempt.

He looked up to Rue again.

"You have suffered a great deal for my vengeance."

"Yes, you have been most successful in your revenge. Don't tell me now that you are sorry of it. I do not think I should be in your place."

"You are astonishing," he said, seeing cold truth in the expressionless blue eyes meeting his so impassively. "But you, you admit that you used me, deceived me, played fast and loose with my honor, my love, my . . ."

"Pride. That too. Yes. I had chosen my course without any regard of the cost, and I have paid, will pay the price." The icy blue eyes widened to take in what Nigel felt was his entire being. "But Varian Temple did not choose to be the object of your revenge—"

"He took you in my house!"

"You had given a portion of that house over to me to be mine. I in turn gave what part of myself was mine to him. *I* betrayed you, not he." Her almost judicial calm cracked. "Send me back to the asylum if you wish, Nigel. I shan't contest your right to your revenge, but preserve Varian from whatever ill my father visited upon him, for your own sake!"

Nigel hurled himself to his knees by the bed, face buried in the counterpane, pale hair laying across it as silkily as Piquant's.

"Oh, God, Rue. I didn't intend any of it. It was the port, the finest ruby port in your, your—in Morgan's study. I've always had a fondness for port, you recall," he said, looking up with dry but red eyes.

"I drank it then and thought of what I had heard, seen, that final night—I didn't know what he'd do. I never dreamed that he'd have you locked away in some filthy place. And T—t—temple. I don't know what Morgan's done with him, can't imagine—"

"There is where we differ, Nigel," she interrupted in a voice heavier than lead. Pagett-Foxx seemed to sink deeper into the counterpane under the weight of her words.

"I'm sorry, Rue, sorry to my soul for it. My house is an empty asylum to me. I tried to lose myself in the country after you were gone, but when the hounds cornered the fox, it had your blue eyes before it was torn to pieces, and the nights were as black as your hair, your heart . . . I couldn't bear it. Rue—"

Nigel's hand uncurled and groped across the linens to her,

his head still buried, his voice muffled. Rue watched his trembling fingers edge nearer as she would a snake.

"Don't touch me," she said breathlessly just as Nigel's fingertips grazed the last hummock of fabric between his hand and her own. "Don't . . . touch . . . me. I have paid for breaking our bargain, and I am free never to deceive you again."

He looked up, horrified at the loathing in her voice, frozen by it as by a basilisk, a Medusa.

"And I played matchmaker at this tragedy," commented Rossford in soft-spoken bitterness. His hands clapped on either side of the kneeling man's shoulders.

"Come, Pagett-Foxx, you have made your confession and must go to your penance elsewhere. I picked you for a harmless sort who would not be too much for my long-lost Rue. But you were too little, and I must make my own penance for that."

The actor escorted his charge to the door and returned to the testered bed to find Rue sitting upright in her lace-trimmed gown, her fingers crooked behind her neck and working a knotted lump of hair there as if it were a worry bead. If he expected an emotional storm now that Pagett-Foxx had gone, he was disappointed.

"Fetch Helia," she instructed briskly, her thoughts abstracted. "I believe I require a shearing."

"No!" objected the shearer when summoned. Heliotrope's hands fisted on her skirted hips and threatened to become permanent fixtures.

"I'll not cut off all of your hair, Rue Morgan, nor even a wisp of it. 'Twill take some untangling, it's true—and a few days—but I'll have it pure satin down your back again."

"I do not have a few days," said Rue, rising and going to a dressing-table stool where a mirror flashed back an image of her taut face. She picked a pair of bright silver blades, pausing to cradle them in her palm, glance again at her face in the mirror, and smile.

" 'Tis self-destructive, mere butchery. It's your most glorious attribute, your greatest beauty, I can't—"

"I trust I have more to recommend me than a few feet of hair. Cut, good Heliotrope, as neatly as you may. And begin here, my reluctant surgeon; amputate this knot."

Rue pulled a wad of hair from the back of her neck and watched in the glass as the blades snapped shut upon it. Those blades continued snipping at the knots that populated her head, steel alligators swallowing sluggish prey.

Rue didn't watch the black halo of hair diminish around her; her fingers were busy tearing at the first severed lump of wool in her fingers. *Hisssss* went the scissors' hinged jaws, then click, shut. Something plummeted past Rue's shoulders to the floor. And again the hiss, the click, the fall of something dark.

When her fingers had finally untangled the knot, Rue glanced up to find Heliotrope fluffing what remained of her once prodigal dark hair into errant curls around her face and neck.

"It will suffice, I suppose," the maid finally conceded.

"Suffice!" laughed Rossford, coming over to survey the damage. "It will be fashion! Rue, you look charming shorn. After the town sees you, half the fashionable ladies of Mayfair will run willy-nilly off to madhouses to attain the Black Rue Morgan look."

She smiled wanly. "I cannot recommend it." Her fingers raised her project up to Heliotrope, holding it above her own head. "This ring, I shall need a chain for it."

"But, Mistress Rue, it is his, his ring!"

"Yes, I know. A birthday gift from my erstwhile father, a token of his esteem and the fact that he had once again taken that which is most dear to me into his power."

Rue Morgan turned from the looking glass, which was well, for she had not really regarded herself in it since her return from the asylum. She faced Rossford, looking up at him with ophidian calm.

"Convene the Basilisks, Quentin. Convene them tomorrow and tell them I will not be satisfied unless they bring news of Varian Temple."

He looked shrewdly into her unquenchably blue eyes, into the dark, dead sapphire depths of them.

"You are a hard mistress to serve, Rue Morgan."

"I have had a hard master."

As it happened, the Basilisks met the next day at Sir Feverell Marshwine's house with the required news. They would not have dared appear without it.

"The West Indies? And alive, you think?"

"Most certainly alive. The crimping-house bullies were warned not to slay him. We would have found them sooner, but we were most distracted by our search for you, dear Rue—"

"You should not have been!" Rue repented her sharpness an instant later. "But, forgive me, Dr. Radclyffe. The Basilisk Club has been my truest ally and could not have served me better."

Here there were many throat clearings and dropped eyes and shiftings of aching legs and backs. And then one smothered sneeze that made Rue bite her lip, blink away her tears, and sit finally at the great round gaming table in Sir Feverell's drawing room. It took great strength of will for her not to pace, especially when her thoughts were striding in seven-league boots half an ocean away.

"The *Ivory Queen*?"

"A slaver," said Colonel Trumbull, blowing his nose. "Very bad business. Barbados-bound."

"Morgan's plantation," added Humphries, nodding sagely. "He'd not killed you, Miss—er, Miss . . ."

Here the Basilisks exchanged cornered glances, not knowing how to address Black Harry Morgan's daughter when she was Quentin Rossford's bastard.

"Miss Morgan will do still, gentlemen. I have, after all, a reputation to maintain, and I do not think Quentin wishes to acquire a namesake so abruptly. Besides, I think it galls *him*, and that is still our purpose, is it not?"

"Assuredly, assuredly."

"Damn well-spoken."

"Hear, hear."

Rue smiled at the new unanimity of the Basilisk Club.

"And you also agree, gentlemen, that I must embark immediately to find Varian?"

"The earl must be rescued, yes," began Dr. Radclyffe, his glance taking silent count of his fellow members' reactions. "But you are hardly fit after your ordeal for such a voyage, such a dangerous enterprise. We must delegate someone—"

"Yes, myself," said Rue indomitably.

"Rossford?" the doctor beseeched.

The actor fanned his hands. "I sired her, sirs, I do not speak for her. Nor could."

"Then Humphries will accompany you. He's our seafaring member. And Colonel Trumbull, our military one."

Colonel Trumbull hawked self-consciously into his ever-present flag of truce at this honor.

Rue smiled, her fingers idly moving to trace circles at the back of her shorn hairline.

"I cannot ask you gentlemen to forsake your interests here to go traipsing off on a purely personal crusade to the tropics—"

"You cannot go alone!"

"But I have thought of an escort, a military man who is perhaps a bit more fit for such a mission than my dear goutish members of the Basilisk Club. Now don't bridle, gentlemen. I've asked you to play gamester and highwayman and cavalry to the rescue in turn. You have earned a rest and shall have it."

As usual when Rue Morgan expressed her wishes, the very act transformed them into everyone else's intentions. The Basilisks grumbled, each in his own inimitable way, but left the room bowing and limping and kissing her hand, and thought little more about how it all had happened.

Quentin Rossford saw them to the drawing-room door, then returned to a decanter and poured a glass of canary for Rue.

"You look paler than in Romney's infamous portrait," he noted, stroking her drawn cheek.

"Quentin! You have seen it?" Her face finally took on a petal-thin wafer of color.

"And blush you should. I have not seen it, but a Basilisk or two has. It was necessary to speak with His Lordship's man, Welles, to discover what had happened to your earl. I have not met the man, but I must say that I admire his taste in paintings—and his wise intentions in taking yours off the public walls. Even being a scandal must have its limits."

She sipped the wine and smiled.

"I confess, Quentin, that—of all my schemes—was the least successful. Poor Mr. Romney. I wish I'd paid for the thing, then at least I could have kept it to myself."

"When do you leave?"

"For Barbados? In a week or so. Even I must make preparations. But, dearest Quentin, you never doubt my resolve. I am touched."

"Rue, my angel, any young woman who would go on the stage can certainly undertake to go to a half-wild Indies isle and take on the local constabulary. I also think you very wise in your choice of escort."

"You know?"

She glanced up at him sharply and found the mirroring blue eyes glancing down at her just as perceptively.

"You slay two birds with one throw, Rue. You allow your first lover to redeem himself even as you rescue your latest. Ah, you would have had great talent as a courtesan, my dear, but I suspect your intentions are to be tiresomely faithful to this earl of yours. There are no great plays made from situations like that. I warn you, your notoriety will vanish like hair powder if you continue to carry on with this revolting constancy."

"Quentin, you waste your talents on me when you go on

so. Do Congreve, I beg of you," she said, laughing and catching his hand.

His face sobered as he looked down at her, at the cap of dark curls as strokable as a poodle's. His hand tightened on hers.

"Take care, my Rue. For every tragedy that ends in comedy, there's a tragedy that is tragedy to the bitter end. You do not know what you will find there on that savage island."

"Quentin."

She glanced up at him, and he saw all the worry he had feared she lacked floating like ominous, fatal islands in the blue sea of her expression.

"Quentin," she said gently, "I do not even know what I shall find in a place so safe as Shropshire."

Chapter Twenty-two

What she found in Shropshire was Graham Winthrop.

At every stage of the journey there, Rue was reminded that the Earl of Argyle's perch phaeton had most likely passed the same route not long before. She fancied she heard its wheels humming alongside her post chaise, a phantom of the road that raced her as the sun did, appearing to run in tandem, even keep pace when it was actually, irretrievably distant.

In every coach yard she glimpsed great-coated shoulders out of the corner of her eye: the earl pausing here to talk to the groomsman about the proper care of his vaunted blacks, his blacks with the red, white, and black ribbons in their fast-flying tails. There. He had sat on that settle and ordered a round of country beer for the company and enjoyed a hasty repast of roast beef and kidney pie before rising abruptly and pushing onward, driving forward to Shropshire.

Rue's coachman did not dawdle and changed horses as frequently as possible, but it was still two days before they entered the limits of that northern country. The chaise was well-sprung, yet Rue brooded as she rattled around on its padded seats. Her fingers now worried at the ring caught around her neck on a golden chain.

Turning this way and that with the motions of the road, of its wearer, it made an awkward token. It was meant to surround a finger, not bounce at the base of a throat, but Rue had tried it on and found that it slipped over her slender fingers with double room to spare. So she wore it at her neck and thought of Anne Temple and of what she would do if she had to have such a ring fashioned in memory of Anne Temple's brother.

Graham's ancestral home hit her starved senses with the impact of a dream seen after it is long relinquished. Winter claimed the rolling landscape. Only well-feathered birds were evident, sitting on branches stripped to the stark, brittle essentials of their form.

The house itself was warm beyond all weather, a much built-upon sprawl of Gothic stone and Elizabethan half-timbering with spider webs of brown, leafless vines still climbing the stuccoed walls.

How pleasant to marry the pleasant squire who dwelled here, to sit of a February night before the fire and speak of gardens to come and the parson's visit, of children and haying and the great house ball. How pleasant it would have been.

How pleasant the hall with its checkered tile floor, dark wainscoting, and low, arched doors leading to places mysterious and inviting. The heavy carved staircase, perfect for small faces to peer through. Rue went to the foyer fire and extended gloved hands to the flames, though she barely heeded their cackle or felt their friendly leap up towards her, like a pack of greeting hounds.

"Rue!"

He stood in the arch of one of the low, little doors, called away from who knows what estate accounts. He was a shadow as dark as the age-stained woodwork, and she was glad.

"Rue, what are you doing here? I was certain you'd wed the earl and I'd never see you again."

"You see me again, and I do pray you see him again, Graham. Oh, I do hope you do."

She advanced with her hands still extended as they had been to the fire, as if she expected some warmth from his greeting that was greater than even the fiercest flaming of mere wood.

He took her hands and stepped down into the hall, looking at her as intently as she tried not to stare at him.

She had traveled without Heliotrope for the first time in her life and had given no thought to her dress. Still it was her red winter redingote she wore, and it became her even more now that her hair was so impishly shorn, a boyish tumble of curls around her pretty, pointed face.

"You look . . . more lovely than ever, more fashionable," he said, dazed, as if he had forgotten what she had looked like at all.

Rue laughed and tightened her fingers on his.

"Oh, yes, and my hairdresser has been M. Lunatic, the mad hatter of the asylum. It is called the Bedlam Snarl—do you like it?"

She doffed her mock-military tricorn with its gold braid and spun for him.

"The madhouse?"

"Yes, my father finally found a suitable residence for me, as he had discovered appropriate treatment of you."

"Let us walk outside. Can you stand it?"

"The cold? I have been colder, Graham."

He led her through a long, ill-lit passage and suddenly into a room at the house's rear that opened out onto a winter-stripped terrace. A spaniel sleeping by the fire rose as they passed through the chamber and followed them outside.

The overcast day threw keen light upon the empty gardens before them, upon the countryside rolling away in bitter rows of brown and sterile gold. It cast better light upon

Graham Winthrop than the kindness of his dusky house. Rue tried to keep from staring at him.

"Your garden must be beautiful in the spring."

"Yes," he answered, "all things are lovely in their infancy."

"Do you think our love was an infant, that I was?"

His ungloved hands twitched a bit involuntarily. If it was a gesture they meant to make, it was a paralyzed one.

"I only know that I am aged beyond belief," he finally said, thrusting his hands into his breeches' pockets.

Rue stared at him openly now that his own attention was cast down to the stick-strewn ground.

He had aged, his light brown hair silvered at the temples, his very face shriveled somehow until all the handsomeness in it seemed to have dried up and blown away. His eye, his left eye, it looked off-angle at the world now and thus saw nothing. Even Graham's frame seemed to have wizened, as if fate had leveled a blow at his solar plexus and kept the fist there so his shoulders sagged and stooped over to cushion the impact.

She turned back to regard the stark countryside. "You would look very dashing in an eyepatch, Graham," she said. "As smart as I when I was asylum-shorn."

"Shropshire does not require such niceties; neither do I."

"You required a great deal once."

"A great deal was taken from me by your father."

She turned back to him, and confronted his one eye.

"He's not my father, Graham, and always knew it, if I did not. I have found my true father, and he is a better man entirely. An actor—can you comprehend it? A most elegant man with more heart than he can hide by all his posing. I wish you could meet him."

"As I met your earl?"

"What did you think of him?"

"I thought him . . . brave, bold, a gentleman of first quality, handsome, healthy, heart-free. What would you have me say, Rue? I thought him blessed and me cursed. I begrudged him every shred of his good fortune and repented the next instant. But I did tell him the truth of what happened at your . . . stepfather's hands. He seemed to think it important that you know of my disgrace."

"Not *your* disgrace, Graham, mine! That is what my earl drove so hard to Shropshire to bring back to me. The truth. Which is that *I* abandoned you, not you me. *I* was found wanting, Graham, not you. I never tried to trace you because . . . because I thought that my father had managed to divert you and thus it didn't matter how. I was not worthy of you, Graham. You were right to fade from my life after . . . after what he did to you. I was too like him to ever accept you back."

"Confessions are good for the soul, Rue." Graham paced a bit on the flagstone, then paused and coughed dryly. "But little else. I as good as died that night, and I don't simply mean my wretched lungs, though the physicians shake their heads ever more dourly with each passing winter month. I have lost whatever it is that makes me a man, a free being with some belief in something called a future and a rôle of any meaning to play in that future. That is why I stayed away, not because of any judgment on you, but because I could not bear to bring the straw man I had become back to the woman who believed that I was cast in iron. Your earl will never break, Rue. I think his mettle is better suited to yours."

"Let us hope he will not break," she murmured.

Winthrop paused in his aimless walk around the terrace, caught fast upon the anguish in her voice.

"It's not old loves you've come to dig up, but—"

"New ones I would never see interred. Graham, I've come to you for help. My father has made disposition of Varian as he once made disposition of you."

"Good God!"

"Not very good at all, I'm afraid, Graham."

Rue's voice broke. She stooped abruptly to pet the accompanying spaniel.

"The Earl was attacked and kidnapped by my, my . . . adversary's crimping-house bullies and put aboard a ship bound to take on slaves at the Guinea Coast, then sail westward for the Indies—most likely Barbados where Black Harry has a plantation."

Rue bowed her hatless dark head and laid it against the spaniel's dappled brown and white back. Outlining the unvarnished realities of Varian's fate before a man who stood half-blind and half-dead from the vengeance of the same man who had plotted the earl's bitter fate made Rue feel suddenly hopeless.

Graham stood still for a long moment, watching her gloved fingers curl into the spaniel's coat. The dog turned a melancholy muzzle over his shoulder to assess this sudden attention from a stranger.

Graham sighed. "And I envied the man."

When Rue's face remained buried in the old spaniel's shoulder, Graham went over, bent to take hold of her arms, and pulled her to her feet. The effort brought on a coughing spell.

Hearing it, Rue simply exchanged her furred pillow for the wool one of Graham's sleeve, clinging there with her eyes shut until the spasms finally stopped shuddering through his body. She opened her eyes to the landscape of navy sleeve directly before them and would look no further.

Graham recovered sufficiently to put his arms around her and speak calmly, his voice flowing out from somewhere above her head, remote and almost magisterial, almost Godlike.

"What can I tell you, Rue? You've seen the color of your . . . of the man's revenge in me. That color is red. Bloody, vicious red."

Her fingers tightened on his sleeve, and her eyes squeezed shut again, but they could not keep out the rising tide that covered her inexorably within, without. Red, the arms holding her. Red-sleeved. For, oh, Redsleeves was all my joy and oh, Redsleeves was my delight . . . Red, red, red is the color of my true love's—what? Coat? Heart? Sleeves? Body? Red with blood. Her entire horizon rose in a suffusing crimson tide, a reverse sunset that soaked upward to the sky. There was red enough in her world to paint Macbeth's incarnadine seas a deeper hue, a gaudy, clotted crimson.

"He most likely isn't dead, Rue," came Graham's soft, distant voice, gentle if it had not been bitter. "Morgan is too cruel to kill."

She broke away to stare into the once familiar, once dear face. Not only abuse had distorted Graham's looks, but a crust of bitterness that had bubbled up from within and hardened slowly without. He still had a cleft chin, though; Rue could barely remember the time when she had doted on this idiosyncrasy as if it were a pearl of great price.

"We will find him," she intoned between her teeth, her nails gouging into his red wool—*navy*, navy wool sleeves. A good omen. Navy blue, sailor's blue, for a trip by water, by sea. A nautical journey and at its end ... Fire. Red. Death. Revenge. An answer, though it be written in blood. Varian's blood.

"You will go with me then, Graham, to find Varian?"

"There is little rhyme or reason for me to stay here, as good to die in one place as another. Of course I'll go with you, Rue. It has not mattered one way or another what I do since the eve of your eighteenth birthday."

"I am nineteen now, Graham," she whispered fiercely, clinging to his lapels and looking deep into the dead gray gaze he presented her.

"And I am ninety," he answered tonelessly. "You may have grown a year or so older and suffered much and learned more—learned even, you say, to love. I do not begrudge you that, Rue, but do not ever do me the disfavor of imagining that there is some renaissance in store for me. I am lost, whether I live or die, and so, you see, it is no great matter to me which I do."

He meant it, every word. He was a kind of animated

corpse, an utterly hollow man. Rue stared at him, realizing that mere kind words from her, mere dependence upon him would not suffice to rekindle his young man's faith in the world.

She tried to imagine what would happen if she found Varian as broken in mind and body as Graham was. She shivered in the navy wool arms so unemotionally enclosing her, shivered violently until it was more of a shudder.

"You are cold? Ay, it is still winter."

The arms tightened on her and turned her to face the house. Graham slowly guided her indoors, his flat voice offering her finally the only words of hope he could muster.

"You mustn't chill before we leave and catch an ague. Come in by the fire, and don't fret. The climate, at least, will be warmer in Barbados."

The droop-eared spaniel rose arthritically from the cold stone pavement and followed them in, his nails clicking behind them like an irritant, a reminder, a clock.

Black Rue Morgan mercifully didn't hear it.

Chapter Twenty-three

The great iron rollers turned, as raucous as carriage wheels, caught the tubes of cane, and drew them into their crushing motion.

The cane came in long, pale stalks, like bone, but it splintered to toothpicks between the rollers. Sweat-polished black arms fed the cane to the grinder as fast as it would take them. Cane juice wept copiously from the shredded stalks and ran like pale sherry down lead-lined gutters to the boiling house.

There the huge copper clarifiers waited to bubble the cane to boiling point until a white foam rose to the surface for mercy. Then all the sweet, pale, clear, amber liquid would be drawn into the grand copper where it would boil for hours into the molasses that made the West Indies Isles the richest source of income in the world for the British Empire.

Rue Morgan, wearing the palest and frothiest of ivory muslin gowns, hatted in a great dipping circle of straw with red ribbons trailing to her hips, holding an organdy sunshade like a walking stick with its ruffled length held shut by another red ribbon, Rue Morgan stood and observed the process with aloof calm.

The noise, the heat, even the stench rose around and seemed to evaporate from her elegant figure like steam. She studied the scene for some time, observing the well-muscled blacks' frenetic pace, the disintegration of the passive cane, the eternal, giant, iron jaws masticating everything that came within reach.

Finally she leaned toward her guide and addressed him by raising her voice above the clamor without seeming to shout, a trick no one yet had mastered in the Barbados sugar mills.

"Mr. Fitch! Mr. Fitch, what, pray, is the function of that person there with the hatchet?"

Her closed parasol rose lazily from the littered floor to indicate a white overseer who watched the proceedings with feet planted wide and arms folded, one hand trailing a short but lethal ax.

Fitch, a beefy man whom Rue had never seen unglossed by a shimmer of sweat, turned to her knowingly.

"Some o' these bloody slackers get careless in harvest time when we keep 'em feedin' the grinders twelve hours a day or more. Gets their filthy black paws in the rollers, you see. Then there's naught for it but ole Sam here's got to hack off whatever's left."

"But this reduces the value of the slave, does it not?"

Fitch, who'd been watching her shrewdly, allowed a broad smile to slowly slice his fleshy face.

"Ay, and you're as sharp as your father. True, hard labor would seem to be barred to the bastards once they got more toes than fingers, but there's other tasks for 'em to do. Mayhap they stick their black pinkies into the rollers deliberate-like so's to shirk the hard jobs," he suggested, winking broadly.

Rue rotated an imperious head to the man.

"Precisely what I was wondering, Mr. Fitch. I can see that my father is well-served in you. Now may we see something other?"

Her guide bowed deeply; when she turned to precede him

out of the millhouse, he surreptitiously wiped his streaming forehead on a grimy sleeve. He was right behind her and obsequious when she turned back to him on entering the Barbados daylight.

"A most peculiar climate, Mr. Fitch," she observed contemplatively. "That alone has made my voyage quite educational."

"Hot as Hades, you're damn right, Miss Morgan, but you do mighty cool in it," Fitch added admiringly, surveying her openly from face to foot.

"You are overkind," said Rue remotely, unruffled by the man's crude familiarity.

He could have been an admirer at Ranelagh with whom she exchanged cool, calculated repartee, rather than a hulking, sweating, transported piece of British roast beef, distinctly middling class and distinctly unpleasant. Yet here on Barbados, he was not an unpowerful man, as dozens of blacks under his authority could attest quite fervently.

Rue's lips smiled slightly at Mr. Leonidas Fitch, but her eyes traveled the broad tamarind-tree-lined avenues leading to a coolly verandahed plantation house. And orange trees, there were orange trees here as well, just as at Ranelagh where once she had strolled with Nigel and feigned headache and gone back to Grosvenor Square to entertain an earl. Rue's eyelids fluttered, and Mr. Fitch took advantage of the opportunity to catch her by an elbow.

"You're quite all right, Miss?"

Her eyes—bluer than the vivid waters of Carlisle Bay, bluer even than the lying eye-whites of a lemon-juice-and-powder-dosed black prettied up for sale by a dishonest trader—flashed open at him instantly.

"It is only the heat, Mr. Fitch. And it was . . . extremely close in the mill." Mr. Leonidas Fitch stepped back a bit.

But Rue truly did feel dizzy, internally dizzy, mind-faint. She felt that she stood simultaneously in two, irreconcilable worlds, and knowing that, feared that if Varian Temple dwelled on this island, she might only find half of him, a shadow.

The others had not felt it, not even Graham, who should know what it was to be split in twain, to have one's mind and body at disbelieving odds.

Helia, of course, had returned to the island of her birth, and of her race's servitude, with more tightly pursed lips and great, slowly widening brown eyes. But Helia clearly knew on which side of the chasm she stood, that much was obvious.

Both she and Graham had remained at the house, entertained by Morgan's overseer, while Rue had insisted on a tour of the plantation conducted by the revolting, but malleable, Leonidas Fitch.

She looked down the falling away slopes to the island's east-facing bay, to the geography that had kept this most westward of the Indies isles safe in British hands. A swift-flowing trade current made approaching the island's only navigable bay at any other than a calculated, well-telegraphed, peaceful pace impractical.

So Bridgetown sat above the bay's placid waters with all the self-satisfied bustle of a home seaport town, like Bristol. Its bow-windowed shops sparkled with the most fashionable jewelry, timepieces, rich fabrics, and rareties from all quarters of the globe, for Barbados's planters were among the world's wealthiest, and they lived like it.

The streets were broad, clean, thronged with gay and industrious people, children threading their way through the crowds like merry circus dwarves. Here and there, one of the island's officers would flash by, a vivid tropical bird of officialdom in gold-braided scarlet coat. Graham Winthrop seemed oblivious to these figures, but Rue's heart leapt up at their appearances.

Why, it seemed like home. Like a happy, safe English town, His Majesty's own on guard, but no outward fortifications because the place's very islanded isolation was a more effective moat than any erected by a medieval lord. Like

England itself, a sceptered isle, safe, homelike. Safe. Civilized as an ... an earl.

Then the party had gone inland to Black Harry Morgan's plantation, and Rue had taken her first step on the unsteady ground of an island split into two, an island halved from the first by its blatant dependence on an alien, transported population to squeeze the liquid gold that was sugar from its terraced canefields.

The few blacks she had seen in Bridgetown, body servants mainly, had been as gaily if raggedly caparisoned as the tropical birdlife, affecting crests and wings of clothing that lay upon their deeply dark bodies like fallen rainbows. And they had chattered like birds, in high, shrill dialects blending English and African into an undecipherable stew of sounds.

The dignified Heliotrope's eyes had grown round with a wonder she had not evinced since childhood and her first being taken to the foggy, dank European isle that was to be her home. Now the strangeness resided in her forgotten origins.

But Graham Winthrop had paced these amazing streets with a leaden foot, as undistracted by Bridgetown's colorful display as a jaded observer is undeceived by the magician's waves with his empty hand.

He was right to reserve his opinion, even as the party traveled in an elegant carriage down hedge-lined roads, up gentle hills away from the bauble of Bridgetown nudging a gently bouncing, ever sun-filled bay of blue water.

For Black Harry Morgan's plantation was known as Barbados's grimmest, on an island reputed for a stiff and whip-underlined policy towards its enslaved black population.

Now every black back the newcomers passed bore the whip's pale scars. Every ebony neck was ringed with an iron collar, a sort of fallen crown. Pale, thick circlets of scar tissue around dark ankles and wrists resembled ivory bangles at a distance, attesting to the arduous middle passage that many slaves had but recently made.

The children, of course, bore no such manacle marks. They had been born here, into durance, and would acquire their body brands from whatever disciplinary measures were deemed necessary to educate them to their lot. The plantation overseer, one Captain Jack Skinner, kept a collection of these disciplinary instruments in a drawing room case and displayed them to his gawking visitors.

"Now here's a pretty collar for you, Miss Morgan, one I vow you've never seen wore by the ladies of Mayfair."

With a festal jangle of chains, he elevated a heavy iron ring hung with links.

"This shortest one leads to an ankle manacle, draws it up against the bastard's lazy back and holds it there so the fellow can only hop about and get a taste of what life'd be like wi' but one leg. Sometimes it's more than a taste, as the putrefaction sets in and we've got to saw him off at the knee. And we've the customary iron cages with spikes, of course, but it's hard to realize their effectiveness unless you see a slave hung out to dry in them. Perhaps we can find a refractory bastard in need of such handling while you remain, Miss Morgan. 'Tis an excellent entertainment to come by day after day."

Captain Skinner regretfully let the chains coil back into their display position and shut the case as if to safeguard its contents against theft, as if his implements of torture were rare and wonderful possessions.

Rue and Graham absorbed this information with dead eyes. Heliotrope, acting as Rue's shadow, as any good island body servant must, was equally expressionless, though even if she had registered the most blatant horror, it wouldn't have mattered, as Captain Skinner never looked at her.

But Rue Morgan looked at Captain Skinner closely.

"Most enlightening, captain," she murmured finally. "I'm sure that you are a master of the arts of persuasion." She examined his immaculate figure, barrel-chested, stiff-legged, attired with almost military smartness in breeches and frockcoat.

"My father has spoken highly of you," she said confidentially, taking a turn around the wide room and leaving Heliotrope and Graham momentarily behind. "He told me before I embarked, 'If you would learn life, and the firm hand it takes to guide the lesser creatures under you through it to your satisfaction, study Captain Skinner.' "

Rue did so with an amazing combination of worldly assessment and girlish admiration.

"You are a fine figure of a man, sir, but it was the qualities of your mind that I believe my father meant me to apprentice myself at. You were a ship's captain for many years, were you not? A very famous one in the merchant trade—Captain Jack Skinner, the scourge of Malta, you were called, I believe."

Captain Skinner clasped his hands behind his ramrod back.

"I had some small fame as a strict taskmaster, Miss Morgan. Overmuch, I fear. These namby-pamby Quakers and do-gooders took exception to my methods, and I had difficulty at length securing a ship, until your fine father installed me here. How does he do now? I have not seen him in some years, since his latest visit."

"He waxes well, Captain Skinner, and is quite as fierce as ever, I assure you." Rue smiled. "You must not fret about his health, sir. That is not why I visit his holdings. I will, if I may impose upon you, explain my somewhat delicate position. You are a man that a young and admittedly inexperienced female may confide in, I trust?"

No females but the most hardened and experienced had offered Captain Jack Skinner anything of any sort in decades. The man's dream of being received in London drawing rooms as a heroic nautical figure suddenly resurrected. He bowed creakingly from long disuse of such social refinements and gestured to a settee near the French doors leading onto a broad terrace.

"I am at your disposal, Miss Morgan," he promised, pleased to see relief rise in her eyes at his declaration.

Rue leaned nearer and lowered her voice.

"You see, Captain Skinner, my father has given me this plantation. I am the new . . . master, if you will."

"I've heard of no such arrangement as that!" he objected, rearing away but drawn back to Rue again by the leash of the perfume she wore, delicately floral over something toothsomely citruslike. The tropical heat released these glisandos of scent from even ordinary colognes. Rue Morgan's perfumes were not ordinary.

Her dark lashes fluttered modestly downward.

"It is a secret transferal. I'm certain you are a man sensitive enough to understand my father's position. I am an only child, his only heir.

"Now it is true," continued Rue, sweeping her hands wide and accidentally letting one fall to Skinner's forearm. She leaned nearer. "It is true I am a mere woman and alien to such responsibilities. I shall have to rely upon you heavily, captain." She demonstrated by leaning even nearer. "Heavily. But my father has implicit faith that you are an ideal mentor for me as I learn the particulars of plantation-owning. And rest assured, sir, I am Black Harry Morgan's daughter, and I mean to squeeze the last drop of"—she drew back abruptly and regarded him through narrowed eyes—"the very last drop of sweat, blood, and sugar from this investment. There'll be no slacking because the master wears skirts. Serve me well, and your lot will be sweet indeed. Try to cheat me, and hell will not be a sorry enough place for you!"

He stared at her, at Black Rue Morgan with more iron in her voice than he had in his curiosity cabinets. She stood then, as snowy and aloof as a mountain, as rock-hard and remote.

"But you are an honest man who has served my father well; such warnings are not for you."

"Certainly not." Skinner belatedly sprang up beside her.

"You may rely upon me, Miss Morgan. I will carry out your wishes to the commas. What are they now?"

"I would tour the rest of the plantation. You need not guide me, perhaps you have an underseer whose fingers are on the pulse of plantation life."

Skinner nodded brusquely. "I have just the man, though he be a trifle crude—"

"Excellent. I am Black Harry Morgan's daughter, Captain Skinner. I have seen things you cannot imagine. And, by the by, it is no longer necessary for you to rattle your little toys at me," she said, smiling calmly. " 'Tis all very well to impress casual visitors with details of island life, but I own this plantation now and am not interested in local legends, be they tales of voodoo and obeah or torments."

He nodded and trailed her back to the room's other end where Graham and Heliotrope waited equally docilely.

Rue drew her white cotton gloves from her reticule and proceeded to don them daintily.

"If I am to tour the premises, I should go properly gloved, do you not think?" she inquired serenely. "Helia, my parasol. Tell me, Captain Skinner, one legend does intrigue me. I heard in Bridgetown of a 'White Slave' "— Skinner's face grew instantly guarded—"and I have reason to know that my father entrusted you with a pet project of his. Can you report anything on this subject?"

"You will see for yourself, I believe, Miss Morgan," said Skinner stiffly, clamping his jaw shut stubbornly.

Rue stared at him for a long moment, then arched her eyebrows, nodded grandly, and swept out to the foyer. Skinner followed and sent a house black for his underseer, the very Leonidas Fitch beside whom Rue now strolled the paths of this island paradise. She glanced to Fitch's rough-shirted form, then drew a lacy square from her reticule and held it daintily to her nose.

"Ay, they're smelly creatures, though we have 'em out and wash 'em down regular; no such nicety as fopperied cleanliness, mind you," he added hastily, "but good, common sense, as it seems to keep the fever from 'em. Blacks abed with the ravings don't cut cane."

"Admirable logic, Mr. Fitch," said Rue from behind her veiling handkerchief.

They were walking farther from the plantation house and sugar mills now, downwind toward the fields. After a walk of perhaps a quarter of a mile, Rue saw a large, pleasant square garden surrounded by rows of palm-thatched plaster and wattle huts that each looked large enough to accommodate a small pony.

"Here's where we quarter the brutes." Fitch gestured expansively around the Lilliputian village. "The garden's theirs, but you can see they've let it go to rack and ruin, which only gives you an idea as to how far they'd let their work slack if they didn't have the leather and powder to keep 'em dancing."

Fitch patted the pistol butt which made a shining wooden hummock above a broad, black leather belt that only underlined the ample belly swelling over it.

Rue Morgan eyed both of these attributes distastefully—mechanical death and the fleshy signs of a life ill-lived.

"They seem docile enough," she commented of the women and children deployed around the compound.

"Ay, they grow sleek on cane greens now, and the harvest is always an excuse for their pagan rituals. Drums, they dance to, half-naked, and screeching and spinning and catching onto one another." Fitch's eyes narrowed as if he were gazing into the nighttime bonfire, as if the charcoal figures were bounding around it already.

"And their women, twisting and writhing they are until they seem half-mad from the motion, the drums . . ." Fitch looked back to Rue and licked his lips. "They're heathen, ugly black wenches, else a man might be tempted to—but they couple like cattle amongst themselves, and white men leave such well enough alone." He spat to the ground ahead of them.

Rue paused and impaled her sharp ivory parasol tip to the

earth. "I'm relieved to find my overseers virtuous," she remarked dryly. "And what do those women do?"

He glanced puzzled to the cabin stoops where slave women seemed engaged in picking over their offsprings' woolly heads and eating some delicacy simultaneously. Fitch laughed, a deep, unamused sound that ran around the village and froze gestures in mid-air.

"Lice! They're crawling with 'em. Their mothers, like monkeys, pick 'em off and eat 'em. You can't say we don't feed our blacks meat, Miss Morgan. Lazy brutes they are. They'd rather strangle themselves on their own tongues than face the lash of honest work. We must watch 'em constant. By luck, cane grows itself, for 'tis a surety if we depended overmuch on these vermin for work, we'd not see a barrel of molasses, much less a bottle of rum for our efforts."

"Mr. Fitch, you are a better education than a university," remarked Rue.

A piglet came running on stout pale legs through the garden, a child as black as the animal was white behind it. The child threw itself upon its quarry and carried it kicking and squealing back to a sty, burden almost as large as bearer.

"These little niggers gather green meal for the pigs; it's good training for when they're old enough to work the fields. But watch these monkeys; they're worse thieves than the urchins of St. Giles and far nimbler."

Rue had wandered to the village center, drawn by the gentle prattle of a stream. This soft constant chuckle at Ranelagh or Vauxhall or in any other English pleasure garden would have been considered a drawing card. Orange, plantain, and other undetermined fruit trees gathered thirstily along the borders of this free-flowing water.

"And that?" she inquired of a laden but foreign tree as luxuriant and alien as if it grew in Eden.

"Avocado pear tree. Greasy stuff," dismissed Fitch. "The kind of slime they eat. I'll show you their quarters for your knowledge, but you'll not want to visit here often for your nostril's sake."

Rue smiled appreciatively and dabbed at these porcelain appendages with her handkerchief. She did not tell Mr. Leonidas Fitch that the stench of the slave huts was precisely equal to the madhouse's overcrowded commonroom's reek. She feared such realities might be overcrude for his delicate sensibilities.

"I have not seen many men," she noted, "save those in the mill and the boiling house. Surely they all cannot have lost arms to the hatchet and feet to Captain Skinner's most remarkable metal devices?"

Fitch laughed, his mouth splitting into a landscape of intermittent teeth, jagged as rocks in the bay.

"Devices, you calls 'em? And what pray do you title a whip, Miss Morgan? A leather ribband? Oh, you're a daughter of Black Harry, all right. Many's the time I've given him a demonstration of my skill with the cat-o'-nine-tails at the whipping post up to the house. I can make it flutter like silk or bite like a flaming fer-de-lance. You'd relish a demonstration, would you not, Miss Morgan?"

"I'm certain of it that you are admirably skilled, Mr. Fitch, a whip-master nonpareil."

He frowned at the Frenchified word, uncertain whether it was praise or ridicule. Her closed lips were curved upward in a taut smile, her eyes the deepest blue of a Barbados twilight.

"Ay," he boasted, "I've made a few of the blacks run red." He frowned, puzzled. " 'Tis so everlasting hot here, not fit for a white man. But they thrive on it, they thrive on thrivin' no matter what. And each day is so like the next, you see—clear sky, bluer than your eye, day after bloody day. And the heat, the heat so high it makes you run water, though the rains never come 'til the autumn and then they come so fast and hard they're like to blow a man to hell and back for the trick o' it." His fist went to the pistol butt at his waist and massaged it. "A man's got to take action to know he's alive here on these cursed islands. An' they're lazy, lying, thievin' wretches with no God but their treacherous witch doctors and nothing to recommend 'em save they breed like rabbits. There's no stoppin' 'em, more and more runnin' about, sullen devils, thinkin' behind their shifty black eyes black thoughts, black plans, black—"

"Yes, I understand you, Mr. Fitch," said Rue very calmly, quite smoothly. "You've had a hard lot of it."

Her white-gloved hand paused, then rested lightly on his grimy sleeve. Fitch's frantic eyes came to her. Muddy eyes they were, as begrimed as the rest of the man.

"I don't consort wi' 'em!" he asserted wildly. "I'm not what you'd call a good Christian, but I been baptized and I stick to my own kind, when it's to be had."

"There, there, Mr. Fitch, I never doubted it for a moment."

Rue watched perspiration pearl his forehead and roll like cane fluid down his florid face.

"Some there is, some highly placed, that come on the Saturday nights off from the fields and, and—your father was one. Come down with Captain Skinner, he would, the two together. Down to the village like common dogs of a night. And I must follow them to see they come to no harm. That's why so many yellow flowers bloom in this garden," Fitch said heavily, his hand leaving the pistol long enough to gesture to the surrounding children.

"Shocking! I'm so grateful, Mr. Fitch, that you have been frank about this. I had . . . no idea," said Rue, still speaking as smoothly as she could, opening and lofting her parasol to her shoulder and spinning it there to distract him.

His eyes flashed obediently to her whirling sunshade, and the madness in them glazed over. Then they rested intently on her.

"You'd not resemble your father in that, would you, Miss Morgan? I don't think I could allow it. You'd never consort wi' 'em . . . ?"

"Heaven forbid! How could I think it, Mr. Fitch? I fear there are some things my degenerate parent has hidden from me. I cannot tell you how appalled I am. Pray let us pause on our tour a moment while I collect myself."

This time she applied her lace handkerchief to her eyes, her hand shaking slightly on the parasol handle. This last touch was not feigned; Rue Morgan had learned to recognize the mad, even when they walked in what was purported to be a sane world.

Fitch stood before her, trembling himself and ultimately reassured by her maidenly repulsion.

Rue learned another thing about this world of her former father's—it, too, rode the razor's edge between one thing and another. It offered a geography of brinks, between madness and sanity, life and death, unparalleled wealth and freedom, and unimagined poverty and impressment. In between dwelt many yellow-faced shadows, half-breeds of the spirit.

She recognized a certain spirit beyond bondage in the communal life of the Negroes Fitch had described, in their dancing and their decidedly unChristian witch doctors, and even in their unique dialect, their deplorably ungentlemanly trait of fighting their masters with lies, theft, and laziness. In the master's contempt, she smelled fear in the most obvious manifestation she had sensed since the madhouse.

"You said some slaves still harvest the cane. I would see these stalks worth their length in gold. Take me to the fields, Mr. Fitch."

"Ay, best be leavin' this hellhole, this stenchhole," he agreed, leading her along the stream and even farther away from the house, from the village, from any human face, whether black or white.

For the first time, Rue Morgan felt a fear that was as great as the hope that had taken her fifteen-hundred leagues.

But Fitch seemed calmer away from the slaves' domestic center and pointed out exotic trees, bushes, and birds to her as if he were a lecturer at the British Museum.

Rue nodded, smiled, and inclined her head inquiringly at all the proper moments. And saw nothing. Barely heard anything. Except in the distance, the rhythmic bawl of laboring slaves, the same gutteral nonsense syllables as were sung in time to their bends and heaves on the Bridgetown docks.

"Hear 'em, do you? An unmelodious sort—another thing against 'em." Fitch patted his pistol. Rue thought she knew why the wood was so shiny; it had been worn so.

"Here we are, Miss Morgan. The cane stands higher than a man when it's growin', but most has been cut for the mills. Save this patch."

Fitch nodded to an overseer who strode booted, pistol-hung, and whip-handed on the higher path bordering the canefield.

Amid the high, pale, tasseled cane stand, a dozen dark backs bent to the task of cutting, machetes swooping rhythmically left and right, cane stalks falling softly to either side of the harvesters' snapping advance.

Every back was lined with the random tracks of the whip, and every back was dark in the Barbados sun, every back and head was bent, every bent head black. The sun even seemed to congeal to ebony in a bright white sky.

He was not here. Varian Temple was not here, in this, the last corner of the plantation to be reached, here among the alien cane. He was not here.

He was not.

"Miss Morgan! You're not going to keel over— ?"

"The sun," she murmured, shaking Fitch's hand away and staring at him as if he were mad. "The sun!" she explained lucidly.

Chapter Twenty-four

Varian Temple paused for a moment to glance slightly up toward the road—a tricky business, for the sun invariably blazed over one's shoulder and blinded one.

The overseer, who had the advantage of having the light at his back, would always spot such unpermissioned movement and send the whip snaking over to stop it.

This time no such rude tap on Varian's cocoa-bean-brown shoulder came. Three silhouettes stood on the road—the overseer's familiar outline; the vicious Fitch's well-bellied profile with pistol butt protruding from it like a nose; and, and another . . . a silhouette of delirium or abomination, something skirted, but with two great fanning saucers atop its head. . . .

The men's forms bent inward toward this vision. Varian straightened further and stopped cutting utterly, letting his eyes endow what he saw with the familiarities of another world, another life.

A woman, a sun-shaded, straw-hatted white woman. Varian stood fully upright for the first time that day. No . . .

not a white woman, a black one. Rue Morgan, Black Rue Morgan.

He was capable of only wonder, wonder and the final apprehension that she had turned her head back to the field and was now staring directly toward him, frozen and staring, either a Medusa or a victim of one.

"I am quite all right, gentlemen," Rue Morgan remarked to the men bracketing her. "The sun, it is merely the sun. Quite hot. And then—that slave, he is staring at me."

"Slave? Staring? Where? The impudent cur!"

Rue Morgan's white-gloved finger rose as if drawn by a magnet and pointed to the only dark figure standing with the cane rather than bowing to it.

"There," she said. "Quite openly."

"Martin, your whip," Fitch growled to his underling.

Rue's white glove slid swiftly to the uncoiling whip butt.

"No. You shall raise cane dust and ruin my gown." She turned appealingly to Fitch. "Did you not promise me a demonstration of your more formal disciplinary measures, Mr. Fitch? Perhaps this is the occasion."

"Ay, he's a contrary one. He'd have been with the renegade Maroons in the hills, save they wouldn't have a white man."

"A white man?"

Rue elevated her parasol to further shade her eyes and minced nearer the edge of the road.

"Why, he's as brown as my morning coffee, and I can see most of him," she noted, studying the frozen figure clad only in ragged breeches. "And his hair is sun-streaked in spots, true, but overall quite, quite black as a raisin. Why, it must be my father's pet charge, for see how it stares and stares at me. It has grown quite insolent. I think it incumbent upon me as new mistress of this plantation to insist on swift retribution for such offenses as stopping work to stare."

Fitch pulled his pistol with the relief of a man finally granted the release his nature required. "Martin, you'd better apply the manacles. We wouldn't want any uproar around the new mistress."

Varian scrambled barefoot up the incline, brown even to his toes, brown everywhere save for the scars along his back and the white of his eyes. Those eye whites remained on Rue Morgan, as blazing as a pair of twin suns, as empty as a glass when everything in it has been drained.

No wonder she had not recognized him. His hair was longer than hers and tied back in a gaily colored cloth. His wrists were similarly decorated with cuffs of figured red material, and his hands, as he extended them for the irons, were filthy, the nails rimmed in black.

He seemed otherwise fit, for while slaves were starved in transport, once arrived they were fed enough to make their work worth it. And the muscles under his once pallid flesh had swollen to the strength required for manual labor.

Rue idly watched the manacling of her discovery, rocking from side to side in perfect boredom and spinning her lace-edged parasol on her shoulder until the shadow of it across her features seemed to be a fast-woven web veiling them.

"Now get along ahead of us, man, and don't look back. The lady don't care for the sight of your dirty brown face, and I can't say I blame her," urged Fitch, prodding his pistol into his prisoner's side.

Varian finally tore his gaze off Rue and started back down the path before them, adjusting his steps to his keeper's convivial pace.

"One must always keep one's eyes open on a plantation such as this," suggested Rue Morgan, ambling alongside the triumphant Fitch.

"Every minute, Miss Morgan." He pointed with the pistol to the bare back ahead of him. "Now this one may have been born white, but he's lived with the blacks long enough to acquire their taint. He's not tricky, like them—oh, no, balkish he is. Plain won't up and do things. We've had our discussions before, him, me, and the leather."

"How persistent you must be, Mr. Fitch. And he. Perhaps

it is the climate; the heat makes us all mulish. Surely you were not born here. Tell me, from where did you spring?"

"Mother England, Miss Morgan, though I now call this pestilent stepchild of hers home. I've sailed under Captain Skinner as first mate and gotten in a spot o' trouble wi' him, too. So we're landlubbers now, and no likin' for it, save the pay be good and there's none to call us up for a too-liberal use o' the whip or the keelhaul."

"The keelhaul. Another disciplinary device, I don't doubt. You must explain it to me, Mr. Fitch."

And he did, Mr. Fitch, as Varian walked ahead, every syllable of their conversation branding itself on his ears more painfully than any pet of circling leather.

She was here, his question and his answer, only now she left no room for doubt. There was only her lilting soft voice, interrogating the sadistic Fitch on his methods of torment both past and present. And he, Varian Temple—or what was left of him after the middle passage and several month's durance as a field slave—must walk ahead of them to the certain agony of the whipping post and the even greater anguish of Rue Morgan's betrayal.

Fools, he considered bitterly, deserved as many whippings as they got, but he would rather be a dead fool than one hung out to dry for the entertainment of Black Rue Morgan. If the renegade slaves in the hills wouldn't have him, the scavengers could. Even crows had a softer touch than the traitorous Rue Morgan. Black, Black Rue Morgan.

He whirled, all flying hair and set face, crouching with animal instinct.

His fisted knuckles were as white as teeth and grinned at Leonidas Fitch as they came rushing up, the chain between them knocking his pistol away, then the crash of both metal cuffs into his jaw.

Fitch reeled backward in the direction that the pistol had arched, toward the path-shadowing orange trees. Varian's double fists rammed Fitch's feather-pillow belly and drove into his white-shirted front as into risen dough.

Fitch collapsed to the road. Varian knelt over him and administered the final blow to Fitch's lolling face, drawing blood from the slack lips and pausing to relish the sign of his savagery.

He turned on one knee and saw the ghost-pale figure of Rue Morgan in the road, her parasol still aslant her shoulder and the long, lethal barrel of Fitch's fallen firearm in her white-gloved hand.

He stood and faced her.

"Varian," she said, her face so stiff and unbelieving and contained that he thought it would crack.

He walked toward her, the length of chain between his wrists chiming.

"Varian," she said again, and the emphasis was entirely different, though what it was he could not really say.

He was directly before her, the cold metal circle of the gun barrel branding his warm, living flesh. She was transfixed by his eyes and seemed not to notice the cyclops she had aimed at his vitals.

He wrested the parasol from her nerveless fingers, the pistol, too, with an expert wrench. Then he spun her away from him, her treacherous face and her expertly assumed wonder. Again he had been as wrong about her Thespian abilities as he had been about her potential as an artist's model. He had been wrong about her always in every respect, and he should not make that same mistake again.

He spun her away from him, threw down the pistol, brought the swag of his chains tight up against her throat, and held her to him, enjoying, loathing the cool crush of her muslin gown against his body, the tease of her shorn, curling hair at his shoulder, even the scrape of her crushed straw hat brim against his neck and cheek.

"I do not need the icy intercession of a pistol with you, Rue Morgan," he hissed into the general area of her ear. "As I told you on the last occasion that you took me captive, a mere tautening of the chains—thus!—and you will be no more trouble to me."

"Varian, Varian," was all she said, over and over, her hands going up to his wrists to stop him from the final, fatal pressure, the perfectly white fingers curling around his deeply bronzed forearms.

He looked at the contrast of her civilized fingers and knew the skin beneath the fabric would look as pale upon him, knew that she had been somewhere cool and as unfeeling as marble while he had burned pieces of his skin away in an ordeal he still could not face whole without fearing for his sanity.

He knew all this, and hated her for it, and himself as well, and still knew that he could not make the last savage, executioner's jerk upon the weapon he had at her throat. He froze in contemplation of this last great truth and great burden of his enslavement: his ultimate enslavement to his own civility, the same impulse that had stayed the wronged boy he was from calling out Black Harry Morgan. Now this identical failing left him utterly defeated before the one woman he had truly treasured hopes of winning.

He was a gambler, Varian Temple, not a killer. He let his arms fall slack.

Once again, Rue Morgan elected not to elude the tokenly imprisoning arms of the Earl of Argyle.

She struggled to turn herself in his still circling grasp to face him, and Varian knew that his survival instincts were keen when he had taken her prisoner from the rear, not running the risk of her unforgettable features, the bright blue dazzle that blinded all who had ever looked at Rue Morgan.

He wondered if even Matthew the Quaker would have been proof against the "rue" his once-delirious patient had prattled of. Certainly Varian Temple wasn't.

He raised his manacled hands over her head, carefully around the swooping straw brim, never touching any part of her or her dress, as if a brush with the brim's raw edge would be as infecting as drawing one's skin across a cobra fang. His arms came down between them, but Rue Morgan didn't seem to notice.

She didn't seem to notice anything—not his lamentable, almost savage dishevelment, not his nearly deadly attack upon her, not the disbelief in his mahogany face, the bitterness in the hazel eyes so light-seeming now in a sundarkened face. She didn't seem to notice or care what he thought of her, what he thought or felt at all. Only that he was there, that she had found him.

"Varian," she said again, neither asking nor telling, simply affirming, as if to herself.

Her gloved fingers winged like white doves to his face and began fanning softly at the edges of it. Her touch seemed sensitive even through the fabric. She was like a blind woman tracing old familiarities, finding new ones—the daily nicks his dull razor made across his jaw, the random bites of vermin. . . .

"Stop." His chains rattled as he reached up to capture her wrists.

She complied perfectly amiably, undistracted from her contemplation of his face, his reality.

For the first time, Varian considered that he might be dealing with a madwoman. She was not behaving as either the foiled schemer who had come down to the fields in muslin to see her vanquished enemy whipped, or the restored innocent with a thousand explanations, demanding five thousand answers.

Varian felt his confusion, only one of many emotions he had beaten back to the bottom of his awareness, bubbling up to his eyes, his lips. He felt himself impelled to do, say a dozen careless things, kiss her, kill her, beg her pardon, congratulate her upon her victory. . . .

"Stop," he said again, knowing at that instant that it was not any particular act of hers that unbraided his better judgement, but the very fact of her existence.

"Varian," she said again, and it was lucky Nigel was not there to hear it, for he would have gone mad at her repetition of that one word, though the bearer of that name had hardly realized she was saying it at all. "I have found you."

He watched the salt water brim to the tidal pools of her eyes. A man could stay afloat in such briny seas a good long time before he drowned, he thought. But it buoyed him up to know she could weep even falsely for him.

"Once again you've made my choice for me, Rue Morgan," he said abruptly. "Fitch will be no friend of mine when he wakes. They have ways of dealing with slaves who raise chains to the overseers. I would hate to defraud you of your entertainment, but shall beg your leave and depart for the hills where the renegade Maroons will or will not admit me to their company. My regards to your father, and thank you for being the occasion of my escape—"

He moved away to the bordering orange trees, but she was as willing to hang onto him physically as she had been with her eyes.

"Varian, wait! You don't believe, you can't believe that I betrayed you into this?"

Her dainty gloved hands had become talons digging into the back of his neck. He pulled them away, but they flew at him doggedly, anchoring somewhere else the instant they were detached.

She did not seem angry or hurt by his lack of faith.

"Oh, Varian, my father's revenge was even more bitter for you than I guessed. For me, there was the torture of wondering if he'd taken you out of this world, body and soul. For you, there was the torment of thinking I still lived in this world, but taken from you, heart and soul. He gave me this—see, another of his bitter birthday tokens. November last it came to me. With no word as to how."

She drew his mourning ring up on its chain and presented to him his own token of Morgan perfidy. His fingers, eyes went to the ring and remained there.

"Yes ... this was taken ... everything I had was taken when I was set upon by the crimping-house gang. You've had it—?"

"Since November. It has been my token—"

"Or trophy." Varian narrowed his eyes to inspect this

alien part of him returned. "The last jewel you wore around your neck was a token of hatred, Rue Morgan. How am I to know that you were not conspiring with your father all along, that you did not lure me into risking an undeniable conspiracy against him to justify the rather melodramatic steps for my removal he has taken?"

He sounded more like the Earl of Argyle again, cool, controlled, and dubious down to his naked toes.

Rue smiled.

"Oh, Varian, you may loathe me to your grave, but I swear I am monstrous happy to hear you distrust me so lucidly. I would rather have you alive and an enemy than dead or even alive and as empty of love or hate as Graham."

"Winthrop? You have seen him?" His hand on the ring tightened into a fist.

"He is here, with me. He was my escort to the New World. He agreed to help me find you."

"Or I found *him* for you, and now you have your old lover back and your new one under your pretty little foot."

"Oh, yes, challenge me, Varian. Disbelieve me. Play deep against me. Always. We were ever well-matched," she said, her eyes blazing a very hot blue. She leaned nearer and tilted her face to his. "And did we not play at other games after?"

"What am I to do with you?" he demanded, pushing her away.

If she had begged, pled, sworn she loved him eternally, he would have felt free to disbelieve her. Instead she dredged up their old games of cat and mouse with either exchanging the predator's role until the next encounter. That was more irresistible to him than all the protestations of truth or love her lovely tongue could curl itself around.

He had to believe her because she was still Rue Morgan, Black Rue Morgan, and her gallows humor, her fire-forged will, her almost masculine gusto for the obvious pleasure she took in the throws of the dice and their bodies together were more reassuring of reality to him than all the insipid declarations of love from the maidens of Mayfair put together. He trusted her just because he thought it was dangerous to do so.

He laughed, the first time he had in many months, and put his arms around her again—this time rudely bumping the accursed hat brim—pulled her very near, and kissed her possibly deceitful mouth, so very sweet for all that.

He stopped long enough for her to catch her breath.

"Very well. Tell me your story, my darling Delilah. If I am to be chained like Samson, I might as well hear the fairy tales that go before from your own pretty lips. What do you say happened? Why are you here? What do you intend?"

They were under the fragrant shadow of the orange trees, and he leaned back against one's trunk, drawing her against him.

"Your Lordship is no Samson," teased Rue, her white fingertips brushing the long sweep of his hair caught back into its crude queue and trailing to his shoulder blades. The gloves began tracing the welts of the whip scars on his back.

He looked down into Rue Morgan's face, knowing he was uncertain whether her fingers were tender emissaries or the light cruel tracings of the winner across the forfeited rouleaux.

" 'Tis you have been shorn, my Delilah," he said, bringing his hands up to either side of her face and burying his own fingers in the soft, satin pelt of her hair.

" 'Tis fashion now. The Bedlam Shear. I owe it to my erstwhile father, Black Harry Morgan, and a few months' holiday in a private asylum, where, I fear, I sadly lacked Heliotrope's benign hairdressing."

"Is that where you've been, Rue Morgan? A madhouse?" He drew her nearer, much nearer, so her bodice ruffle was crushed against the dark hair of his chest, as though even these frothy barriers were too great when he wished to be close to Rue Morgan.

She dropped her black lashes and her lower lip slightly in

reply. Yes, her gestures replied, now make me madder than the maddest of the mad in reward.

He kissed her as only a man who has been denied all physical pleasure for months, who has been isolated among an alien people can. It was sufficient for Rue Morgan.

Her eyes twinkled into his again when he released her, as wickedly satisfied of herself as the sapphire had been of its precious perfection, hard and sparkling and infinitely desirable.

Varian could almost see the intervening candlelight on her face when she had stumbled back from him in her Grosvenor Square rooms, inviting him nearer with every step backward.

"Tell me more of your tale," he urged softly, as if impatient of interrupting it again.

"He is not my father, that man. And so he informed me on the way to the madhouse when he would not inform me of what he had done with you. He also admitted he knew that I was not his child from the very first. And he made plain that certain parental restrictions to behavior no longer applied ... He was most forward, Varian," she added, her eyes dropping.

He drew her close again and brought his face totally under the shadowing brim of her hat.

"With Black Harry's knowing no blood stood between you, I must salute his self-control for its duration," he murmured at her ear and kissed her in reward for this latest indignity.

She seemed to be smiling even when he kissed her; certainly that smile was always there when he drew back enough to see her entire face.

"Your mouth," she said, distracted from her narrative. "It tastes ... spicy." She leaned near again, but his hands tightened on her back to stop her.

It suddenly came home to him, his last months of agony and loneliness when no human around could mirror back as simple a fact as that, that despite his deprivation and his suffering, his mouth was sweet to a lover. It had the primitive poetry of the song of Solomon. It struck him to the heart, the humanity. It made him love Rue Morgan, though it be a fatal occupation. She accepted his sweat-streaked, grimy arms around her and reveled in his scented mouth.

He shook his shaggy head.

"A native bark. All we slaves chew it in lieu of tooth-brushing. It may not be German cologne, but I am glad it pleases you."

"Yes," said Rue simply. "But to continue, for I fear our time grows positively dwarfish; Quentin Rossford is my father, the actor who introduced me to the London stage—"

"And introduced London to its loveliest Lydia Languish—"

"I thought that you agreed with Quentin's lamentable assessment of my Thespian abilities—merely passable?"

"Obviously Rossford's daughter would have acting talents, though perhaps not entirely suitable for the stage."

He kissed her again, and Rue considered that the Barbados climate was really quite superior, that the island was a balmy, fragrant place more perfect for lovers than the most artificed natural bower at Ranelagh or Vauxhall. She resented that circumstances forced her to the conclusion of her tale.

"At any rate—if Your Lordship will desist from these disgraceful attentions—I was ultimately rescued from the asylum by Heliotrope, Quentin, and the entire Basilisk Club—"

"The Basilisk Club to the rescue? Another comedy you have played in, dear Rue; how shameful that I was unable to witness it. But I was . . . detained elsewhere."

"Indeed." Rue's hands rested on his iron cuffs like a softer variety of manacle. "So the Basilisks, your portly comedians, discovered from the crimping-house bullies how you had been captured and sent on the *Ivory Queen* for Barbados. I enlisted Graham as escort, took Helia of course, and came in search of you."

"Piquant?" he asked seriously.

"What?"

"Did you bring Piquant?"

"Dear me, no. Piquant resides with Sir Feverell Marshwine until my return. Even I would not bring a lap dog on a rescue mission, my dear Varian. You wound me."

This last was another flagrant invitation to address his apologies to her lips, which he did for some time.

"And what of the exceedingly tiresome Mr. Fitch?" Rue finally inquired.

Varian grinned.

"I fear my somewhat, er, repressed feelings were overefficient with Mr. Fitch. He should not wake for some hours."

"Excellent. Then we have only to return to the house, overthrow Captain Skinner and any of his loyal underlings, take control of the plantation, and you will be utterly free."

"Is that all? My dear Rue, you make the best of generals. Your plans are magnificently vague, and their execution is left to the mad improvisation of others."

He brought his hands over her hatted head to release her and stood away from the tree.

"And what if your tale is so much sugar foam, a mere deceptive scum over your true intentions, to be swept away in a moment? What if you are truly Black Harry Morgan's daughter in body and soul? And have always been devoted to my overthrow, only saying such pretty things now to lull me into safety so I do not take advantage of the fact I have you in my power here? I could love you or kill you as my whim dictated, free myself and flee to the hills, even slip into Bridgetown, leave the island, and go back to be an earl of England without you, then turn all efforts fourfold upon you and your vile sire."

She looked into his eyes for a long moment without answering, without moving. Even the frail hat brim seemed frozen from dipping in the soft breeze that whispered through the glossy leaves above them.

"What if all this is true, and I return to the plantation house chained, with you?"

"Then, Your Lordship," she said finally, quite seriously, "I expect that you shall have quite a nasty whipping out of it. And the great humiliation of having been deceived, which stings far greater than even Mr. Leonidas Fitch's inventive whip, I suspect."

He regarded her. She was as icily contained as she had been at Brooks's when he'd first seen her, when he had first—or always—suspected that they would be lovers. Or haters. Or both.

"I gamble upon you again, Black Rue. Will you not even give me advantageous odds upon it?"

She put her hands to his shoulders.

"Varian, I love you utterly, wantonly. Even if I were all that you in reason have a right to suspect, that would remain. Perhaps you are right not to trust to that. I will never blame you for it. You will simply have to throw upon me again, Your Lordship, and I pray you roll a six."

She leaned up on her toes and kissed him lightly on the lips, her eyes open and staring into his the entire time.

He nodded. Varian Temple, gambler, would game again with Black Rue Morgan, who may or may not be truly a Morgan, may or may not be black-hearted at bottom, but who certainly, he felt in the deepest level of his heart, was worth the game.

They moved back to the road, both suddenly efficient, isolated in their separate roles.

"Does he have a key?" she asked, gesturing to the prone Fitch. "You'd better give it to me for later."

Varian crouched over Fitch's satisfactorily crumpled form and felt over the revoltingly slack belly until his fingers traced the cryptic shape of metal in a breeches' pocket.

He returned to Rue and presented it gracefully, like a magician flourishing an illusion to the audience. He reflected that the illusion might be in his own mind. But she smiled at him as if she knew what he thought and dropped the key into the frothy folds of her fallen sunshade, which she then retied the ribbon around.

"I had better carry the pistol," she suggested, brushing off the cane dust that she had acquired from his embraces. "We will tell them the infamous . . . 'Shellman,' was that it?"

"I'll tell you of that later."

"Anyway, the most contrary Shellman attacked the valiant Mr. Fitch, and only by capturing the pistol was I able to prevent a lamentable escape and—"

Varian went over to the roadside, stooped to the weapon, and brought it back, polished pistol butt politely pointed toward her. She took it and leaned toward him.

"—and prevent this wily slave's escape and, most likely, prevent this creature's having his way with me before he fled, a most thorough ravishment in the road."

He kissed her again as they exchanged the weapon. Before, shuddering leaf shadows had veiled their passion. Here in mid-road they kissed in broad blinding daylight under a sun as ardent as their emotions.

If Black Rue Morgan's lips were lying under his at this moment, Varian Temple deserved no more chances at any kind of hazard.

They parted. She wordlessly gestured with the pistol barrel, swinging her parasol before her like a cane. They resumed marching down the center of the glaring road to the time of Varian's chiming chains. Rue brought up the rear with a level pistol and a cool competency that should go far toward impressing Captain Jack Skinner, the Scourge of Malta, with the new mistress's formidable will.

Captain Jack Skinner himself awaited them on the house's broad, pillared verandah. He was rocking back and forth on his heels, a habit Rue had often noticed in her erstwhile father, the habit of those who have power and enjoy exercising it to its fullest.

"What's this, Miss Morgan? Mr. Fitch has undergone a most startling transformation in the course of your walk."

"Mr. Fitch's transformation is even more startling than

you imagine, Captain Skinner," said Rue. "He has determined to take a nap at the foot of one of the shady orange trees, although I must admit that the sandman was forced to put him rather urgently to sleep."

"Sandman? More like the Shellman. Causing us trouble again, are you? And while the new mistress visits. You'll pay dearly for this," growled Skinner to Varian. "Though on the high seas we'd've keelhauled you for it."

Rue, with Mr. Fitch's graphic account of this disciplinary measure still ringing in her ears, grew sterner and paler. The pistol, it was apparent as she spoke to Captain Skinner, no longer pointed at her prisoner.

"This is no way to address the new master, Captain Skinner. I confess myself quite taken with him and elevate him to senior overseer, or Lord High Admiral of the Bounding Cane, or whatever title is sufficient to see that you do not attempt to overthrow it."

"This scurvy lot?" demanded Skinner incredulously.

"You wound me," noted Varian, shaking his head and his manacles.

"He's a miserable debtor sent over by your father to sweat off his bond, an' other than'ee be white and a man, has nothing to recommend him further."

"He's an English earl, my dear captain, and though the courts of the motherland may be distant, the crack of their justice snakes its way even to these outer islands eventually. I would look to your own position, if I were you. Perhaps if you were to quietly steal away and leave the plantation to us—"

"Mutiny!" thundered the fierce seaman. He lifted a narrow brass whistle to his lips.

"He'll make a fight of it," warned Varian, hurling himself at Skinner and cutting off the piercing whistle in mid-shriek.

They rolled down the steps together, Skinner still clutching for his whistle, and Varian's chained hands clawing at it as desperately. It flew suddenly in a canary-yellow arc to the shrubbery edging the walk. Varian began hauling the winded sea captain to his feet.

"You should work the cane, brother Skinner," he said sardonically. "It does wonders for the constitution. Perhaps we'll put you to it before we leave."

Rue calmly unfolded her parasol and bent to shake out the silken folds. "A moment, dear overseer, and we'll make a new man of you indeed. The key must be here somewhere . . ." She set down the pistol and shook the sunshade even more diligently.

A sudden pounding of the ground around the house's corner brought her eyes up. Three, no four, five men came running around the far pillars, dark athletic figures like those on an Attic vase come to ominous life.

"Damn, his whistle was call enough for the trained maneaters Skinner keeps. Where's the key? Quickly!"

Varian kept his fingers curled in Skinner's crushed stock and dragged the man over, using him as a shield between himself and the advancing plantation guards.

"Not here, not anywhere! Oh, Varian!"

That was all Rue could say before the men were upon them. Varian thrust his captive at the first two like a bowler aiming a particularly unwieldy ball at the pins. They reeled a bit, but remained upright, then came crashing bodily into him. He staggered backward, knowing that if they bore him to the ground, his chained wrists would become anchors too heavy to let him rise easily again. He swung the manacles in a deadly arc, and his attackers danced away a bit.

Beyond them, Rue had stood to meet the next installment. Two men headed directly for her at Captain Skinner's shrieked orders. She finally discharged the pistol, directly into the center of the first oncoming man. The red exploded on his yellow linen shirt like a Ranelagh firework. He fell.

Rue backstepped, then leveled her parasol at the second man as if it were a lance. He ran stomach first into its cunningly wrought ivory tip in the likeness of a unicorn, screamed agonizingly, veered off, and doubled over. But the impact had jolted Rue backwards and snapped the parasol's ebony stick.

"Shivered your timbers, have you, Miss Morgan?" smirked Captain Skinner, advancing on her.

Behind him, another pair of thugs were running in answer to the sounds of the scuffle. Rue glanced over her shoulder. Varian was still keeping his pair of bloodhounds at bay, but they yapped ever nearer, heads lowered and fists curled around thick blunt knives.

Varian suddenly sprang away and caught Rue's hand.

"The house, quickly!"

"But the key—"

"Forget the key!"

She lurched up the steps in his urgent grasp and into the shadowed house. They slammed the door shut after them and locked it, but—

"The French doors—" began Rue.

"Yes, I know. These confounded tropical houses were constructed to let in breezes and battalions. And if you think the blacks don't know that—where's Winthrop?"

At that instant, Helia came clattering down the broad white staircase.

"Helia! 'Tis a revolt, join in," called Rue as Varian dragged her hastily toward one of the downstairs rooms.

Heliotrope snatched up a heavy porcelain figure of a cock from a sidetable and swept into their wake even as the front door began heaving to the rhythm of blows from without.

"Where's Graham?" asked Rue, turning to ensure the door still held.

Helia nodded succinctly. "Where His Lordship leads us, the great drawing room."

"With the French doors all around? Varian, you hear, they'll come pouring in like a high tide. We should go upstairs."

"They'll find us anywhere," he growled, neither turning nor pausing in determinedly towing her forward. "Either we win here or we lose everything. And with Winthrop, we've a chance as long as their pistols are empty."

The party burst into the drawing room, looking like a dance chain from a mad costume party. There was the savagely naked earl, the pristinely attired Rue still dragging her fractured sunshade, and lastly the fastidious Helia, her face carved into a frown as forbidding as jungle drums, with the gaily painted ceramic rooster clutched threateningly in her hand.

"My word," said Graham Winthrop, slowly turning from an idle perusal of what few books Captain Skinner kept on his ample, but mostly empty shelves.

"We'll need more than your word," said the earl briskly, turning to slam shut the door, then manhandle a delicate Sheraton secretary in front of it. He hurled himself half-across the room at the long settee sitting a few feet from the French doors in question; both he and sofa skidded resoundingly against several of them. Rue and Helia joined in, dragging Chippendale chairs and Hepplewhite consoles over to barricade the curtained colonnade of doors.

Graham put down his book, a rather dry dissertation on some of the more repellent of tropical diseases, and came over to them.

"Temple?" he asked of the agile brown figure still engaged in wrestling furniture to the room's limits. "Rue?"

She passed him distractedly, looking frantically around the room for something. Even the stately Helia only paused in her motion long enough to give him a level, reassuring look, then resumed her rooster.

In another instant, all explanations were moot. A phalanx of booted men charged the doors, splintering glass and driving back the dainty furniture with the snap of breaking wood. In a moment, their dark boots were scaling sofa backs and kicking contemptuously at fractured table and chair legs.

"Damn the key!" swore Varian, plucking a decorative pirate's cutlass from off the painted paneling and clutching it two-handed. "Arm yourself, Winthrop!" he ordered, but Graham still stood uncommitted in the room's center, a dreamer from another room and another time, a hurricane's eye in a world whipped into winds and waves of death.

Rue stared at Graham, then ran over to the wall and leaned up desperately to unfasten the weapon's mate. She would have offered it to Graham, but a man had breasted the waves of furniture and came charging toward them.

Rue took a grandiose swipe at his midsection and had the reward of seeing him jump quickly back. But three more men had entered the room and were drawn to Varian as flies are to molasses, while Captain Skinner was stepping most delicately over the furniture shards to survey what he knew to be a contest determined only by a matter of time.

He had never noticed her, Helia, the new mistress's effacing black shadow. She was not worthy of notice, being a black female servant. Unless, of course, he had a sudden taste for two of those qualities. So he did not notice her now, the woman poised as absurdly as a blackamoor statue in a London entry hall, arms raised, face frozen, hands holding some overcolored pagan artifact. . . .

The rooster flew in a gaudy arc and shattered quite completely on the back of Captain Skinner's unobservant head.

Rue flashed Helia a triumphant smile, then took rapid calculations. Five then. Skinner out of it, and the man she'd shot. And this slow fellow, did he not bear the brunt of her parasol's charging unicorn? And the three, no, four now around Varian. Ah, he nicked one, a cutlass being ever so much more serviceable than their quarrelsome seaman's daggers. . . .

"Graham!" Rue urged, glancing just briefly over her muslin shoulder before launching herself at the backs of the men encircling Varian.

She, too, wielded her cutlass two-handed; it was damned heavy. Her stinging arcs upon the men's backs drew two away. Helia gathered up the fallen Skinner's empty pistol, the one Rue had dropped, and joined in harrying Varian's attackers from the rear.

But one man turned, maddened, and used a mahogany chair leg to parry Rue's blade. It turned not only the attacking steel, but caught Rue's wrist hard against the sword's cumbersome haft. The weapon went spinning away to the edges of the room, and Rue retreated hastily.

The man followed up his advantage, pinning Rue behind a chair in the room's corner. When Helia came over to aid her, his frequent swipes with his dagger kept them both cornered, weaponless.

So it was over the hulking shoulders of this cornering adversary that both Rue and Helia saw Varian retreat ever nearer the windows, saw his manacled cutlass thrusts swing ever lower with fatigue, saw finally the weapon miss its target and stick fast in a broken console table like the sword in the stone that only Arthur could free. It vibrated there, all that lethal metal now unhanded.

One of Skinner's men tried to reclaim it as Varian retreated past it. At least it was faithful to him, stuck fast, resolutely neutral in a contest coming inescapably down to fists, knives, and sinew. Down to Varian and three unchained men.

Rue danced forward at her human barrier. His taunting pass with the blade tip ripped a horizon in her muslin sleeve. Her own personal sun rose there, spreading red morning in her own blood. Helia leaped forward in outraged defense and was awarded the same badge. And beyond this maddening, pricking fence of flesh that caged them, Varian's defenses were slowly softening, his attackers always coming nearer, their blows landing a bit more often, a bit harder.

Rue's rage rose scarlet throughout the room; it seemed to color everything crimson. It seeped up Graham Winthrop's stooped shoulders and coated them red as they had once been. Gay, gallant red.

"Graham!" she called. "Graham!"

He stood unengaged in the room's center, still a maddeningly contained observer. He did not see Rue and Helia at the cruel dagger pricks' bay; perhaps that would have moved him, but his eyes were only on the four men contending against the farther wall.

Contending was perhaps too generous a word for it—it was more like playing fox and hounds with the pack clearly in the advantage. Even as he watched, two men caught Varian by the upper arms and the third administered a brutal blow to his midsection. Varian bowed away from it in what seemed a graceful, frozen ballet, falling sprawled, dazed upon the damask settee, from which he was plucked to be positioned for the application of an inevitable fist to his cheek.

His dark head snapped back, grimacing sideways, spinning away through time and motion. Varian fell to the floor, the straw, sweet-smelling hay in the lanternlight, and all the lanterns of pain bursting around him in hot, red, unbelievable glory. . . .

"Graham!"

So spoke a screech owl in the rafters of Black Harry Morgan's stables. A wise, remote old bird. It shrieked his name, though he could barely hear it, while against the farther wall, thrown there by the lanternlight, the shadow figures were wrestling, punching, breaking, twisting, making a rag doll of a man. . . .

"Graham!"

He turned away from the fray, from the irritating sound of his name. He faced the last untouched piece of furniture in the room, the great, glass-fronted display cabinet in which Skinner kept his disciplinary trophies.

Graham Winthrop couldn't see these clearly, but he saw a faint figure reflected in the glass. Himself, in the silent island on which he'd chosen to reside since the November night more distant than time. He saw himself and heard the clamor still echoing behind him, the blows landed, the shocked expulsion of breath at each contact.

Always shocked, even when the blow was seen coming for a lifetime. He raised his wrists, which were not manacled, but he raised them together as if they were, and brought them crashing through the glass and the delicately arched mahogany struts that made a sort of cathedral of the doors.

Glass and blood splintered from the blow in glittering rich red fragments. Graham reached in and caught up a thick iron collar dripping lengths of chain. He whirled back into the room, into reality, into the lanternlight, swinging the chains like Samson his jawbone.

Into the crimping-house men he waded, the chains chiming in his ears now, landing brutally on backs, arms, legs, heads. The dark shadows fell away from him one by one, reeled back into the bloody straw. One came lurching from his blind side, and he felt a momentary impact, but it was a remote blow. He was strangely anesthetized to it, as he was to the bloody rivulets snaking down his hands, to the rebound of the swinging chains around his own forearms where they wrapped themselves like friendly serpents before he shook them free for another foray at the shadows, those damned shadows that had never given him a chance to fight them before.

He could hear the crack of bone. His bone, their bone. He could see only the light and the red and the figures ebbing before him. They were slipping away from him, deserting him, leaving him empty and enemyless in the center of the stables ... He stumbled across one, still dark and crouched at his feet, one that wriggled a bit yet. He knelt over it with the collar and pressed the metal to its throat, then held it down, down, down where it belonged—hell. The hands came weakly up to his own. Hideous hands—he should never forget them—large and unshapen, thick-knuckled and tufted with a smothering scrollwork of black hair, wrought-iron hair, hands like those should never make him stop, never draw mercy from him—

"Graham, stop! It's over. Graham, you'll kill him. It's not necessary."

She was back, the screech owl hovering over his shoulder, his red-coated shoulder, fanning her wings at him, her eyes a very unbirdlike blue. Why was she there? She shouldn't be there. . . .

"Graham!"

Despair—he heard it in the voice, he knew its tones. Despair like that makes one press on. Graham leaned farther onto the dark beneath him. He would make it give, break, stop threatening to rise up and swallow him whole—

"Graham, the man's down, done. They're all done. We've won," insisted the owl, still flapping for his attention.

He looked down to his mad, disembodied hands on the dark thing beneath him. A dark brown bird, not an owl this time, fluttered to his own wrist and perched there. This hand had nothing to do with the stables or the past. He followed it up the curve of arm to the face connected to it, a face as warm and soothing as chocolate somehow, infinitely firm, infinitely unafraid.

"Captain Winthrop," said Helia, looking very intently into the one blazing gray eye focusing puzzledly on hers. "It is done."

Graham looked to his victim, Captain Skinner as it turned out, who had unwisely awakened to rejoin the fray and become the last of Graham's prey. Skinner's breath sawed in ragged rasps through his bruised throat, his face dewed with drops of blood flung from his attacker's cut hands. Graham spread those hands with their gloves of blood.

"You must have them bound," said Helia firmly. And Rue, leaning over her shoulder, nodded solemnly, then flew over to the room's other side where Varian sprawled groggily on the askew settee, nursing a bloody mouth and his red-bandana-wrapped wrists, which oozed another shade of red now.

Graham rose stiffly to his feet, ignoring the convenient

human cane of Heliotrope standing beside him. He eyed Varian across the room's wreckage.

"We've . . . won then?"

"You've won," said Varian, slowly and painfully. "You annihilated them single-handedly, my dear Winthrop. I was most grateful of the rest. My darling Rue," said Varian to her. "Do you think that at your leisure you could repair outside and search for the bloody key? I am finding being a prisoner somewhat tedious, even with such a lovely jailer as you."

Rue hastened outside apologetically and spent a good part of an hour on her knees before she retrieved the misplaced key.

"I thought it a clever hiding place, Varian," she said when finally turning reluctant metal in metal. "How was I to guess the key would take such wing? There, now we can bestow your irons on the last unchained man, and you may do it personally."

Graham looked up from the remnants of a console table at which he sat while Helia bound his hands.

Neither man had allowed his hurts to be tended until the unconscious Skinner and his bullies were neatly enchained in the more ingenious devices from the trophy chest. Graham's eyes rested on the whip scars along Varian's bowed back as the earl crouched to pass his irons on to another.

"Is it truly you, Temple?" he asked as if assimilating the persona of the recent drama for the first time. "You, you look—"

"Worse for wear, I know, Winthrop," said Varian, rising slowly and giving a wry smile that nevertheless flashed like a pirate's in his uncharacteristically bronzed face. "If only they could see me now at Brooks's."

Graham studied the earl's nakedness of limb, his savagely darkened skin and shaggy hair—so different from the fashionable frock-coated figure who had visited him in Shropshire and coolly extracted the humiliating details of Graham's treatment at Black Harry's hands.

Graham felt himself infused with pity toward creatures other than himself.

"Is there nothing we can get you, man? Anything?"

Varian grinned and stepped to the center of the room, automatically holding his wrists a bit awkwardly close as if he still expected bonds.

"Get me?" He paused to consider it with some of the old connoisseur's air about him. "I think . . . some brandy. A bath. Beefsteak. And Black Rue," he finished precisely, his eyes finding hers.

"And not necessarily in that order."

Chapter Twenty-five

His Lordship, the Earl of Argyle, was forced to take two of his desires in proper sequence—the brandy and the bath.

He lolled in this latter, a great tin affair imported to the plantation house's spacious master bedroom, with a towel modestly draped across it while Heliotrope officiated at his shearing, as she had done for Rue only weeks before.

Rue knelt by it, alternately holding up a mirror while Varian shaved his tender jaw or offering him sips of the wished-for brandy.

She also took the opportunity to admire the gleaming expanses of his new muscles, those of a bronze figure of a Greek God, and to study, now that both manacles and bandanas were absent, the odd pale bands of untanned skin circling his wrists like ghostly irons, like the last bonds of civilization and civility.

Heliotrope snipped off the final shaggy hanks and nodded briskly, her face a burnished brown moon in the mirror. Varian submerged, rising again with his dark hair sleek as a seal's.

"Ah, you have no idea what a comfort it is to see hot water," he commented, diving again.

Rue and Helia traded glances at this eccentricity. But the black woman was gone by the time Varian bobbed up, and Rue had the brandy glass ready to toast his lips.

"Gad, that stings," Varian noted even as he took a healthy swallow, "but I was never one to draw back from a pleasure because of a risk," he said, looking very significantly at Black Rue Morgan.

Nor did he draw back on this occasion, and it is true that the freshly changed bedlinens got excessively damp, which would not have happened had the Earl of Argyle taken the trouble to dry himself thoroughly first.

Rue and Varian lay tangled, watching the last of the bath steam dissipate into the already humid tropical air. Their union, as their recent reunion, had been forced and hasty. They had come together as if the most necessary thing were to prove that they could still unite in this specifically physical way. The earl had not spent long in preliminaries, and he had spent himself soon after entering her.

"I'm sorry, Rue—" he had begun in apology, but she only shook her head to silence him.

A certain raw urgency of satisfaction was as fulfilling in its way as all the languid, liquid, silken dalliances of the senses. So she simply wrapped her arms around him more tightly, buried her head on his shoulder, and pointed out that he had yet to have his beefsteak.

"Damn the beefsteak! How can you care about such a trifle when there are serious matters you have not dealt with? Are you sure you do not resent that I mistrusted you, even for a moment?"

"Varian," said Rue serenely, "of course you mistrusted me. What reason had you not to? I should not care for you half so much were you not an eminently sensible man. Knowing whom my supposed father was, knowing you and I had been locked in a battle of wills from the first, I consider it implicit faith that you even allowed me to conduct you back to the house as my prisoner—"

"Your supposed prisoner."

"At any rate, degrees of faithfulness are only for debate to those capable of degrees of faithlessness. Varian, I am content," she said, bringing her face up to his and kissing him excruciatingly lightly on the lips, for she knew how sore they were.

He sighed, knowing that he was enmeshed in his Black Rue's web, as he had first suspected he would be when he had made her kiss him of her own volition in Grosvenor Square, and her touch then had been as fugitive, tender, and winged as it was now. Because she was so formidable, it was always her vulnerability that would ensnare him. And his own.

He returned her kiss, hard despite his discomfort, until whatever edge there was to his pain was blunted on the rim of Rue's mouth. He consumed the draught that he had always wanted to abstract from her, and that he had ever to fill to keep it flowing—love, which like luck, came only to those who truly cared to have it.

"And Rossford's your father?" he asked finally, breaking away, for there were more questions always elbowing away his answers.

"Yes," said Rue complacently.

"And I libeled your Thespian abilities!"

"So did he," confessed Rue. "I see that I shall have to return to the Basilisks for honest admiration."

"From now on, you shall get all the admiration you require here quite honestly," vowed the earl, taking her so pressingly into his arms that it was pointless to speak, so she didn't.

The earl took his beefsteak later that day at the table with Graham and Helia. The quartet enjoyed an exhausted but triumphant dinner, secure in knowing that the villainous overseers rested chained in a sugar shed. The house staff had been assembled and acquainted with its new residents. Varian had aided Graham in choosing an assortment of bondsmen and slaves to serve as temporary overseers until the plantation's reorganization.

After dinner, Rue and Varian strolled down the orange-treed walk and stared into the serene evening sky spangled with southern stars.

"I've talked with Graham," said Varian. "We agree that certain basic repairs must be made to the plantation. Can you bear a stroll toward the slave huts?"

"Pacing Rue walked farther and in worse surroundings at the asylum," she reminded him.

"Dear Rue." He stopped to take her face in his hands. "You have told me so little of that."

"And you of this," she answered, nodding toward the stench that even now drifted toward them.

They walked onward in silence for a bit.

"A sewage trench would relieve the sanitary conditions," he finally said. "And, of course, the huts need repair."

"I still can't believe people live in such boxes. And did you have one?"

"The honor of a solitary hut is generally reserved for the couples, but I managed to acquire one. See, it is the only one without a fire; these Africans will not sleep without the comfort of flames, no matter how hot the night. I'm surprised some hutless wretch has not claimed my quarters—oh, well, step in, and see what I can honestly term my humble abode."

Rue bowed her head to the low thatched roof and stood inside a dark narrow room. Varian quickly lit a primitive lantern, which cast shadows upon the wooden pallet that passed for a bed, a few hanging gourds for decoration, and ribbons of bright cloth fluttering everywhere.

"I won these," he said, running his hand nostalgically over a limp strip of fabric.

"Won them? In this Godforsaken place you gambled? Varian!"

"Men gamble in hell, Rue," he said, laughing. "And my fabled luck was the only attribute that did not desert me during my enslavement. You wondered why they called me Shellman. Here, this is why."

He dropped something very light into her palm, and Rue examined it in the fire flicker. Not one, two. Two shells marked with a varying series of dots.

"Dice! Varian, these are dice."

"A bit primitive, to be sure, but adequate. They won me food, some bright clothes, these half-dull pieces of razor so I could shave the vermin off my face. Small comforts, I think the civilized world calls them."

"I'll keep them," said Rue, her fist closing very tightly around the shells. She bent to the door and bowed herself back into the deepening night. Varian followed her, holding his homemade lantern aloft.

"What is that? That larger hut there?"

"Ah, observant Rue. That is where Captain Jack Skinner and certain of his overseers—and even the absent Morgan when he would visit the plantation—go to take certain of the slavewomen when they have a yen. It is a trying climate and unravels inhibitions. Against both pain and pleasure."

"Varian, did you—were you . . . ?"

He laughed.

"No. They would have killed me for it, even had I been inclined. I was never one of them, you see. They always sensed that I was but a step away from the other side of the chains. And they were right. But it is not so barbaric as you think. These slaves are not ridden with our sense of morality and propriety. They couple quite changeably among themselves, so I think it matters less to the women if the masters come for them. There is the possibility of their children's being freed, or even themselves. And we English never claimed to cart blacks to the Caribbean for the honor of saving their souls as the hypocritical French and Spanish do. They're here as a sturdy, inexhaustible work force. If fornication be a side effect, so much the merrier."

"Varian, you have become cynical."

"And you have become as dour as Jonathan Flemming. No, I have become many things, but cynical is not one of them. I'm thinking of looking up Wilberforce when we return home."

"The Quaker abolitionist?"

"Exactly. I ran into one of his followers in my travels—At any rate, I might bestir myself in their cause if they let me."

"The Earl of Argyle an abolitionist? I can understand your concern, Varian, but what will they think at Brooks's? 'Tis worse than gambling with scandalous Rue Morgan, Your Lordship. Next you will be telling me you are for the separation of Ireland and the liberation of the Irish—"

"Perhaps I am."

"And the, the emancipation of women?"

"Oh, indubitably."

Rue stopped and gave herself over to laughter.

"Oh, it will be better than the elephant bone episode when poor Quentin was forced to play the reluctant lover before me and the rampaging fiend of lust before Dr. Radclyffe and Black Harry."

"You doubted Rossford's virility? Rue, the man is notorious—"

"Ah, but I didn't know he was my father then. And so when I came to him and made the same offer you found so difficult to refuse—"

"Rue, Black Rue, you offered yourself to your own father? I can forgive you Sir Nigel, but this is shocking even for you. Poor Rossford must have quavered to his buskins. And tell me more of this elephant bone affair. It sounds intriguing."

"Ah, I fear it is too ribald for your delicate ears," said Rue, skipping up the path ahead of him until he caught up and regaled her ears with assorted ribaldries that she found most instructive.

* * *

Later that night the earl quite earnestly proposed she marry him before they returned to England.

"Marry? Morgan's daughter? You cannot."

"You are not Morgan's daughter."

"But I am Rossford's bastard daughter."

"First I am told that I cannot marry you legitimately, then that I cannot marry you illegitimately. You roll two-faced dice, my dear."

"You cannot marry me at all. You have a position, a family honor to maintain. I have destroyed mine."

"Then you must be grafted to mine."

"No," said Rue, leaving the bed.

For the first time, Varian took her protest seriously.

"But I wish it."

"And I do not. I will come home with you, though, and live with you and be your love—"

"Don't quote the bloody Cavalier poets at me—they were ever a caviling bunch. Rue, I mean it."

"Then throw for it. Here are your shells. Six or below, and I wed you. Above, and I merely love you. Is that not enough?"

"I will not gamble for you anymore, Rue. Put down the dice and come to bed."

"Then I'll cast for you."

She did, throwing the primitive shells out onto the little table with its silver tree of candles.

"They're very difficult to read . . . a three, and, and . . . a four. Seven. I win. I always told you that seven was your lucky number. So I will not marry you, but I will come to bed. You will have to be content with that."

He was.

On the third day of their successful uprising at the plantation, Graham and Varian returned from Bridgetown with the news that their prisoners had been safely deposited as impressed sailors on a suitable out-going vessel.

"And," crowed Varian over his beefsteak, which had been

his daily request for dinner, "we've the best cabins reserved on the *Barbary Allen* bound for Southhampton in two day's time. I am set upon enjoying my return voyage from a different perspective than the first."

"Excellent idea," said Winthrop vaguely, cutting his own beefsteak into smaller and smaller pieces.

Rue noticed his abstraction, but dismissed it as Graham's usual melancholy. Besides, there was Varian to watch, Varian to speak with, plot with, stroll with, to do everything with but worry. No more worry for them. It was home to England and a staggeringly successful confrontation with her ex-father.

No doubt when faced with his erstwhile victims, even Black Harry Morgan would quail and meekly relinquish his Barbados plantation and whatever else they demanded, all the while cringing obsequiously.

The image was so satisfying that Rue forgot even Varian for a while and let her eyes focus on the shuttered windows.

The following morning Rue and Varian came downstairs to find Graham waiting for them in the restored drawing room. He was wearing an eyepatch—Rue wondered where he had unearthed one so conveniently—and a worried expression.

"I'm not going," he announced as though resigning a commission.

"Not going? Where?"

"To what you call 'home.' England. London. Shropshire. I'm not going."

"Graham, you can't mean it," began Rue, but something in the set of his shoulders made her protests stop.

"It's no use. I always told you there was nothing for me there. I think there may be something here. The weather—I find it agrees with me. And my lungs. And . . ."—he looked at Varian then, and something passed between them that Rue could not intercept—"and the work."

Graham smiled, and Rue realized that the light tanning the

sun gave him somehow softened his worn features, that he did indeed look very gallant in an eyepatch, that he looked altogether better than he had since their reunion in Shropshire.

"You'll need an overseer, Rue," he went on a little less stiffly. "I can only see with one good eye, but perhaps that's what's needed here. I'd like to try turning this inferno into . . . well, a working plantation that doesn't have to grind human beings body and soul to turn a profit. I don't want to leave."

Rue thought for a moment, then took Varian's arm preparatory to their morning stroll.

"I can't quarrel with you, Graham. I thought that I should never hear you say you wanted a blessed thing again. 'Tis a sweltering, deceptively smiling place with more drunken white men per square foot than Gin Lane in London, but if you wish to claim it, it's yours to oversee."

He bowed mutely as she swept past him. Rue's eyes on Varian were vivid with suppressed comment.

Another barrier in their path appeared—Heliotrope at the curled birdcage of spindles ending the stairs, her hand loosely poised upon the newel post as upon a canetop.

"I stay also," she said in a declarative sentence that left no room for argument.

Rue stopped, stunned.

"You? Not coming back? Helia, why?"

"It is the place of my birth."

"Yes, but that was so long ago."

"Do you return to Black Harry Morgan's house?" asked Helia implacably, sternness shoring up her resolve.

Rue started to answer, then paused. She appealed to Varian, but he was irritatingly remote from these defections. First an old lover. Then an even older servant. A friend. Rue felt her lower lip trembling and a tantrum coming on. Stamp the little foot. I want my Helia! Stamp. The only person in Blackstone House she had trusted, loved. Now staying behind in this heathen Eden of an island.

Staying with the heat and the sugar and the lilting blue sea and the black slaves in the fields, the brown slaves, the brown

bubbling molasses and the mosquito netting and the odd foreign things that Rue could never love, never understand . . .
And Graham, staying on with Graham. How queer. . . .

Her hand tightened on Varian's sleeve.

"You are free, Helia," she said a bit regally, "to do as you
wish—"

"As I must," interrupted Helia, stepping down the last
stair to Rue's level.

"Very well. As you must." Rue smiled. "But Piquant will
be most snappish at losing a bed-partner. Varian, my before-
breakfast turn," she ordered, and he rapidly piloted her out
on the broad porch and down the shallow steps.

Rue's eyes blinked like semaphores in the sunshine.

"The light," she explained with great dignity. "It is excessively bright."

"Just so," he said, setting a slow pace down the garden
walk.

She was still for some time, and when she next spoke,
she stopped.

"Varian!" She turned to regard the distant house, as white
and dazzling as a wedding cake in the tropical sun. "Varian,
you don't suppose that, taking everything together, adding it
up, as it were, that—"

"Dice usually tumble in pairs," he commented obliquely.

"Varian! Is it possible that Graham and Heliotrope, that
they—"

"In the tropics, anything is possible."

"But it is most unconventional."

"Why not? They have been taught by a mistress of the
unconventional."

They walked on again in silence. Rue finally broke that
quietude presided over only by calling birds above them.

"I suppose," she conceded glumly, "that I am fortunate
that you deign to return to England with me. Or is there
something that you wish to tell me?"

He laughed. And turned her to face him. And then told it
to her without words. And at great length.

Chapter Twenty-six

"A toast, my dear colleagues, to the loveliest lady to grace a coffeehouse and our own humble circle, to—to—oh, dear. Ah, ah, ah, ah . . ."—and he sneezed, Colonel Rutherford Trumbull, still hoisting his glass and muttering his last preposition doggedly through the typhoon of his malady. "—To the loveliest lady to, to, to—"

"To play hazard at B—B—Brooks's," interjected Sir Merivale Fenton-Mews triumphantly.

"To play highwayman," added Hookham with a bow.

"To play upon the boards at Drury Lane," said Quentin Rossford most sincerely, as his critical faculties had never had to hedge at his daughter's beauty.

"To play a false father false," said Dr. Radclyffe with a wicked, nostalgic twinkle.

"To, er . . ." Poor Sir Feverell Marshwine was running out of options. "Ah . . . to play matchmaker for a footman and a housemaid!" he ended victoriously.

"To play, play . . . play mad among the mad and outwit them," barked Lemuel Humphries, gruff at having to resurrect a dreary episode.

"To play for a man's heart and lose her own," said Varian quite accurately.

"I have no heart, gentlemen," said Black Rue icily, sitting very still in the red leather club chair in the earl's library as they had risen one by one with their topaz glasses raised high. She stood as well. "I have quite sliced it up into eighths and given it all to you. The only conceivable way to reach my ambition of having no heart, I have found, is to sublet it. I really cannot possibly tell you of my gratitude, my fondness for you all, that I, I . . ."

Rue no longer wore a sapphire at her throat, but her eyes glittered as solemnly as a gemstone, though more softly now, and her voice teetered on the ragged edge of breaking.

"No speeches, Rue. They were never your long suit at Drury." Quentin came to put his hands on her shoulders and press her gently back down into her seat.

"Your honesty is overwhelming," she said, resting her hand for a moment on one of his. "I find it quite refreshing in a parent." Quentin winced as Rue laughed, recovered.

Varian came over, too, to stand by her other side. Perhaps he feared some evil fate would whisk her away from him again.

Rue felt an inutterable security even without looking at him, just knowing his impeccably tailored figure was there. She could see the dark ring on his small finger curled around the clear crystal glass stem. His hands had grown larger from his servitude; odd how things that changed the spirit changed the body as well.

She thought of Anne Temple, whom she seemed to know ever since sensing her presence in the asylum. She blended Anne's image with that of her unremembered mother. Only these two of Black Harry's victims were not alive to witness this triumph, this reunion.

She was the only woman who had survived Morgan's worst efforts. She, Black Rue, had been the only one perhaps whose life had been overshadowed by him from birth, and thus she had learned how to cast his own evil back at him.

They were talking of him above her head, obliquely, and she had not been listening.

"... meets with his accursed orgiasts tonight."

"But tomorrow—"

"Will she go as well?"

"Try to stop her, gentlemen."

That was Varian's voice drifting down past the brandy glass at his chest, drifting familiarly over the dark hovering oval of his ring to Rue's abstracted ears.

She was tired, but she must not fade out from the culmination of all her plotting now. Yet the voyage had been long, and even revenge was a tonic she had to remind herself to taste. She looked up to Varian. He was still Barbados-bronzed; indeed, on his return to Brooks's he had actually been momentarily denied entrance by a footman, having been taken for a mulatto servant.

There had been a great deal of "Your Lordshiping" and abject apologies when the mistake became known, Jonathan Flemming had reported to Rue later. But the earl had simply absorbed it all icily, then smiled wickedly and said, "My dear fellow, I have gamed at Brooks's with Black Rue Morgan; one day I may hazard with someone who is black in body as well as in beauty, and I daresay it shall take more than you to stop me."

And then he had gone in and won prodigiously, won everything in sight and a great deal that was not, which had to be conveyed by promissory note. A good number of these items were jewels and such that ought to decorate Rue quite nicely the next time he brought her to game at Brooks's.

"He has become an uncontrite nonconformist," lamented Jonathan wide-eyed to Rue.

"Wait till you see him in Parliament," was all she would say and very cryptically.

But for now their brief two days in London had been all reunion and appalling tendencies to lapse into raw sentiment. Varian had instantly taken a liking to Quentin, and vice versa, something that relieved Rue, for she had every intention of making her new-found father a cornerstone in her life.

In a sense she, the bastard, was acknowledging him rather than the other way around. That was something old London town was probably not ready for, this open admission of illegitimate relationships, but then this capital city was not ready for a great many things that Black Rue certainly intended to do.

"You seem abstracted, Miss Morgan—I say, what do we call you now?" blustered Humphries, embarrassed.

"She won't be Lady Argyle, despite my most lordly beseechings," said Varian, running the backs of his fingers ever so lightly down her cheek.

"Call me Rue, Rue Rossford," she said impishly, glancing up to Quentin. "It will be the joy of my esteemed father's declining years."

Quentin stared heavenward to the pagan-inspired paintings on the ceiling. "My decline is being hastened by such premature advertisements of my advancing years. I warn you, if you go by the name of Rossford you shall have some scandal-making to do before you catch up to this 'old codger.' 'Ave'ee a penny?" he whined in Bartholomew Fayre fettle.

Rue playfully slapped away his begging hand.

"You are all incorrigible. No wonder I missed you so prodigiously. Helia remained behind, you know," she added suddenly with a sigh. "I shall miss her a great deal. But," she looked up at them again, "I have you all and, and there is always that rascal Piquant, my last refugee from Blackstone house. You have him, do you not, Sir Feverell? He has grown, no doubt, as fat and pampered as a Basilisk. You must send him to me as soon as possible."

A sudden, hovering silence. All the Basilisks' eyes, supposed projectors of stone-provoking terror, fell down to their glass rims, their swelling stomachs, their shoetops.

They kept silent to a man. Rue glanced rapidly from Varian to Quentin, both still outposting her chair and both puzzled and somehow foreboding-looking.

"You do have him? Piquant. He's not . . . died?"

The silence held still, growing guiltier by the second. Rue stood, as pale as her ivory silk wrapper.

"Rue," began Addison Hookham, his supercilious voice surprisingly compassionate. "Rue, he was . . . kidnapped. The dog. Shortly after you sailed for Barbados, after—"

"After *he*, after *that man* learned that I had escaped the asylum! And he could not find me anywhere so he, he . . . took Piquant. Because Varian was already gone. And I. And Helia. And there was nothing left for him to wreak his revenge upon—even my canary had escaped in its own way— there was only Piquant, only my dog . . ."

"The footman was walking him around Grosvenor Square garden. Two bullies accosted him," explained Marshwine. "He put up such a gallant defense, poor Moll had to attend him afterward herself—it was James Frankson as it happened, your amorous footman. But they took the little beast. I'd grown fond of him, quite honestly I had. I wouldn't have for the world—had I known, suspected Morgan would be that petty. Damn it, Miss M—m . . . Rossford, I'm bloody sorry about it."

Rue just shook her head dazedly, her still-short curls glossy from the motion.

"Piquant? My fat, lazy Piquant . . . Just to have him? Or, or kill him? Sacrifice him at one of those satanic orgies to which he wished to bring me as he threatened in the carriage . . ."

She was nearer to tears than she had ever been with any of them before; they fairly shrank in helplessness. Rue finally looked around them all, mutely, horrifiedly, and looked last to the earl. "Oh, Varian," she said in a blend of disbelief and pleading, and then fled sobbing from the room.

They heard her pattering footsteps echoing through the marble-lined passage and up the hard uncarpeted stairs.

They heard her sobs scatter behind her in hard, sharp little bursts, like a string of gems that breaks and goes rolling down the stairs, the echoes of their shattering clicking down some timeless, endless hall.

They remained quiet for some time after that, the eight men who remained in the room all looking down, not after her, not at each other.

"Something," came Quentin Rossford's voice finally, like a baritone gauntlet into the center of their loosely formed circle, "must be done about that man."

They looked up then, one by one, and looked at each other, one by one. And when every eye in that room had met every other eye, the earl nodded once, grimly, and strode out of the chamber.

The others remained for a long time until he came back. And they stayed on a great deal longer until the candle wicks sputtered in hot clear pools of beeswax and the tall-case clock in the entry foyer chimed its muffled time in very low numbers. And then they left Cavendish Square, one by one.

It was nearly dawn when the Earl of Argyle finally went back up to Rue's bedchamber.

She was awake, though she said nothing to him. He did not undress or get into bed with her. He sat by it in a Chippendale armchair and drank the last of the brandy in the glass he had brought up with him.

And he waited, as she did, until it was light and there was some excuse to get up and pretend it was a new day and not the same old nightmare replaying again and again.

Chapter Twenty-seven

She picked up the pistol, the wooden butt as polished in her palm as satinwood, and let it weigh to the bottom of her black velvet reticule, a kind of muffled anchor.

"Really, Rue, how did you manage to hang on to that?"

"It was among my things when Heliotrope removed them to Sir Feverell Marshwine's house. I found it with the petticoats."

She laid the heavy reticule on the dressing-table edge and adjusted the sapphire taffeta bow of her sweep-brimmed straw hat. Early spring in London meant mist of a morning mingling with the heavy coal fog that blanketed the commerce-packed streets. She would wear her blue taffeta redingote.

"Rue, I must object again. 'Tis folly."

"When has what I have done not been folly?" she countered, smiling from under her buoyant brim at the earl.

He paced, as formally dressed as she, frockcoated in fine maroon wool and booted instead of shod. The streets were wet and mucked of a spring, and at any rate it was to Black Harry Morgan's house they were going. The earl paced, his gleaming black boots sinking into the pale figured carpet of Rue's dressing chamber as into sand.

"There is no need for you to confront the fellow. And I ardently hope that you won't shoot him! Newgate is no place for a lady, though I swear it's the only place you have not yet honored with your presence. This is not necessary, Rue."

She picked up the anchor-heavy reticule and slung its strong, silken cords over her wrist.

"I am going, Varian. I take a pistol because it is best not to enter Black Harry Morgan's house unarmed. As for what I will accomplish, I want our escape to force him to surrender the Barbados plantation quite legally so that Graham can captain it, and the crusading Earl of Argyle shall have a model abolitionist paradise to point to in Parliament. And I want him to know that he has not won."

"Who can win against you?" The earl threw up his well-manicured hands and stepped into the connecting room to summon Welles.

"To Blackstone House then, Rue," he conceded reluctantly, trailing her downstairs to the foyer.

The valet scurried to assist the earl into his greatcoat and extend a black beaver hat and cane.

"But surely it's a bit early to go," he stalled, coming over to put his hands on her redingoted shoulders. "You look as if a chimneysweep's thumbs had brushed your tears away," he said more softly, noting the pale blue bruises of fatigue under her eyes.

Those eyes narrowed to deep cerulean.

"You talk as if you were making a social call, Varian. I have no qualms about rousing the monster from his sated slumbers. And I know all about his demonic club of similarly depraved roués—good God, Varian, I *invented* the Afridisiac affair! In fact, I wish the stuff had been fatal, for *he* would have swallowed enough by now to slay several elephants. Of course, Quentin would not have appreciated any side effects." She drew on her gloves and smiled. "Dear

Varian, it is you who were naïve; you go to Morgan's house unarmed."

He flourished his cane. "*Au contraire*, my dear barbarian. *Voilà*." His thumb flicked at the heavy silver-worked canetop. The rosewood stick slipped off like a sheath to reveal a lethal giant of a stickpin, a short sword. The earl made a graceful pass at Welles standing by patiently with his greatcoat. The little man sidestepped as anxiously as a nurse snatching a charge from an oncoming carriage.

"Excellent reflexes, my dear Welles. We'll make a Tartar of you yet. Well, Rue, if you must you must."

The earl sheathed his blade pointedly, finally accepted the coat, his black kid gloves, and hat, and escorted her into the slightly dank air.

The vaunted blacks stood ready at an almost funereally gleaming black equipage. It was a gig for two; the earl would drive himself.

"I am fortunate it is not a perch phaeton," remarked Rue as the lackey handed her up onto the tufted crimson leather seat.

"You are fortunate that you do not ride the luggage rack behind the rear wheels," noted the earl, assuming his own seat and picking up the whip for a starting flick at the glossy black hindquarters before him.

"How did you know *where* I rode on your kidnapping night?"

"Hookham told me at great length. That is the advantage of making peace—your adversaries know such intriguing tidbits."

"You do not have to sleep with Hookham," Rue warned.

"A fact for which both he and I are supremely grateful," the earl conceded, drawing up the skeins of leather and starting the blacks smoothly along the mist-drenched pavement, which shone pearl-gray in the prenoon overcast.

Their banter ceased during most of the drive to Black-stone House. The nearer they got, the paler Rue's face grew, until it seemed but an extension of her glacial expanse of fichu and cravat. The morning mist muffled them, made the gig's almost supernaturally smooth progress into a kind of apparition of gloom.

Even Blackstone House cooperated in the mood. It had never been more than a dark, stately place, stone-faced and smudged by wisps of London grime that darkened its facade as tarnish blackens silver.

Now the fog choked its foundations, wove through its wrought-iron fence, slid softly off its blank mullioned windows, a smoke-gray alley cat that was not wanted here.

They paused before the gray stone steps and waited for the lackey to see Rue down and the groomsman to take the horse's heads. No one came. Rue shifted the black velvet reticule on her lap.

The horses pawed the cobblestones, shook their mist-damp necks, and snorted impatiently, steam hissing from their nostrils until they resembled coursers from hell and it was possible to imagine their eyes rolled red in their coal-dark faces. The Earl of Argyle slammed the whip butt into its brass socket, the leather hissing a bit in the thick air like a blade through a candle.

"It looks . . . deserted," Rue observed as he lifted her down.

"Looks deceive," said Varian grimly, offering her his arm and balancing his lethal cane lightly in his other hand.

They faced the great coffered door together, he ringing the bell-pull with the same abrupt challenge with which he'd tabled the driving whip.

No one came. The earl suddenly fanned his gloved fingers and pushed on the painted wood, like a man striking the chest of an opponent preparatory to real challenge. The hinges squealed protest, but the well-balanced door swung open, completely open.

Rue crossed the threshold into a house she had not seen in the eighteen months that had elapsed since her eighteenth birthday.

It was the same. She had expected it to be webbed in a

dozen sinister memories of what had happened since her contention with Black Harry Morgan had moved from the domestic shadows into the bright light of public warfare.

But it was only the same, only a house, only a familiar assembly of tiled floors and the staircase she had once climbed like a mountain and all the blank white doors neatly closing off the great drawing room where her heart had broken, the library where Morgan had first met his cuckold in the form of Barty Fayre, the foyer through which Rue and Heliotrope had come and gone in elegant passage, the halls where Piquant had waddled along on clicking toenails like a dandy on mincing heels. . . .

They explored the deserted first floor, Rue lightly brushing her gloved fingertips over the dusty cut-crystal contours of the library's infamous decanter of port, the finest port fit for crimping-house men.

She paused in the arch of the drawing room after Varian had thrown both doors open as if exorcising the place's musty air. She studied the great Italian marble chimneypiece across the room and smiled back at the frozen-faced cupids disporting there. She looked to the earl.

He sighed.

"The Basilisks said Morgan had deteriorated. That elephant bone scheme of yours, Rue, seems to have maddened the man. He can't have been far from it. The countryside had heard disturbing tales of late, of dark rites and servant defections and frequent deportations to Bedlam. I can't say I'm surprised at the state of the place. Morgan may have erected his own destruction. Let us leave him to it—"

"I haven't seen all the house," she said, sweeping back to the foyer on a crisp taffeta rustle.

She paused at the foot of the stairs, then began mounting them methodically. The earl halted at the newel post, as if his stationary presence could drag her back down, out of the house and into the exterior fog.

"You don't have to perform a post-mortem on the entire house, Rue," he urged softly.

But she was plodding upward, as if into high, thin air where it became ever increasingly difficult to breathe. The earl shrugged and followed her up.

Rue glided down the empty hall, past the slim console table where her slipper had rolled when she had kicked it there on the night of her eighteenth birthday. She expected to see it there still, webbed with dust, a lowly trophy of her former father's victory. But some servant had tidied it away long ago.

Now the house was empty, chill, only old ashes in its grates. Rue paused again before a door, a door familiar in every irregularity of feature, the chips beneath the white paint, the tracks of scratches below the knob. Piquant, like Nigel, had ever been impatient of admittance.

She pushed it open. It swung on silent, well-oiled hinges as if this room were the only tended chamber in the house, as if there were something secret and dark about that fact.

This was not her pale and airy girlish bedchamber within, but a scarlet, circled temple draped in heavy brocades, furniture cleared away save for an oddly swollen arrangement of sofas and a central malachite-topped table so simple in its lines it resembled . . . an altar.

The floor was painted with great crude paths of scarlet and gold and azure in cryptic signs—astrological signs, though the centaur that was Sagittarius drew back his bow to point a phallic arrow, and Virgo the virgin lifted her skirts, and Scorpio's stinger was equally suggestive and aimed aggressively toward Aries the Ram, whose horns were those of a medieval cuckold.

Rue hovered on the threshold, then plunged over it into the air murky with forbidden incense and ritual. Even the ceiling was draped with fabric, a lid against the eye of heaven. Rue was aware of the dark glitter of iron scattered about the place, chains and bonds and machines. She had not sensed such an ominous metallic presence since the night she had met Graham Winthrop in the Morgan stables.

Then the snaffle bits and harness rings had echoed his careless laughter with chiming mockery.

She moved to the richly veined green of the ceremonial slab and saw the bronze bowl in its center, rusted red.

It was here that Black Harry Morgan would have inevitably imported Pacing Rue, here that he had perhaps sacrificed Piquant to his frustrated vengeance, his artificially erected lust ever in need of more exotic stimuli.

Her white-gloved fingertips trembled against the corroded red bottom of the empty bowl, and she leaned over the clean green gulf of malachite to study incredulously the obscenities that weighed in Libra's scales.

A heap of fallen ruby brocade lay crumpled upon the design behind the monolithic table, more than a mere discarded curtain. It was a very human crumple she now noticed, yet growing from one end was something very unhuman, something gray and soft as moss, bulbously shaped—or unshaped—with a great long, puckered tentacle undulating across the gaudy floor.

She screamed, shrieked, a high, piercing wail of disbelief that sliced through the heavy draperies to find good hard solid wall behind to rebound off.

Varian's short sword was suddenly before her and whatever she saw, piercing the mystery should it leap. "What? Or is it merely the evil of the place?"

She pointed, her small, white-gloved hand as neat as a child's indicating some novelty.

"What is it, Varian? What have they called up? It's not real, it can't be."

He went around the hard-edged altar and prodded point-first at the fabric.

Suddenly he dropped his weapon, knelt, and heaved the stuff over. It was a roll like a carpet, and the velvety gray stuff at one end overturned to become an oddly sinister elephant mask with a flaccid trunk lying askew the man's mouth beneath it, the man whose hands were unmistakably hair-matted as they flopped upright. And the dagger, curved like a steel smile from the wicked East, the ceremonial dagger driven haft-deep into the man's robed chest, an eternal erection of steel and death.

Varian looked up at Rue and she at him for a very long time. He rose. "We'd better leave."

She backed obediently toward the door, step by step, each one sounding like slaps against the uncarpeted floor, past the grinning zodiac debauchees underfoot.

Varian bent once behind the somber malachite; she gasped at his disappearance as if he might have been swallowed. But he stood again almost instantly, pulling down his frockcoat in what seemed an oddly nervous gesture for the self-collected Earl of Argyle.

He retrieved his cane and strode toward her. Rue continued to back away from the chamber with its hideous past and deadly present, continued backing away until she came up against a wall of flesh, started and turned with an inaudible gasp.

"I 'eard the screams and knew I could come out, Mistress," said the wizened old woman who swayed on the threshold. "Clean screams, they was, not like 'em others. No, just clean, clean 'orror. So I knew it was safe. Good day to you, sir. Such a fine gentleman, a fine lady. It's the little Rue, yes, sir, so it be. There's naught to fear. I always knew she'd come back one last time and give her a-birthin' scream and then go to her rest, poor creature, yer mother, little Rue. Only old Rebecky Bartle remembers. They've all gone. Even 'im at the last. Last is best. Last is sweetest, eh, Miss?"

The woman's face, as webbed with lines as her face, tilted at Rue and the earl. She shuffled away from the threshold.

"Wicked is as wicked does. And wicked dies as wicked does. 'E's gone to 'ell and I 'opes 'e stays there, 'deed I do. They'll not be lettin' 'im out; they don't get such evil easy nowadays. You was born in that room, little Rue. She died in it soon after. Rebecky Bartle knew. Always knew 'e'd meet 'is demons there."

Rue ran her hands down the woman's meager arms, testing her corporeality.

"Yes. It's old Rebecca who's been in this house longer than I. Where are the servants? What happened here? To him?"

"Servants?" The cackles grew softer. "Ay, servants they called us, though we 'ad little choice in it. The young 'uns he sent for to 'ere," she said with a savage nod to the room behind them. "Them as that liked it. And them as that didn't. And then it was 'ard to get servants after a time with 'is gentleman friends comin' once a fortnight, then every week. Oh, they were up to no good above, I could tell. But they left old Rebecky out o' it. Even those gentlemen had some nicety left. And someone must clean up after them, wash out their bowls, you see, and 'ear nothing, say nothin'. . ."

"You stayed on alone?"

"Ay, it was not done, you see. They came last night—the gentlemen fiends, I call 'em. 'Tis a small wordplay. Gentlemen fiends. They come as usual, and there is great noise, tumult as they says in the plays. And then they leave. Early, it seems. They leave. And old Rebecky knows better than to creep in until the light is up. And what do you think, fine lady, fine gentleman? She finds 'im dead, she does, stuck through his black 'eart like an 'og for the meatdresser . . ." Her bony fist drove repeatedly into her stringy palm. "Again an' again an' again until 'e's a right royal red pincushion."

"Varian—?"

"It's true. More than one blow killed him—"

"Made mincemeat o' 'im, didn't they? It'll keep for Christmas, oh, yes. It'll keep. And now Rebecky can go."

"Why did you stay?" asked Rue incredulously. "You could have left earlier."

"No, no, not so. Couldn't leave. Oh, no. That would be

losin'. Couldn't leave this 'ouse until '*e* left. Until nothin' but ghosts prowls these passages. Rebecky's not a ghost, she's flesh and blood, and now she'll be leavin'. Good birthday to you, little Rue. 'Tis never a November without a wind, though." She leaned very near and caught Rue's wrist with her clawlike fingers.

It was then that Rue heard a faint, persistent rustle, a nearing scraping sound, soft as the brush of rat claws on pavement, the play of fingernails across a door when someone makes a genteel scratching to get in. Or out.

Rue stared over Rebecca's stooped shoulder down the dim, deserted passage. The sound came from the dark and grew louder. Her own hand went out for the security of Varian's frockcoat lapels behind her. Finally it came into view, the maker of those sounds, a bedraggled tangle of dirty blond hair.

"Piquant!"

The dishevelled dustmop plodded over to her gown hem, suddenly hurling itself into frantic turns and leaps and welcoming yaps. Rue knelt to the little creature and elevated him to her knees.

"He's so thin, so tangled—so affectionate. How is it that he is here? And safe?"

Rebecca Bartle rocked smugly on her feet.

"Ay, fooled 'im again, I did. Brought it 'ere and forgot it for a while, didn't 'e? I told 'im I cooked it and fed it to 'im for dinner! And 'e believed me, great wicked creature 'e was. 'E thought it a great joke and promised to fetch me more such meat to serve 'is Royal Order o' the Elephant or some such thing as 'e called 'is wickedness. But this plump little beast was safe in the coal scuttle, wasn't it, though? I knew you'd be back for the little dog, the little Rue. And now old Rebecky can leave. Got no use for the November wind, an' I 'aven't got to stay to face it. No use at all . . ."

She shuffled off down the corridor, her bent and dark-clothed figure already vanishing into the endless dark.

"Wait! Where will you go? What will you do? Come home with us."

"I've other to do, other to go," came back the waning answer punctuated by a high-pitched laugh. "Don't fret for old Rebecky, I sees to myself. And sometimes to some'un else. 'Ware the November winds . . ."

And off she whined, a feeble, somehow prophetic gust of elderly sibyl and outright senility. Rue stood with Piquant in her arms. The Pekinese rolled out the pink carpet of greeting so incessantly that he managed to include the earl's impeccably shaved cheek in his circle of attentions.

Varian reared back. "I see Black Harry Morgan was incapable of teaching this one any manners, too," the earl remarked dryly. "Well, Sir Feverell will be greatly relieved that you have recovered the beast, though I can't say as much for myself."

Rue looked up at him with tear-polished eyes. "You are not distracting me from what has happened here, Varian, though it is a gallant attempt."

He took her arm before relieving her of the reclaimed Piquant's wriggling bulk.

"Then I shall have to find other means," he promised, conducting them both firmly down the long passage, down the stairs and out the ajar door into the drive.

The mist had cleared.

Chapter Twenty-eight

Bow Street was duly notified of the crime at Blackstone House. In a day or two, a respectful representative of the law's long and often overextended arm called upon Rue Morgan at Cavendish Square.

"Your Lordship," said this functionary, bowing first to the earl, who stood behind the brown leather wing chair, and then to Rue who sat upon it.

Functionaries are ever impressed by titles. That may be why his manner was impeccable to the woman who most unconventionally resided at number three, Cavendish Square.

"I am most sorry to report your father's death, Miss Morgan," he began conventionally enough. "It grieves me further to relate that your late father had taken up with evil company. It is these whom Bow Street suspects of complicity in his, er, demise. Please accept my condolences."

Rue inclined her dark head solemnly; the official was obtuse enough to mistake the gesture for bereavement and clucked sympathetically. The Earl of Argyle's hand curled almost protectively over the shoulder of leather, a somber ring flat black upon it. The official was most impressed by the air of mourning investing these two.

"That is all there is to say of it?" inquired the earl.

"I fear so, Your Lordship. Reports indicate that these, er, suspected parties have fled abroad. They have little recourse, you see. Their social habits were most reprehensible. I would elaborate further, but I do not wish to disturb the ears of the lady." He bowed again, congratulating himself on his finesse.

The lady in question smiled tautly. Clearly, she had already heard more than she could bear. The official bowed himself out discreetly.

Rue rose after he had gone and went to stand before the wine decanter. Varian read her gesture and poured a burnished glass. For himself, he poured brandy.

"I rather feared they would ... well, question our motives," he said as much to the brandy snifter as to Rue.

"Obviously we overestimate Bow Street. How much easier to blame a group of dissolute ruffians than a Peer of the Realm. No, we are safe enough there, but—"

"But?"

"I do·not believe it."

"Believe what?"

"That his fellow pachyderms killed him."

"You heard the Bow Street man; they fled."

"So do rats a sinking ship. It does not mean that they are the captain."

"I'm afraid you must face the truth, dear Rue. You are not only *not* a suspect, there is an even more unpleasant role awaiting you."

"A role? What?"

"Heiress," said the earl succinctly, savoring his brandy.

Rue regarded him blankly. "You mean?"

"That if officialdom overlooks your possible reasons for slaying your imposturing sire, they will also likely overlook any barrier to your inheriting his estate. You are his only apparent heir."

"But Varian, that means that—"

"That you have your Barbados plantation without a whimper, you have a merchant fleet you can now divert from the slave trade, you have crimping houses you can close, and you have a rather prodigious fortune. Whether you can keep it without resorting to the corner-cutting of your so-called father will be an interesting exercise for you."

"But it means that . . . that to the world I shall always have to be Rue Morgan. If I would have his wealth, I must keep his name!"

"Unless you become Lady Argyle." The earl smiled.

Rue sat upon the venerable leather. It gave the small squeak of the aged, a sound which very well expressed her astonishment.

"Poor Quentin. You know, despite it all, I think he would have delighted in a namesake. He is not nearly as jaded as he pretends."

"I know." The earl smiled. "It runs in the family."

"But what shall I do?"

"You must decide where your sentiment lies—whether you wish to bestow the Barbadian hellhole that Morgan made upon Winthrop for his reclamation, whether you wish his ships to carry cargo instead of souls, or whether you prefer to recognize Quentin Rossford as your true father. I warn you, if you keep Morgan's holdings, I fear you will be thought quite respectable, quite legitimate."

"What a quandary." Rue sipped from her wine and kicked up the hem of her skirt in frustration. "It is as if that man reaches from the grave and lays some claim upon me still. His name—I can strip him of everything he had and misused, but I must bear his name."

"Will you do it?" he asked narrowly, for even he was not sure.

"You did not christen me 'Black Rue Morgan' for nothing," she answered staunchly. "As the Bard of Avon said, 'What's in a name?' "

"A Rue by any other name would still be as sweet," paraphrased His Lordship in reply. He took her hand. "And this Rue needs a rest," he said, "and needs to forget Black Harry Morgan."

She forgot Black Harry for two days, as prescribed, and on the third she went to the Basilisk Club.

"Pray stay seated, gentlemen. Surely my attendance is not so formal an occasion? You did not think that I would forget you?"

The Basilisks bobbed up and bowed anyway, except for Sir Feverell Marshwine, who was so firmly wedged between table and Windsor chair that anything other than a gentlemanly squirm was impossible.

Rue was splendidly gowned that day in a rose silk shift topped by a short black velvet spencer jacket. Her jet curls were allowed to unfurl only so far before being beaten back by the scissors now, and the "Bedlam Shear" was indeed as fashionable as Quentin Rossford had predicted—although it was beginning to be called the "Morgan Mop."

Rue had taken to stringing assorted silk flowers and ribbands through her waves of tossing dark hair, and this too spawned a trend to such fashionable flotsam. Altogether she looked in the very blush of health, though a faint line ran from each of her eyes. It was what Addison Hookham privately called her "taming of the shrewd" look.

"Yes, hot chocolate would be quite fine. Thank you, dear Sir Merivale. I had quite forgotten how to be spoiled."

She smiled all round and twisted the black satin cords of her reticule on her rosy lap. They beamed back at her, even Hookham allowing a self-congratulatory expression to soften his perpetual semisneer.

"It is so pleasant to be among you again, my dear Basilisks," said Rue, wriggling her toes upon the little footstool like a stretching kitten and sipping demurely from her flowered cup.

"And, Sir Feverell, you did know that I have reclaimed my darling Piquant?"

"Yes, yes, I'd heard," he replied, wriggling restively. "Damn fine canine, damn fine. Wouldn't mind having the little nipper myself—though, of course, I'd not dream of depriving you, that is, you'd hardly consider giving him up," he added most hastily.

"Oh, I don't know, Sir Feverell," said Rue, very roguishly. "Since our separation he has become quite prodigiously affectionate. He must be by me constantly. His Lordship, I fear, grows impatient."

The Basilisks considered the image of the Earl of Argyle contesting a determined Pekinese for the privileges of Rue's bed. A series of suppressed smiles were tucked firmly into mouth corners all round the table.

"But," she continued, "I am grateful for Piquant's safe return, although I must admit that the conditions in which we found him were far from pleasant."

Here faces fell on cue.

"Most distressing, Miss, er—"

"Morgan, I fear, Colonel Rutherford. For financial reasons, you understand."

"Quite."

"See here, Miss, ah, Morgan. You mustn't fret about this ritual murder thing. The man deserved it, God knows, and the Devil, too, quite likely. It was predictable that his vile associates would turn on him and rend him rib from rib—"

"Was it?" demanded Rue sharply. "Was it, indeed, Mr. Humphries?"

That gentleman's face drowned in an even more crimson tide than normal.

"You left Cavendish Square the night of our reunion quite late, I believe, did you not, gentlemen? And did you not likely repair to a tavern to discuss, oh, matters unsuitable for discussion in front of me?"

"A tavern? Certainly not," objected Dr. Radclyffe. "I for one went directly home."

"And I."

"Yes, we all went home, one by one."

"Quite alone."

Rue considered, and sipped chocolate. "One by one. Then none of you can vouch for the other, can you, sirs? Surely one of you could have slipped unseen to Blackstone House and had a purely rhetorical confrontation with Black Harry Morgan? One could have, shall we say, rammed home his point and then have left quite unseen?"

"One could have," said Addison Hookham, leaning his chin on the heel of his hand, "but is it likely that one would have? You said yourself we were a goutish lot, more ready for freezing veins than glances. We are innocent by virtue of your very assessment of us."

"Yes," concluded Rue slowly. "Then all."

"A—a—all?"

"Heavens, Sir Merivale. I thought you were Colonel Trumbull and attempting a sneeze. Yes, a—a—all. All of my very dear Basilisks could have left Cavendish Square quite unobtrusively and arrived at Blackstone House just as surreptitiously. There were, after all, a good many thrusts of the dagger in Black Harry's body. Methinks the slayer was possessed of a stutter."

Sir Merivale opened his mouth to reply, then shut it firmly and sank far back in his chair, his high forehead pleated with concern.

"My dear Rue," remonstrated Hookham even more suavely, " 'tis true that London teems with a number of ridiculous societies nowadays—from the Royal Society of the Beefsteak to our own association to Morgan's rather ribald club. But the Basilisks are hardly members of the Morgan Murderers."

"Why not? You are a syndicate, gentlemen, and had been long before I met you. I do not blame you for any mayhem you may have committed, I merely wish to know of it."

"There is nothing to know," protested Dr. Radclyffe sternly. "We can swear to you that not one of us is responsible for plunging the dagger into Black Harry Morgan's heart."

"Not one?"

"Not one of us, we swear it."

"You . . . all swear it."

"We do," they answered in chorus, placing hands over hearts and regarding her quite steadily.

Rue sipped her chocolate. "Gentlemen, you persuade me of your sincerity," she said as she smiled and rose, taking her leave.

Within the half-hour, her carriage was poised outside the Drury Lane, and Rue was inside the theater posed on Quentin Rossford's best guest chair.

"Quentin, you are not listening to me."

He paused in applying his makeup for the matinee pantomime.

"An actor always listens; it is half the art. Speak to my profile, dear Rue, it is my best side anyway."

She sighed. "Vanity, thy name is Rossford."

"Yes," he agreed, regarding his mirrored image quite complacently.

"You do understand about my still using *his* name, Quentin. It is only an accommodation—"

"I am always most accommodating, Rue. Names do not matter to me."

"Precisely how accommodating are you, Quentin?" she pursued, leaning forward on her chair, her hand on his arm to stop his eternal fussing about the fringes of his face.

He glanced at her. Damn dressing rooms. Despite the candles flickering at either side of the looking glass, the side light was quite bad, and she could barely read his features.

"Most inventively accommodating," he replied.

"Does your invention bear a blade?"

His motions paused the merest fraction of an instant, but he kept his profile to her, a flat, unrevealing image as unreal as a painted proscenium.

"My weapons are words, gestures . . ."

"You left Varian's house, alone?"

"We all left, alone."

"One by one."

The head tilted, still in profile. "Each by each."

"And you went straight home?"

"Rue . . . You know better than to question a gentleman. Even a father must be discreet."

"And it was not Lady Death you courted?"

"We all court Lady Death. Why are you asking me these rather oblique questions?"

"Because I do not think a roistering lot of rakehells killed Morgan, Quentin. I think someone we know did, that it was one of us with a motive for revenge—"

"You exempt yourself, I take it. What a relief."

She smiled. "I must. I, too, went straight to bed. Alone."

"Please, no details of your domestic arrangements," he mocked, fanning his hands in surrender. "What are you asking me? Say it direct."

"Did you go to Blackstone House to kill . . . him?"

Quentin Rossford finally turned his face from the mirror. He looked into hers, which had drawn nearer on every question until it hovered over his shoulder. He took her face in his hands and shook his head sadly.

"You have no talent for dissembling, my dear; it is why you will never make an actress. Did I go to Black Harry Morgan's house?" He kissed her forehead and drew back to smile at her quite gently. "I tell you, 'No.' "

"Quentin!" she protested. "You are an actor!"

"I fear so." He had returned to the mirror and his makeup. "Since you are an actor's daughter, you will have to put up with it."

She rose. "Very well then. I believe you. But since I am an actor's daughter, you will never be certain whether I do or not. Adieu, dear dissembler, and we expect you for dinner on Thursday next."

* * *

For the last time that day, the carriage rolled up before a door not the Earl of Argyle's. It was number twenty-one, Grosvenor Square, and Rue peered discreetly out the lowered window for a long time before nodding to the footman to help her disembark.

She stepped slowly to the pavement and followed the be-wigged footman to the great front door, once so familiar, so taken for granted. It swung open, that deceptively sunny yellow door, and Rue asked meekly to see Sir Nigel Pagett-Foxx if he were in.

She was conducted to the first-floor study where were kept books and port wine and certain country squires sick of city life. Nigel was wearing an almost deliberately noisy figured waistcoat and was sunk into an overstuffed chair. He rose on her approach.

"Rue ... Missssh Morgan, that is. Or is it Lady Argyle by now? No, I don't mean that. How fare you? You found him—Temple, I mean. 'Tis all over London, his return. Even I heard of it," he remarked bitterly. "Some port, very fine port, ruby port. No? What can I offer you then? Only a seat?"

"Thank you."

She sat, a flick of her lids instantly measuring the ebbing level of the port decanter. She chose to survey her former lover instead and saw that as the wine sank in the crystal, it rose in him, painting his square face ruddy and bloated, swelling out his waistcoat, giving a tremor to his hands. Rue folded her own hands over her reticule and recalled that she was alone in a darkened study with a man who had once betrayed her into unspeakable exile. But she had to know.

"Nigel, I—"

"How fare you?" he asked again, obsessive.

"Well," she said noncommittally.

"You are with the earl?"

"Yes."

There was an awkward pause. "You will wed him?"

"No."

His glass suddenly clinked against the decanter as he turned roughly to pour another stream of wine into it. He lifted the rim to his lips, then paused.

"There is a country squire's daughter in Norfolk. Neighboring family, you know. She's eight-and-twenty, quite plump as a pigeon, and has pale straight hair. Like hay, I suppose. I could wed her, retire to the country, you know. Her father has her cap set for me—or no, that's not the right expression—she sets her father's cap at me ... Anyway, there's a great deal of sizing-up has gone on. I might go back. And wed her, you see."

"It is better to marry than to burn," said Rue.

"Burn. Yes, I know about burning," he said then intensely, his pale eyes feverish upon her.

"Nigel," she said, so softly that he had to lean forward in his chair and the wine sloshed against the very glass rim. "Nigel, you offered me your adoration and your lust. There is a great deal in between. I earnestly beseech you to seek for it. Elsewhere."

He slumped back into his chair, the fingers of one hand crushing the damask. "I'm sorry, Rue. God knows I'm abjectly sorry. When I, I saw you after that place ... I'd have done anything to make it up to you, anything—"

He was fighting back tears, or sobs, or whatever it is men fight back when they are drunk and feeling maudlin. Perhaps it is only honesty.

"Anything?" she whispered, leaning toward him.

"Anything," he swore in his anguish.

"Nigel, did you ever think of going to Black Harry Morgan's house and—"

"And telling him how contemptible he was? How I knew that he'd used me, how he'd abused you in that asylum? Yes, yes, I thought it a thousand times! A hundred thousand."

He had set aside his glass, and his hands were throttling the arms of his chair. He was leaning toward her, but seeing far beyond her to the man who always stood behind her in most people's imaginations, Black Harry Morgan, as immortal somehow as hatred.

"But only once, Nigel. Did you actually do it only once? One night, three nights ago. Did you go to Blackstone House and push open the unattended door and walk upstairs and find Black Harry Morgan alone in ... in a very bad place, a place as twisted and hateful as he was, with a dagger there and a bowl—were you there, Nigel, were you?" Rue demanded, watching his feverish nodding throughout her recital as if he recognized and affirmed each step of the path she described.

"Yes, yes, yes!" he said. "I have been there, in such dark places. I know it. A thousand times ..."

"You were there? That night? In that place?" asked Rue, standing.

"Yes. I have seen it all. I know that place." He buried his face in his equally square-shaped hands. "It is called hell!"

Rue's breath suddenly hissed out. She came and stood over him. "Not your generalized hell, Nigel. A particular hell. Black Harry's Hell. It was in his own heart, his own house. I want to know if you killed him."

"I don't know, don't know ..." he mourned. "I have thought it. Many times. Dreamed it. I was in his house, and he handed me the gleaming red globe to play with—so sweet, so satisfying, and I have longed for satisfaction ... I have dreamed of smashing his pretty red ball at his feet. It was a lure, a betrayal. I am sorry for it. And then smashing and smashing and smashing Black Harry Morgan."

He looked up from dry, red-rimmed eyes. "But I don't know, you see. Don't really know anything." He shifted leadenly back deep into the chair's embrace. "I am thinking of returning to Norfolk, did I tell you?" he said remotely. "There is a squire's daughter there I would wed. She is very fair. I will send for you to my wedding if I do."

"Yes," said Rue, moving slowly to the chamber door. It stood ajar and let in a slice of fanlight-lit air. Once through it, she would be in a normal corridor of time, of being. She would not be with Nigel in the room that remorse and port wine had erected for him.

He did not know. He may have dreamed the knife and its plunge. He may have rode upon it. But one thing was eminently clear—Nigel himself did not know. She left, and Nigel didn't know.

"You look melancholy, my dear," said the Earl of Argyle to his mistress, Black Rue Morgan, after dinner that evening.

They had dined alone and repaired to the earl's sitting room where the fire entertained them with its fiery acrobatics and reminded them of another evening spent before it.

"Oh, Varian," said Rue, leaning her head on his shoulder. "I'm not sad, I'm fatigued. I have spent the day trying to pry the truth from my dearest friends—and one enemy—and it has been most exhausting."

He laughed, put his arm around her, and drew her closer.

They reclined on an ivory damask settee, both shod, but dust on the damask was hardly a matter to occupy their attention at the moment.

"Which enemy have you been bedeviling now?" he asked, tilting up her chin.

"Nigel."

His eyes, still a smoky drift of autumn colors, fastened on the blue skies of her own expression.

"Rue," he chided, "hasn't he proven dangerous enough for you already? Stay away from him. He may be unhinged."

"I had to know, Varian. Or try to know. You always said gamblers were overcurious."

"I am the gamester, Miss, remember it. What did you have to know?"

"Who really killed Black Harry."

A frown grooved itself over one of the earl's dark eye brows.

"Varian! It wasn't any besotted circle of Satanists, I know

it. It was someone who finally thought Black Harry had gone too far—"

"What has stimulated this conclusion on the part of people who'd been wronged by him for decades to suddenly drive home the dagger?"

"Oh, I don't know, perhaps Piquant—"

"Ah. Now, rushing to the defense of the wronged Pekinese, a noble band of Basilisks, aided no doubt by the consummate actor Quentin Rossford and the dejected and pathetic Pagett-Foxx—this determined group speeds headlong to Blackstone House to wreak bloody murder upon the now deceased Morgan."

Rue kept silent a moment, finally playfully fluffing the lace of his cravat.

"Don't forget the Earl of Argyle," she cautioned.

"You think I—? 'And then he plucked up the dripping blade and drove the steel home, saying: "Die, thou villain and pay thy price," quoth he.' "

"You tease me, as Quentin does. But neither of you look me in the eye," said Rue, half-rising above him quite threateningly.

"In my case, that's because I've better things to regard," he replied, pulling her down to kiss her and slip her wrapper off her shoulders and in general distract her quite effectively.

"Varian!" She broke away, half-laughing, half-ready to shed tears of frustration. "You can't deny it, you didn't come back to my room until almost dawn."

"Ah, you suspect infidelity already . . ."

"No. But the Basilisks left soon after our reunion gathering learned of Piquant's fate, and I so rudely ran out and left them all to themselves. And you, and Quentin. They left soon after, but you did not come up until hours later. I know. I was awake, I waited."

He caught her close and buried his fingers in her hair, and still she could not quite see his face, his eyes.

"I was distraught. I stayed below and nursed my brandy

and cast my cursed dice. And no matter what I threw, they always came up sapphires."

He bent to kiss her again so speedily that she felt she was dodging a fractured series of images, that he was smothering himself so close to her so she could not draw back and read any objective answer in his eyes.

"And speaking of sapphires . . ." He rose and went over to the mantel, returning with a long, narrow box.

She meld it mutely before her as if it were a weapons case she contemplated. "White moiré. Why do jewelers always use that? Or is it dice with which you present me?"

"If it is, it is double eights and a singleton for luck. Open it."

She did cautiously and saw again, reunited, the seventeen perfect sapphires of her mother's necklace strung perfectly along the light blue silk down to the great teardrop of blue that formed the necklace's center.

"But he took it! That day in the carriage. Varian, how did you get it? Or is it a, a replacement?"

"There should be some secrets between a man and his mistress," he asserted, taking the gems out of their box and fastening them around her neck, although he unwittingly caught a strand of her hair in the mechanism. She forbore to tell him.

"I'm not sure I want these." Her fingers tripped over the glittering constellation like a blind person's.

"They're whole again. And cleansed. They're yours. How I reassembled them does not matter."

"Perhaps." Her hands hovered over his. "But, Varian, my other question does. Did you, did any of them—all of them—go to Blackstone House that night and—"

"Hush. We will have, according to you and my sincere intention, a great many years to trick the truth of that out of each other. Let us not overwager early on, Black Rue. There are other tactics we can employ that are much more useful," he said, kissing her in such a way that she knew that it was useless to debate anything further, that it was useless to do anything other than kiss him back at her great and good leisure.

At their feet on the pale settee came a bound of springs and a sudden presence. Their eyes flew open to see Piquant steadily clambering his way across their legs and up toward their laps.

The earl fanned his hand across his eyes to delay the approach of this strawberry-blond vision.

"My dearest Rue," he demanded in an injured tone, "how can you ever have suspected me of killing Morgan if it meant any chance of recovering this creature? I would rather sail the hold of the *Ivory Queen* again, cut cane till the dust flew, find myself sequestered with the most dangerous woman on any island including the one that is my heart, I would—"

"Yes?"

"Rather discuss it further in the morning."

Piquant, having worked his way up to their laps, settled there with a contented wheeze. It was, he concluded, a most satisfactory arrangement for the night.

It must be said that the years passed on Cavendish Square, and that Piquant, perhaps hastened by his deprivations, did not endure for too many years thereafter, although he was greatly pampered while he clung doggedly to what comforts he could.

And the second-story windows of number three, Cavendish Square, often blazed late into the night—sometimes, perhaps, because its occupants were debating the exact events of a certain night and a certain sensational crime.

But most of the time, the yellow squares blazed on either side of the darkened windows in between, and Rue Morgan sat at her neat writing desk and composed the latest chapter of her searing novelization of the horrors of the madhouse, titled *The Abominations of the Vanished Cloister*, which featured ghostly monks, certain overlarge species of spiders, and other suitably thrilling ingredients.

She had interested a publisher and soon thought herself ready to challenge Mrs. Radcliffe herself at outré events in fictional form. Her other activities involved such enterprises as cajoling the earl into sponsoring a trans-channel balloon flight straight into the teeth of the French. She would, of course, be the first female to accomplish such a crossing.

And though she missed Heliotrope dreadfully, more than anyone might guess, they corresponded frequently. Very soon after having left Barbados, Rue began receiving letters in which references to "Captain Winthrop" degenerated quickly into mentions of "Graham," and those were most excessive.

Rue, at least, had found another factotum in the form of Mad Agnes, who fetched and carried and generally meddled in her vague way into the more domestic of Rue's affairs— although not long after her freeing from the asylum, she had demonstrated herself quite sane and even shrewd.

As for the earl, he had interjected himself into some of his day's most unpopular political causes, and the triumph of an honored title like his on the side of the humble Quaker abolitionists had instilled new fire into the movement to free the slaves and even, by God, the Irish. They predicted that monumental gains would be made within the next twenty years.

In the meantime, the earl sat at his desk on the other side of the bedchambers he and Rue shared, and he wrote speeches for Parliament and persuasive letters to Peers of the Realm quite unceasingly.

Unceasingly, that is, until he rose from his labors, extinguished his candles, and passed through the darkened room to where her last flames were guttering, and they did not always go out after that.

It must be confessed that when those final candles did extinguish, it was not by the hand of a servant, nor even by some fugitive gust of November wind snaking through an unguarded chink.

And when those candles did go out, it was invariably with a wink.